WITCHES
AND
KINGS

WITCHES & WARRIORS: BOOK 2
J.H. WEAR

To My Mother, Hetty Wear
Her courage, strength, and intelligence will always live on.
Her mark on this world was captured by a TV documentary on her titled,
appropriately, "Remarkable Hetty".
Rest in peace.
1924 - 2022

1

"Mother, hurry. I want to have a good spot to see them."

"We have plenty of time." Ululla took her daughter's offered hand and smiled. Ayleth had busied herself earlier that morning, brushing her long, golden hair and even rubbed a pink pigment made from flowers on her cheeks. Ululla didn't know why she was so eager to see the king and the royal family when they came to visit the city of Jital.

The witches in King Grayson's Kingdom normally avoided direct contact with the king and the king's army, wanting to show they were independent of the laws of the kingdom. Although the Allisure Kingdom was one of the kingdoms that allowed witches to operate freely, recognizing them as a positive influence. That contrasted with the Dwykath Kingdom, who wanted to exterminate any witches within its borders.

Ayleth and Ululla stepped out of the terradomus into the bright sunlight and made their way down the stone pathway to the street. As Ululla expected, there was plenty of space for them to stand alongside the cobblestone roadway. They picked a spot to stand, and Ayleth immediately peered down the street, showing her anxiety as she twisted a wood carving in her hand.

"What is that you have in your hand, dear?" She saw a small piece of carved wood with a leather cord attached to it.

"An Ego Taue." Ayleth looked up at her. "I asked Brother Ukail to make it for me."

"I see. Ego Taue means 'I am yours'. Are you planning to give it to the king?"

"No. How much longer will they be?"

"It will be a while longer." She traced her fingers through her daughter's hair. *Even at twelve, her beauty is showing. She's going to be a beautiful woman. Too soon for my liking.* She looked across the street and saw Orienla standing with her son, Dorian. Ululla offered a smile and a wave at them. Dorian was Ayleth's stepbrother, and the two got along very well. Ululla's husband, Alric, had become a positive influence on his son, wanting the two families to spend time together. Ululla was at first apprehensive, worried that Orienla's good looks would make him feel tempted by the ex-lover, but those fears never materialized into a problem. As time passed, Ululla became friends with Orienla as well. What prevented the families from becoming even closer were the restrictions placed by the two competing orders of witches. The Whiterose and Darkrose witches tolerated each other, sometimes supported each other, but at other times battled with each other. Their distrust with each other manifested in subtle ways. In this case, they stood on opposite sides of the street to view the royal procession.

Time passed as a lonely cloud drifted overhead, giving a short period of shade. The king's entourage made its way in the distance, cheered by the people, as the sun reappeared. First were four uniformed horsemen, riding as pairs, ahead of the royal carriage. Inside the decorated, open carriage sat the king and queen. They waved at the cheering population. Following the carriage was another smaller one. The open carriage held the two princesses, who giggled and waved enthusiastically. A governess tried to keep them from jumping up and down on the seat cushions.

Following the second carriage on horseback were the four princes. They were more reserved in their waves but appeared to enjoy the attention of the townspeople. Foot soldiers walked next to the princes, ensuring the crowd stayed away. Following the princes were four more horsemen. Like the lead horsemen, their hands were on the hilt of their swords, ready to protect the royal family in the unlikely event there was an attack. The population loved and respected the king and trouble wasn't expected.

The first of the horsemen came by Ululla and Ayleth, and the crowd increased their cheering, with shouts of 'Long live the king!'

Ululla noticed Brother Bruhamoff was standing close by. She saw tension in his face, as if the royal family was of significant emotional experience to him. Ululla didn't notice Ayleth had slipped away until she heard the crowd gasp. She saw Ayleth step forward toward the royal family.

The foot soldiers looked at lost what to do as the slim, blonde girl walked past them and straight to the last prince. Prince Terrowin stopped his horse and stared at her. He bent, reaching with his hand to take her offered gift. She spoke to him, and he nodded, looking surprised.

Ayleth turned around and returned to her mother.

Ululla heard the crowd buzz with excited whispers. The young girl had broken all protocol in approaching the prince and the guards acted as if she had the right to do so, not even offering a verbal warning to stop.

"You gave him the Ugo Taue. What did you say to him?"

"I will wait for him until the time is right."

"What made you say that and give him the Ego Taue?"

"Mother, don't you understand?" She looked up at her. "Prince Terrowin will be my husband someday. He needs to know that."

2

Brother Bruhamoff was barely aware of Tersica standing next to him as he waited for the royal procession to go by. Even when she held his arm, his attention didn't waver. When the first carriage rolled into view, he peered behind it, trying to pick out the horse riders following it.

Finally, the princes came into view. He stopped breathing as the youngest prince, Terrowin, approached where he stood. Despite his young age, he was as tall as the third oldest prince. It shocked Bruhamoff when he saw Ayleth walk boldly up to the prince and pass him a gift.

What did she give my son? Bruhamoff recalled the time he spent as a royal guard, his rendezvous with the queen, and her subsequent pregnancy. He left the royal guards, knowing it would be too difficult watching his son being raised without ever being allowed to acknowledge him.

He realized a repeated question, and he looked at Tersica.

"Are you okay?"

"Yes, I'm okay. I apologize. I was lost in thought."

She continued to look at him. "What was it about the royal family that bothers you?"

"I was a royal guard at one time. Just memories of my time there."

"Brother Bruhamoff, you have often told me to always tell the truth. Are you telling me the complete truth now?"

"Tersica," he held up a finger, "that is not what I have told you. One should not lie, but when speaking the truth, one should make sure the truth spoken does not cause harm and not just to increase one's importance."

Tersica nodded as they walked together back to the terradomus. "I understand, Brother Bruhamoff. But I'm still curious what happened when you were a royal guard that's causing you sorrow. I can tell. You're unhappy about something."

He noticed she was using the tile of Brother to address him, meaning she was upset with him. "There are some things in the past that are best left there. My moment of reflection is something I do not wish to share at this time."

"Okay, but I'm very curious about things. Someday, I'll find out what secret you're hiding."

Bruhamoff looked sternly at her. "That is not for you to find out. I will tell you when and if it is appropriate for you to know."

Tersica sighed. "I like you a lot, Bruhamoff, but you can be rather frustrating."

He reached for her hand. "Tersica, I will tell you everything you need to know about me. If I hold any information back, it is because it may break the confidence of another."

"Now I'm really curious."

———

"Ayleth, tell me what you meant when you said Prince Terrowin will someday be your husband." Ululla sat with her daughter in the dining room, sharing a pot of tea with her. The room was half filled, with witches sharing conversations or reading in solitude. She preferred the conversation be with her in the dining room, rather than in their suite, where it would appear to be more of a lecture. Ululla knew Alric heard about his daughter passing the gift to Prince Terrowin, but he didn't inquire why. She decided she should have a talk with her before discussing it with her husband.

"It's true. I've always known that Prince Terrowin will be my husband. It won't be for a long time, but it will happen."

"How do you know this? Was it a vision? Or just a feeling?"

Ayleth took a sip of her tea. "It is in my dreams. It's many years from now, but I'm by his side."

"Do you dream of anything else?" Ululla watched her daughter sit quietly composed, drinking her tea. She acted years beyond her age, and sometimes appeared to be amused by her mother's questions about what she saw as being obvious.

"Of course. I also dream of a time of war when many, many people die. The skies are troubled as they fight the battles."

"Why haven't you told me of these dreams before?"

"I didn't want to worry you, Mother. There is going to be a horrible battle between good and evil, men and witches. We cannot prevent it, so I didn't want to tell you, as all you would do is worry about it."

Ululla reviewed what Ayleth said. *She's trying to protect me from bad news.* "As a leader of the terradomus, I am prepared to accept news and information, good or bad. The more information I have, the better I can prepare for events."

"I understand. But this battle won't occur for many years. You cannot stop it." Ayleth finished her tea. "Is that all you want to talk about?"

"Just one more thing. Have you told anyone else about your dreams?"

"Yes. I talked about them with Dorian."

"Why Dorian? What did he say about them?"

Ayleth let out a small sigh. "Because Dorian has those dreams, too. We will fight together when the dark one strikes."

———

Alric listened to his wife's recount of her conversation with Ayleth. "And you didn't find her troubled by her dreams?"

"No. It was almost just as if she was reciting a passage from the Book of Redemption about a prophesy."

"Do you believe what she said will come to pass?"

"Our daughter is very smart, and she shows abilities in magic beyond what I have taught her. Yes, I believe her."

"Many years ago, I went to visit one of the Blackrain cabins, located deep within the Lowieza Forest. The pastor told me the key pieces in the next great battle would be my offspring. He said when they reached adulthood, the true battle would begin."

"Is there anything we can do, should do?"

"I remember my time as a warrior. A warrior does not get to choose when he fights. When the time arrives, he knows he will be in battle. A warrior cannot avoid a confrontation when it arrives. That is for kings and gods to decide. What a soldier can do is to be prepared. Keep his sword ready, know how to use his weapons, and focus on the task at hand.

"To protect our daughter, and my son, we must prepare them for a future battle. There's no point in trying to avoid a battle already written in the stars."

———

Prince Terrowin received teasing from his brothers about the blonde girl giving him a gift. He blushed as they chanted that the young prince had his first girlfriend. They ignored his denials.

Part of his discomfort was the memory of when he looked into the eyes of the young girl. He felt like it trapped him in moments of time, each moment distinct from the next. A wave of emotion isolated him from anything but the girl. When their fingertips briefly touched, there was an odd feeling of familiarity, like a forgotten dream.

I know her.

3

Dorian walked back to the terradomus with his mother after the Royal Procession had gone by. "Why did we have to stand on this side of the road? I wanted to stand with Ayleth."

Orienla took her time answering. "I know it doesn't seem fair, but sometimes there are rules we follow that don't always make sense."

"I just want to stand on the other side of the road. Why is there a rule against that?"

"If you were to go to the other side of the road and stand with Keeper Ululla and Ayleth, Altus Rector Carlton would believe you might switch allegiance to the Whiterose."

Dorian remained silent until they reached the terradomus doors. "Maybe I should switch to Whiterose."

"Hush. Never let anyone hear you say those words." She grabbed his arm and bent down to stare into his eyes. "Do you understand?"

He nodded, surprised at the strength of her voice. "Yes."

They entered the terradomus. Dorian wondering why they had to shun the Whiterose and spoke only about the order in less than complimentary terms. During the times he spent with Ayleth, she indicated to him he was always welcome to visit the Whiterose terradomus. He knew he could never reciprocate the offer to her. They did not trust the Whiterose witches to enter the Darkrose terradomus.

"Sister Orienla."

They turned toward the speaker, a male witch.

"Yes, Brother Jardel?"

"Altus Rector Carlton wants to see you. Please follow me."

"Dorian, go to our room." She looked at Jardel. "What is this about?"

"I don't know, but it is important if the altus rector wishes to see you."

Orienla frowned and followed him. They walked to the rear of the terradomus and descended the worn stone steps two levels. The large room had a high ceiling with several torches and candles, giving sufficient light to make the various designs on the walls visible. The floor was a mosaic of coloured tiles that told of future and past events. Jardel escorted her to an older woman sitting behind a desk.

Orienla remained standing near the desk after Jardel left. The woman continued her work of examining a ledger, making small notations as she read. Orienla recognized the book as one the keeper used to make records of the terradomus activities.

"Pardon me, Altus Rector Carlton requested to see me."

The woman looked up briefly. "I know. Wait." She resumed her reading and notations.

Orienla considered walking out but knew the repercussions would be severe. She continued to stand and wait.

The woman stopped writing and stood, giving Orienla a stern look. She proceeded to a heavy wood door and pulled a leather cord hanging from the centre. A bell rang, and she opened the door.

Orienla heard a whispered exchange between the woman and the altus rector. The woman beckoned Orienla to come, standing by the open door until Orienla passed by.

The heavy-set older man did not look pleased at her standing in front of his ornately carved desk. "You took your time arriving here, Sister Orienla."

"I arrived as soon..."

He held up a palm toward her. "Apology accepted. In the future, when summoned here, respond immediately. Understood?"

"Yes, Altus Rector Carlton."

He settled back into his leather chair and gestured to a wood chair in front of the desk. "Please, sit down."

Orienla sat.

"It has come to my attention that your son, Dorian, is spending much time with a person of the Whiterose order. While we allow conversing with Whiterose members, we do not encourage close association. I am concerned young Dorian's views may be corrupted by time spent with the Whiterose order."

"Dorian is only spending time with his sister. They're just children playing."

"That may be true, but by extension, he is also spending time with his stepsister's family. The mother, Keeper Ululla, is in a position of high authority in their terradomus. We are worried they may unduly influence him."

"I am Dorian's mother, and I assure you I have the most influence on him. There isn't any danger of him being corrupted by outsiders. I firmly believe Dorian has benefited from his time with his sister. Keeper Ululla's only influence is that of a caring woman. She has never pushed ideology."

"That you may know. The Whiterose have their methods to push their views. I understand Dorian's father is also a Whiterose. No doubt the boy looks up to him as a role model. I am not saying that as a negative, but I believe it would be prudent to have a male figure here for Dorian to spend time with."

"I don't understand what you are suggesting."

"I don't know if you know Brother Mihai. He recently arrived at our terradomus."

Orienla shook her head.

"He is slightly older than yourself and is of excellent character. He can be a positive influence on Dorian. I would like Dorian and you meet him."

"I don't need a stranger to help me raise my son." Orienla's face was flushed.

"Sister Orienla." He raised a finger. "There is no need to get upset. We all want to do what is best for Dorian. We have given this serious consideration, and all that we ask is you meet with Brother Mihai. Perhaps you will find you have something in common, besides being Umbravox witches." He spread out his hands. "Will you at least meet with him?"

Orienla felt pressured to accept. "I will meet with him one time."

"Thank you, Sister Orienla. This evening, please sit at an empty table at dinner time. Brother Mihai will find you. Remember, this is for Dorian."

Orienla stood.

"Peace be with you."

"Peace be with you, Altus Rector Carlton."

As Orienla reached the door, she heard him call out.

"On your way out, please tell Sister Guilia I wish to see her."

Orienla closed the door behind her, noticing Sister Guilia was drinking tea at her desk. She looked at her but didn't get a response. Orienla continued to walk by, exiting the floor when she reached the stairs.

———

In the evening, Orienla took her son to the dining area. After receiving a tray of food, she picked a table near the outer perimeter of the dining room. The table could sit eight, four on each side, and Orienla sat next to Dorian, facing the other tables. It wasn't long before a male witch approached their table.

"Hello, I'm Brother Mihai. May I sit with you?"

Orienla nodded. "If you wish."

He placed his food on the table and sat across from Dorian. Orienla appraised him. Average height, soft, thinning brown hair. His reddish beard was patchy, partially disguising a scar on his cheek. She would have considered him average looking, except his brown eyes were visible as mere slits.

"You must be Brother Dorian. I am pleased to meet you."

Dorian stared at him.

"Dorian!" Orienla gave her son a sharp look.

"Hello." Dorian frowned at him.

Mihai gave a brief chuckle. "I can see it takes a while for you to get used to strangers. I understand. When you read the Book of Destiny, you will learn to appreciate new people that come into your life."

"I have read the Book of Destiny."

"Really? The entire book?"

"Yes, every page. The book discusses meeting new people and accepting their differences. It also warns about those who have their own interests."

"Are you suspicious of everyone you meet?"

Orienla listened to the exchange. It surprised her at Dorian's response to Mihai. Normally, her son stayed quiet when they met with other witches, observing and listening without adding his own thoughts. This time he was taking an adversarial position.

"No."

"But you are suspicious of me?" Mihai spread his hands. "Why?"

"You just sat with us, like you were supposed to all along. I think you're planning something."

"I assure you; I mean no harm to your mother or to you."

"Then why did you sit with us?"

"I want to know both of you better and perhaps be your friend."

Dorian ate slowly, took a drink of water and finally spoke. "I still don't trust you."

———

Mihai stood in front of the Altus Rector Carlton's desk. "I met with Sister Orienla and her son. It was a challenging situation. The boy is distrustful of strangers."

"You must try harder to befriend him."

"I will do so. And Sister Orienla?"

"She is not inconsequential, but Dorian is what you must consider first. The Book of Destiny tells us he will be of great importance."

"His half-sister Ayleth is also prominent, according to the scriptures."

"Of course. We are concerned Dorian will feel pulled toward the Whiterose order because of his stepsister. This must not happen. You must ensure that he sees the Umbravox as the only means to advance his beliefs." The altus rector paused. "You must not fail here, under any circumstances. Use what ever means to ensure success."

"Understood, Altus rector Carlton."

4

Orienla was not surprised about Dorian's request.

He quietly spoke as they ate their lunch in the dining hall. "I want to spend a day with my father. Just him and me."

"I understand, but it may take a while to arrange it. The elders of the Umbravox would prefer minimal contact by us with the Whiterose. However, we should not separate a son and a father. I will see that it happens."

"Thanks. I don't understand how if both the Book of Destiny and the Book of Redemption talk about love and peace, there's so much anger between the orders of witches. It just isn't right."

"Maybe someday it will change. Eat your lunch. This afternoon, I will contact Sister Ululla about your visit."

———

Orienla left the Umbravox terradomus alone, knowing her departure would be noted and the information sent to the altus rector. If she left with her son, she suspected they would have followed her.

She reached one teahouse along the main street and entered. Orienla looked around and spotted two Whiterose witches sitting at a table, identifying their order by the lighter colour of their clothing. She approached them, giving a small bow when they noticed her.

"Pardon my intrusion. Could one of you give Keeper Ululla this note?" She extended her hand with a folded yellow paper.

"You must be Sister Orienla. We have heard about you." She smiled as she took the paper. "I'm Sister Rashie, this is Sister Petra. Please sit and join us."

It surprised Orienla at the invitation to join them. "Thank you. That is kind of you to offer." She sat.

"We are often told to be kind to strangers when we meet them. To me, it would seem peculiar not to offer the same to another witch," Sister Rashie responded. "I assume this note is of importance. I will go now and give it to Keeper Ululla. Why don't you stay and keep company with Sister Petra until I return?"

"Thank you, I will. Peace be with you."

"And to you."

Orienla turned her attention to the younger witch. "It is good to meet you. Are you originally from Jital, or have you journeyed here? I'm from a small village called Kunua, a three-day walk from Jital. The Jital Terradomus is my second posting."

"I was born in Kireland and became a witch there. This is my second posting as well."

"Kireland was the site of a battle. That would be an unsettling experience."

"My parents were killed there during the takeover."

Orienla placed her hand on Petra's. "I'm sorry for your loss."

"It is why I became a witch. I want to do my part to bring peace to this land."

"A worthy cause."

Orienla found it easy to converse with the Whiterose witch, reflecting they had much in common despite being in different orders.

"I see Sister Rashie has returned with Keeper Ululla."

Orienla stood, smiling at Ululla as she crossed the floor. The two women hugged each other, and Orienla was sure one of the Umbravox witches in the teahouse would quickly report the incident.

"Come, Sister Orienla, tell me more about this note." She led the way to a vacant table.

"I shall come to the point. It won't come as a shock to you that Dorian wants to spend more time with his father. Specifically, he asked to spend time alone with him."

Ululla nodded. "I'm sure Alric would welcome that as well. I know our orders will wonder about them spending time together, but that is not our concern. Dorian deserves to spend time with Alric, and Alric deserves to have time with his son."

"Thank you for those sentiments."

"I don't believe we need to be underhanded on how we arrange this meeting. Let us pick a morning, say in two days' time, and have them meet here."

"Dorian will be followed. They don't trust he won't fall into the false notions of the Book of Redemption." She smiled. "I think they also believe I'm a poor influence on him."

Ululla laughed. "No, you're a truly wonderful mother, raising a very special boy."

"According to the scriptures, our children will someday change the world. We both have an enormous responsibility to ensure they stay safe. Shall we agree to meet here in two days' time? An hour after sunrise?"

"Yes. If you wish, we can spend time together with Ayleth. She is very curious about you."

"Me? Why?"

"You were Alric's first love, and you're raising Dorian alone. She sees you as a remarkable woman."

Orienla blushed. "I had little choice but to raise Dorian, not that I regret that."

"Yes, but you did it through strength and refused to let anyone control you. I, too, admire you." She smiled. "We will see you in two days."

———

Two days later, Alric went with Ululla and Ayleth to the teahouse. He saw Orienla and Dorian were already sitting at a table, and both stared at him as he entered.

After a few minutes of talk, Alric invited Dorian to accompany him.

"It will be easier for us to talk if we take a journey around here."

Dorian readily agreed and followed him outside. Alric noticed two male witches followed them as they walked away from the teahouse.

"How are you doing, Dorian? Are you and your mother doing well in the terradomus?"

"We would do better if they would just leave us alone."

"Who are they?"

"The altus rector and the elders. They keep having other witches watch us. There's this witch, Brother Mihai, who tries to sit with us at meal time. He keeps asking me to go for walks with him. I don't like him, and he keeps bothering me and my mother."

"Have you told him you don't want to spend time with him?"

"I've tried to, but he keeps showing up."

"As a witch, you must be respectful of others' feelings."

"I know."

"Good. Because you can inform Brother Mihai that he isn't respecting your feelings of wanting to be left alone."

"Oh, I wonder what he would say to that." He grinned. "I'll also tell him he isn't respecting my mother's wishes."

"Careful, you don't speak for her unless she wants you to. Your mother, I'm sure, can inform him if he is bothering her."

"You used to kill people as a warrior, didn't you?"

"Yes, but the circumstances were different then. I never wanted to kill. It was necessary for me to live. I prefer being a witch than a warrior." Alric turned down a different street, one slightly busier than the one where the teahouse was located. He stopped.

"I understand. But I was wondering how you won. How do you beat someone who also has a sword? Is there a trick to it?"

Alric thought of the long practices he did with his sword, a sword of superior quality. He also had an enormous horse, Darkian, that liked to charge into battle. His own height on the horse gave him advantage over most opponents. "It's a skill I learned. In a sword fight, the first thing to do is to protect yourself. Defend first, then strike when you see an opportunity. I hope you're not planning to become a soldier."

"No, but someday I may have to fight. I want to know how you do it."

Alric stopped walking and turned around. "Wait here." He approached the two witches that were following them.

"Stop trailing us."

"We wish to make sure the boy comes to no harm."

"I can protect him better than both of you. If you continue to follow us, I will go to the Whiterose terradomus. I'm certain you won't follow us inside there."

One witch looked shocked. "You can't do that."

"I can and I will if I see either of you following us again. Now turn around and leave."

Alric watched them leave and returned to Dorian. "I'll tell you the first rule of fighting."

"What is that?"

"Avoid it. If that doesn't work, follow the second rule. Don't get yourself hurt. Keep yourself calm. Wait for your opponent to make an error or reveal a weakness."

"Okay."

"Dorian, whether you're fighting with swords or with words, keeping calm is the best road to victory."

———

Dorian enjoyed the long walk with his father, stopping at the edge of the Jital where the farmland began. He listened to Alric as he described his new life as a carpenter in the Whiterose terradomus.

"Is it hard to work with wood?"

"One can acquire it just by learning." I enjoy working with wood. I find it relaxing and gives me the satisfaction of accomplishment. Whether it is making furniture or a wood spoon, I enjoy the task."

They returned walking toward the city centre.

"We should have dinner, but then I must return you to your terradomus. I promised to have you back before dark."

———

Dorian hugged his father, who walked him right to the edge of the terradomus property. There was an unwritten rule that neither of the opposing orders of witches approached close to the property of the terradomus.

To Dorian, that showed his father would break rules to be with him. With a feeling of pride, he strode up to the entrance doorway. His mother was there to greet him.

"How was your visit?"

"It was great." He hugged her, seeing the disapproving faces of the nearby witches. "They don't look happy."

"That is their problem. I'm happy for you, Dorian."

5

Prince Terrowin rubbed his bruised left shoulder. He grinned at his older brother, Prince Rupert, who sat on the ground holding a broken wooden sword.

"I think I finally won."

"Only because my stupid sword broke in half." Rupert stood. "Nice counter-swing."

Terrowin was improving rapidly on his sword fighting and horse-back riding. He found his height advantage worked well in giving him a longer reach and easier to apply a downward strike during the heavy workout. He extended a hand and helped Rupert up. "Thanks. You were right. I had a lot to learn about sword fighting."

"I want you to be ready if war happens. I don't want my baby brother to die because he didn't know how to defend himself."

The intensity of the workouts had increased over the last few months as the possibility of war increased. King Grayson had kept his army well-trained and insisted every man knew how to use a sword in at least rudimentary fashion. There were monetary rewards for showing proficiency in archery.

Despite the preparation for war, the kingdom continued to prosper, with the marketplace bustling with goods. The royal family didn't stop doing visits to various parts of the kingdom, although the travel was restricted to the closer towns and cities. King Grayson considered allowing the populace to see the royal family strengthen the kingdom. Staying only within the confines of the castle walls, he believed, separated the kingdom from the people he ruled.

Terrowin walked with Rupert back inside the castle, past the usual on-lookers. Besides their battle, there were several other matches between soldiers. Crowds were interested in the fighting as entertainment. There were also many women who waved at the princes as they left the courtyard, and a few called out their names.

"You should take advantage of the ladies that show an interest in you." Rupert put his hand on Terrowin's shoulder.

"Maybe sometime I will."

"You still pine for that blonde witch. I get that she's pretty and likes you, but you need more than one lady friend. Maybe one who lives close by."

Terrowin grinned. "Yeah, I might do that." His thoughts returned to Ayleth, looking forward to the visit to Jital in a few weeks.

A servant quickly helped him change from his workout garments and armour to the more formal dress expected of a prince. He decided to have something to eat before turning to studies. As a member of the royal family, they expected him to have a broad education and be knowledgeable on several diverse topics. Not that he ever expected to be king. His three brothers were all older and the next king would be the oldest son. If that son could not fulfill the duties as king, it would go to the next oldest son. As the youngest son, along with the princesses, they expected him to support the king by whatever means he had available. Unlike some of the other kingdoms, there was little likelihood of sabotage by any of the princes to move closer to be in line to be king.

After his meal of beef and roasted vegetables, Terrowin went to the main library. He studied the history of past kingdoms, some of which were now part of Allisure. One city kept being mentioned was Jital. The ancient city had survived countless battles and had been part of different kingdoms. It was home to the two orders of witches and existed before the split of the two orders from one. The Umbravox became the Darkrose and the Whiterose orders, although the Darkrose still referred to themselves as the Umbravox. To Terrowin, it seemed

Jital was the site of many ancient battles and would be the centre of many more.

Another ancient book referred to King Terrowin and his special relationship to the Whiterose order of witches. It implied, but did not confirm, King Terrowin himself was a witch.

King Terrowin was a commanding figure. The ink drawings of him had him sitting tall in the saddle, peering at the landscape beyond. Another had him standing in front of his throne. His beard and height made him a regal figure. Stories told how he united the warring lands around him and forged a prosperous, peaceful land.

The return of King Terrowin was mentioned in many books, but the prophecy was vague. Terrowin carried the same name, but he was certain they gave his name to him as a tribute to his ancestor, and not because anyone expected him to become the reborn king. The other part of prophecy was there were rarely any timelines given. They spoke part of the prose of the circle of life and time, having the past repeat itself in the future. The reference to King Terrowin sometimes implied it was in the past, with echoes of the future.

The short, but strongly built dark-haired Prince Nicholas, known for being light-hearted, entered the library. His lack of seriousness was a contrast to his oldest brother, Prince Kumar.

"Terrowin, you may turn into paper if you spend much more time in here."

"There's a lot of interesting material to read."

"And an even more interesting world outside of these walls. Come, I'm going on a deer hunt. We can test our skills with a bow and arrow."

"Sure." Terrowin stood. "Fresh air will be good."

———

"You're shooting too low," Nicholas lectured. "The arrow will arc, no matter how hard you pull back on the string. If you pull too hard, you'll lose accuracy. Relax and aim higher."

Terrowin watched the small herd of deer scatter and he returned to his horse, where several royal guardsmen waited. "Why didn't you shoot?"

"I want you to get the first one. My aim is excellent. You need the practice. You can hit a target during training, but it's different when you have to strike under pressure."

Terrowin and the others rode the horses, circling around the herd of deer. Quietly, Terrowin and Nicholas crept toward the grazing animal.

"Easy, pull slowly. Picture the arc of the arrow. Adjust for the wind."

Terrowin carefully shifted the position of his bow. He held his breath and released the string.

The arrow flew true, striking a buck just behind the shoulder. Nicholas fired a second arrow into the beast. The deer ran around in a frantic circle and then collapsed on the ground.

"Well done, Terrowin. You learn quickly."

Terrowin walked with Nicolas past the grove of trees positioned inside and across the grassy ground. "Why do you like spending so much time hunting? You also practice with a sword a lot."

"I'm trying to hone my skills as a fighter. The Dwykath kingdom is preparing to war with us and is building up their army. When the war breakouts, I want to be ready to contribute to protecting our kingdom."

"You took me hunting to help me improve my shooting."

"True. When the war comes, and it will come, you need skills to defend and to protect yourself. You should practice against the royal guards. They are highly skilled, and you will learn much battling against them."

"You make it sound very serious."

"It is serious. The enemy wants to kill you. What skills do you have to defend yourself? You need to be prepared."

———

When Terrowin asked the sergeant of the royal guards if he could have a practice battle with one of his men, he could tell that the sergeant was amused.

"With all due respect, Prince Terrowin, we don't wish to cause any harm to thee, even in a practice setting."

"I understand, but I wish to improve my fighting ability. I thought a practice session with the best would help me learn."

"Of course, Prince Terrowin." He pointed at one of the younger guards. "Mason, you are to have a practice session with Prince Terrowin."

Terrowin looked at the shorter, lightly framed man. The man with thin lips drew them tight and his brown eyes showed an intense look. They squared off, with the rest of the royal guards watching.

The learning experience for Terrowin was a series of bruises. He learned that besides the wood sword, the shield could be used as a weapon. Mason used his shield to batter and push Terrowin. Several times, Terrowin toppled to the ground, with Mason standing above him. The wooden sword inflicted damage on him as well. As he picked himself up from the ground for another round, he didn't see any smugness on the royal guard, just the same fierce glare on his face.

This time, Terrowin reacted better to Mason's attack. Instead of retreating when Mason's shield hit at his sword arm, Terrowin pivoted. For a fraction of a second, Mason's side became exposed when Terrowin turned in response to his attack. He swung his sword down, clipping Mason's arm and his hip.

Mason stumbled for a moment and Terrowin took advantage by striking his back with his sword.

The sergeant stepped toward them, holding up his arms. "The battle is over. Mason, you're dead. Thank you, Prince Terrowin, for your fine showing in our practice session."

Terrowin saw the scowl on Mason's face.

"Sir, it is I who should be thankful. Royal Guardsman Mason taught me how to fight in a battle. I was fortunate at the end, but the truth is he won each of the previous battles."

The royal guardsmen saluted Terrowin as he limped away. He soaked in a hot bath before getting dressed. *Nicholas was right, I wasn't prepared for a fight against soldiers. My ego and my body sure took a beating today by a man smaller than me.*

His hand gripped the cloth he was using to wash himself, and then relaxed. At least in a few days, I get to see Ayleth. He smiled. *I hope she likes the gift I have for her.*

6

Bruhamoff carefully flipped the page of the book he was reading. He sat at his favourite table, near the back of the library where there was less noise from other library users. He became aware of someone standing in front of the table and looked up.

"Tersica. What brings you here?"

"I knew I would find you in the library." She sat in the chair opposite from him. "I have arrived at important decision, and you should know about it."

"Are you wanting my advice?"

"No, I don't want advice. Bruhamoff, I am going to stop taking praevent tea. I want to get pregnant."

"I see." Bruhamoff pursed his lips.

"Do you? We are sharing a bed. Now I want a child. Are you prepared to be a father?"

"Yes, I think so."

"You think so? I hope you would be more certain than that." She stood. "Let me know when you're sure." She walked away, leaving Bruhamoff feeling perplexed.

He closed the book and returned it to the shelf. A walk down the hallway led him to the office where Ululla sat behind her desk.

"Brother Bruhamoff, what brings you here?"

"Keeper Ululla, I need your insight into a problem I have."

"Of course, what is it?"

"Sister Tersica has just informed me she wants to have a baby, and that she has stopped taking the praevent tea. She asked me if I was prepared to be a father."

"What did you say to her?"

"I said, 'I think so' and she didn't like my reply. She got angry with me and left. Keeper Ululla, this came a surprise to me and I wasn't sure how to answer and now am at a loss at what to do."

"Brother Bruhamoff, you are a smart, well-read man who knows the Book of Redemption. It is one thing to understand the words inside, and another to apply them to everyday life. May I ask if Sister Tersica ever mentioned about having children before?"

Bruhamoff frowned as he thought. "Yes, there were occasions when she mentioned it would be nice to have children, and she did make a fuss when she saw a baby and remarked how nice it was to hold it."

"The Book of Redemption teaches us to listen and observe. If you apply those words to what you just told me, what are your conclusions?"

"That she wants to have a family."

"Yes, so it should not have been a surprise to you that she stopped taking the praevent tea. You share a room with Sister Tersica. She wanted more than a "I think so' reply."

"I understand. I was not paying fully attention to her words. I understand now why she was upset with me."

"Good. Now what do you want to do about it?"

"I don't know."

"Brother Bruhamoff, you have reached a fork in the path. If you stay with Sister Tersica, she will become pregnant with your child. If you leave her, your relationship will end. Which does your true self lean to? That is a question only you can answer. Do not stay with Sister Tersica out of obligation, as that will lead only to misery in the end."

"I do love her."

"That is good. Do you love her enough to have a family with her?"

He nodded. "I have considered asking her to marry me in the past, but I was looking for the right opportunity."

"Marriage, for witches, is very serious. As you know, witches can marry only once, for we believe it will be to our soulmate. A divorce is not recognized in our order. Are you certain you wish to marry her?"

———

Bruhamoff left the terradomus, walking down a street filled with merchants and shoppers. He entered a teahouse he knew Tersica frequented, finding her sitting at table by herself in the crowded room.

He stood next to her. "Sister Tersica, I have given our earlier conversation much thought, and have concluded my reply to you was inadequate. Please forgive my lack of judgement."

"I do, Brother Bruhamoff. I was hoping for a different response from you, but I understand you have your own priorities."

"You are correct, I do have priorities in my life. One of them is you, Tersica." He dropped to his knees. "Tersica, this comes from my heart. I love you. I want to marry you. I want to be the father of your children." He heard the scraping of chairs as others in the teahouse shifted position to watch his proposal. A silence overcame the room.

Tersica hugged and kissed him. "I love you too and want to be your wife."

A ripple of applause crossed the room.

Bruhamoff kissed her back.

"I want you to travel with me to meet my parents. They will be happy to learn of my marriage."

"Travel to meet your parents?"

"Yes, you do want to meet them?"

"Of course." He let out a quiet sigh.

———

Dorian spoke to his mother in her room. "I would like to be with my sister when the royal family goes by."

Orienla put down her teacup. "I don't have a problem with you doing so, but others in our terradomus may believe you are being too close to the Whiterose witches. There may be questions afterward."

"She is my sister. Why should anyone care why I'm standing on the other side of the street?"

"Dorian, we have talked about this before. Perception is very important to the altus rector and others in the councillium. They are worried you will become too familiar with the Whiterose."

"But we're all witches. We should know each other."

"I agree, but not everyone sees it that way. You have my permission to be with your sister. I assume your father will be there as well." She smiled. "It is good for you to spend time with him."

"Thank you."

"Just know they will probably question you afterward."

"That's okay. You won't get into trouble, will you?"

"No more than usual. It seems they already blame me that your father is a Whiterose witch rather than a Darkrose."

———

Ayleth looked up at Dorian. "You made it."

"My mother said I could. I could be in trouble with the altus rector later, but this is important. I can feel it." Dorian looked down the street, not seeing the royal procession yet. He was aware of Ululla and Alric standing behind them. Dorian was tall, as tall as most adult men, but Alric still was a head above him. "Are you going to give that to Prince Terrowin?" He pointed at the flower she was holding.

"Yes, I want him to know I'm thinking of him."

"I think he knows that."

"He does, but it's still important I show him."

Dorian relaxed as they waited, feeling content. Part of him enjoyed the illusion he was part of this family. Then a wave of guilt washed over him. *I'm sorry, Mother.*

"I see your mother standing across the street." Ayleth spoke. "Do you think we should invite her over to be with us?"

"The Darkrose wouldn't like that. I guess I may be in trouble for being here. I don't care."

The crowd sent a murmur along the street. Dorian looked and saw the lead guards on horses of the royal procession. The dust surrounding horses gradually faded, revealing details of the riders and the carriages behind. As the royal family drew closer, cheers went up and the people lining the streets waved.

The guards walked alongside the first carriage, occasionally pushing back a few enthusiastic spectators. After the first carriage containing the king and queen, a second carriage arrived with the princesses. Following them were the princes riding on horseback.

Dorian saw Ayleth step forward as Prince Terrowin went by. He followed her, but guards quickly blocked him. He watched as Ayleth walked past the guards, who ignored her. She reached Prince Terrowin, who stopped his horse, and jumped off. She lifted the flower to him, and in return, he bent his head to give her a small wooden box. They exchanged words Dorian couldn't hear. They walked together, with Terrowin leading his horse. Shortly later, Ayleth gave him a kiss on his cheek. He climbed back on his horse and waved goodbye.

Ayleth returned to where Dorian was stood. He looked at the small box she clasped in her hands against her chest.

"What is in the box?"

"I don't know. It's a gift from Prince Terrowin."

Dorian stared at the box. From what he could see, the wood box was inlaid with a gold design. "Open it."

With deliberation, Ayleth opened the hinged cover. Inside, rested a gold ring with a green emerald mounted on it. "The ring." Her hand shook as she carefully placed it on her finger.

After the royal procession went by, Dorian said goodbye to Alric and Ululla. He noticed Ayleth appeared to still be in a daze and had to touch her arm before she acknowledged him.

"Sorry, I was focused on the ring Prince Terrowin gave me."

"That's okay. That ring must mean a lot to you."

"Very much so."

Ululla stepped up to him and gave him a hug. "I hope someday you will join us for dinner in our terradomus. Perhaps your mother could join us as well."

"I don't know if we could ever get permission for that. Thank you for your offer."

Dorian walked across the road, meeting his mother.

"Did you enjoy being with your sister?"

"Yes. I'm sorry you had to be by yourself."

"That's all right. You have the freedom to be wherever you choose.

But there may be consequences. The altus rector likes to control everyone. Come, let us get something to eat."

Dorian walked with Orienla into the Darkrose terradomus. He saw long glances directed toward him.

The dining area was half-filled, and they made their way to the front counter. The young woman on the other side of the counter passed over plates of food.

"Be careful. The altus rector is not pleased you stood with the Whiterose witches." She turned away to fill another plate.

Dorian carried his plate to an empty table, anger rising as by the time he sat. He jabbed at his food with a fork.

"You need to remember the teachings of the Book of Destiny. Your anger will block you from seeing the light." She took a drink of her tea.

"It's not right. I wasn't doing anything wrong."

"I know that, but sometimes it is the perception of wrongdoing that causes others to be anxious. You did nothing wrong. Just give it time for others to see it that way."

"For how long? They have been watching you for as long as I can remember. They treat you like you're spying for the Whiterose. All the witches treat you different." He used part of his bread to mop up part of the stew on his plate.

"I'm okay with the surveillance. I know who I am. They do not."

"You deserve more respect." He took a gulp of his tea.

A male witch walked to their table. "Altus Rector Carlton would like to see you." He looked at Dorian.

Dorian took another bite of his bread.

"He wants to see you immediately." The witch rose his voice.

"I will finish eating first." Dorian looked straight ahead and continued to eat.

The witch clenched a fist and glared at him. "I'll report your disrespect."

Dorian grunted and finished eating. He saw the worried look on his mother's face and stood. "Let's go."

Dorian was taken downstairs to where the altus rector's office was located. He stopped in front of the desk of the secretary. The woman behind the desk looked up and returned to writing notes.

"Excuse me, I was told to see the altus rector."

She looked up. "You will wait and be quiet until I have time to deal with you. Sit and be still." She returned to her work.

Dorian frowned and went to one of the three wooden chairs, sitting as he watched her ignore him.

After a duration, the secretary stood and tapped on the door behind her, opened it and spoke a few quiet words. She turned around and, using her hand, summoned Dorian to enter the second room.

Dorian walked reluctantly into the altus rector's office, closing the door behind him.

"Brother Dorian, please sit. I have a few things to discuss with you."

Dorian sat, feeling a mixture of worry and anger. "What do you want to talk about?"

"You're old enough now to understand the Umbravox teachings. One of them is to accept others in our life's journeys. We may not always understand the role another person brings to us, but later on, we can see how such encounters benefit us. Do you understand this concept?"

"Yes, I do. What you said is on page one-hundred and sixteen in the Book of Destiny."

"Excellent. It is one thing to have read the teachings and recite them. It is another to practice them. Brother Dorian, since you have read this section of the Book of destiny, then I must express disappointment on how you have treated Brother Mihai. He has offered to be your friend and help guide you through your difficult years as a young adult. Yet you shun him, and to be serious about this matter, been rude."

"But he just shows up without being invited to sit with us. We don't always want him around. I don't want his advice."

"Brother Dorian, are not all friends someone who at one time were strangers to us? You should suggest a time when it is convenient to be with him. Talk with him. He is an adult male who can provide much guidance to you."

"I don't need his guidance. I have a father, and he tells me what I need to know."

"Brother Dorian." The altus rector raised his voice. "Your father is a Whiterose witch and thus has no suitable knowledge to pass on to someone devoted to the Umbravox. You may speak with him but be aware he wants to lead you down an uncertain path, a path that will lead you to great sorrow."

"I trust my father more than Brother Mihai."

"Yet it is Brother Mihai who comes to you with an offer of friendship. Remember, your father's loyalty is the Whiterose order, his wife and to his daughter. He may be fond of you, but understand he chose Keeper Ululla as his wife and not your mother. You and Sister Orienla are not his first family. In fact, your mother and you are nothing more than an obligation to him."

"That's not true!" Dorian stood, ready to run out of the room.

"Sit down!"

Dorian sat.

"If the truth hurts you, I am sorry, but it had to be said. Henceforth, I want you to be careful with your dealing with Keeper Ululla, Brother Alric and Sister Ayleth. They are part of the Whiterose order. You are not. I want you to be more accommodating to Brother Mihai and know he has the best interests for you and your mother in his heart. You need to trust him and accept him as part of your life."

Dorian took slow, deep breaths through clenched teeth.

"You may go now. I fully expect to hear from Brother Mihai that you have made amends with him."

Dorian left as fast as he could. He ignored the others he passed and went straight to his room, where he sat on his bed, shaking with anger.

7

King Hadrian paced around the throne room, receiving nervous looks from the guards. "Where the devil is he? I don't like being kept waiting." He went over to a long table and picked up a goblet, draining the contents in a single gulp. "More wine and be quick about it."

He didn't speak to anyone, but a servant ran outside the room.

A guard then entered. "My lord, you have a visitor, Master Diablo."

"Send him in."

A tall figure wearing a dark grey robe with a hood covering most of his face entered the room in an unhurried manner.

"You're late."

Diablo snorted and glared at Hadrian. "No, time is of no consequence to me. I'm here now, and therefore I'm not late. You forget who you are dealing with. I am the master. Don't put me in a position where I must exert my authority."

Hadrian thought the room appeared to be darker, as if Diablo had absorbed the light. "You sent me a note about increasing my army in the battle with the Allisure Kingdom and said that you could assist in the finances with it." Hadrian licked his lips.

"Yes, I knew you would be concerned about that." He let out a sigh. "I will arrange for a quantity of gold to pay for your army. In return, put together an army strong enough to eliminate Allisure. Be aware, I expect success and don't accept failure."

King Hadrian grunted. "I don't need extra incentive to destroy Allisure. I just need enough gold to make a bigger army."

"Give me a private room and two men."

King Hadrian summoned a guard. "Take the Master Diablo to my private dining room and have two men report to him."

The guard quickly bowed and led the way to the king's private dining room.

"Master Diablo, I will send two men shortly." The guard hurried away, not enjoying being in close proximity of the evil looking Diablo.

———

King Hadrian scowled as he peered out on the balcony attached to the throne room. "What is he doing with those two men?" He turned to one guard. "Knock on the dining-room door and find out how much longer he's going to be."

"Yes, my lord." He bowed and left.

A few minutes later, he returned. "King Hadrian. I knocked on the door, but there wasn't an answer. I opened the door, and he was not there." He swallowed. "King Hadrian, you may wish to see for yourself what is in the room."

King Hadrian snarled and went to his private dining room. As soon as he entered, the smell of decay assaulted him.

On the dining table, the bodies of the two men rested. Their faces looked as if they had died months ago. Sharing the table was a pile of gold coins.

King Hadrian swore and went to the gold coins, a smile creasing his lips. He spoke to the guard standing in the doorway. "Get rid of these bodies." He fingered the coins and laughed.

8

Ululla sat with Orienla in the teahouse, where they met several times previously. As was their custom, they sat around one of the square wooded tables. Nearby, Dorian and Ayleth sat at another table. Ululla caught fragments of their conversation, which included both giggles and serious moments.

"They sure squeeze in a lot of conversation during their visits," Ululla remarked.

"It's great they get to spend time together. How is Alric doing?" She smiled. "He didn't want to join us for the meeting?"

Ululla laughed. "He's fine. The one time he joined us, you could tell how bored he was. He's more of a doer than a sit and talk man."

"I recall him looking at the door, looking for a reason he could leave." She looked at the doorway and saw Brother Mihai enter. He looked slightly out of breath. *I had hoped he hadn't discovered where I went.* Orienla had tried to leave the terradomus without Mihai seeing. She suspected the terradomus' watcher had informed her of their leaving, and he correctly guessed they went to the teahouse where she usually met with Ululla and Ayleth.

Mihai approached their table. "May I join you?" He pulled out a chain and sat.

34

"No, Brother Mihai, I'm having a private conversation with Sister Ululla."

His jaw dropped slightly. "Sister Orienla, I just want to join you and Sister Ululla in a cup of tea. Surely, there's no harm in that."

"Brother Mihai, I must ask you to leave. We do not invite you to sit with us."

He drew in a slow breath and stood. "You are being most rude."

"No, it is you that is holding that end of the stick. You chase me down here and sit without regard to my feelings. Witches should not impose themselves on others, or did you forget your teachings in the Book of Destiny?"

Mihai's hands shook for a moment. "Do not lecture me, Sister Orienla, on the Book of Destiny. I shall take my leave." He pointed a finger at Ululla. "Keeper Ululla, I know you're trying to subvert Sister Orienla and Brother Dorian to the teachings of the Book of Redemption. Know that we are watching and will take steps to prevent your distorted messages from the Whiterose." He stalked away, sitting at a vacant table nearby, glaring at them.

"I'm sorry, Ululla. This is what I have to endure."

"You handled the situation well." She used the clay pot to add more hot water into the teacups. "So, how is my conversion working on you so far?"

Orienla laughed. "I'm getting more tempted after Brother Mihai's visit."

"Do you have friends in your terradomus you can talk to?

"Yes, there are a few witches I am acquainted with, but most are careful in not appearing too close to me. I am considered a bit of an outcast. One exception is Keeper Truman. He has always been friendly and kind to me." She looked over at Dorian and Ayleth, who had resumed their whispered conservation, after stopping during Mihai's interruption. Orienla watched as Ayleth poured a small amount of water on the table and spread it out with her fingers. The damp surface was used to write out symbols. Dorian nodded and added a few strokes of his own.

"I wonder what they're talking about, and what is that writing they're doing?"

Ululla whispered, "Ayleth discovered something in the Book of

Redemption. She is being secretive about it, telling me she wants to be sure before she tells me about it."

"I want to ask you something that we have discussed before. If things continue to get uncomfortable for Dorian and myself, can we join the Whiterose order? I don't want to make things difficult for Alric and yourself."

"Sister Orienla, you and Dorian are part of my family. Of course, you are welcome to join us at our terradomus." She looked at where Mihai was sitting. His unrelenting gaze made her feel uncomfortable.

———

Orienla walked back with Dorian to the Umbravox terradomus. She was aware of Mihai walking behind them a short distance.

"That seemed like a pleasant visit with your sister," she said in a soft voice.

"Yes, it was good."

"Can you tell me what you talked about?"

He looked behind them. "Yes, but not here. I don't want him to hear anything."

"Okay, I understand."

They entered the terradomus and Dorian announced he wanted to go to the library. "I want to check on some things Ayleth said."

"Okay. I'll see you later at dinner."

Orienla went to her room, observing Mihai was following Dorian. *I wish he would leave us alone.*

———

Mihai approached Dorian as he read part of the Book of Destiny, flipped a few pages, read another section and jumped ahead a few pages again. The library contained several tables and chairs scattered around the perimeter of the two-story room. In the centre of the room, the Book of Destiny sat on a pedestal. The rest of the room contained books devoted to the study of the Book of Destiny and the philosophy of the Umbravox. There were also paper and writing instruments available for self-study and note taking. The second level of the library contained older texts and scrolls. A catwalk, accessed via a set of stairs, allowed users to reach the upper-level reading material.

"Can I offer you help in finding something, Brother Dorian?" Mihai asked.

"No." He shook his head. "I can find what I'm looking for."

"What is it? Perhaps I can offer you my insight into the teachings of the Book of Destiny. I have studied the book for many years."

Dorian didn't turn around as he went to another section of the thick book. "I don't need your insight. I know more about this book than you do."

"How is it possible that you, a mere boy, can know more than a scholar such as myself? That is a ridiculous statement."

Dorian turned around. "Okay, page number two-hundred and seven. What does the third paragraph say?"

"I don't know. If you open the book there, I can give you my interpretation of it."

"It says, 'Understanding weather is important when planning. When planning, it is important to understand how weather can influence planting crops, traveling, or holding celebrations. There are many indicators that the weather may be changing. Examination of clouds, the moon, the wind and even animals will tell us of a change in weather.'" Dorian stopped reciting. "I can tell you what is on any page. I don't need your help with anything."

"You possess an excellent memory, but do you understand what the words mean? Their hidden meaning?"

"I understand more of the hidden meanings than you do. Now please leave me alone." Dorian returned his attention to the book.

Mihai glared at him and left the library, going straight to the altus rector.

———

Dorian met his mother for dinner, joining her at a table.

"You look tired, Dorian. Did you find what you were looking for in the library?"

He nodded and took a bite of his food. He whispered, "I found a hidden message in the Book of Destiny. It's also in the Book of Redemption. Ayleth discovered it in the Book of Redemption and told me to look for it in our book."

"What was the message?"

"Not really a message. It's a spell. And there's more than one."

"What do the spells do?" Orienla glanced around, checking to see if anyone was trying to listen to them.

"I'll show you later. Brother Mihai was with me, trying to discover what I was up to, but he learned nothing."

"He is being very annoying."

"But he's not very smart. I liked how you told him off in the teashop. That was funny."

"Thanks, but I don't want to make enemies with him or anyone. I needed to establish a boundary with him."

Dorian finished eating. "Let's go to your room. I want to show you the spell I learned."

Orienla walked with Dorian to her room. His room was further down the same hallway on a lower level of the terradomus. A series of shafts allowed light and fresh air to enter the spartan rooms. Dorian's room was not large, with only a bed, a dresser, and a desk that could be used as a table. Orienla's room was larger, in part because of her seniority, and it was the room they gave her during the time she raised Dorian. A separate room, separated by a beaded curtain, contained her bed and dresser. The main room held a table with two chairs and a desk. Like all rooms, a leather-bound book rested on the desk's surface. The book contained short lines of inspiration centered around the teachings of the Book of Destiny.

They entered her room, and she closed the door.

"Okay, what is this spell you learned?"

Dorian pointed at the desk. He mouthed a few words and extended his hand, spreading his fingers. The book suddenly rose in the air, twisted around, and floated to the table where it dropped.

"Dorian! You have used the turpis force. Only the most senior witches are capable of that."

"I can make it much stronger." He opened his hand at the desk. As he raised it, the desk lifted. He lowered the desk back to the floor. "I have found other spells as well. One that improves my eyesight like a hawk."

"Dorian, it is important you keep this knowledge to yourself."

"You're the only one who knows."

"Does Ayleth know this spell? Can she use the turpis force?"

"Yes, she told me about it. She said she can only move small objects, but I feel I can move almost anything. I can feel the force inside me. It's like a string on a bow. I can unleash it at anytime."

"Be careful. There are those who would be very envious of your power."

"I know, especially here. I think the Whiterose order may be more understanding of who we are."

"You may be right but keep those opinions to yourself. The Umbravox don't like anyone promoting the Whiterose."

Dorian left for his own room, deep in thought.

9

Orienla made her way across the main floor of the terradomus. She had enjoyed lunch with her son, Dorian, and decided a walk outside would pleasant way to relax before meeting Ululla at a teahouse. She heard the tapping of a cane behind her. Recognizing the sound, she turned and smiled at the approaching older man.

"Keeper Truman. How nice to see you." She smiled at the average height, slimly built man. Orienla knew he required a cane because of one leg being shorter than the other. She first met him when she was in her teenage years. She had become drunk and passed out on the streets when Truman took her into the terradomus for her to recover. Truman was a watcher responsible for observing the area around the terradomus. He maintained his relationship with Orienla even after being promoted to keeper. He was one of the few witches who readily gave her a smile and informed her she was doing an excellent job raising her son.

"And to you as well. May I walk with you?"

"Of course. Is there something you wish to talk to me about?"

"There is. The watchers have been instructed to observe Brother Dorian and yourself. My understanding is there are witches that will continue to follow you even after you have left the terradomus."

"I'm not sure what to make out of this."

"Don't worry about it. No one is likely to interfere with your activities. You just need to be aware of the situation. I would suggest you carry on as normal as much as possible."

"I don't like the thought of being followed."

"They're supposed to be discrete. You could make it more difficult for them by changing your route when outside the terradomus. If you're planning to go to the market area where the tea houses are located, take a circular route and travel where there are crowds that make following you difficult."

"I will do so."

"Remember, you can come to me anytime to talk."

"Thank you. I wish you were the altus rector and not the one we have."

"I am content in my role as keeper. Peace be with you, Sister Orienla."

"And to you, Keeper Truman."

————

Orienla turned left instead of right after she left the terradomus. She walked a block before turning down a narrow lane between a garden and the rear side of vendors. The vendors were in two story, extensive buildings with living quarters above and merchant shops below. When she reached the half point of the lane, she turned around and saw two witches from the Umbravox following her. She quickened her pace, and after reaching the end of the lane, mixed in with the crowd shopping.

After a few minutes, she reached the end of the vendors, and made quick strides down another block. After checking she had lost her pursuers, she changed direction again and headed to a teahouse.

"I'm sorry I'm late, Keeper Ululla. I was being followed by witches from my terradomus. I didn't feel they should know where I was going, so I took a longer route to lose them." She sat across from Ululla, sharing a four-chair table.

"That is all right, Sister Orienla. Why are they following you?"

Orienla looked around the large tea house, seeing a mix of regular patrons and a few witches. She noticed her table was the only one with both orders of witches sharing a conversation. "They are suspicious of me." She smiled. "Partly because I regularly meet with you. You and Ayleth apparently are bad influences on Dorian and myself."

"I'm sorry. It must be difficult for you to always be scrutinized."

"It's not so bad for me, but Dorian is getting upset at the constant interference."

"Is there anything I can do?"

Orienla took a sip of her tea. "Support me if Dorian and I decide to become Whiterose witches?"

"Unquestionably. For your sake, I hope it doesn't come to that."

Orienla enjoyed the rest of the conversation with Ululla, bid her goodbye and returned to the terradomus. *It's good to have someone to talk to, even it is of the Whiterose order. I wish Dorian wasn't subject to the paranoia of our elders. They believe he will be part of the great battle against evil, but he's just a boy. They should let him grow up without so much interference.*

After she returned to the terradomus, Orienla noticed a witch carrying a knapsack on his back standing in the entrance way.

"Hello, you appear to be new here. Do you need help? I'm Sister Orienla."

"Yes, thank you. I'm Brother Trav. I have not been in such a large terradomus before, and I'm not sure where to go to be assigned a room by the keeper." The tall, dark-haired witch gave a sheepish smile.

"Keeper Truman is on the lower level. I will show you."

"You are most kind."

"Where are you from, Brother Trav?"

"The Equisurbem Terradomus. Previous to that I was at the Kireland Terradomus."

"It seems you are a bit of a wanderer."

"I guess I am, although I hope to stay here for a while. Thank you for showing me to the office of the keeper. Peace be with you, Sister Orienla."

"And to you." She walked away, but after a few steps turned to look back. He was looking at her, and they exchanged a smile.

———

Dorian ate his stew and bread with his mother. He was worried about her welfare, and decided having meals with her gave him the opportunity to help protect her. She was treated as an outcast in the terrado-mus, and he wasn't sure why.

It did not surprise him when a male witch approached him, telling him the altus rector wanted to speak with him.

"I will, after I finish my meal." He slowed down his eating, enjoying the angry look of the witch. *I don't enjoy being ordered around.*

The male witch lectured Dorian as they made their way to the altus rector's office.

"When the altus rector summons you, you do not have the luxury to finish your meal or continue with whatever the task you're doing. The altus rector deserves the utmost respect and his time is valuable. You should feel blessed he has chosen to speak with you."

Dorian remained silent as he plodded alongside the witch.

They reached the altus rector's office.

"Brother Dorian to see the altus rector. He is sorry for being tardy. The witch left Dorian standing by the secretary's desk.

"Sit. I will summon you when it's time to see the altus rector."

"I prefer to stand." Dorian put his hands behind his back.

"I told you to sit."

"I won't."

"This is outrageous. You will sit immediately, or else there will be severe repercussions."

"I will stand here. I don't have to obey you."

"I am a senior witch, the secretary to the altus rector and you will obey my orders." She stood, raising her voice.

"No."

"We'll see about your attitude." She stomped to the office door of the altus rector, pulled a leather cord, and went inside. Moments later, she returned. "You're in serious trouble. Altus Rector Carlton will deal with you now."

Dorian shrugged his shoulders and entered the office. He stood in front of the altus rector's desk. The desk had an open book in front of the altus rector. The thick, wood covered book had large black print with a drawing of road leading to a castle on an adjoining page. On one side of the desk was a pot of tea and a cup. On the other side of the desk was a lantern, the yellow light giving sufficient illumination to read by.

Dorian recognized the book as an interpretation of some passages in the Book of Destiny.

"Sit, Brother Dorian. Or do you want to have an argument with me on that request?"

Dorian sat.

"I keep hearing troubling reports about your behaviour. Despite my earlier suggestion that you be more open to Brother Mihai's offer of friendship, you recently spurred his offer of help while in the library. In fact, you foolishly claimed you knew more than he did about the Book of Destiny.

"Then there is the matter of you standing with the Whiterose order during the Royal procession. To be clear, that gives the impression you prefer their company over ours.

"Brother Dorian, your continuing rejection of the Umbravox principles is a cause for concern. Be aware that it is not only you who will face measured discipline but also those who are close to you. Your mother has tried to protect you, but now she put herself into a situation that can be unpleasant."

Dorian stood. "I will not have you threaten or harm her."

"Sit down. You will not tell me what I can and cannot do. You made unfortunate choices and now must be prepared for unpleasant consequences. This is to help your development as a proper member of the Umbravox. If I should choose to extend your discipline to your mother, you must understand it is because you have failed to understand your obligations."

Dorian took a deep breath. He extended his hand, spreading his fingers, and in a quick motion, swung it to his side. Suddenly, the pot of tea and the cup flew off the desk, shattering on the floor. He swung his hand in the opposite direction, causing the lantern to crash onto the floor.

The altus rector gasped.

"You will not threaten me or my mother again!" He shoved his hand forward.

The altus rector and the chair he was sitting in slid back until it reached the wall behind him. He moaned at the impact.

Dorian moved his hand again, sending the heavy book into the altus rector's chest. Blood dripped from his nose and his jaw was slack. He groaned as his head slumped forward.

"If you ever cause any harm to my mother, I will end your life!" He pointed a finger at the altus rector. He heard a sound behind him and turned to see the secretary rush in as Dorian walked out of the room.

————

Altus Rector Carlton looked at the concerned face of his secretary and became aware she was speaking to him. "The altus councillium. Notify them immediately. We have a demon in our midst!"

10

King Grayson listened to the messenger, who had arrived breathing hard. The messenger had come from near an outpost of the Allisure kingdom.

"King Hadrian has amassed troops between the Dwykath and Allisure border along the River Lewis. They have set up tents and look to be prepared for a long battle. It appears they out number our troops by two to one. Lord Trey has sent additional troops to the area for support, and they will arrive in two days' time. Allisure troops will be still outnumbered, but our soldiers are better trained."

"Let us hope we can prevail and hold them. We don't have many troops between the River Lewis and our castle." He turned to Captain Hawkins. "Are our Royal Guards in good order and prepared for battle?"

"Yes, my lord. We are ready for any eventuality."

"Any eventuality covers a lot of possibilities." He frowned. "I admire your confidence. However, we must assume King Hadrian may have a few surprises. I want you to ensure my sons will not be at the front lines defending the castle. I do not want them exposed during the first attack here. They need to be kept in the castle's interior and not at the perimeter walls."

"I understand. Your sons are brave men and will want to defend the castle, but I will ensure they understand we do not need them at the castle walls."

———

Queen Elissa approached her husband, King Grayson, in the throne room. He acknowledged her with a smile.

"What brings you here?" He gestured at the throne chair next to the one he sat in. "We aren't planning to receive any guests today."

"I'm not here for any pompous ceremony." She sat next to him in her oversized chair. "But there is something I need to talk to you about."

"Our sons."

"Yes, I don't want them fighting against King Hadrian's army. In particular, Nicholas seems too eager to want to engage in fighting. I want you to order them to stay in their rooms during an attack." She was careful not to use Terrowin's name, not wanting him to think he was the main reason for her seeking their protection. The truth was, the king was suspicious of who Terrowin's father was, but not enough to accuse the queen of infidelity. It was common knowledge the king had mistresses, but the queen was supposed to remain faithful. If he was to accuse her of being unfaithful, she would lose her title of queen and be removed from the royal court. The king was not willing to go that far on mere suspicion, but as the years passed, facial features on Terrowin were less like his brothers or the king.

King Grayson sighed. "I cannot do that. Our sons are men. We did not raise them to hide from their responsibilities. If there is a battle, how would it look for our sons to be hiding in their rooms? How can our people respect them as leaders afterward?"

"I just don't want them to be hurt or killed."

"Neither do I. They will be protected, but I will not shelter them."

Queen Elissa stood. "I have said what I wanted to. Please don't let our sons come to harm because you want them to be men."

She walked away, leaving the king upset.

11

Dorian went straight to his room after his confrontation with the altus rector. He sat on the edge of his bed, taking deep breaths of air. *I overreacted. I shouldn't have threatened him. I will disappoint mother when she learns what I did.* He left his room and knocked on his mother's door.

"What is it?" She saw the scared look on his face. "Did they do something to you?" She stood away from the doorway, gesturing for him to enter.

Dorian closed the door and leaned against it. "I'm sorry. I lost my temper and used the turpis force on him. I hurt him badly."

"Who? The altus rector?"

Dorian nodded. "He said because of me, he was going to punish you. I got so angry, and I, I hit him with the turpis force. I don't know what to do now."

"The first thing to do is to calm down. Sit, I'll pour you a tea. Remember the teachings of the Book of Destiny. Meditate and find the calm within you and let it expand."

Dorian sat in a simple chair by the table. He closed his eyes and spread his fingers, lightly touching his chest.

"Are you feeling better now?"

He opened his eyes and saw the offered cup of tea. "Yes. But I still don't know what to do."

"You will. You must wait for the next event to appear and react accordingly. One cannot plan to do something of a thousand possibilities. That is a waste of your energy. Whatever happens next, I will be with you."

———

Dorian sat with his mother in the dining room. In the two days since his incident with the altus rector, none of the senior members of the terradomus approached them. No one challenged them, but they received some stares and whispered comments.

"I don't understand. Why hasn't anyone said anything to me?"

"I don't know, except I suspect the elders are viewing their options on what to do with us. They may be concerned about your ability to use the turpis force."

"Do we just act as if nothing has happened?"

"For now. We have to be wary of any changes in how they react to us."

She looked around and saw a familiar face carrying a tray. When he gave her a smile, she beckoned him to their table. "Brother Trav, please join us. This is my son, Dorian."

"Brother Dorian, it is good to meet you." Trav sat. "It is good to see you again, Sister Orienla. How have you been?"

"We have been fine. Are you adjusting to our terradomus?"

"Yes, the witches I have encountered are very friendly."

Dorian asked, "have you noticed anything different with our terradomus compared to others?"

"It's bigger." He laughed.

"I mean, is our place quieter than others?"

Trav looked around. "Well, it is quieter than normal here. There could a be a good reason for that."

"You mean something bad may be happening?"

"Not necessarily." He gave Orienla a wink. "It may mean something good."

Altus Rector Carlton ventured into the Hall of Sentential. He paused at the entrance to the large hall, where circular bench seating could hold hundreds. At the front was a raised planform with a long table that could seat seven on one side. Carlton recalled sitting at the table when he addressed the assembly. Waiting for him behind a table sat three members of the altus councillium. The woman in the centre looked up at his entrance.

"Altus Rector Carlton, please take a seat."

Carlton sat in the single chair facing the table.

"We are concerned about why you reported Brother Dorian is a demon. Can you go through what happened that drew you to that conclusion?"

Carlton cleared his throat. "One of my responsibilities, besides the orderly running of the terradomus, was to ensure the safety and the well-being of Brother Dorian. In that light, I endeavoured to give him, and his mother, additional support. The Whiterose order's teachings may have drawn his attention, which concerned me. His father is a Whiterose witch, and I tried to reduce their interaction as much as possible."

"Pardon for the interruption, but Dorian's father, Brother Alric, has the right to interact with his son. From my understanding, he would be a positive influence. Keeping a father and a son separate from each other is not something we teach in the Umbravox."

"Yes, of course, but I was concerned Brother Dorian would want to join the Whiterose order. I asked Brother Mihai to befriend him and his mother, Sister Orienla. Unfortunately, Brother Dorian repeatedly refuses to accept his overtures of friendship. When I challenged Brother Dorian on his refusal to befriend Brother Mihai, he became argumentative."

"Altus Rector Carlton, you understand the Umbravox does not believe in forced or prearranged marriages?"

"Yes, of course."

"Then, in the same vein, why would you believe we should force friendship? Shouldn't friendship be natural?"

"Yes, I suppose so. I was only trying to help him appreciate the ways of our order."

"Continue. Why do you believe he became a demon?"

"During my last meeting with him, he became angry and used the turpis force. It was disturbing use of its power, pushing me to a wall and sending a heavy book against my chest. I believe only a demon could harness such power. His anger was immense. He threatened to kill me."

"May I ask what you may have said to provoke such a reaction from him?"

"I merely stated his behaviour would have consequences, and not only for himself, but also for those he was close to, such as his mother."

"Altus Rector Carlton, was it your intention to cause Brother Dorian to fear for his mother's safety if he didn't obey your suggestions?"

"Yes, he needed to know the full measure of what happens when one doesn't follow the Umbravox's teachings."

"From what we can ascertain, Brother Dorian was protecting his mother after you threatened him and her. I would not classify that action as a demon." She paused and continued after looking at a paper in front of her. "You are the replacement of the previous altus rector that was found wanting of honesty and devotion of the principles of the Umbravox. We respect your strict observation of the Book of Destiny, and your desire to extend those beliefs to Brother Dorian. However, it would appear your relationship with Brother Dorian has been harmed enough to become a source of constant conflict. You are aware, Brother Dorian is part of the prophecy in the Umbravox teachings. It is important that he feels comfortable here and not tempted to join his father in the Whiterose order.

"It is with this in mind, we have changed the altus rector at the Jital Terradomus. Altus Rector Carlton, you are being reassigned as the altus rector at the Drumon Terradomus. This new posting is effective immediately."

Carlton stood, his face flushed and his lower lip quivering. "I..." He swallowed. "I accept your decision and will make haste for the Drumon Terradomus." He turned and hurried out of the room.

12

Orienla sat with her son, Dorian, in the common room. It was quiet in the afternoon, with only a scattering of chairs being used. Most of the users were drinking tea, sharing conversation or reading scrolls.

"Something is happening here," Dorian commented. "The elders were whispering among themselves, and it feels quiet in the hallways."

"I know. I heard the altus councillium was visiting. When they arrive, it usually means something important is about to occur."

"Are they here because of something I did? I know I overreacted when I met with the altus rector."

Orienla frowned. "Perhaps, but they could be here for other reasons. No matter what happens, I will be with you. Together, we will be fine." She thought about the wink she received from Trav. *He acted like he knows something he can't tell us.*

They continued to drink tea, with Dorian announcing he was hungry. "Let's go to the dining room."

"Sure, it will be good to have a fresh cup of tea."

Orienla sat at a table while Dorian went to the kitchen counter to obtain bread and cheese.

"Hungry again?" the witch on the other side of the counter smiled.

She was fair skinned with blonde hair and appeared slightly younger than himself.

"Yes." He returned her smile. "I'm Brother Dorian."

"I know. Sister Bethena is my name. Maybe we can have tea sometime."

"Sure, that would be nice." He returned to his table with an extra tea for his mother.

"You look happy." Orienla looked over at the kitchen and saw the young lady who served him. "Oh. Did you ask her for a date?"

"No, she asked me." He grinned.

Orienla laughed. "Well, you are getting popular with some witches."

Dorian ate the bread and cheese, not wanting to extend the conversation. Shortly after he finished, a female witch arrived at their table. "The altus rector would like to see both of you." She gestured with her hand to follow her.

Orienla and Doran carried their cups and plates to the receiving counter and followed the witch, an older, slim woman who moved at a brisk pace.

A middle-aged male witch greeted them as they reached the office of the altus rector and stood at their approach.

"Sister Orienla, Brother Dorian." He gave a friendly smile. "Please wait a moment while I inform the altus rector you're here."

Orienla commented to her son in a low voice. "This is much better than my last visit."

The man returned and said, "The altus rector will see you now." The witch stood at the door and gestured for them to enter.

Orienla entered, recognizing the new altus rector immediately. "Keeper Truman! You're the new altus rector!" She took quick steps as Truman stood and stepped around his desk. He used his cane to aid his journey, grasping her hand as they met.

"It is wonderful they have given you this position. I know you'll make a great altus rector."

"Thank you for your confidence." He looked at Dorian. "Your mother and I have been friends for a long time, as you know. I am now in a better position to help her and yourself. Let's sit down and talk." He lifted his cane. "I'm not able to stand for long periods."

They sat around the desk and Truman grunted as he dropped into his chair. "I'm glad this chair is padded. I have a lot of work to do here." He pushed a few of the scrolls off to the side.

"As a former keeper, you must be used to doing written reports." Orienla smiled as she sat.

"True words. There is a sequence of events that has occurred with my promotion to altus rector. One is that I have to fill the former position of keeper I held. I've decided on Sister Evaline. She is a bright woman and is still relatively young. I didn't want to promote someone who saw the role of keeper as a retirement position."

"Sister Evaline was a watcher, was she not?" Orienla asked.

"Yes, which leaves an open position for a watcher." He paused and looked at Orienla. "I would like you to be our new watcher."

"Me? I would be honoured."

"It involves long hours, as well as nighttime work. Lots of strong tea helps with those after sunset duties."

"I believe I can endure those conditions." She smiled. "Thank you so much for thinking of me for this."

"You are a resourceful woman who observes what is going on around her. Keeper Ululla of the Whiterose order is friends with you. We need witches in positions of influences who are not prejudiced against others because of their beliefs." He focused on Dorian. "This leads me to my next request. Brother Dorian, I know of Sister Ayleth is of the Whiterose, and you're very close to her. The altus councillium wants a less hostile relationship between the Whiterose and ourselves. In fact, they believe it is time for our two orders to work together.

"Brother Dorian, I ask you to take on a special assignment. Will you help bring our two orders together?"

"Yes, Altus Rector Truman. I will do my best."

"Excellent. We are facing troubled times. We must join forces that are good at fighting the evil ones.

"I know the Umbravox has not always made you feel trusted, but I assure you, I see you as a valued member of the Umbravox."

———

Orienla left with her son. She felt light on her feet as they walked.

"Altus Rector Truman has given you an important task."

"I know. I have a plan to bring the two orders together."

"What is it?"

He grinned. "I'll tell you later."

She watched him walk away to the library and turned toward the common room. Near a seating area at the back, she saw Trav sit with two other witches, sharing tea and conversation. Orienla walked over.

"May I join you?"

"Of course," a witch replied. "Brother Trav is new here."

"We have met." Orienla sat and chatted with the witches, surprised how friendly they were to her.

After the two other witches left, Orienla asked Trav, "you knew something was going to happen with the altus rector."

"Perhaps I just thought a change was about to occur."

"A coincidence then, you arrive, ask to speak to the keeper, and shortly later he is made altus rector."

He smiled. "Well, since the Jital Terradomus will be my new home, it is good that there is a strong and fair altus rector."

"Your home for how long?"

"I hope this will be my final stop."

She stood. "I hope you will be here a long time too. Peace be with you, Brother Trav."

"And to you, Sister Orienla. Oh, and congratulations on being named a watcher."

13

Elsh, soldier second class, tried to peer through the downpour of the cold rain. The day had started with just a few clouds, but as the time for the battle came near, angry clouds formed ahead. When the battle horn sounded, the rumble of thunder accompanied it. The sky lit up with lightning, and the growl of thunder sounded like an angry beast. He pushed on; his sword raised at unseen enemies with the sticky mud hindering each step.

He thought about his young wife and child back home, and wished he didn't have to join the army to make enough coin to put bread on the table. Elsh knew he wasn't skilled with a sword and was scared. Each step took him down the slope where the creek now was awash with mud, rock and water. If he could make it through the stream of debris, he would have to climb the steeper slope and engage the enemy.

Elsh made it to the water's edge, stepping around a body of a comrade with his head submerged in the cold water. He could just make out the battle ahead. Men on horses were trying to climb the bank on the other side, but the enemy held the high ground, keeping them at bay. Despite starting out with a higher number of soldiers, they were losing to King Grayson's army. Bodies of men and horses fell back into the water.

What chance do I have of surviving this? He thought of his wife and daughter, clutching his sword like a lifeline.

He crossed the torrent of water and advanced up the muddy rise, stepping on bodies of fallen soldiers. *Forgive me.*

He looked up through the rain and saw a large man, his beard bursting out of his helmet like a mushroom held up-side-down. The bigger man grinned at him, beckoning him to advance. *I don't have any chance in a battle with him, even if this was level ground.*

"Move up! Move up!"

He listened to the impatient shouts of those soldiers behind him, urging him to sacrifice himself so others could step on his body to move up the muddy bank.

Suddenly, the faint blast of a horn, signalling to pull back, reached his ears. He almost wept with joy at the opportunity to return to their miserable camp. *I'll live another day. Thank you, Almighty, for your mercy.* He turned around, not wanting to even look at his adversary one more time.

———

Commander Willis growled as his lieutenants filed into the large tent. A table held a large map with multiple markings on it. Behind the table, a canvas sheet hid where his cot sat.

"What in hell's fury is going on out there? We had to pull back, like bloody cowards." He pointed a finger at one of his men. "Talk! What happened?"

"Sir, it was impossible to cross that damn stream. The rain washed out the sides of the bank and the stream is flooded. Even horses had trouble crossing it. We could barely see a sword's length in front of us, it rained so hard. When we reached the other side, the enemy found us to be easy targets." Lieutenant Savard stuttered out his explanation.

"It's not raining that hard here."

"True, but as we approached the stream, the rain became harder and colder. They have placed a curse on us."

Willis thought of the time a few months ago when dark magic was used to help his troops in battle, only to find a counter-spell had been used to remove it. Soldiers didn't like the use of magic in battle. Even if it aided them to win the day, there were often consequences to be paid later. "That may be so, but our king has ordered us to cross that stream and claim the territory in his name." He walked around in a small circle, causing his lieutenants to take a step back. People knew he had a bad temper, so it was better to keep a distance when he got disappointed.

"Okay, here's what we shall do. Have a messenger carry a white flag and inform them we need to bury our dead. We don't need vampires or ghouls feeding on them. Go downstream in case the river carried away some bodies." He pointed at another man. "Go up steam and have a bridge made that will cross that bloody stream. Strong and wide enough to carry to horses one at a time. Make sure it's far enough away King Grayson's men don't see it. And get me a messenger to send the news of our battle to King Hadrian."

A messenger appeared in the tent after the lieutenants had gone. The young man spoke nervously, fidgeting with his hands. "You desired to see me, Commander Willis?"

"Yeah. You must travel with haste to King Hadrian." He passed a rolled note to him. "In case the king prefers not to read my message, inform him we have repelled the first attack by King Grayson's army and are preparing for the second assault. King Grayson's army is employing dark magic against us, using storms to try to defeat us. We are holding our own and hope to counterattack soon. Now go."

Willis watched the messenger run to a waiting horse. He hoped his king wouldn't remember they were the ones who'd initiated the attack, and therefore King Grayson's army repelling them. As far as the dark magic was concerned, he wasn't certain magic was involved, and if it was, by whom. The Allisure Kingdom was not known to use magic in battles before.

———

Kylye ran his horse hard, and not just because Commander Willis told him to make haste. Once he left the camp's boundaries, he heard the whines of ghouls as they travelled where the dying and the dead could be fed on. Vampires were a concern as well, but they preferred the weakened state of the dying for a meal. Ghouls became excited at the smell of death, and sometimes would attack the living. The fact he was alone, and not well versed in fighting with a sword, made him feel vulnerable.

He sat low on the saddle, watching for areas of ambush, such as riding underneath a tree limb, or along a swamp area. To his left, he glimpsed the pale skin of a ghoul just ahead, hiding behind a tree stump. He reached for his knife, knowing he didn't have time to draw his sword. He wouldn't have time to react even with his knife, except his horse saw the danger as well, swerving to the right. The precious second slowed the leap of the ghoul. The black-nailed fingers were a contrast to the white skin as they reached out. Instead of Kylye, the claws dug into the horse's hide. His knife swung wide but connected to the neck of the ghoul. It leaned back, howling, showing off sharp, yellow teeth. He saw the skinny creature had small breasts. The female ghouls were no less aggressive than the males, only smaller. The knife blade pressed past the hard muscles and the ghoul dropped away, howling in her rage.

His hand shook from the encounter, but he refused to sheath his knife. The moon, at three-quarters, provided enough light for him to keep a steady pace. The ghouls were quieter, and he assumed that as he moved away from the camp, he was less likely to encounter them. He hoped he would have the chance to rest before he arrived at King Hadrian's castle. The trail through the bush led to a dirt road, and he gratefully directed the horse on the easier route.

Under the moonlight, he could see blood on the horse's flank where the ghoul had attacked. It pleased him his knife stopped the creature from continuing its strike. He considered it would not so easily to have deterred a werewolf. A three-quarters moon wasn't as likely to cause a transformation of a human to a lycanthrope form, although he had heard some were more sensitive to the moon light than others and could change format less than a full moon.

———

The ghouls and other creatures of the night disappeared as he increased his distance from the fighting. He steered the horse to higher ground, finding an open area along a hill. Kylye slid off the horse, tying the reins to a tree branch. He placed his back to the same tree and slowly slid down the trunk until he was in a sitting position with his legs sticking straight out in front of him.

Now that I'm away from those cursed ghouls, this is a lot better than fighting in rain and the mud. I just need a few minutes to relax and then I better get going.

Kylye woke up with a start. He saw the horse try backing away from the tree branch. Kylye jumped up, reaching for his sword. He stared past the sparse trees around him and saw several glowing eyes peer at him.

Wolves.

He yelled at them. "Get!"

They didn't move, continuing to stare. He picked up a rock and threw it at the closest one. The wolf dodged the stone, but slowly turned and trotted away. The rest of the pack followed it.

Kylye let out a sigh of relief. As a farm boy in charge of protecting a flock of sheep along with a pair of farm dogs, he knew wolves were careful about what they attacked and avoided confrontations with humans. Unless they were hungry, then they could be more aggressive. Still, noise and showing the wolves he was not afraid usually deterred them from coming too close.

He climbed back on the horse. "Come on. Rest time is over."

The horse didn't need encouragement to leave the area, galloping until Kylye slowed it down. "We may need your energy later if we encounter any more creatures."

Daylight arrived, and he continued his journey past a scattering of farms, a village, and the outside wall of the Kingdom of Dwykath. Two guards watched him without a comment as he passed the outside and followed a stone road to the inner barrier. Here he was stopped by one of the four guards.

"What is your business here?"

"A message for the king about the battle with the Kingdom of Allisure."

The bearded guard sized him up, decided he was telling the truth, and told him to proceed.

Compared to his encounter with the wolves, Kylye felt worried. Addressing the king with information about a battle that was not going well was not something he looked forward to. When he reached the castle, he dismounted the horse and went up the steps to face another set of guards.

He again explained he had a message for the king about the battle.

"King Hadrian does not like being disturbed, especially with bad news." The tall guard with a scar on his left cheek sneered at him. "But if you want to risk your balls, that's up to you." He grabbed Kylye's arm and pulled him along.

Kylye felt the strength in the guard's hand as it squeezed him at the elbow. Up they climbed a staircase and along a wide hallway.

"Wait here." The guard ordered and entered a double set of doors.

Kylye heard him address the king, informing him a messenger was here about the battle with the Kingdom of Allisure.

"Then send him in, you idiot!"

They pushed Kylye into the room. He stumbled to his knees, and he looked up at the king.

"Well? Are you going to speak, or should I have it beaten out of you?" The king shouted at him.

"Yes, my lord, sorry." Kylye licked his lips. He held up the rolled parchment that the king roughly snatched away. "Commander Willis' troops have successfully repelled the advance by the Allisure forces. The Allisure side is using magic, causing heavy rain to prevent the advancement of our soldiers."

"Magic, you say? Rain?"

"Yes, very heavy rain that makes crossing the river difficult. We have to climb a muddy, slippery bank where the Allisure troops have the high ground."

The king grunted and read the message on the rolled paper. He tossed the paper on a table. "So, they used magic. I doubt their magic can match what I plan to unleash." He pointed a finger at a servant. "Send me a scribe immediately."

The servant disappeared, returning with an old man carrying a roll of paper, plus a pen and a clay pot. He sat at a table and soon had added ink to his pen from the vessel. He wrote in quick strokes, listening to King Hadrian's instructions. After he finished his writing, he handed the paper to King Hadrian, who grunted with satisfaction as he reviewed the note.

He looked at Kylye. "Inform Willis that he is to hold his position. I will send more troops and may send the devil himself to rectify things. Ensure his men are ready for a full assault in three day's time." He handed the note to him. "Now go!"

Kylye hurried out of the room. He wished he could have a rest before returning on his journey. Reluctantly, he went to the stables, requesting a fresh horse. He wondered what the note said but didn't dare read it.

14

Kylye stopped the horse by a small stream. Up to his point, he had not pushed the beast, preferring to delay the time he returned to battle. The rest of the journey to the camp would have ghouls and vampires waiting for the weak. The desperate ones would attack a healthy horse and rider. He slipped off the horse and waited as it drank.

I wish I didn't have to return to the battle. He kicked at a rock, sending it skipping down the path. Shortly later, he climbed back on the horse, urging it to gallop, rather than trot.

The first sign of he was approaching the campsite was the dark-grey smoke drifting in the sky. He knew the ghouls would become more prevalent as he travelled closer to the battlefield. The horse showed signs of nervousness as they approached a grove of trees, shying away from entering a pathway. Kylye tried turning the horse around, but again, it refused to enter.

"Damn!" He pivoted the horse in a new direction, running past the tree line. Another pathway appeared between the green foliage. "Let's try this one." He pulled out his sword and urged the horse forward. The horse hesitated but obeyed, twitching its ears as it travelled deeper into the forest.

Kylye relaxed as they went deeper between the trees, occasionally coming into a small clearing. He hoped that he could get to the camp without incident as the smoke in the sky became closer.

The screech from the attacking ghouls jarred Kylye from his focus on the surrounding forest. Several creatures jumped on the horse as it tried to run. Kylye killed one attacker with his sword, but another one hit him on his shoulders. Claws dug into his skin, and he used his elbow to hit the ghoul. The creature fell off, screaming at him.

The horse bucked, trying to get rid of its attackers, and reared up on its hind legs, throwing Kylye off. It ran, leaving him sitting on the ground. He quickly shifted to one knee, holding his sword at arm's length. He pivoted and saw a ghoul lunge at him.

The creature's howl was cut shout as his sword plunged into its chest. Kylye watched as the ghoul lay dead. Black blood pooled on the ground and a stench from it made his eyes water. He stood, holding out his sword as he looked around. The horse had disappeared into the woods. He hoped it survived and he could retrieve it later.

Kylye's instinct was to make for the woods and hope the rest of the ghouls wouldn't be searching for him. He felt alone, not seeing, or hearing, any animals or birds as he made his way toward the battleground. The quiet worried him.

A howling sound behind him caused him to turn around. He saw half a dozen ghouls scamper through the forest toward him. He ran, with little hope they would give up. He reached a small clearing among the trees, and he chanced a look behind him. The ghouls had stopped at the edge of the trees, snarling but not approaching.

That's odd. Is there something about this area? He turned around and saw what stopped the ghouls.

Two women wearing light green robes stood quietly. Both were slim; one with dark hair and the other a mixture of grey and blonde.

Witches. He took a cautious step forward, believing the witches were less of a threat to his life than the ghouls.

The older witch beckoned with a hand. "You best hurry. I'm not sure how long we can keep them away."

Kylye made a quick decision and ran to the witches.

"You may put your sword away. It is of no use now." The younger witch smiled. "Follow us."

Kylye trailed after them, looking behind him. The ghouls were still watching him. The witches took him deeper into the woods, paused at one of the largest trees and pulled open part of the trunk. He peered into the dark interior, making out a set of steps that disappeared underground, lit by a yellow light from a lantern.

The younger witch went down first, and Kylye followed next. When he reached the bottom, he heard the door above him close.

"Where are we going?"

"To our terradomus. My name is Chatlene. Sister Nollium is behind you."

"Oh. I'm Kylye."

"We know. That's why we rescued you."

He peered ahead, seeing the curved top tunnel was higher than he was tall. The walls of the tunnel were made from tightly fitted bricks. There wasn't any sign of water leakage, indicating the tunnel was well made "How far are we gong?"

"It's a long walk. We will give you food and water when we arrive at the terradomus." Chatlene turned her head to direct a question at him. "You're not scared, are you? We won't hurt you."

"I've been scared ever since the first battle I was in. I guess it's part of me now."

"You are safe now. The fear will disappear."

It surprised Kylye how long the tunnel was. He noticed a second tunnel branched off from the one they were travelling, but the weakly lit interior didn't give a hint where it went. Kylye was impressed by how the well-designed the tunnels were fairly straight. He wasn't sure how long they were walking when the tunnel rose and shortly later Chatlene opened a heavy wood door, revealing a large chamber. Kylye saw dozens of other witches, who turned to look at him.

Kylye saw they made the rectangular cavern from bricks. Light came from several torches attached to the wall and openings that allowed sunlight to enter.

"Follow me. The altus rector will want to speak with you." Chatlene led him up a flight of broad stairs, opening up to another rectangular room. As with the lower room, wall torches and openings provided light. They went to a room with a doorless entry. An older woman sat at a desk, looking up at them with a smile.

"Welcome to Westerly Terradomus. I'll inform Altus Rector Normand you are here."

He watched her rise smoothly and turned to closed oak door behind her, giving it a quick knock before opening it. He heard her announce, "Altus Rector Normand, warrior Kylye is available to see you."

Shortly later, Kylye entered the second room, decorated with a few simple paintings on the walls. The desk was plain and large. Two wood chairs faced the desk. When the altus rector stood, he made the desk seem smaller.

Kylye stood at attention, placing his hands together in front of himself.

"Relax, Kylye. There's no need to be concerned. Please, sit."

Kylye sat. "Thank you. I don't know why I'm here, or even where I am."

"You are where you're supposed to be. Fate has carried you here." Normand sat. "Allow me to be less obtuse. On your person, you are carrying instructions for your battle commander." He paused for a moment. "A Commander Willis, I recall."

"Yes." Kylye produced the rolled-up parchment from under his shirt.

"May I see it?"

Kylye passed over the document. "I haven't looked at it."

"I can tell you what was written." Normand peered at the scroll. "Commander Willis is to prepare to launch an attack during the night of the next full moon. There is a claim the rain will stop, and the enemy will be incapacitated. There are some additional instructions, but fortunately, he won't hear about them until later when a Master Diablo sees him."

"What does that mean?"

"It means a few things. One, King Hadrian, is planning to use powerful magic to win this battle. Two, now Commander Willis and his men don't know about this message. Three, we will counter their magic and ensure the battle will be fair and the Allisure forces will prevail."

"That's good, I suppose. What about me?"

"Ah, King Hadrian will assume they killed you on your way back to the battlefield. That means we need to keep you away from the Dwykath Kingdom. It wouldn't be good if they discovered you're alive."

"Does that mean I can't go home again? My family..."

"Not forever. Perhaps the better part of a year. We can send word to your family you're alive."

"Can you tell me where I am?"

"No." He smiled and shook his head. "We pride ourselves on a certain amount of secrecy. For a few days, you will be our guest here. Later, you will travel to your new home. I assure you that you will be safe."

After exiting the meeting with the altus rector, Kylye was escorted to a dining area where he finally had enough to eat to fill his stomach. Although the witches were reserved in their dealings with him, they were still pleasant to him. He felt relaxed for the first time in months, and he was grateful he wasn't heading to battle soon.

15

Commander Willis noticed the change in the weather. The rain that he cursed at in the early morning finally stopped. As the clouds parted, he made his way to the edge of the river and peered across. The Allisure forces waited there, daring his army to make their way across the muddy banks.

"Commander Willis, you have a visitor."

Willis turned around and faced Lieutenant Savard. "Who the hell is it? A messenger?"

Savard made a sour face. "He calls himself Master Diablo. I don't like the looks of him."

Willis frowned and went to his tent. Inside, he saw a tall figure wearing a hooded robe waiting for him.

"What do you want? Who sent you?"

"I'm assisting King Hadrian. That is all you need to know. I have put an end to the spell that was causing the rain. King Hadrian sent you a message. Have you completed the preparations?"

"I didn't receive any message from King Hadrian." Willis saw the glare from Diablo's eyes and wanted to take a step back. *This man is full of evil. I can feel it.*

"Your kingdom is full of incompetence. I was hoping you and your men could follow simple instructions." His lips curled back, showing yellow teeth. "Here is what I want done. Do not fail me this time."

Willis listened to Diablo, barking out demands in a sour breath. He wanted to run his sword through the arrogant figure, but fear prevented him from doing anything but nodding his head. After Diablo left, Willis went to ordering his men to complete the instructions.

———

Fear gripped Elsh, making him even more terrified than when he was in battle. He felt ill as he joined three other soldiers escorted by armed men went to the location where a temporary bridge had been built. The narrow walkway was composed of trees tied together by ropes. It appeared to Elsh it would be strong enough to hold people, but insufficient for horses.

The four men stood, surrounded by the soldiers, who didn't look pleased at their task. They waited until a hooded figure approached them, carrying a pot and ladle. One of the armed men reluctantly took the pot and ladle and approached Elsh.

"Swallow this."

Elsh looked at the red mixture. "What is it?"

"I don't know, and I doubt I want to. Eat."

The thick liquid tasted like rotten meat, with flavour remaining in his mouth after he forced down the vile paste. The other three men were required to accept the ladle as well, with one man being prodded with a sword before sipping from the ladle.

Elsh felt light-headed. A tingling sensation began in his hands, travelling down his arms.

"Strip off your clothes," the soldier holding the pot commanded.

Are they planning to kill us here as a sacrifice? Elsh slowly removed his clothes, wondering what was to happen to him. He heard the hooded man chant phrases that had no meaning for him. He stood, wavering like a drunk with the other naked men.

A heavy feeling enveloped him, and he fell to his knees, tumbling slowly to the wet, grassy ground. He was dimly aware of a man's low voice, giving instructions.

The pain went through his entire body. Elsh felt distorted as he extended an arm. He opened his eyes to a moon-lit night. His moan came out as a growl. Slowly he drew himself to a crawling position, and he looked down, seeing fur covered paws with long fingers ending in claws. He stood, partly bent-over, and looked around.

There were two other werewolves by him, staring at the surrounding landscape. Another creature lay on the ground, still, a strange combination of human and wolf. The upper body was that of a wolf, the lower half of a man.

He heard one werewolf howl, and he joined in. Suddenly, Elsh sprinted toward the bridge. He knew his task; to kill the king and his sons. His companions raced with him, their claws tearing up the muddy fields and crossed the newly constructed bridge. They didn't see many soldiers at first, but as they neared the Allisure castle's boundary, they spotted guards and peasants bustling around their tasks in the dim light.

Elsh bounded over a low stone wall, racing through a market area. Most of the stalls were empty, but as he ran, dogs barked. A man shouted at him as he approached the next barrier, a high stone wall. He sprinted along the wall with his companions, approaching the entrance protected by two guards. The upper position of the portcullis, made of a lattice of iron, was maintained.

A guard screamed as a werewolf leaped at him, its jaws tearing away at his face. The second guard died without crying out as a were-wolf clamped its mouth on his throat. Elsh didn't slow down as he ran to the castle. He avoided the front entrance, where four guards stood in front of the heavy double doors. Instead, he leaped up to a balcony, tearing into an empty room. Seconds later, he burst into a hallway, scrambling on four paws to gain purchase on the marble floor.

He heard men shouting and women screaming as he ran up the wide stairs. He ignored those who pressed to the stone railing along the stairs, but when a guard raised his sword to defend, he launched himself. The blade of the sword cut at his shoulder, but the force of his leap knocked the soldier down. Seconds later, he ripped out the throat of his adversary.

He left the guard gurgling his last breath and turned to a hallway, sensing a prince was nearby.

Another werewolf sprinted past him, growling as a pink tongue fell out the side of its mouth. The second werewolf didn't hesitate as it turned a corner to another hallway. Elsh followed.

Two princes stood, each holding a sword. Four guards stood in front with swords held high. The two werewolves leaped at the guards, determined to reach the princes.

Screams and howls followed.

Elsh reached one guard, making quick work of the feeble attempt to defend. He bit the guard on the arm, ripping off the uniform, skin, and muscle. The guard moaned on the floor and Elsh attacked the next guard. A wild swing with the sword by the guard struck him at his side, slicing him at the hip. Elsh pounced on him, using his front paws and teeth to tear open his chest. The man yelled out a death scream.

A prince tried to back away, but Elsh didn't waste a moment. He charged into the chest of the prince, knocking him down. The prince struggled underneath the snapping jaws. He dropped his sword and tried to use his fists to beat off the monster, to no avail. Seconds later the prince lay dead, and Elsh looked around. He saw the other werewolf had locked its jaws on the neck of a dead prince and was shaking the body. A guard, his left side covered in blood, slowly rose to his knees. He drew back his sword and lunged forward. The sword pierced the side of the werewolf holding a prince. The creature howled in pain and dropped dead.

Elsh ignored the dead princes and werewolf. He searched out the hallways for the king and the remaining princes. The other werewolf joined him. Elsh sensed the king was behind a set of wood doors and threw his body weight at them. The doors shuddered but held. He clawed at the wood and pressed against them, but couldn't force his way in. Snarling, he turned down the hallway, where two princes stood behind four guards.

The other werewolf raced past him, absorbing an arrow into its shoulder. It didn't slow him as he burst between two guards, leaping at a prince.

Arrows flew at Elsh, keeping him at a distance. He growled as he watched the other werewolf absorb swords and knives as he attacked a prince, pinning him to the floor as it used its teeth to tear flesh away from bones. Elsh heard the screams and tried to advance, but several more arrows punctured his body. He yelped in pain and slipped to the floor on his side. He rolled and got back on his four legs. Blood poured on the floor, and he knew he was dying.

Clarity of who he was suddenly came to him. He stood on his hind legs and lifted one fur covered arm. Elsh slowly spread both arms. The prince held his bow with an arrow and stared at him. Elsh spread his arms wide. *Make your aim true.*

The arrow flew into his chest, and Elsh crumbled to the floor. In his blurred vision, he saw his outstretched arm change to a human arm. He rolled on his back, seeing the last remaining prince stand above him, holding the drawn bow and arrow pointed at him.

Elsh took in a shuddering breath and whispered out his last words, "Thank you."

16

Commander Willis swore as he surveyed the battleground. The Allisure forces had decimated his troops. Rather than extend the battle to the evening as the plan laid out by Master Diablo, Willis called an early retreat in the late afternoon.

Damn if I'm going to sacrifice my men so he can do his dark magic.

"Commander Willis, we secured the camp and are tending to the wounded."

Willis turned and saw Lieutenant Tybalt standing with his arms crossed. He didn't look pleased at delivering the report.

"Tybalt, I know you're upset, but none of this is on us or our men. That slimy Master Diablo used us as a diversion so he could send his creatures to the Allisure castle. He didn't care our men were killed. All he wanted was for as many of the Allisure troops as possible to be engaged with us, so there were few guards left at the castle. As a result, we are now pinned by two fronts."

"What do we do? If we fight, we die."

Willis frowned. "I don't know yet, but one thing I will not do is send more of our men to be killed on a cursed diversion tactic. Tybalt, our focus now is to keep our men safe long enough so we can fight again."

———

Prince Terrowin stood over the dead man. Only a minute earlier, he was a werewolf, threatening his life and others. Now the naked body showed no signs of being a monster, other than blood around his mouth and hands. His last words, "Thank you," haunted Terrowin.

"You need to come with me, Prince Terrowin."

Terrowin felt the hand of a royal guard on his shoulder and pushed him down the hall. "Where are we going?"

"To the king's chambers, Prince Terrowin."

They arrived at King Grayson's bedroom, where the royal guard pounded on the door and announced he was with Prince Terrowin. After they went past the door covered with claw marks, his mother hugged Terrowin.

"Thank God you're alive." Tears rolled down her cheeks.

"Prince Terrowin killed the last werewolf himself with a well-place arrow. He showed great courage in taking down the beast," the royal guard announced.

"Well done, Terrowin." King Grayson placed a hand on his back.

"My brothers and sisters. Are they okay?" When he didn't hear a reply, he broke from his mother's embrace and faced the king.

Tears flowed from his eyes. "Terrowin, your sisters are safe and unharmed. Your brothers..." Grayson took a moment to compose himself. "Your brothers died bravely, defending the kingdom."

Terrowin closed his eyes and clenched his fists. "I cannot believe they are gone."

The king put a hand on each shoulder. "It has happened, and now we must protect you at all costs. Terrowin, I must send you away from here, far away from the battleground."

"I want to stay here and fight and seek my revenge."

"That may be what you want, but you must trust me when I say you need to stay safe. You are to be the next king. We must act accordingly."

Terrowin heard the conviction in the king's voice. He said goodbye to the king and queen and was led by the royal guard to a door, a door he recalled that joined to the queen's chambers via a private, short walkway. Instead of going to the queen's bedroom, the royal guard pushed on a wall, revealing a stone staircase.

The guard handed him a torch, and Terrowin peered down into the darkness.

"Go straight. Don't take any of the side tunnels. At the end, you'll come across a wood door."

"Where am I going?"

The guard handed him a canteen. "It's a long journey, but it ends at the Whiterose Terradomus in Jital."

Where Ayleth lives.

———

Terrowin walked in a daze down the stone tunnel, processing the recent events. After a period, he noticed they made the tunnel of rectangular stones fitted tightly together. The tunnel's construction featured a floor that was mostly level, while the sides and roof were curved. Insects and mice were his only company as he walked down the long tunnel.

Periodically, he came across an unlit torch. When his torch died down, he exchanged it for another one. He noticed the smoke from his torch didn't just linger at the ceiling but disappeared between spaces of the rocks. Terrowin took a drink of water, wondering how far he had to go. He knew by horse it was a full day's ride to Jital from the castle, but the route was full of curves and twists. The tunnel was more or less straight, and he felt he could arrive at Jital by morning.

He was unsure what time it was, but the events of the day fatigued him. He used his torch to light another one along the tunnel and sprawled out against the wall, falling a sleep quickly.

His sleep was restless, and he woke up to the flickering flame of the torch. He rose, stretching out stiff muscles. After lighting another torch, he resumed his journey. Periodically, he noticed a shaft of light in the tunnel through a gap in the stone walls. After examining the separation between the rocks, he concluded they did it on purpose and not a failure of the wall structure.

He passed a side tunnel and peered down the dark interior, not seeing anything. He continued on and came across a wood ladder. Above, a speckle of light filtered down. He climbed to the top of the ladder, and he saw what appeared to be a door latch. Terrowin looked through a cluster of wood branches covering an opening the size of a man's head. He saw green vegetation and trees. It tempted Terrowin to go outside and breathe in the fresh air, but decided he needed to stay on his journey. He climbed down the ladder and resumed his walking.

His walking didn't give him a sense of time, or how far he had travelled. He passed two more side tunnels, otherwise there wasn't any variance in the stone walls. He came across a large wooden door, which surprised him. He didn't see a door knocker or a bell cord, just a simple door latch he lifted. The door opened, and he met a smooth stone floor. As he stepped inside, a male witch greeted him.

"You must be Prince Terrowin. I am Altus Rector Howrand. Welcome to the Jital Terradomus. May your stay here bring you peace."

Terrowin looked around in the candle-lite cavern sized room. *Is this what the rest of the terradomus looks like?* "Thank you. I don't know how long I have to be here before I go back, but I'm grateful for allowing me to stay."

"You are sincerely welcome to stay as long as you need to. Allow me to show you to your room and arrange for refreshments. You must be tired after your long journey."

The room was spartan but clean. A pitcher of water and cup sat on a wood table. He gulped several cups of water and sat on the edge of the bed. The thin mattress didn't promise any comfort, but he soon decided he needed rest, and stretched out on it.

Terrowin fell into a deep sleep. When he woke, he saw Ayleth siting in the lone chair in his room, sipping from a cup. She gave him a smile.

"How are you feeling?"

Terrowin rose to a sitting position. "I'm okay." He shrugged. "I'm still getting over what happened. They killed my brothers."

"I know." She put down the cup and went over to him. "I'm so sorry for your loss." Ayleth sat on the bed and gave him a hug. "Come, you should have something to eat." She took his hand and led him to a rectangular table with four chairs. A plate of bread, cheese, and meat slices sat on one side of the table.

The hunger showed up as soon as he took the first bite. Terrowin also finished a pot of tea by the time the plate was empty.

"I see you're wearing the Ego Taue I gave you."

"I always wear it. I don't know what it is, but I think it's important I keep it with me." He paused. "Maybe it's a good luck charm."

"It may be that as well, but I gave it to you to tell you I am yours." She extended her hand. "I always wear this."

"The blue sapphire ring is from my grandmother, Queen Lythea. My parent's emphasized the ring's uniqueness and instructed me to give it only to someone deserving. I always liked the blue stone. It looks wonderful on your finger."

"It's beautiful." She touched the sapphire with a fingertip. "I appreciate your gift knowing part of it came from Queen Lythea. That is very generous of you."

"I'm sorry to interrupt, but I need to speak to Prince Terrowin."

Terrowin turned to see the altus rector and a tall woman, one he recognized as Ayleth's mother.

Altus Rector Howrand indicated the woman next to him. "This is Keeper Ululla. May we sit at your table?"

Terrowin nodded, noticing the exchange of looks between mother and daughter.

After they sat, Ululla spoke, "Prince Terrowin, we are all sincerely sorry about what happened during the attack at the Allisure castle. It is now our honour and duty to protect you from any harm. Please understand. We are in contact with King Grayson to decide on the best course to take."

"What does that mean?"

"Try not to worry about anything. Rest and take this time to heal and prepare for your next steps in life. Your next journey will be a difficult one, but one you will succeed."

17

A Royal Guardsman approached King Grayson.

"General Ricard is here to see you, your highness."

Grayson looked up from the table he was sitting at in the main library. A map lay flat in front of him, marked with charcoal lines on the coloured features. "Send him in."

Ricard stepped inside the room and dropped to one knee, bowing his head. "Forgive me, your highness, for the terrible tragedy that has fallen on the kingdom. I take full responsibility for not preventing the attack on the castle by the Dwykath forces."

"Rise and tell me what happened during the battle."

Ricard stood and swallowed before speaking. "Your highness, the Dwykath army received new recruits just before the battle. From my vantage point, they appeared to be disorganized, not acting well-trained at all. They made what I consider was a foolish battle strategy. They spread their front line too thin. I found the arrangement of the troops unusual, not something I expected from Commander Willis. He is my enemy, but I respect him. He is ruthless, cunning and knows how to engage in battle."

"What are you inferring?"

"Commander Willis was deploying his troops to entice as many of our soldiers as possible to engage in battle. That left the castle without a full complement for defence, allowing the attack of the werewolves easier. Their battle strategy was a sacrifice to allow the werewolves easier access to the castle but decimated the Dwykath army.

"I am sorry, my lord, that I did not consider this possibility during the battle."

"I do not put blame on you. How were you to foresee the dark magic of using werewolves? Creatures of the night sent by an unknown evil." He slammed a fist on the table. "What is the condition of our army and that of Dwykath's?"

"Our army is powerful, especially with Lord Trey joining us. Commander Willis and his troops are weak and would unlikely withstand a full assault. I suspect he will withdraw his troops, whatever is left of them, and retreat from the battleground. At least, that is what I would do under the circumstances."

"I want one part of our troops to finish the Dwykath army, and another part to bring me King Hadrian and any of his court advisors. I will have my revenge."

"It will be done."

———

Commander Willis stood in the command tent, his hands curled into fists. He shouted at his two lieutenants. "If that Master Diablo shows his ugly face here again, I will slit his throat myself. Under his orders, we lost most of our men. All to provide a diversion for his damn werewolves." He stomped around the tent. "I ain't going to lose any more men in a battle that serves only the devil."

Lieutenant Savard asked, "What are we to do, commander? The enemy is likely preparing an attack soon. Do we just wait for them?"

"No. At first light we break camp- hell, maybe even before that. I have studied the map, and there is a position south of here that we can easily fortify to defend against attacks. We will regroup there and decide on what to do next."

———

King Hadrian peered at the landscape from beyond the balcony. Beyond the perimeter walls of the castle grounds, he could see Lord Trey's army. They had amassed the day before, blocking any exits from the castle. He wondered if they were planning a siege, when a movement at the walls showed ladders being placed at the walls. Hadrian knew he didn't have enough reserve troops to prevent the invaders from flooding over the barrier. Once again, he called out for Master Diablo to appear and give him help, but the result was the same.

"Order the men to defend the castle at all costs. No one must breech the castle itself!"

A guard ran out of the room to relay the order.

Hadrian turned to his chancellor. "Butker, I want this room fortified. Pick our best men and have them stationed here."

"Yes, sire." Hadrian was alone with three servants as the heavy-set man left the room.

The king walked back to the balcony, watching the enemy flood the courtyard. Soldiers raced to the castle's main doors after the gates had been opened. "Where is that cursed Master Diablo? He made promises. Curse him and his black magic!" He stepped back into his throne room, seeing Butker had returned with four guards.

"The situation is desperate, King Hadrian. Our men are no longer fighting, dropping their sword and going into hiding. We can barricade the doors, but it will be only a matter of time before they break through. May I suggest negotiations?"

Hadrian sat in the throne chair, rubbing his forehead. "Secure the door to this room the best you can. In the meantime, let me think." He looked around the spacious room, seeing the four guards had closed the double doors and placed a wood beam across the centre. A clattering noise drew his attention, and he saw an arrow had landed on the floor. "Close the balcony doors!" he shouted.

A guard ran to the balcony and shut the doors. Moments later, another arrow struck the wood shutters.

Hadrian could hear the victorious shouts from the courtyard below. Thuds from the throne room doors showed the enemy was trying to break down their last line of defence. The wood splintered and suddenly a gap appeared in one door.

King Hadrian gave his last order. "Kill anyone who attempts to enter this room. Fight to the death!"

The doors burst open. The guards stepped back and dropped their swords, raising their hands.

Hadrian seethed with anger. He stood. "I am King Hadrian, and you will treat me with respect." He defiantly stared at the enemy captain.

"You are a king no longer." The captain stepped up to him and knocked the crown off his head, sending it spinning across the room. He turned to two of his men. Take him and his chancellor. Put them in chains and escort them to the cages.

Hadrian was jostled as he was pushed and pulled down the corridors of the castle. The chains on his ankles caused him to stumble occasionally. When that happened, a guard roughly pulled up on the chain between his wrists.

"Come on! Are you losing balance as well as your kingdom?" The guard laughed.

After they pushed him forcibly out of the throne room and down the stairs, his servants and members of the court watched in silence as they marched him through the foray. When he stepped outside, cheers rang out. The crowd threw stones and pieces of wood at him. A large cage on wheels awaited him and Butker. They were shoved inside, raising more shouts and cheers. The cage moved and as it made its journey to the outside wall. The jeering crowd hurled rocks and vegetables at him.

Hadrian stared at the iron cuffs attached to his wrists as he sat in the cage.

His chancellor looked at him. "It seems you have lost the support of the people."

"Shut your mouth."

"I don't believe you can order me or anyone to do anything. Your power has evaporated."

———

Hadrian endured the bumpy travel over two days. The captors gave them tasteless food between the bars of the cage and periodically provided water from a metal tankard. None of the captors would say a word to him, forcing him to try a conversation with his chancellor.

Butker had little to say to him, and most of his comments were of contempt of the former king.

"You sold your soul for power by aligning with Master Diablo. You are now getting your reward for dealing with the devil."

Hadrian thought his time with Butker was over at the end of the journey, but they were both taken to the same cell in the dungeon. He cursed Butker. "You faked being my supporter for a title at the court. If I had known who you truly were, I'd have your head."

Betker laughed. "No one ever liked you. They only stayed with you out of fear. There's no one in your entire kingdom that was loyal to you. Well, perhaps, Commander Willis. But he was more loyal to Dwykath than you. He was a good soldier, taking orders from a selfish king."

———

Morning came and guards escorted the two men, taking them on a long route to the throne room of the castle. They forced Hadrian and Betker to their knees, facing King Grayson.

King Grayson, sitting next to Queen Elissa, peered down from his throne chair. "Chancellor Betker. You are an enemy of the Allisure kingdom. Is there a reason I should spare your life?"

"King Grayson, I ask for mercy. I was following orders from a king who knew no decency. If I had refused to do his bidding, he would have ended my life. I am sorry for any harm I may have contributed to. If you decide to spare my life, I promise I will avail myself to the proper path and be a loyal subject of the Allisure kingdom."

Grayson pointed a finger at Hadrian. "And you, do you have anything to say?"

"King Grayson, as a king myself, I want to remind you that we always grant clemency to royal figures. When we captured Kireland, I gave their former king land to rule as a lord. I shall be a loyal subject to you and the Allisure kingdom. I assure you I will rule any land you give me will be for what is best for Allisure. I am sorry for any harm that occurred, but Master Diablo tricked me into doing his bidding. If I had known what he was up to, I would most certainly have ignored him. King Grayson, let us work together to restore peace and prosperity to the people of Allisure."

Grayson frowned. "Chancellor Betker, I accept your apology. I shall spare your life. For the rest of your days, you will work at the royal stables. It will be unpleasant, hard work, but you will have your life.

"Hadrian. Your lies continue to spew from your mouth. I have nothing but contempt for you. Your involvement with the devil led to the deaths of three of my sons. I wish I could kill you three times." He sighed. "Instead, I will have to be content with you dying once. I sentence you to death by hanging tomorrow at dawn. We will not bury your body and instead leave it in the woods for scavengers. He raised his hand to him. "Guards, take him away."

"You can't do that! I have protection of a king!" Hadrian shouted as they dragged him away. "I demand you reconsider. Please, mercy. Mercy!"

King Grayson looked at Elissa. "I hope you will not ask me to show mercy."

"Not in this case. He should be executed ten times for what he did."

————

Hadrian kicked and struggled the entire journey from his cell to the platform in the courtyard. He yelled as they put a noose over his head and tightened it around his neck. He stared at the grim face of the executioner and at King Grayson standing a few feet away. "Please, please, spare my life."

"Go to hell." Grayson gave a signal, and the executioner pulled a lever, causing a trap door to open.

Hadrian fell a short distance, choking out a gurgle of words as his body wiggled at the end of the rope. The gathered crowd cheered and jeered as Hadrian's jerks became less violent and then stopped.

18

Terrowin was bored, eating meals and spending time reading parts of the Book of Redemption. His visitors included Altus Rector Howrand, Keeper Ululla, Ayleth and Alric. His time with Ayleth was one he looked forward to the most, although his advances toward her were restricted to hand holding and kisses.

When he asked about her reluctance, she told him it was dangerous for them to become too intimate, and his needs would have to wait for a later time.

Alric's visits comprised lessons on sword fighting. Wooden swords were used, and Terrowin quickly found out Alric was an expert in sword fighting. Even without a sword, Terrowin found Alric a tough opponent in hand-to-hand combat.

Terrowin hit the floor on his back, looking up at Alric. "Damn, that hurt," he squeezed out the words as he gulped for air.

"Sorry, but you need to learn how to fight. It takes a few hard hits for the lessons to be learned." Alric offered a hand to help him up. "Let's stop for a drink."

Terrowin limped over to a table where two tankards waited. He looked over at a wall where Ayleth stood, looking concerned. He lifted a tankard and drank the wine and water mixture, finishing it in a series of swallows.

"Are you okay?" Ayleth placed a hand on his arm.

"I'm fine. Just a little sore."

"Just a little?" She turned toward Alric. "Father, is it really necessary to hurt him so?"

"He needs to learn how to fight. These lessons may save his life."

"Not if you kill him first. Having him lose every battle will only teach him he's not good enough."

Alric frowned. "You make a good point. Confidence is essential in a fight. Terrowin, I apologize for being too hard on you. Tomorrow, we shall focus more on your strengths and how to use them to your advantage."

After Alric left, Terrowin commented, "Your father is an excellent fighter. Isn't that unusual for a witch?"

"He used to be a warrior. He still has that ability. I'm sorry he hurt you."

"When I trained with the royal guards, they took it easy on me, and I'm not sure how much I learned. Your father showed me I have a lot to learn. I needed that."

"Okay. I just want you to learn how to protect yourself without getting injured."

He knew the altus rector and his secretary were observing them, but leaned over and gave her a kiss.

"I'll see you later, Terrowin. Maybe you should rest after your workout."

Terrowin watched her leave the room. *I wish we could spend more time alone.*

———

The training went better for Terrowin as Alric showed him how to use his height and arm reach to his advantage.

"Much better. Lean into your opponent. An enemy off balance makes it easy to target a vulnerable area."

Terrowin nodded, understanding Alric's lesson on positioning. "Why am I being taught how to fight? Am I going back to the castle? I am prepared to fight for my family and Allisure Kingdom." He straightened his back. "The sooner I return, the better."

Alric sighed. "Prince Terrowin, no, you're not returning to fight. I'm teaching you how to protect yourself for a different reason. I believe you need to have a talk with Altus Rector Howrand." He pointed toward the altus rector's office. "Come with me."

Terrowin sat across from the altus rector with Alric standing near the entrance.

"Brother Alric has been aware of the situation but promised not to tell you the complete story." He leaned forward in his chair, folding has hands on the desk.

"How are my parents and sisters?"

"They are doing as well as one can expect. The Dwykath army was repelled and decimated during a counterattack. The rest of your family, and the Allisure Kingdom, are currently safe."

"Then I should go back and help restore what we have lost."

Altus Rector Howrand frowned. "I am sorry, but that may not be possible. An evil man, who uses the title of Master Diablo, wants to destroy the Allisure Kingdom and rule the world. According to our prophecy, you shall become king and lead the Allisure kingdom to a new era of prosperity and peace. Master Diablo is determined to find you. He needs to kill you at any costs."

"Am I to remain here?"

"No. Eventually, he will discover you are here and attack. He has the power to force others to attack you, so you may not be safe here, even from witches."

"Where can I go then? Is this why Brother Alric is training me on how to fight?"

"Yes, there's the reason for your fighting lessons. After consultation with the altus councillium, we feel it is best you go far away from here, where it's difficult to find you. Master Diablo has spies and ways to find you, but if you keep moving, he will only know where you've been and not where you are. It takes a lot of effort to find a person using magic and he can't devote all of his energy to discovering where you are. In time, he may become more desperate, but for now, he is likely to use spies to look for you."

"Where is this far away place? When would I return?"

"You are to go to places that are often only spoken as a fable, but actually exist. A strange land where witches don't live, and men look and act different from us. When you will return, I cannot say. You will know when it's time."

"How do I get to this place?"

"A ship makes a journey to the tip of this land occasionally for trading. You can travel on the ship and leave when it makes port. When you arrive at this new land, you shall live there until it is time to return home.

"It will be difficult for you, but we believe it will be safer for you than staying here. The port you need to go to is New Kireland. It is a small city, but our reports indicate it is well run. You may choose to live in the city, or the surrounding area. The important thing is for you to be safe. We will prepare you the best we can."

"How will I know when it is time to return? How do I return?"

"You will know when to return when you discover who you are. As for returning home, you can choose one of the ocean ships at the port of New Kireland."

Terrowin sat, not saying a word. He felt Alric's hand on his shoulder.

"Do not underestimate what you're capable of, nor forget the power of witches to protect you, even at a distance. You will succeed."

———

Terrowin didn't sleep well. Morning came, and he yawned as he sat at the wood table outside his room. Instead of the altus rector bringing his breakfast, Ayleth arrived carrying a tray.

"Good morning."

Terrowin immediately sat up straight. "Hello, Ayleth. How are you?"

"I think I'm doing better than you. I heard they are sending you on a journey. You must be worried." She put the tray on the table and sat across from him.

"I guess I am. I don't know what to expect."

"Life is not meant to be without unknowns. Another way to look at it is that you have a chance of a glorious adventure, while others live a life without change. Terrowin, you will be an outstanding leader. Embrace what is before you."

He nodded as took a piece of dark bread. "I have little choice. I shall try to not be worried about what is happening next."

"Good, because I want to put a spell on you."

———

Ayleth spoke words that Terrowin didn't understand. He sat without his shirt on as she drew small lines on his chest using a brush with blue paint.

Terrowin felt the paint warm as she uttered phrases. Suddenly, the smoke appeared from the paint, and he yelped out in pain.

"It's done." She wiped the excess paint off him with a cloth, leaving red and blue marks.

"What does the spell do?" He touched the sensitive skin.

"No matter what language people speak, you will understand them and speak in their tongue."

"Oh, I guess that will be good. Ayleth, you mean so much to me. I want you to be by my side always. I promise..."

Ayleth nodded and held his hand. "Terrowin, I've told you I can see events that have not yet passed. I know someday we will be together. Understand, I know for you to survive, you may be required to do... things...you don't want to do. I want you to live. You need to do whatever it takes for you to come home again."

19

Commander Willis snarled as he looked at the map rolled out on the table. A rock held each corner of the coloured pencil drawn map.

"We are almost trapped." He turned around, facing the two officers standing at the entrance of the tent. "Prepare to break camp tomorrow morning."

"Where are we going?" Corporal Nevis looked at the map and back at Willis. He didn't see an obvious route away from the Allisure forces.

"In a direction no one will expect us to take." He jabbed a finger at the map. "Jital."

"Jital is a city controlled by the Allisure forces. Isn't that going into a trap?"

Willis looked at Tybalt. The tall, dark-haired soldier had proven to be a competent officer. Willis knew he was a friend of Alric many years ago and helped him escape the army. That was treason, punishable by death. Instead, Willis kept him close to his chain of command. If there was one thing Willis prized above anything else, it was loyalty. If Tybalt would risk his life to help his friend, that was a man he wanted to help lead his troops. "A good point, but the army at Jital has never been in a fight. Our smaller numbers may prevail. If we can capture Jital, that may at least give us time until help arrives."

He left unsaid that help may not arrive. In the past few weeks, there had been no communication from King Hadrian of the Kingdom of Dwykath. That did not bode well in his mind, but it may have been to factors he was not aware of. The king himself may have been replaced by a coup, and in that case, his loyalty would be the new king and to the Kingdom of Dwykath. That meant he had to continue the war.

Tybalt placed a hand on his own shoulder.

Willis recognized it was a habit Tybalt had when he was thinking. He recalled it was the shoulder injured in battle. Witches had healed the shoulder, Tybalt later confided.

"Jital has several main roads leading to it. The authorities guard and maintain the main roads leading to Jital well. But there are many smaller roads that lead to it. Farmers use dirt roads to move livestock. That may be our best hope of sending in our troops."

"A good plan. This map doesn't show all those roads and pathways. We need to send scouts ahead to find the best route."

"I will send men before we set out and find out what will be our best option to enter Jital."

"Good." He spoke to the other officer in the tent. "Nevis, make sure the men are ready to leave at first light. If I hear any late-night activities, it better be the horses."

———

Willis didn't like the muddy terrain, the muggy air, and the constant buzzing of insects as he rode his horse. The good news was the enemy would be in the same conditions. Leaving the battlefield also meant there would be less likely the appearance of ghouls or vampires, although they usually left large groups of men alone.

His plan to attack Jital was spoken with more assurance than he thought. Although the army at Jital had little in the way of fighting experience, they were well trained and equipped. His best hope was to catch them unprepared for such an audacious attack. His speech in the morning to the troops had them raising their fists, ready to win the day. Nevis joined in the fist raising, holding his sword high in the air as he shouted, "Victory will be ours!" Willis saw Tybalt was more subdued in his cheer, and Willis knew the officer had seen how desperate their situation was.

The sun continued to heat the land, driving some insects away. The odour of horses, unwashed men and the dirt assailed his senses to the point he didn't notice them anymore. So far, the Alliance forces had not followed them, or at least had remained out of sight.

He wondered if his life would end at the next battle. In truth, he hadn't expected to live as long as he had. *Bloody miracle. I don't know if the lord is keeping me alive out of mercy or the devil to punish me.* He hummed an old verse popular with soldiers, then sang the lyrics.

> *I've had my thrills*
> *I've had my spills*
> *I've shared my bottle of wine*
> *But I've reached my time*
> *It's time to say goodbye*
> *And lay down my sword and die*

Willis considered the reality that within a few days, he would likely be dead. *I don't mind dying, but this is an ugly place to take my last breath.*

———

The forest, scrubs, rocks and mud gave way to flat ground where the grain was growing. They marched through the yellow fields, destroying the crop. A man stood outside near a log home, staring at him. Even from across the field, Willis could see he was angry.

"Shall I have a couple of men dispatch him?" Nevis asked.

Willis considered the man wasn't likely to cause them any harm. "No, let him be." He grunted. "He'll never know how lucky he was today." *A few months ago, I would have him, and family killed and their home set on fire. Maybe I'm getting soft as I approach my last days.*

A cooling breeze made travel easier, and a wide stream gave an opportunity to rest the horses and men.

Tybalt came up to him. "This is too open to make camp, but one scout has found a group of homes clustered together. It's about a quarter day's travel from here."

"Is it a village?"

"No, just homes. I suspect they're together to provide mutual protection against ghouls and wolves."

"Take a dozen men and secure the homes. No one is to leave until I arrive. I don't want any unnecessary killing but put the fear of God into them."

"Yes, sir."

Willis watched him round up a few men and took a long drink from a flagon. *At least we should get a decent meal tonight.*

———

The last light was fading when Willis and the rest of the troops arrived at the four farmhouses. They were all constructed out of stone, with heavy timber used as support at the corners and the top of the walls. The roofs were all made from woven straw and mud.

Willis entered the closest home. The men of the four homes were sitting on the floor, glaring at him. Another man was lying down on the floor, holding his side where blood seeped through his shirt. A woman kneeled next to him, stroking his head. She appeared to be weeping and didn't turn her attention to Willis.

"If you don't cause any trouble, no one else will be hurt. My men are hungry." He pointed at a group of women huddled together. "Prepare food." He watched them leave, signalling two soldiers to follow them. Willis turned to Tybalt. "Tell our surgeon to attend to him. We don't want to be attracting any ghouls if he dies."

The medic carried a cloth bag into the house. He gave a curious look at Willis and examined the injured man. The kneeling woman moved away, clutching her hands as if praying.

The surgeon took no notice of her, or the man's moaning. He poured wine on the open wound, causing the patient to cry out. Honey was applied to the red skin, and he wrapped a cloth around his torso.

"He needs to lie still for a while. Give him wine to drink so he can sleep. He will live." The surgeon stood, waiting for Willis to speak.

"Don't question the reason I'm giving aid to a civilian, or you'll be needing some healing powers for yourself," Willis snarled at him.

———

Willis made sure he had the first choice at the prepared food, using wine to wash down the heavy meal. After he had his fill, he found a bed in the house to sleep on. *I don't need anyone thinking I'm getting soft. The next time someone even gives me a sour look, I'll give him a beating with my own hands.*

20

Morning came and Commander Willis woke from troubled dreams. The dreams faded away as he stood and stretched but left him feeling uneasy. *Death is coming for me in my dreams. Soon it'll be here when I'm awake.*

Willis pushed his way to a table set with plates of food. He grabbed portions of meat, bread, eggs, and cheese and lumbered to the common room. "Get me something to drink," Willis snapped at the woman standing with her hands clasped in front of her.

A soldier quickly stood and gave up his chair for him. He plopped down and ate with his fingers. The woman nervously handed him a metal cup of wine. He gulped down its contents and shoved it back at her. "More."

After he had his fill of wine and food, Willis told his lieutenants to order the army to prepare to march. "We need to make headway. The enemy is likely close behind."

Willis finished another cup of wine and strolled toward the front door. A woman came up to him, whom he recognized as the one weeping over the injured man.

"Thank you for saving my husband's life." She clutched his arm.

He grunted. "It was to give our surgeon something to do."

"Bless you all the same. Peace be with you."

Willis swallowed. "Peace is only a dream for fools."

———

Willis brushed away an errant fly as he rode his horse. A scout had earlier informed him there was a village a few hours ahead, and he decided it would be a suitable spot to stop for the night. He sent a dozen soldiers to secure the village and ensure there wouldn't be any resistance to their occupation. He recalled the name of the village on the map he studied earlier, Negotia.

"After the village, we should be close to Jital." Nevis stated as he rode next to him.

"It won't be much further."

"Have you worked out a plan to take the city?"

Willis didn't tell him an assault at the well-protected Jital did not have high odds of success. "I have a few ideas on the best way to attack." He ignored the questioning look from Nevis, focusing on the road ahead of him. He knew his men were tired from the long battles earlier and were wondering what their fate would be. Unlike many of the surrounding soldiers, Willis didn't have a home or family to return to. The battlefield was his place of residence, and his family were only fellow soldiers that often had a short life span.

He wondered if the troubled dreams were a vision of a tragic end for him. Willis was far from a spiritual man, but he wondered if it was too late to make amends before his demise. *I will surely go to hell for what I've done, but perhaps a few good deeds will give me a reprieve.*

He took a drink from a flask containing whisky and water. *When I die, I hope I'm drunk enough not to realize it.*

Negotia was larger than he expected. The road did not go through it but formed the border on one side with several smaller roads entering the village. The village was a trading post for farmers to exchange their goods for monies or other supplies that saved them a journey to Jital. Negotia had pens for livestock and bins for grain and corn. The heavy odour of horses, cattle, pigs filled the air, causing Willis to take shorter breaths of air.

As the army closed off the entrance to the village, men and women gathered outside, facing and pointing at them.

"Do not kill the villagers unless they attack or resist." Willis gave the order to Nevis and Thybalt, who would relate the command down the ranks.

"Some of those villagers look like witches. We don't want to mess with them," replied Thybalt.

Willis looked closer at the villagers, spotting what Thybalt thought were witches. The long-robed figures looked at them without fear. He knew many of the warriors refused to attack witches, worried a curse would be placed on them.

"Move with care, then. The witches won't be a problem if we leave them be." He moved his horse toward a teahouse. The main floor served food, while the upper two floors held rooms to rent for the night.

The teahouse was less than half-filled when he entered, with the guests staring at him, but didn't show any urgency to leave. Willis frowned at their lack of fear of him and his army. A woman of middle-age and with light blonde hair approached him. He recognized her as a witch with her long, soft-green robe.

"Would you like something to eat and drink?" She gestured to a vacant table.

"Yes, but I won't be paying for any of it." He sat. "My men are in need of nourishment as well."

"I see. We don't turn anyone away, regardless of their ability to pay. Do you prefer wine or tea?"

"I prefer whisky."

"Wine it is."

He watched her walk away, not acting perturbed at his demand or his appearance. *These witches are a strange lot.* He sat at a table and looked around, seeing the teahouse was being served by several witches.

The blonde witch returned to his table, setting out a bowl of stew, bread, cheese, and a mug of red wine.

"I've arranged for your men to be fed. We don't have room for them to eat in here, so we will serve them outside. It will take some time to make sufficient food for all of them, so I hope you're not in a hurry." She stared at him without smiling.

He grunted. The stew smelled good, and the dark bread looked like it would be filling. "Thanks. Just so you know, we don't intend to harm anyone here. We just need food and a place to rest."

"Good. But we don't fear you. Enjoy your food." She turned and walked away.

Willis gulped down his food and drink, enjoying the best food he had in months. The witch returned to refill his wine mug from a metal pitcher.

"Thanks."

"I was wondering if you had enough manners to acknowledge our gift of food to you and your army."

It shocked him by how little fear she had of him. *She sees me as a nuisance and not a threat.* "Let me know if my men cause any difficulties. I'm Commander Willis." He took a long drink of the wine, wanting to avoid confronting her.

"Sister Caletia. I run the teahouse and boarding rooms upstairs. We are part of the Order of Whiterose."

"Your food and drink are very good. My compliments."

She surprised him by sitting across from him. "Tell me, Commander Willis, what are you doing here? You're obviously not part of the Allisure army."

"The Allisure forces are our enemy. We are part of the Dwykath Kingdom."

"You are far from the Dwykath Kingdom. Your men look tired and not well equipped." She peered at him with questioning eyes.

"We were battling the Allisure army a few days ago. We are changing our position to better engage them."

"Commander Willis, and I ask this not to mock you, but do you seriously believe you can go into battle?"

"It matters not. I am a soldier and must be ready to fight the enemy at anytime."

"Even to your death?"

"Yes."

"For what cause? So your king can enjoy more riches? Commander Willis, it does not have to be this way."

"Caletia, once a man becomes a soldier, that becomes his life. He is a soldier until he dies."

She smiled. "That is simply not the truth. In our order, we have a man who used to be a soldier. He shed his warrior clothing and became a man of peace."

"A deserter."

"No, a man who followed his beliefs. It takes great courage to walk away from what he was and to follow his destiny."

"His destiny?"

"Yes. In the Book Redemption, they wrote of a warrior who leaves the battlefield and becomes a witch. His offspring are part of the great battle against evil."

Willis raised his eyebrows. "I'm not much for soothsayers."

"One does not have to be a soothsayer to know your life is extremely dangerous. Surely, you must know your life would be better not being a warrior. You have served your kingdom. Perhaps it is now time for you to consider your own life."

Willis took a gulp of his wine. "What you say has merit. But consider this. My parents threw me out of our home when I was just a lad. I joined the army as a means of living. The army has been my whole life. I have no other skills but as a warrior. I have no family or home. My only friends are soldiers, and often they have a brief life. So, as you can see, I have no one who cares if I live or die and no place but the army to live."

"You are wrong."

"How so?"

"I care if you live or die. I would like it very much if you could live to an old age. As far as a place to live, we need more workers to help us here."

Willis was silent, staring at the witch across from him. He felt her hand touch his own. He took in a deep breath. "Why do you care?"

"Does it matter? Just that I do. I see a troubled man who deserves a chance to live in peace."

He kept his hand in place on the table, relishing the gentle touch of her fingers. "It doesn't matter what I want. I have a duty. I made an oath and must follow it to the end."

She stood. "You also have a duty to yourself. A dead man serves no one."

Willis watched her walk away, wishing he could follow her advice.

———

Later that day, Willis checked his army, pleased the men didn't have any complaints about the food they received. He emphasized his orders to the soldiers that they must not harm the villagers. The horses were to be taken to a nearby stream to make sure they had enough water.

He took Nevis and Thybalt to the side. "Make sure we are ready to move at first light. I know the enemy can't be far behind us and I want to reach Jital in time to launch an attack by tomorrow." He walked to the teahouse. "I will spend the night inside. You and the rest of the men stay here. Post a few guards for nighttime duty around the perimeter. We need to watch for any surprise attack. Sleep with your swords close by."

Willis entered the teahouse, spotting Caletia working behind the counter that led to the kitchen. "I would take another bite of food and drink, and a room." He pulled a few coins from a leather pouch, holding them in his hand. "This should cover it."

"Keep your money, Commander Willis. I would feel guilty taking coins from the man who may be dead in a few days." She pointed at a table. "Sit. I will bring you nourishment."

Willis sat the table, watching the witch move behind the counter. He admired her fluid motions. Even though she appeared young, he suspected she was almost as old as himself. *War has really aged me. Or at least, being a witch has made her appear younger. She's being nice to me, and I don't know why. I'm the opposite of her, but she acts likes she cares about me. I can't remember a time when someone cared whether I lived or died.*

He watched her place a bowl in front of him and a mug next to it. She sat across from him, watching as he ate the mixture of noodles and beef.

"This is very good." He took a drink from the mug, surprised to find it contained whisky and water. "Ah, my favourite drink."

"I thought you deserved a good meal and drink. It may be one of your last." She frowned. "I don't understand why you believe you must die to serve your king."

Willis opened his mouth, prepared to say, 'My duty and honour require me to do so,' but decided it would sound like a weak excuse. "I made a commitment. My men depend on me to lead them."

"To their death? Commander, you know you don't have to engage in battle. You have already proven you are a brave and strong leader. Please reconsider."

He nodded. "I will think about what you have said."

She left the table, returning to refill his mug. "It's getting late. After you finish your drink, I will show you to your room."

Willis drained the mug and stood. Caletia indicated for him to follow her. They went to the back of the teahouse, where a set of stairs took them to the second floor. Another set of stairs went to the third floor, but Caletia turned down a hallway. Doors lined both sides of the wood walkway. She reached back and took his hand.

"I will give you a corner room. It's larger and has a better mattress."

The door to the room had a simple wood latch and wasn't lockable. He entered the room and glanced out the window, seeing only a night sky. He turned and saw Caletia standing by the door.

"Sleep well, Commander Willis. Please think about what I said."

Willis stood, staring at the door after she had left. *Maybe that witch put a spell on me.*

———

Willis rolled out of bed in the morning, sleeping better than he expected. Fragments of a dream chased him, a dream where he faced a choice of pathways in a forest. He knew what the dream meant but couldn't recall which path he took.

He made his way downstairs, where breakfast and tea were prepared for him.

"Did you sleep well, commander?" Caletia asked.

"Yes, it was one of my better sleeps."

"Are you still leaving to go to battle?"

"My duty."

"One that serves no purpose but to lead you to your death. Take care. It has been good to have met you." She walked away.

Willis finished his breakfast and joined the rest of the army. He mounted his horse, continuing to look at the teahouse for a sign of Caletia. Only after the army left Negotia, and he looked back, did he see her.

He waved to her, and after a moment, she waved back.

Have I made the wrong choice? He snorted. *I know I have. But I won't have my troops see me as a coward and turning away from a fight. When I die in this battle, no one can say I lacked courage.*

————

"It appears your warrior has gone to battle after all, Sister Caletia."

Caletia remained standing at the doorway, watching the army disappear over a hill. She acknowledged the voice behind her. "Yes, Sister Honora. I tried to persuade him, but he has a sense of honour that drives him to do battle."

"We have sent word to the Jital Terradomus of the army. The Jital forces should be able to defeat them, although there will be much bloodshed. In addition, more Allisure troops will be arriving. Your warrior is not likely to survive."

"That is true. I regret I could not convince him to lay down his sword. When I first spoke with him, I just wanted to stop the battle and save unnecessary deaths." She frowned and turned to speak to the smaller woman behind her. "Commander Willis is a troubled man. I felt sorry for him. He feels alone in this world, but still feels loyal to the awful king who sent him to battle."

"You did your best, Sister Caletia. You can show the path, but you cannot force a person to walk it."

"I know. I believe he was close to making the right choice. I just needed more time to push him. I told him I cared about him, and that surprised him. I don't believe anyone ever told him they loved him."

"Come, let us share a tea and offer your warrior a prayer of hope."

21

Ululla watched her husband rub the grey cloth along the sword. He had gathered his old weapons from a storage box in their room and began cleaning them.

"Alric, I had forgotten you had kept your sword and armaments."

"I never thought I would ever need them again, but I didn't know what else to do with them."

"Do you plan to give them to Prince Terrowin?"

"I am."

"Have you considered that by giving him weapons it may make him more conspicuous? That sword may draw unnecessary attention to him."

"Prince Terrowin is a tall man. The royal faces are known. I have doubt he could hide in a crowd. There will be those who may try to do him harm. At least with a sword and knife, he will ward off some attacks."

"Is he versed in using a sword?"

"He has had some training already. Regardless, I've been showing him what I know." He put down the sword. "I've sharpened it and cleaned it. It may be a few years old, but it's made well."

"Good. Let's go for lunch."

"That is something I could use. Where's Ayleth? Spending time with Terrowin?"

"Of course. She believes he will be her husband and wants to know more about him. I told her that was fine, but she was not going to spend the night with him." She sighed. "Ayleth acts so much older than her years."

"She does. She has informed no one, including Dorian, about him, has she?"

"No, she understands secrecy is extremely important, even from her brother."

Alric breathed in the aromas of cooking as they entered the dining room. "I feel hungry now." He made his way past the tables and to the counter.

Suddenly, bells sounded.

Alric looked at Ululla. "So much for food. We better go to the meeting chamber."

The circular chamber was filling by the time they reached the circular auditorium. The altus rector stood at the front, waiting for the room to be filled.

Alric tried to be patient, wondering what the alarm bells were for. He hoped it wasn't anything to do with Terrowin, who remained hidden on the lowest floor of the terradomus. Very few knew he was under the protection of the altus rector.

He sat near the front on the curved, backless bench with Ululla and Ayleth.

Altus Rector Howrand cleared his throat and spoke. "Witches, I have news to unfold to you, but please do not be concerned. The last army of the Dwykath Kingdom is approaching Jital. They stayed last night at the village of Negotia and continued on the road that leads to the city's eastern gate. Fortunately, the witches at Negotia have provided us with information on the size of their army and how well they are prepared for battle. I relayed the information personally to Captain Pickett of the Allisure forces stationed here. Normally, we do not get involved in armed conflicts, but I felt it was prudent in this case to inform the captain of the situation. He was most appreciative of our help. I have also informed the Darkrose order of this development.

"Captain Pickett has assured me they enjoy superior weaponry and will defeat any challenge. In addition, the Kingdom of Allisure is sending additional troops to Jital. That is all the information I can report at this time. I shall advise that we should stay close to the terradomus in case of the conflict becomes an issue. I'm sure everyone is aware the Dwykath Kingdom has a strong dislike for witches."

Alric waited until most of the crowd had dispersed before approaching the altus rector. Ululla and Ayleth followed him.

"Excuse, Altus Rector Howrand, I was wondering if you have any more information on the Dwykath army."

"Not too much. The army, while large, appears to be physically in poor shape, with many of the men having various injuries. Sister Caletia tried to convince their leader, a Commander Willis, not to go to battle and surrender. She believes she almost succeeded, but apparently the commander was determined to fulfill his duty as a soldier. A pity. No one should feel an obligation to die for another man."

"Commander Willis? I know him well." He turned to Ululla. "I must see if I can talk to Willis. Maybe I can convince him to lie down his sword."

"You want to enter the conflict? That's very dangerous, and as you know, the Dwykath Kingdom does not like witches. They may kill you as soon as they see you."

"I understand why you're worried, but if I can save lives by meeting with Commander Willis, then I must do so."

Ululla stared at him, deciding she could not change his mind. "Please, please be careful."

———

Captain Pickett, tall with a medium build, stroked his brown beard as Alric made his request.

"I know Commander Willis, and I believe I can convince him to surrender. I ask you for permission to approach his camp, and to offer him acceptable terms of surrender."

"And what would those terms be?"

"To allow them to live, for one. Perhaps you could absorb them into your own army. These are good, experienced fighting men. To punish them for being born in the wrong kingdom would be an injustice."

Pickett laughed. "You sound like you have a soft spot for them."

"I do. I served under Commander Willis as a soldier."

"Really." Pickett raised his eyebrows. "And now you're a witch that wants peace. Quite a change."

Alric shrugged. "Fate is hard to fight. Now I find myself in a position to do good. Do I have permission to try?"

"You do. I think you're foolish to try, but as you point out, it is likely to be worth the effort. I will have two of my men escort you to the perimeter of their camp. From there, you will have to hope their reaction to a witch won't be too aggressive."

Alric mounted a horse lent to him, carrying a pole with a white cloth attached to the top. Two soldiers rode next to him. One rider, after eyeing him for a short time, spoke. "I'm surprised how well you ride. I didn't think witches normally rode horses."

"Thanks. I rode horses in a previous life. It's something that you never forget to do."

They reached the Dwykath camp and stopped, waiting for acknowledgement from the enemy soldiers.

"Who you be and what is it you want?" The old soldier addressed Alric as he peered at him.

"I want to speak with Commander Willis about the upcoming battle."

"You're a witch, ain't cha? What do you know about war?"

"I know no one wants to die needlessly. May I speak with Commander Willis?"

"Stay there, I'll ask."

Alric and his two escorts waited. Finally, the old guard returned.

"You can see him. Off your horse and follow me."

Alric dismounted and walked through the camp, receiving curious gazes from the soldiers. They arrived at a dirty white tent that Alric wondered if it was the same one Willis had years ago when Alric was still in the army. He pushed the tent flap aside and entered.

Alric stood and met the gaze of the three men eyeing him.

"Alric? Is that you?" Thybalt took a few steps toward him.

"It is I." Alric closed the gap between them and clasped his arm. "I'm glad to see you are alive and well."

"I never thought I'd see you again." Thybalt stepped back. "A witch of all things. Strange."

"You know deserters are executed, don't you?" Willis's voice boomed out. He walked toward Alric and his mouth broke into a grin.

Alric gave the big man a hug. "It is good to see you again, commander."

"So, a witch offers conditions of surrender. That's something I never thought I'd live long enough to see."

"I hope you will live long enough to see other unusual things. Commander Willis, your army is the last of King Hadrian's troops. The Allisure forces have defeated the rest of the Dwykath Kingdom. You are all that is left of the Dwykath Kingdom. Please consider this offer for peace."

"And what, pray tell, is this offer?"

"A promise to treat your soldiers fairly. None shall be punished for being on the wrong side of the battle. Please allow your men to either become civilians or join the Allisure army. No one should die for a lost cause. That includes yourself, commander. You deserve a day without worrying about a forthcoming battle."

Willis nodded. "I get weary of fighting every day."

"It takes a brave man to lie down a sword, even when it's the right thing to do. Commander Willis, you never lacked courage."

"If I decide to surrender, none of my men will be harmed?"

"This is what I was told. That goes for yourself, as well."

"Perhaps it is time to retire my sword."

———

"Sister Caletia, you have a visitor."

Caletia stopped preparing vegetables for a stew. "Who is it, Sister Bueno?"

"I think you go and see for yourself." She gave a smile.

Caletia put down the knife and exited the kitchen. She immediately recognized the nervous man standing in the middle of the dining room. "Commander Willis, you have returned."

"It is just Willis now, Sister Catelia. I have resigned from the army. I have decided I need to do something other than wield a sword."

She approached him, placing a hand on each of his arms. "We could use a strong man here."

"It would be my honour to work here."

"Come, Willis, allow me to show you around our village. It will give us time to talk and to learn more about each other."

22

Terrowin changed into clothes normally worn by shopkeepers or workers. Alric had given him his sword he had used as a warrior, and Terrowin used a leather belt to secure it to his hip. He secured a knife in a holster at his waist. He finally added a robe that witches wore. The loose-fitting robe partially hid the sword.

Ayleth stood with Alric and Ululla as Terrowin approached them from his bedroom. "You now look like a witch instead of a prince." She smiled. "I hope you are comfortable wearing the robe."

"I understand it's necessary for a disguise."

Ayleth reached up to him and gave him a hug. "I will wait for your safe return."

"I shall miss you."

"Do whatever you need to do to return home."

Alric beckoned him. "Come. It's now late afternoon and we have travelling to do."

Terrowin followed him to a tunnel entrance located one floor above where he was staying. He wondered how many tunnels led from the terradomus. The tunnel looked much the same as the one he had used before, except this one split into two tunnels immediately after the entrance door.

They walked in silence, passing another side tunnel, and Terrowin noticed the tunnel slopped downward before levelling out.

"How many tunnels are there?"

Alric laughed. "I'm not sure anyone knows the answer to that. I saw a map of the tunnels leading to and from Jital. There were a lot, and each terradomus has several tunnels attached to them. Plus, the Darkrose witches have tunnels as well."

"Do the Darkrose tunnels ever run into one of ours?"

"No, but I understand some of their tunnels run parallel to ours."

"Do these tunnels go everywhere?"

"Just about. They can go under small rivers, but not lakes."

"It certainly makes it safer for witches to travel about."

"It does. Not so much now, but at one time, it wasn't safe for witches to travel on the open road."

"What is our next stop?"

"A farm. Although not devoted followers, the family living on the farm are Whiterose witches. They will give us food and shelter for the night."

The entrance to the farm was by a ladder that led to inside a toolshed. Alric went first, pushing up the trapdoor. He offered a hand to Terrowin from the ladder, and together they made their way to a farmhouse. The evening air was cool, with a threat of rain, when they knocked on the door.

A short, but muscular, man opened the door.

"Good evening. Can you spare food and lodging for the night for us?" Alric asked.

"Of course. Witches be welcome here."

Terrowin followed Alric through the small common room and into a crowded kitchen, where four young children stared at them. A woman, short and of slender build, placed bowls of food on the table.

Alric and Terrowin took a place at the table, requiring two of the children to stand to eat. "Thank you for your trouble. I am Brother Alric. This is Brother Rowin."

Terrowin said little during the meal, keeping his hood on to help hide his identity. He saw the younger members of the family stared at Alric and himself but said nothing to them. After the filling meal, they were taken to the barn to sleep.

"Sorry, we don't have no extra beds. But the hay should help keep ya warm and comfortable enough. Come to the house in the morning. We'll have breakfast for ya."

———

Terrowin found he slept well. The sound of the rain helped him relax, and he fell into a deep sleep.

Breakfast was filling, and the farm couple made a lunch for them to take on their journey. They left via the same tunnel under the toolshed and walked until they reached another door, this one opening to another terradomus.

Alric whispered to Terrowin, "This terradomus is in the village of Kroteen. The village is small and not much of importance, but the terradomus is quite old and is home to many witches."

Leading the way, Alric spoke to a watcher, who took them to the altus rector. They waited at the outer office, with the friendly secretary politely asking them to wait.

"In the meantime, may I offer you tea?" The male witch rose and went over to a small table. "The tea is only warm, but it's brewed from a special leaf and berries," he said. It's very soothing."

Altus Rector admitted Alric and Terrowin to his office shortly after they accepted the tea.

She stood behind her desk. "My apologies for making you wait. We had recent reports of unusual military activity and I needed to ensure it was not a concern for the terradomus. I am Altus Rector Eliison."

"I understand, and we are sorry to interrupt your work. I am Brother Alric. May I inquire about the military activity?"

"Of course. It appears a major conflict between kingdoms has been, for a lack of a better word, resolved. Soldiers of the Allisure kingdom are celebrating, partaking in the consumption of ale to excess. This is understandable, if indeed conflict is over. Although my experience is that another conflict will soon arrive."

"I suspect you may be right but let us hope peace lasts for a while."

"I agree with those sentiments. One benefit of this time period of peace is the increase of goods and food from the port city, Edwin. The ships are no longer forced to stay away from the port because of military conflicts."

"That is good to hear. Altus Rector Eliison, this may sound like an odd request, but I assure you it is also one of utmost importance. I ask you to keep our stay here a secret, that no one knows we are here. We will be here only one night, but we would be in danger if our presence here became known."

"I can ensure your privacy. I will also inform the watcher to remove any reference to your visit here."

"Thank you. I assume there is a tunnel that goes to Edwin."

"There is. It is about a half day journey. The terradomus there is near the wharfs."

Alric and Terrowin stayed in bedrooms on the lowest floor of the terradomus. The altus rector brought a tray of food for them, informing them no other witches were aware of their presence.

"The watcher will be discreet and not tell others of your arrival and departure." She smiled. "I will leave you in peace, you and your silent companion."

———

Terrowin reflected on the rapid change in his life as he rested on a straw-filled mattress. His bedroom in the terradomus was simple, containing only a table and chair beside the bed. The food he ate for dinner was filling, although the turnip and rabbit were not his first choice for a meal. The heavy robe was too warm for his liking, but he understood it provided a good disguise. As far as he knew, no one knew he was actually a prince. He hadn't shaved since his escape, and sparse whiskers helped change his appearance.

Morning came, and the altus rector brought food to them on a tray.

"I hope your night was restful. If there's anything I can do to help you with your journey, please don't hesitate to ask me."

Alric assured him they slept well. "Thank you for the food. You have helped make our journey easier."

After they had eaten, Terrowin followed Alric through the terradomus and to the door that led to a tunnel. He kept his hood over his head and refrained from looking anywhere but straight ahead.

This time the tunnel wasn't empty, with witches travelling in both directions. Terrowin noticed the tunnel was much the same as the others he had used, but he also saw some stones had names carved in them.

"Alric, did you see the names on those rocks? Did you know that witches put their names on them when they were assigned to help build or repair a tunnel? I guess it gave them a sense of immortality."

"Yes, new witches, were often given a task of working tunnels. How did you know that was the reason for inscribing the names there?

"I'm not sure. It's like something I just remembered."

The tunnel didn't go in a straight line but turned at an angle several times. Terrowin wasn't sure where they were, but reasoned they had travelled far enough that they should be near their destination. It surprised him when Alric pointed at a ladder to use as an exit.

"I think it will be better if we use this, rather than go to the terradomus. Fewer people will see us this way."

The exit was a narrow space between two rocks inside a cave. The cave was on a rocky hill with vines covering the entrance. Terrowin looked down from the hill and could see the port city and the ocean beyond it.

"We made it to Edwin."

"We did. Now we need to find a ship for you to catch a ride on. Some ship captains don't like witches, others don't care. It may take a while to find the right ship."

―――――

Terrowin noticed unfamiliar smells as they moved through the streets. The ocean had its own presence, but there were also fish, fresh vegetables, and farm animals in the market. Mixed in was the odour of food being cooked by merchants that lined the market square. Terrowin had become used to people not stopping to bow to him as he went past. He found it more relaxing, now not worrying about his posture or if his clothes fitted well.

He stood behind Alric as he made inquiries at the docks, moving down a line of ships. The largest ships were at the end of the dock.

Terrowin had seen the ships used on rivers before, but these ships were much larger, boasting three masts.

Terrowin listened as Alric spoke to a captain of one of the large ships, nodded and proceeded to the next.

"He didn't want a witch on his boat. Do you think I should remove this robe and go as a worker instead?"

"You may have to, but the robe helps hide who you are. Let's try the other boats first."

At the next ship, the Oceanum Ore, the captain was willing to accept him as a passenger.

"To be clear, the reason we don't have many passengers is because we go to the end of the Earth, where no man wants to travel, and creatures live that you thought were only in your nightmares. Some captains fear witches will bring a curse on their ship. I'm more of the thought a witch may help preserve us with a kindly spell." He grinned. "If one were inclined to believe a witch has that power."

Terrowin took a liking to the old captain of medium height. His shoulders and hands showed the years of hard work. "I'm Brother Rowin."

"Captain Nikols. Welcome aboard."

Alric gave the captain a few coins to pay for the fare and passed Terrowin several more coins.

"I don't know if you'll need them, but you'll have them just in case." He gave Terrowin a hug. "Stay safe and come back in one piece, or Ayleth will be very upset."

"I don't want her to be upset. I'll be okay."

"Peace be with you."

"And to you."

Terrowin boarded the ship, climbing the wood ramp. The lower part of the ship had similar ramps that hard working labourers used to load goods. He found the passenger cabin below the captain's quarters, holding four beds in two bunk beds. The top of the cabin was just above the deck, allowing some light to enter through small glass windows.

He took a top bunk and stretched out, feeling tired after his day's journey. He relaxed but didn't fall asleep. Another man came in, nodded at him, and tossed a knapsack on a lower bunk. The young man looked wiry, although his jerky movements gave the appearance of being nervous and unsure.

Another man entered, older and heavyset. He pointed at Terrowin. "I want that bunk. Get off."

"No." Terrowin didn't hesitate in responding, deciding he wasn't going to be intimidated.

"Then I shall remove ya, witch."

The intruder reached with a large hand to the collar of his robe.

Terrowin reacted with the fighting skills Alric taught him. His fist snapped forward, striking the man's forehead. The man staggered back from the blow, clutching his head.

"If you come within an arm's length of my bed again, I'll make you wish you never came on board."

The would-be fighter turned away, sitting on a spare lower bunk. "What kind of witch knows how to hit like that?"

"One that who knows how to survive. This is my bed. Don't even think of lying on it again."

The man glared at him but remained silent.

Much later, Terrowin decided he had enough rest and left the cabin. The ship had finished loading, and he looked over the railing around the perimeter. A rowboat with two paddlers used a rope to pull the sailboat away from the dock and toward the ocean. They deployed only one sail on a mast, easing the ship toward the open water.

I guess we're on the way.

Terrowin stared at the water and walked around the bow of the ship. After repeating his journey a few times, he came across the captain, standing with his hands behind his back, searching the open waters ahead.

"Are you looking for something in particular?"

Nikols glanced at Terrowin before returning his attention to the front. "No, not one thing. Many things." He shifted his head as he peered at the ocean. "I have been part of the ocean for my entire adult life. I know the signs of the water and sky. What am I looking for? The colour of the water. The size of the waves. Are all the waves moving as one, or are they in chaos? What are the fish doing? Are they jumping out of the water, or are they hiding? What does the water smell like? What is the sky like? What type of clouds are above us? How high are they?"

He turned to Terrowin. "You seem like a smart lad. As a witch, I'm sure you see things I don't. The ocean is my domain. You may see only water. I see a living creature that needs to be respected and understood."

"I hear your wisdom, captain. I didn't realize there was so much to see."

"You will understand more about the ocean as we travel. As we head to warmer waters, you will see a change in the surface."

"How long is our journey?"

"In this direction, a full month and then a bit. We make two stops before our last one, New Kireland Port. There we load up and return home. The journey home takes longer. More tacking against the wind, pushing against the waters. Two months of travel. Will ye be going home with us, or are you staying there?"

"I don't know for sure. Likely staying a while."

"The ports are fine, and usually safe. But the jungle around the ports is not for the timid. Monsters that can eat a man in one gulp be there."

"Real monsters?"

"Creatures that are more teeth than body. Beware."

23

Dorian stepped out of the main terradomus doors and walked on the stone pathway to the edge of the boundary of the property. In one hand, he clutched a scroll of paper; in the other a piece of dried meat. There were only horses and human traffic on the quiet road that he looked up and down. He continued to watch for a few minutes and strolled along the road.

He paused and whistled a high note and repeated it. Shortly later, a dog with gold fur came bounding up. Dorian dropped to one knee and petted the tail-wagging dog, enduring the attempted tongue licks. He gave the dog the meat and waited until it finished with its treat.

"Okay, good boy. Now you know where to take this."

The dog took the offered a roll of paper and ran off.

Dorian watched the dog until it turned a corner and disappeared behind a building. *I might as well go to the teahouse and wait.*

———

Watcher Tarra approached Keeper Ululla in the dining room where she was drinking a tea.

"Excuse me, keeper, do you know where I might find your daughter, Sister Ayleth? That dog was barking outside the front door again."

"At least she isn't hiding her meetings with Dorian. Sister Ayleth is in the second-floor library." She stood.

"Please sit, Keeper Ululla, and finish your tea. I'll inform her. I'll enjoy the walk to the library."

Ululla nodded, understanding a watcher often sat in a small room for hours at a time, and a chance for a walk would be a welcome change.

Tarra entered the library and spotted Ayleth reading a small leather-bound book at a long table. Three other witches were also in the library.

"Sister Ayleth, that dog has appeared again at the front door. He's waiting for you."

"Thank you, Watcher Tarra." Ayleth quickly closed the book and returned it to a shelf. She hurried out of the library.

———

Ayleth stopped by the dining room and got a soup bone. She gave a wave to her mother and continued to the front doors of the terradomus. Outside she called out to the golden furred dog. "Bragi, do you have a note for me?" She bent down and rubbed the dog's flank and took the note. She gave the dog the soup bone. "Thank you for the note." She watched as Bragi ran off with the bone.

Ayleth opened the note, not surprised by its contents. She went back inside the terradomus, found her mother in the dining room.

"I'm going to meet Dorian at a teahouse."

"Okay, don't be too long."

Ayleth left for the teahouse, hurrying.

The teahouse was one of several along the long block that included merchants and taverns. Dorian and she would choose different teahouses along the road, not wanting to be too predicable in case they were being watched.

She entered the teahouse, looking around in the dim interior. She saw Dorian wave from a table near the back making her weave past the tables placed at random intervals on the worn wood floor.

The chair she sat on wobbled slightly from her weight. The chairs around the square table didn't match, and she swapped her chair for another that didn't threaten to topple over. She saw Dorian already had a teapot and two cups and took a cup after he filled it.

She used hand signals Dorian and her had developed to greet him.

He returned with hand signals in return, informing her that he had exciting news.

"It'll be faster if I just told you." He grinned. "We have a new alter rector, one that wants our two orders to become closer. He asked me to help do this."

"That's fantastic news. That's great to hear."

"I have a plan and need your help."

"Sure. What do I have to do?"

"The Whiterose has an open sermon once a week. I want to have the Umbravox attend, and afterward our two orders can meet and see that we're both witches that are pursuing peace."

Ayleth took a drink of her tea. "That sounds good, but how do you plan to get the Darkrose, I mean the Umbravox, to attend a sermon? They don't seem to trust the Whiterose. I can't see many wanting to attend and meet Whiterose witches."

"The Umbravox study the Book of Destiny as a guide to the future. The most important passage is the prophesy of the warrior. A red-headed warrior who dies and sires the boy and the girl who will be part of the great battle against evil."

"Us."

"Yes." Darian paused. "What if the warrior himself was to give the sermon? I know the Umbravox would want to hear him speak."

"You want our father to give a speech? You know he's a private person and speaking in front of a crowd is not something he would want to do."

"It's for the greater good."

"Yes, but he's a stubborn man. You know that."

"I'll bet his daughter can convince him to give a speech." He gazed at her.

Ayleth frowned and closed her eyes. "You know him. He'll do almost anything I ask him to."

"That's great."

"I don't enjoy doing that to him. I'd rather he'd agree to giving a sermon other than my pleading with him."

"Ayleth, I have endured a difficult time with the Umbravox, partly because we both agreed it was best if I remained in their order to help facilitate change. I have done my part. Now you must do yours."

She shifted her hands and fingers, signifying her answer.

He responded with his own hand signals.

———

Alric watched his daughter approach him as he worked on a chair in his workshop, located in one of the lower levels of the terradomus. He put down the rasp and gave her a smile. "You decided you want to learn how to work wood after all."

She laughed. "No, I don't want to have hands like a man." She held up her hands, spreading her fingers. "Someday, I'll be a princess. I can't have fingers like yours."

Alric chuckled. "I suppose you take after your mother that way."

"I do. Can I ask you for a favour? A huge favour that's very important for everyone."

"What kind of favour?"

"Something to help bring people together, especially witches."

"Are you going to ask for the favour, or are you just going to tease me with how important it is?"

"It is very important." She smiled and put a hand on his arm. "Papa, would you please give a sermon at an open house? We are going to invite the Darkrose witches to attend."

"I'm sorry, but I'm not good at speaking in front of others."

"Please?" Ayleth lowered her head and looked up at him. "It's really important. It was Dorian's idea, and I know how much he looks up to you."

Alric let out a long sigh. "Damn. All right, I'll do it."

24

Alric watched as a steady progression of Darkrose witches enter the terradomus temple. He heard the quiet voices of the witches as they went to sit on the curved benches. When the doors were first open, only a few of the rival witches' order entered. Alric thought at first that he would speak to only to a few brave Umbravox witches that entered their terradomus. As the morning progressed, more Darkrose witches entered until they used the seating up. Several witches ended up standing on the steps between the seating.

"I think it's time for you to speak." Ululla gave him a smile and squeezed his arm.

He nodded. "I don't want to do this."

"You promised."

"I know." He went to the podium and tried to take a slow, deep breath. Alric saw hundreds of eyes stare at him.

He cleared his throat. "When I was a soldier, the moments before a battle, no matter how much I prepared the night before, I felt a hard knot in my stomach." He looked at the intense faces peering at him. "Although I am not going into battle, that same knot in my stomach has returned."

He heard the laughter, smiled, and continued. "Earlier, after agreeing to speak here, it was hinted that I should enlighten everyone on my journey from being a warrior to a witch. To be honest, it was more stumble than a journey." He paused as the audience laughed. "First, the reason I became a warrior was not because I felt a sense of duty to the kingdom. I chose to be a soldier because I thought being a woodworker, like my father, was too boring. The other factor was that young women liked soldiers on horses." After a brief burst of laughter, he continued.

"It turned out I became an excellent fighter with a sword and a very good horse rider. I was a good soldier, but it didn't make me happy. After I received promotions, I saw the commanders of the army were not happy men either. I wanted to leave the army and become a boring wood worker, but if I left, they would consider me a traitor. They executed traitors. It seemed I doomed my life to fighting until I died.

"But fate took mercy on me. I kept coming across witches. They became part of my life. It was odd; me, a warrior, befriending witches. One witch, she was of the Darkrose order, told me the warrior in me must die so I could live. At first, that sounded like nonsense, but later I understood I needed to fake my death as a soldier. I did so with help from a friend and escaped the army.

"I can imagine my father laughing when I returned to being a wood maker, likely wondering why it took me so long to figure out what I was meant to do.

"I was still hesitating on becoming a witch. But when I was in a teahouse, a man in old clothing sat at my table. He told me not to fear of making a commitment. That opportunity may only come by once. This man, he was of the Blackrain order. He urged me to become a witch." He heard the gasps from the crowd at the mention of Blackrain. A group feared to be warlocks with their own designs on the world. "I have met the Blackrain several times. I believe it is best we don't pass judgement on them. They, from what I can understand, are prepared to battle the evil forces that are trying to invade our land. One thing that stands out to me is his message that sometimes we only find ourselves in the right place only once. Brothers and sisters, we are here now, together. Let us seize this moment."

Alric stepped in front of the podium. He smiled and spread his arms. "Please, let us enjoy tea together and share the gift of friendship."

He felt shocked when the audience of witches stood up and clapped their hands. A wave of emotion swept through him as the crowd moved toward him. Hands reached out to touch him. His son made his way to him, hugging him.

"A new day has begun. Glory to peace."

———

Alric sat in the dining area, filled with witches of both orders, talking and making new friendships. His son and daughter, as well as Ululla and Orienla, sat with him. They all appeared to be watching him.

"I feel I'm being scrutinized."

Ululla laughed. "No, it's just we're so proud of you. That was an amazing speech. This may be the beginning of the joining of our two orders."

"Pardon my interruption. I am Altus Rector Truman."

Alric looked up at the friendly face. He stood. "It is an honour to meet you, Altus Rector Truman."

"The honour is mutual, Brother Alric. Thank you for your role in giving us hope to make the Umbravox whole again. I hope you will come to our terradomus when we open our doors, and our hearts, to the Whiterose order next week."

———

Dorian put his arm around his mother as they returned to the Umbravox Terradomus. "I'm so happy with the way the two orders got along! They sat with each other, talking and laughing. I believe we can be one order again."

"You did well, Dorian. I'm so proud of you arranging the meeting between the witches."

"It was my father's speech. He really spoke to us about the need to accept one another and to take this opportunity to achieve peace."

"That he did. Your father has seen much and understands how life may only present opportunities once. But don't undervalue your own accomplishment in this. They gave you a difficult task to do and yet you succeeded."

"Others helped me. Ayleth was the one who convinced father to make that speech."

"Yes, and credit to you for getting others to help you and not trying to do everything yourself."

They entered the terradomus, and for the first time, the witches greeted him with smiles and hellos. There weren't any side glances, frowns or avoidance when they saw him.

"There is still work to do, Mother. We have the Jital orders now willing to join, but now I need to spread the word of what we did to everyone in different cities and towns."

"That is a very ambitious plan. Make sure you discuss this with Altus Rector Truman. He may have an insight on how to accomplish this."

"I will. This never would have happened under Altus Rector Carlton."

"True. Let us hope he finds peace in his next posting."

25

Terrowin walked around the ship's deck. He kept out of the way of the ship's crew, who worked unhurriedly as they washed the deck and inspected ropes reaching high to the sails. After a couple of days, he had adjusted to the roll of the ship.

There weren't any more challenges to his bunk bed, although his earlier adversary glared at him a few times. Terrowin went to the railing at the perimeter of the deck, staring at the endless small waves. Occasionally, he saw a fish leap briefly out of the water. It was a calming experience, and it startled him when a voice spoke next to him.

"My name be Karl. I don't want to cause no trouble, witch, but I need to ask ya for a favour."

Terrowin looked at the man who had attacked him on the first day on the ship. "Speak."

"I know it wasn't right for me to try to pull ya off that top bunk. I wanted that bunk for a reason. It scares when I'm in small places. Your bunk has a window. I really want that bunk. Please. I cannot sleep. I am scared to be in my bunk."

Moments passed as Terrowin considered the request. "I am not one to be cruel. I will trade bunks with you."

"Thank you, witch. I have heard that witches have a kind side, and you have shown this to be true."

Terrowin watched him walk away. *At least they believe I'm a witch. This is a good disguise so far.*

Terrowin resumed his slow walk around the ship, reaching the stern. He looked up at the billowing sails. Above them, white birds with grey trim flew above, circling. He had noticed the birds had followed them since they left port. The ship dragged nets, catching fish for the crew. They tossed overboard the remains of the fish, resulting in a feast for marine life and the birds.

He continued his journey, retracing his steps toward the stern. He saw the captain looking up, and as he approached him, turned to see what he was looking at. At first, he saw the same mostly white birds. Then he saw two black birds flying higher than the other birds.

"Them a bad omen," Captain Nikols stated.

"Those black birds?"

"They were following us since the morning." He peered at Terrowin. "I heard witches bring bad luck. Now this."

"Maybe they're just birds flying around."

"They ain't here for the food and they keep watching us. I heard about these birds before. They be called black-watchers. Magic men send them to find people or things. Maybe they're looking for someone special here." He pointed a finger at Terrowin.

"I'm just a witch. Why would they care about me? Maybe it's someone else they're watching for."

"Could be. I just hope the damn things go away."

———

It pleased Terrowin that the black-watcher birds had disappeared later that afternoon and he hoped that was the last he would see them. As he stared from the bow of the ship, dark clouds drew his attention that covered the sky.

Without a build-up, the wind increased in velocity, accompanied by thunder. Rain followed, and Terrowin staggered his way across the slippery deck against the wet wind. He doubted he could make it to the cabin before being swept overboard.

"Grab a rope and hang on. It's going to get worse!" the captain shouted.

Terrowin reached a mast and gripped a rope. He wrapped it around his waist to the mast, just as the ship tilted at a sharp angle. He saw the ocean spill over the sides, and as the ship swung back the other way, water poured over his legs. The force turned him toward the stern of the ship, and he saw sailors frantically pull-on ropes, lowering the sails. It amazed him they could stay on the deck and work on the ropes.

The fury of the storm seemed relentless. Lightning cracked the sky with jagged slivers of white.

Then, as quickly as it came, the storm receded.

———

Terrowin waited until Captain Nikols looked to be free from directing his crew before approaching him.

"Thanks for telling me about using the rope."

"I didn't want to lose a passenger." He frowned. "Sorry, I shouldn't have said it that way. I'm glad you be safe."

"Anything I can do to help?"

The captain gave him a curious look before responding. "If ya want, join the crew in pulling on the ropes. We need to raise the sails again."

Terrowin joined two sailors in pulling on a long, thick rope. The sailors barely acknowledged him, grunting as they worked. At the end of raising the sails, Terrowin's arms ached, and his hands had developed blisters. He felt good when Captain Nikols gave him a compliment.

"You did good there. I never expected a witch to offer to do hard work, but you really helped out."

Terrowin walked to his cabin, seeing the other passengers standing just outside the door. One, the quiet smaller man, had a cut on his forehead.

"Did everyone survive the storm okay?" Terrowin asked.

"Lots of bruises and hurts, but no broken bones. Where were you?"

"I tied myself to the mast."

"We thought you'd fallen overboard." He paused. "Not that was what we wanted. I told the others the witch gave me his bunk. They thought I was mad for even asking a witch for a favour."

"As long as we're all safe."

Terrowin went past the other passengers and went inside the cabin, feeling exhausted. He climbed into a bunk bed and soon fell asleep. He dreamt he was in a room where brick walls faded into a fog as he sat on a stone bench. Next to him sat Ayleth.

He looked at her. "Where are we?"

"A place between dreams and reality."

"Why am I here?"

"Because you wanted to see me. This is a place where we can visit."

"Is this real?"

"Of course. Whatever we see is real, whether it's in a dream or when we're awake."

"But when we wake, the dream disappears."

"Rainbows disappear too. That doesn't mean they weren't real." She reached out a hand and touched his. "We are here now. This is real."

Terrowin nodded. "I miss you."

"I know. That's why you sought me out. And I miss you."

"I don't know where I am or if I can get home again."

"You're where you are, where you must be. You will return home once you're ready. Believe in your path."

"I love you."

"I love you. Stay true to who you are. Remember, to be with me again, you must ensure you survive. Understand?"

"Yes."

Ayleth leaned over and kissed him.

———

Terrowin woke up, still feeling the warmth of lips on his own. He used his finger to touch his lips, wondering if the dream was real.

It's real enough.

26

Terrowin looked out from the bow of the ship, watching as they drew closer to a single pier that reached far out from the green land. The horseshoe-shaped bay water changed colour, becoming emerald under the strong sun. There was only one other ship at the wood pier, smaller than the Oceanum Ore. The town stood out, with the buildings made of a white material.

The Oceanum Ore slowed, drifting toward the side of the dock. Workers on the pier ran along the length, preparing for the docking. They set two rowboats out to help guide the ship's position. Ropes from the ship were tossed to the workers on the dock, holding it in place.

"We will leave tomorrow at first light; in case you want to wander around the town." Captain Nikols continued to speak as he motioned his arms at a crew member. "It's a big town with a few places to eat and drink. I won't leave without you, but don't make the ship wait too long."

By the time Terrowin reached the dock, goods were being unloaded from the ship. He stepped out of the way of the determined-looking workers and left the harbour area. He climbed a wide ramp made of rock and entered the town, enjoying the change of room from the ship. Most of the town people were tall with light-brown skin. The men wore cloth or leather vests and shorts, while the women made use of colourful wraps that went from below their shoulders to almost to their knees. He drew little attention, and Terrowin assumed foreigners were common in the port.

He passed various vendors selling food and merchandise. Some of the food was fish, but others sold meat and fruit. He felt the tangs of hunger and entered a teahouse. He breathed in the air, smelling fish, and exited. *I don't want to eat fish. I've had enough of that on Oceanum Ore.* A second teahouse looked more promising as he saw a woman carry a plate with a slice of meat on it. He went to a table and sat, and soon a young woman came to take his order.

"Strong juice or tea to drink. Food today is the tail of gilizard."

"Juice. What is a gilizard?"

"A reptile that lives along the beach, twice as long as you're tall. The meat is good."

"Sure, I'll have that." He held up a silver coin. "Do you take these for payment?"

She took the coin and peered at it. "I can use it. We get lots of different coin here."

His eyes adjusted to the dim interior, and it surprised him to see two people sitting at a far table wearing robes. *Witches live here? I wonder if they are Whiterose or Darkrose.*

His food and drink were set on the table, and it intrigued him to see what the meat would taste like. The white flesh was light, and he could cut it with a fork. He found the flavour light with a fishy taste. Besides the meat, there was a scoop of a yellow potato-like vegetable. He discovered that the drink was fermented juice. It was pleasant tasting, but he turned down a second offering of it after he finished his meal.

"Hello, may we join you?"

Terrowin looked at the two witches in front of him. "Of course."

"I'm Brother Gerical and the is Sister Horeen."

"Brother Rowin. I wasn't expecting to see witches here."

They sat, and Horeen replied, "We are a small, and not a widely known, order. We used to have several witches visit us at one time, but since the war between kingdoms in the established region, there have been far fewer ships coming to our port. It appears we are a forgotten group of witches."

"Are you of the Whiterose or Darkrose order?"

"Both," Gerical answered. "At one time, there were Whiterose and Darkrose terradomus in Durban, which is the name of this port. The situation was we were both small in numbers, and eventually both orders joined, adopting the old title of Umbravox. We still have two terradomus, and a tunnel joins them."

Horeen continued. "Witches love tunnels." She smiled. "We are continuing a tunnel along the coast. We aren't sure where it will end, but everyday we advance a shot distance. What order are you with, and what brings you here?"

"Whiterose. I am just travelling, seeing different parts of the world."

"That is unusual for a witch. Did the altus rector or altus councillium send you on a special mission?" Horeen leaned forward.

Terrowin hesitated. "I cannot say."

Gerical stood. "Come, let us show you our terradomus."

Terrowin walked with them down the twisted stone streets. None of the buildings were tall, with few over two levels. They reached what appeared to be a large, two-level home. Wood timbers accented the white exterior and had a single, wide front door.

When he entered the terradomus, a dozen witches greeted Terrowin. He noticed the robes the witches wore had different shades of brown. He tried to act calm but was worried they would ask questions that would expose him as not being a witch. The witches acted excited having an unknown visitor, insisting he sit in a common room and tell them what was happening in the established region.

The altus rector took control of the informal gathering, informing the other witches they were making Terrowin feel he was under interrogation.

"Brother Rowin needs time to relax." He turned to Terrowin. "How long will you be staying?"

"Not long. I leave in the morning."

"That makes your visit rather short, unfortunately. Perhaps we can take a few minutes to have a private chat."

"Of course." Terrowin followed the altus rector, a middle-aged man of thinning hair and slim build. They left the common room and went upstairs to an office.

They sat on a pair of wood chairs in front of a desk.

"I am hoping you may have some news for our order. We have not heard from other witches in a long time. Can you tell me of the situation where you come from? I understand it is from the established region."

"There are still battles between kingdoms, but there is hope for peace."

"I see. Are you on a special mission, one you cannot reveal to us?"

"Yes, that is true."

"Very well. I accept your need for secrecy. I noticed you have what appears to be a sword under your robe. Did your altus rector suspect you may be in danger during your travels? Are you aware of strange creatures, some that would call monsters, live in the lands and seas where you are going?"

"I heard there are strange creatures where I'm going."

"Be alert. Some of those creatures can kill a man instantly. While your sword will be of use to you, it is best not too many people know of it. Witches may carry weapons to protect themselves in some situations, but others may think a sword of as excessive."

––––––

Terrowin return to the ship late that evening. He discovered only Karl remained on the boat; the other passengers had stayed in the port. He went to his bunk to rest, curious about the warning given by the altus rector.

He had hoped he would have a dream of Ayleth again, but he woke up with the ship leaving the dock. Terrowin left the cabin, and the saw the dock was receding from view. The water was calm and the winds light, making the outward journey smooth.

Soon, the captain had ordered all sails to be deployed. Terrowin went to the bow of the ship, looking out at the expanse of water. He watched as the occasional fish leaped out of the water. Above him were the familiar white and grey birds. *This is peaceful.* He looked up again and saw two black specks. They grew bigger, revolving into black-watcher birds. He didn't realize how large they were. Previously, they soared higher than the other birds. Now they flew lower, and Terrowin guessed their wingspan was as wide as a man was tall.

Terrowin had a distinct feeling the pair of birds were observing him. He wandered along the top deck of the ship. The waters were calm, and he found it easy to keep his stability on the tilting floor. As the weeks passed at sea, his balance allowed him to move about the ship easily. He wasn't as surefooted as the sailors, and he admired how well they moved as they worked. He made sure he didn't get in their way, although the sailors seem to be tolerant of him. They were amused he was carrying a sword under his robe, telling him there weren't any pirates where they were sailing.

He stared up as a sailor climbed near the top of the mainmast, impressed when he used the rope ladders to reach a lookout platform. It wasn't something he would like to do, deciding a life at sea wasn't for him.

Terrowin sat against the short rail that circled the perimeter of the deck, watching the clouds and birds. The two black-watcher birds stood out from the white and grey seabirds circling the ship. The large birds with talons and hooked beaks seemed capable of attacking small animals rather than the fish that was plentiful in the waters. They swooped lower to the boat, dropping just above the mainmast. Then they turned away, disappearing.

An old sailor peered at them and wandered over to Terrowin.

"Bad luck, them birds. No business being this far away from land."

"Why do you say they're bad luck?"

"Dark magic. Them birds were sent to spy on us. No other reason for them to be out here." He paused. "Someone bad looking for you?"

"No, I'm just a traveler."

"You have a sword under that robe. Makes me wonder if you expect trouble."

"The sword is my uncle's. He gave it to me as a gift. It's all I have from my family."

The sailor nodded. "All right. You look too young to have made enemies."

Terrowin was glad the ship's captain and crew didn't know the truth. *They may throw me overboard if they knew I was Prince Terrowin and fleeing for my life.*

———

The food on the ship was simple but filling, comprising of fish stew with thick bread. After dinner, he knew it would get dark soon and there was little to see other than the half-moon and a scattering of stars between the clouds. He went to his assigned bed and rested. Sleep was still far away. Boredom settled in and he stared at the dark wood beams above him. A few lanterns gave off yellow light, casting shadows that moved as the ship gently rolled with the waves.

He was in the twilight of sleep when he heard her voice, a soft whisper coming from inside his head.

"I'm praying for you. Stay safe."

"I'm safe. I wish I knew what was going to happen next."

"Be prepared. The dark is seeking you."

Terrowin thought of the black-watcher birds. "They may have found me."

I'll try to safeguard you. I love you."

"I love you."

His eyes opened, and the voice in his head disappeared.

Was I dreaming? He watched the shadows flicker above him and a few minutes later, fell into a deep sleep.

The following morning, he went to the deck. The sun was bright, and he blinked a few times after stepping on the wood deck. He walked toward the spot where they handed out water and bread to him.

Terrowin took his usual spot along the rail and sat, watching, but not seeing anything as the wind pushed the ship. He noticed all sets of sails were being used, and the boat rocked more under the higher speed. The captain came out of his cabin twice to inspect the sails and peer at the horizon. He spoke to a few of the senior crew members, pointing to an area off the starboard side of the ship.

A few minutes later, the ship gently turned, and he heard the splashing of water along the sides.

An old sailor approached him. "Boy, best be ready to hold on to something. Maybe rope yourself to the railin'."

"Why, what's wrong?"

"We being chased. A monster known as the cetus. It has many arms, each as thick as a man's body. Once it has ahold of you, you can't escape. The damn monster can take down this entire ship. If you have a god, pray to him now."

Terrowin stood at the rail looking at the water rush past the edges of the ship. The sails were all fully engaged as the ship turned toward the port side. He looked back at where the captain was shouting commands from the quarterdeck as he held the wheel.

A grey-green tentacle rose above the deck, waving around until it slapped down hard on the deck. The arm was as thick as a man's waist, and it slid on the wood floor until it wrapped around the second mast.

Terrowin saw the underside of the tentacle had suction cups as sailors began beating the tentacle with any object they had. Brooms, wooden poles and even knives were used to fight off the attacker. Terrowin staggered across the shifting deck, lifting his robe to retrieve his sword as he approached the tentacle. With an overhead swing of the sword, he brought the blade down. It sliced the end of the arm off, spilling out blue blood. The chopped end of the tentacle twisted around on the deck. A sailor used a broom to push the fragment off the ship.

The severed tentacle lashed into the air, knocking a sailor down before it disappeared off the ship. For a moment, the crew cheered at the withdrawal of the tentacle, and a sailor clapped Terrowin on the back.

"Well done! Ya chopped it clean off!"

The ship suddenly listed on the other side. Several tentacles reached over the ship and two began pulling at the masts. Other tentacles moved about the deck, wrapping around sailors and carrying them, screaming off the ship and below the water.

The ship continued to tilt on its side. Terrowin slid across the deck, grabbing desperately at a rope. He replaced his sword in its sheath, worried he might lose it. Shouts, wood splintering and rumbling below the deck unnerved him. At first, he thought it was the monster making the noise, then he realized it was the cargo sliding in the hold.

The ship righted itself and tilted again. The repeated motion of the tilted ship caused cargo and crew to spill off it. During a sequence of the ship being tilted, Terrowin saw the struggling sailors slide off the decking and into the water. Tentacles reached through the waves to pull them under to quickly end their attempts at swimming.

Terrowin looked around the sea, which was getting closer as the boat listed on its side. He felt this time the ship wouldn't right itself.

I'm a poor swimmer, especially with this sword hanging at my waist. He spotted a wooden crate almost his length and half its width floating in the water. As the water sloshed at his feet, he let go of the rope and jumped to the crate. His chest absorbed most of the blow, although his chin took a knock. He wrapped his arm and legs around the sides of the crate, hanging on tightly. His weight caused the crate to sink lower, but it kept him above the water.

He waited, expecting a tentacle to reach for him. A splashing sound drew his attention. He saw two men in a small boat rowing frantically. Terrowin watched as a tentacle broke through the water by the side of the boat, reaching up and around one rower. Moments later the tentacle dragged him down under the water, muffling his cries as his chest was compressed. A second tentacle arm appeared and removed the other sailor.

He saw Karl swim frantically when a tentacle gripped him and pulled him under without him having time to shout out a scream.

Time passed, and Terrowin didn't see any more of the ship's crew. He heard a gurgling sound, twisted his neck to look behind him, and saw the ship disappear under the sea.

Now I'm alone. He watched the empty rowboat, the end of oars hanging into the water. *The boat would be a better place than hanging on to this crate.* He drifted with the boat ahead of him, wondering if the sea monster was still close by. He thought if he stayed still, the monster wouldn't take notice of him. It seemed to be attracted to the crew members who were swimming or using the rowboat.

The sea remained quiet. Terrowin carefully looked around, not wanting to upset the crate he was holding onto. The white and grey birds had disappeared, and he assumed they had little reason to be around without the ship to help provide fish scrapes. He saw two dark spots that soon revolved into birds. *They're checking to see if I'm still alive.*

As the birds approached, Terrowin slipped off the crate on the opposite side of their approached. He kicked his legs and secured himself to the side of the crate with his fingers. He found the robe restricted by his movements and wished he could discard it. He thought the black-watcher birds would circle to where he was next. Terrowin took a deep breath and dropped under the crate. Slowly he went to the other side of the crate, and when he desperately needed air, broke the surface of the water. He blinked and looked around, not seeing the birds initially. Then he spotted them flying away, their bodies just black smudges.

The sun had moved past the high noon position and after he climbed back on the crate, paddled with his hands to the rowboat. Slowly, he came closer to the boat. When he pulled alongside of it, he clambered aboard the small craft. He removed the wet and heavy robe and took a deep breath. *I feel a lot lighter without that robe, but it helped disguise me. I guess I should be thankful for that.*

After a few minutes, he took the oars and tried a few strokes. He looked behind him and saw a green smudge of land. *That's as good a place as any.*

He found he could row faster facing backward, occasionally looking to see if he was moving in the right direction. He thought he detected movement on one island, but it was too far to determine whether it was human or a large animal.

Terrowin continued to pull at the oars, his back and arms protesting the strain of paddling against the choppy water, worried that the ocean currents would take him to an unknown destination if he stopped.

Behind him, and in front of the bow of the boat, he could make out the green smudges of trees on the land. He increased his efforts, drawing in deep breaths of the salty air.

The land became more distinct, the jagged edges of the rocks becoming more in focus. He knew if there were rocks in the shallow water near the land, it could sink his lifeboat before he reached the shore. He switched his position on the boat, deciding the less efficient method of rowing of facing forward gave him the opportunity to avoid rocks. The land looked to be rising high with small patches of vegetation. He also saw people among the rocks but was unable to discern what they looked like. It didn't matter if they were friendly or hostile. He felt exhausted and needed to rest soon.

Hands grabbed the front of his boat and faces appeared, staring at him. It shocked him at their appearance as their heads rose above the boat's side.

Beautiful women with long hair grinned at him, showing off pointed teeth. He looked at their hands, the long fingers ended in claws, with web skin between them. He stopped rowing, wondering what they planned to do.

27

"A lone sailor. Shall we play with him first, or just dispose of him?" a red-headed woman asked.

"He's rather good-looking. Perhaps I can make use of him for a while." A blonde licked her lips.

"Please. I mean no harm. The ship I was on sank and I'm only trying to get to land."

"You understand us?" The blonde acted surprised.

"Yes, I do. Please let me be."

"No, I don't think so." The blonde lifted herself into the boat, facing him, revealing a tail of gold scales instead of legs.

Mermaids.

She flipped her tail toward him, pressing her tail fin against his chest.

Terrowin leaned back, feeling the strength of her legs as she pinned him to the back of the boat. His hand rested on the end of the tail, and he could feel the bones of her foot underneath the skin.

"How come you can understand us? Very few humans can." She pushed harder with her tail.

"It was as a spell. Magic." His back protested against the wood of the stern of the boat. He looked at her face, red lips and dark-blue eyes.

Fine bones framed lovely cheeks. Her breasts were large compared to her slim, muscular body.

"A spell? By whom?"

"The Whiterose witches."

"Tell me more. Why did they give you this spell?" She slid her tail down, pressing on his stomach. "What is your name?"

Terrowin grunted. He tried to push at the tail but found there was too much strength pushing on him. "Please," he gasped, "I'll tell you."

The tail reduced the pressure a fraction.

"My name is Prince Terrowin, son of King Grayson. The Whiterose witches helped me escape and saved my life."

"Why would they help you? How are you special?"

"I am the last heir to the kingdom. They told me I am part of a prophecy to battle evil during the next great battle."

"Are you a witch, then?"

"No."

"But you like witches?"

"Yes." He gave a painful smile. "I'm in love with one of them."

The blonde mermaid looked amused. "You're too young to know true love." She withdrew her tail, allowing him to sit. She looked at the red-headed mermaid. "I want to keep him for a while. Help me undress him."

Terrowin watched as the second mermaid climbed into the boat. Despite not having legs, they didn't have any trouble moving in the boat. He didn't resist as their fingers undid his clothing. He was aware the claw fingers could have simply ripped off his clothes, but reasons unknown to him, they were almost gentle with him. Though they were smaller and slimmer than he was, he felt they were both as strong as himself.

He sat naked as the redhead slipped out of the boat and pushed it to the rocky shore, avoiding the rocks that would have damaged the hull. The blonde held his arm in one of her clawed hands, ensuring he would not escape. "What's your name?"

"Carassius." She smiled, showing off the pointed teeth again. "Are you scared?"

"Yes."

"You should be." She pointed to a path leading up past the rocks. "Go. Stop at the first plateau."

He stepped out of the boat and followed the path. It wasn't too steep and curved to the right before leading to a flat area of sand and tough grasses. He stopped and waited. Moments later, Carassius joined him, moving efficiently on her hands and tail.

"Lie down, Prince Terrowin."

Terrowin obeyed, lying on his side to face the mermaid.

"We may decide to let you live, but we want more information from you first. The fact you are a friend of the witches has given you a chance to survive your encounter with us. Witches are the only humans we believe understand the reason for life. Tell me why the witches like you and want to protect you, besides the prophesy."

"I don't know. Except Ayleth told me I was her soulmate."

"This is the witch you're in love with?"

"Yes. I also have dreams of being a leader fighting against evil forces. Perhaps those dreams are of my future."

"To stay with Ayleth, would you become a witch and give up being a prince or a king?"

"Yes." He answered without hesitation.

"Stay here. I'll be back."

Terrowin watched her roll away and back down the path from where they came. He stood, looking around. From what he could see, there were numerous mermaids. They varied in skin tone and hair colour but were usually slim. They were all beautiful, as they took turns leaping into the water or sunbathing among the rocks. He didn't see any mermen, and he wondered the reason for that. He was nervous about his predicament and wasn't comfortable without his clothing. He pushed aside the idea of trying to escape as he waited for Carassius to return.

When she returned, he was sitting again.

"I conversed with our elders. It seems the witches may have a special interest in keeping you safe."

"Does that mean you'll let me go?"

"Not right away. We have ways of conversing with witches. We need to check out your story. You'll be my prisoner for a few more days."

"Why do you want to keep me?"

"I like you. I want to play with you." She reached out and stroked his shoulder. "Lie down."

Terrowin laid on his back, lying passively as Carassius touched him. She kissed him, starting on his lips and working down to his chest.

"You may touch me as well." She laughed.

He slid his hands up and down her body, mechanical in his efforts. He was aware she was more amused than aroused by his efforts.

She rolled on her back. "Sailor, I need to return to the water soon. You're ready, and that will have to do." She pulled on his arm so he was on top of her, and she reached down to guide him.

Terrowin didn't need any encouragement to finish. A minute later, he rested on his side.

She kissed him. "Considering the circumstances, you did well. I must go to the water now. You may rest."

Terrowin watched her leave, and rested on his back, soon falling asleep.

———

He woke up to the redhead mermaid staring at him. "Hello."

"You slept a long time. It's now morning." She gave him a smile.

"Oh."

She pointed to another path, away from the water. "If you go up there, you'll find fruit trees and berries to eat. Unless you like raw fish. I can get you those."

"No, I prefer the fruit." He stood. "Is everyone here a mermaid? No mermen?"

"We are part of a pod of mermaids and a merman. He looks after us."

"So there are very few mermen?"

"There are far more mermaids than mermen. There are unattached mermen who live alone or with just one mermaid. Sometimes mermen swim together for companionship."

"What happens if your merman dies? Do you just find another merman?"

"What a horrible thought that our merman would die. We all love him. He's part of our pod, our family. But to answer your question, if we need a new merman, we send out a signal we are looking for one. Several mermen will apply. We will choose one for his physical and mental qualities."

"The mermen don't fight to be chosen?"

"No, that is primitive. Mermen wrestle, but out of sport, not to main."

"I see. That's a good way to do things."

"For a man who carried a sword, you are very perceptive. We will talk later." She went back down the trail to the water.

Terrowin climbed up the rocky path. At the top, as promised, was an abundance of fruit trees and bushes full of berries. Terrowin ate until he quenched his thirst and filled his stomach. By climbing a tree, he looked as far as he could and observed that the rocky island was elongated towards the mainland. The mermaids were taking turns swimming and sunbathing. *If any ship comes near, the rocks will probably break apart it under the water's surface. The poor sailors will find out those beautiful mermaids will be their last sight.*

He returned to the lower plateau and found Carassius waiting for him.

"Are you feeling stronger, Terrowin?"

"Yes, I feel better now."

"Good. Maybe you'll please me better this time."

"I'll try."

Carassius laughed. "You are a funny man. You must do more than try. You must learn to do things right, whether it is rowing a boat, fishing, or making love. You have fingers, lips and a tongue. Use them to touch me. Everywhere."

Terrowin followed her directions, gaining confidence as she made sounds of pleasure. A few times, she gripped him in her claw-like fingers, causing a trickle of blood to form. That encouraged him more, and he enjoyed making her react to his efforts.

"Now, Terrowin."

He didn't have a choice as her arms pinned him to her, her claws digging into his back. He was glad when she let out a primal cry and relaxed. He could finally breathe again.

She lay panting and turned to him. "Much, much better. I want to keep you even longer now." She laughed. "But no, I shall give you your freedom. We have checked with witches, and they have confirmed your tale about a prophesy. If you are really Prince Terrowin, we won't take your life. But I still want to keep you around for a while longer."

"Why me? Don't you have the merman to take care of you?"

"He does. But it's not my turn yet, and I have a strong need right now for a man. Even a human."

He stared at her.

"Someday you'll understand. I'm coming of age when I want to have a child. You're not a merman, but you're still a man. I'll see you later."

Terrowin watched her leave. The mermaids were more agile than he expected on land, using their powerful tail muscles to lurch over the ground.

He picked more fruit to eat and sat under a tree. He felt bored, but there was little to do but stare at the ocean and sky. He returned to the lower level and rested, enjoying the warm sun.

Carassius returned, her hair wet. "Come with me."

Terrowin stood and followed Carassius down the path to the water. He saw his boat still secured to the rocky edge of the land. He watched Carassius dive into the water, joining several other mermaids.

"Come in," Carassuis said.

Terrowin was aware of the amused looks from the mermaids as he ventured into the water. He kept to the rocky shore, standing on the sand and stone mixture, with his shoulders just above the surface.

"Come on, we won't let you drown." The blonde mermaid swam up to him and pulled on his arm.

"Please. I can't swim well."

"You can learn." She circled her arm around his neck and slowly dragged Terrowin away from the shore. He turned on his back, floating with his head on her shoulder. "See, you're safe."

"Maybe."

"Relax. Your body will float."

Terrowin tried to relax, spreading out his arms. He took in slow, deep breaths. Moments later, he saw the blonde mermaid swim past him, and he realized he was floating by himself. He tried moving his arms to propel himself and was pleased he could maneuver through the water.

"Turn over and try moving through the water. Don't worry, I'm next to you."

"Okay, but I'm not sure what I need to do."

"Terrowin, mermaids are humans that adapted to living in the water. All humans can swim. You just need to relax."

He rolled over, taking in gulps of air as he used his arms to pull at the water and kicked his legs.

The blonde mermaid laughed. "Stop splashing so much. Glide your arms and don't kick at the water. Move your legs slower."

Terrowin tried following her suggestions. He was swimming, surprising himself. Glimpses of the surrounding mermaids, who were amused by his efforts, caught his attention while he swam. He was tiring and orientated himself toward the shore, discovering it was the same spot the mermaids gathered where they left the water. Before he reached the shore, he found he could stand on a pebbled bank. He was aware of the mermaids, and there were also several offspring among them, watching him. He stopped where the water ended and sat, facing it. When he looked behind him, he saw they were close by.

Carassius smiled at him. "They're curious about you. Don't be concerned. They won't hurt you."

"Thanks for teaching me to swim but I find it tiring."

"You must keep practicing. Also, you need to learn how to swim underwater."

"I'm having enough trouble staying above it."

She laughed. "You tell funny jokes, Prince Terrowin." She held out her hand. "Come, let's play in the water."

Terrowin went back in and played with her and the other mermaids. That is something he never would have expected to happen.

———

The days passed, and he spent more time in the water, increasing his ability to swim. He also tried short durations underwater. The mermaids enjoyed teasing him, occasionally bumping into him, gliding under him and sometimes pulling him underwater.

As Terrowin's head broke the surface, he looked up as he shook the water from his face. High above, he saw a pair of birds. They circled and seemed to be peering at him as they spiralled lower. *Black-watchers. They've found me.*

"What's wrong?" Carassius asked.

"Those black birds." He pointed with his hand. "They were sent to find me. They're called black-watchers. Something bad is going to happen soon." He told her of the storm and the attack of the cetus after the appearance of the black-watchers.

"Then we must make preparations to keep you safe." She gave him a grin. "You're my prisoner and I'm not going to let you come into harm. Unless that's what I want, of course."

"Thanks. But if you set me free, I can go where the birds cannot find me."

"I'm not ready to let you go yet. You'll be safe with the mermaids, I promise you."

———

He discovered they made use of fire and occasionally cooked food. Set away from the water and on the high point on the rocky land, they placed stones against each other to form a long, narrow bed. Inside the walls were the remains of burnt wood. On top of the walls were flat stones laid across.

The mermaids laughed when he gathered enough dry wood, and using a flint rock, started a fire to cook fish and potato-like roots.

"We usually eat our fish raw," Carassius informed him as she watched him turn a fish over on the flat stone with a stick.

"I know, but my stomach digests cooked food better."

She took an offered piece of cooked fish from him, still steaming as it dangled on the stick. "Cooked fish is good too, but it takes too long to prepare."

He ate his dinner. "How long have mermaids been mermaids? It seems to me at one time mermaids had legs and walked on land."

"There isn't any memory of a time when we had legs. A legend tells how a god was jealous of a seashore village of beautiful people and made us all into half fish. I don't know how true that is. Sometimes a mermaid is born with legs instead of a tail. So, it seems we have a common ancestor."

"What do you do with the mermaid born with legs?"

"We give her, or him, to a fishing village. We ask them to care for it. It is all we can do. In return, we help protect the village when they venture out to sea."

They allowed him to sleep with the rest of the mermaids, and he learned several of their names. There were mostly female, although there were also two mermen, both juveniles.

At night, Carassius slept next to him, resting her head on his shoulder. Other than a few kisses, she didn't express interest in physical contact with him on the land. In the water, she told him to follow her a distance away. When they were alone, she indicated it was time for intimacy.

He thought of Ayleth, feeling guilty. It wasn't just the love-making. He knew he was falling for the beautiful mermaid.

It was during one morning he met the merman as he swam in the shallow water. The dark-haired man had a thin beard of long whiskers.

"Are you trying to take over my pod?" In his hand, he held a spear with a tusk tied to the end.

"No, no, I'm just, just..."

The merman laughed. "I know. I was told earlier about you. My name is Bardo."

Terrowin wasn't sure how tall he would be if he had legs, but his arms implied a long stature. He saw the mermaids had clustered nearby, looking happy about Bardo's return. After a quick conversation with Terrowin, Bardo swam toward the shore.

Unlike the mermaids, who were graceful in their swimming and rolled between stomach and their back, Bardo surged through the water. He stayed on his stomach, disappearing under the water briefly before almost leaping from the surface.

The mermaids, save one, all followed in his wake. Carassius stayed closed to Terrowin.

"What do you think of him?"

"He seems all right. Friendly enough."

"I'm glad he likes you. I wasn't certain what he would do when he found out you and I were close."

"Oh. I hadn't thought of that."

"Tonight, we will have a feast and celebrate his return." She turned toward the shore. "Come, you can help us prepare the fire."

———

The party, celebrated on both land and sea, was a success as far as Terrowin could tell. It lasted late into the night, and while there wasn't any alcohol, the sea people acted as if it intoxicated them with happiness.

It the morning, life returned to normal for the mermaids. Terrowin was careful with how close he stayed with Carassius in the water, suspecting Bardo may be watching them. Later in the afternoon, Bardo approached Terrowin.

"It may be best if you stay on the island for a bit."

"Is there a problem?"

"There's a ship approaching. It seems suspicious it is coming soon after you arrived here. This ship may be searching for you. The mermaids and I will see if we can deter them."

Terrowin swam to the island and climbed to one of the higher points. He peered at the horizon, spotting a pair of masts of a ship. As he watched, the ship became larger, and he made out the ship's crew moving about. Terrowin knew most of the mermaids were in the water, as the beach area where they liked to sunbathe was almost empty.

The ship continued to get closer. The crew took some sails down to slow the speed of the ship, and Terrowin wondered if they were aware of all the sharp rocks just underneath the water's surface. To the port side of the ship, mermaids waved their arms and partially leaped out of the water. The boat turned toward where they swam, with the crew members clustered at the bow of the ship to watch the frolicking mermaids.

Suddenly, the ship lurched, turning on its side. As it tilted, some sailors jumped into the water. A rowboat was lowered and filled with crew members. The mermaids and the merman attacked, dragging the sailors below the water. The rowboat overturned and the mermaids soon overtook the surviving crew members as they tried to swim to shore.

Terrowin looked but didn't see any survivors. The ship itself had disappeared under the water. He watched as he saw the mermaids return to the island. Carassius went to the beach area and signalled him to join her.

"We have eliminated the ship and its crew. The ship's captain confessed they were looking for you."

"You killed them all?"

"Yes. Most humans are our enemy, and we don't feel any remorse in killing them. You, and witches, are the exception. Prince Terrowin, it may not be safe for you to stay on our island. Bardo and I agree it's time for you to go to the mainland. You'll be safer there."

At the end of the night, Carassius snuggled next to him. "Tomorrow, I will set you free. Sleep well, Prince Terrowin."

———

The morning arrived, and Terrowin made his way to the water's edge. Carassius swam close by and stopped to speak with him.

"Prince Terrowin, it is possible I am carrying your child. More than just a possibility."

"How do you know that?"

"Mermaids can tell when a union has been successful."

"I'm going to be a father?"

"Yes. Well, in about a year's time. It takes longer for a mermaid to develop. Also, with a human, there's a greater chance of it not coming to full-term."

"I wish I could meet her, or him, someday."

"Someday it may happen. I thought you should know, even if this is the last time we meet."

They led Terrowin back to his boat. Several mermaids were there to watch him leave. Even the merman was present. Bardo was hairless, except for long hair and a beard. In one hand he held his spear. Muscles rippled in his chest as he waved at Terrowin.

"Good luck on your journey. The black-watchers will likely return, looking for you. I suggest after you reach land, we scuttle the rowboat."

"Thank you."

Carassius leaned into the boat to give him a kiss. Then she and another mermaid pushed at the back of the boat, propelling it rapidly away from the island. When it landed at the mainland, Terrowin dressed. He watched as the mermaids turned the boat on its side. It soon disappeared below the water. He waved goodbye and headed inland.

28

Altus Rector Carlton used a tunnel for only a short distance. He didn't want to pass by other witches during his walk to the Drumon Terradomus. *I am leaving in disgrace. I don't want to see their accusing eyes as I leave.* He left the tunnel, climbing a ladder that exited at the back of a blacksmith shop. A man pounding a piece of iron with a hammer barely looked up at his appearance.

Carlton went past him, not making eye contact, leaving through the oversized open doorway. He felt invisible among the crowd due to the narrow streets being crowded. Carlton made steady progress down the flat stone street, keeping his hood over his head and looking straight ahead. The road ended in a T intersection, and he turned to his left. This road was wider but made of hard packed dirt and gravel. There were fewer travellers but more horse-drawn wagons. Carlton was mindful that most people, outside of witches, would not recognize him as an altus rector. When a wagon passing by him stopped to offer him a ride, he accepted. Carlton sat at the back of the wagon, saving him from conversing with the couple at the front and explaining why he was travelling.

Sparsely placed homes with extensive gardens were replaced by farms as they left the Jital urban area. Carlton reflected on the change of his fortunes. *The previous altus councillium chose me to ensure order and bring discipline on our teachings. That Dorian, he failed to show respect or follow directions. And his mother! She refused to entice that warrior, Alric, to be part of Umbravox. Because I tried to enforce our rules and the Book of Destiny, I get replaced! Dorian may not be a demon, but he is clearly under their influence. I shall learn from this deceit. From now on do what's best for me and not just the Umbravox.*

The sun moved across the sky and toward the horizon. The man at the front called out, "We be near the village, Cuttery. We are stopping for the night."

"Thank you. If you can stop near a teahouse, I will be most thankful."

The village was larger than he expected, with a small market area. He jumped off the wagon and thanked the couple.

"You giving me a ride was a kind deed that I won't forget," Carlton said and clasped his palms together at his chest. "Peace be with you."

He waited until the wagon moved away and frowned as he looked for a teahouse. *I was hoping they would offer me food and a place to rest.*

Carlton walked down the cobble street, entering a busy teahouse. He found a square table near a window and sat, waiting to be served. Carlton pushed off his hood, no longer worrying about being recognized. Across the room a pair of Whiterose witches sat, but not any from his own order. He decided he would not make use of the Cuttery Terradomus as a place to eat and rest. *They would know me there, and I have no intention of enduring their peering eyes.*

A woman approached him, offering a choice of watered-down wine, or ale. For food, they gave him a choice of chicken or pottage.

"Wine with the chicken." It tempted him to drink the ale to dull his mind but decided on the wine. The wine was weak in taste, with the alcohol in the wine meant to purify the water and making it safer to drink.

A few minutes later, the half chicken was placed on his table. He began tearing the meat from the chicken, occasionally taking a drink. Near the end of his meal, a young, dark-haired woman approached him.

"Pardon me, may I converse with you? I feel troubled and need help with your teachings."

He looked up at the pretty face, smiled, and gestured for her to sit. "Of course. How may I be of help?"

She sat. "My name is Darla." She gave a modest smile.

"Brother Carlton."

Carlton listened to talk about her failed relationship. She used hand movements as she spoke, occasionally brushing back her long hair. She acted shy, prompting Carlton to ask questions and assure her he was not blaming her for her troubles.

"I assure you, I know too well of being blamed for situations not of our control. Please continue and know I have sympathy for your difficulties."

"At first, he was nice to me, but later he used angry words and a firm hand to make me do things he wanted. I finally left him, but I wonder if I should have stayed with him. Am I good enough to attract a nice man?"

"Of course. You deserve someone who cares for you."

"Thank you for your kind words. May I ask why if you are travelling or staying in Cuttery?"

"I am travelling, actually, I am going to Drumon."

"Oh, that is a sizeable town. Is that where you will stay?"

"Yes. I will be the altus rector there."

"You are a very important witch. Have you been to Drumon before?"

"No, it will be my first visit."

"Oh, so they don't know what a nice man is going to be their altus rector."

"Well, I'm sure they will get to know me after I arrive and provide the proper leadership."

"Thank you so much for listening. You have truly made me feel better. May I impose upon you one more favour?"

Carlton spread out his arms. "Please, just ask."

"Would you walk with me to my boarding room? It isn't far, but I worry about walking by myself at night. A man, such as yourself, would keep troublemakers away."

"It would please me to accompany you."

Carlton walked with Darla to the exit of the teahouse, pushing open the wood door. He found her proximity inviting as they walked down the road. There weren't any sidewalks, causing even closer contact when a horse and wagon went by.

She used a hand to hold on to his arm as they continued their journey. "I feel so much safer with you close to me."

"I am glad to provide you with protection."

"After my last relationship, I find your company most pleasant. You are an interesting man."

"I find you attractive as well, although I am much older than you."

"Age difference is not as important as the quality of a person."

Carlton's earlier anger at being forced out as the altus rector at the Jital Terradomus turned to musings about Darla's company. As they passed a brick building, it surprised him she stopped and faced the gap between the next building.

"Tell me, Altus Rector Carlton, do you believe in the after life?" She smiled.

"Yes, I..."

From behind him, a hand covered his mouth. It muffled his attempt to cry out as a knife pierced his back. He sagged as he was pulled back into the dark gap.

"Great news, Keela. He's the altus rector going to Drumon. They don't know what he looks like either."

As his vision faded, he wanted to curse her, but instead passed away.

———

Keela walked along the road alone. He carried the dead witches' robe in a backpack until he reached the town of Drumon. When Wizard Crimson hired Darla and himself to pose as a witch, he felt it was a task he could do without much risk. When Master Diablo learned of the opportunity of Keela impersonating an altus rector, he ordered Crimson to change their plans.

Pretending to be a witch and gathering information was a task Keela felt he could do. Pretending to be an altus rector wasn't something he looked forward to trying. But he was scared to refuse Crimson or Master Diablo.

After stopping at a tea house, he went behind the building where a dirt path travelled between the various market shops. A quick glance showed he was alone, and he put on the robe. *I hope the blood stains show little at the back.* He thought back to how Dara had tried to wash out the blood and sew the tear in the back of the robe.

Keela reached the middle of Dumon and approached the large temple-style building. He hesitated at the front entrance. Several witches moved past him, and he finally took a bold step and entered the terradomus.

He wasn't sure what to expect. Witches moved about in a large foyer. The marble floor looked worn near the entrance way. High above, sunlight came down in beams from glass openings in the ceiling. He walked toward the centre, seeing several archways that led to other parts of the building. Near a side wall, a large entrance showed a dining room with a kitchen at the back. He didn't know what to do; if he was supposed to announce he was the new altus rector or wait for someone to approach him. He stood, looking at the ornate, bowl-shaped ceiling. *What do I do now? Where should go?*

A woman approached him. "Hello, I am Watcher Rainela. Are you in need of help?"

He stared at the tall, brown and grey-haired woman. "I need help to locate where I'm supposed to go. I'm Carlton, the new altus rector."

She appeared to consider his response for a moment. "Come with me, Altus Rector Carlton. I will be pleased to take you to our keeper."

Keela walked with the watcher across the floor and to a set of stone steps, where they descended to a lower floor. He saw the ceiling was high and made of white marble. Light came from lanterns and sunlight that was directed to the lower floor by use of slits and angled cut-outs. The walls were adored with paintings and written passages from the Book of Destiny.

Near the end of the room, Keela saw several doorways. Two were closed, but the other was an open archway. As they approached the open doorway, he saw a man sitting behind a desk. Moments later, the man stood, eyeing Keela.

"Keeper Rehoat, this is Altus Rector Carlton." She paused before adding, "Altus Rector Carlton came through our front doors and appeared uncertain where to go. We weren't prepared for his entrance."

"Is there a reason you choose to arrive through the front entrance rather than the primus tunnel, Altus Rector Carlton? That was rather unusual." Keela studied Rehoat's face. The older woman with dark features didn't give a hint what she was thinking.

"I wanted to see how ordinary witches are greeted when entering the terradomus."

Rehoat looked at Rainela and spoke to Keela. "I see. Have you chosen a day for the ceremony for the new altus rector?"

"No, not yet. Perhaps in a few days after I get used to the duties here."

"Altus Rector Carlton, please sit and relax. Watcher Rainela, please inform other witches our new altus rector is here."

"Of course."

Keela tried to relax with a cup of tea, aware Rehoat was watching him closely. He hoped the keeper wouldn't ask for any details about Carlton or his past, as he was unsure of what to say. He was pleased Rhoat was willing to sit quietly as well.

Watcher Rainela returned with four male witches.

Rehoat stood. "I don't know who you are, but you're obviously not Altus Rector Carlton. We don't have a ceremony for a new altus rector, nor is there any primus tunnel. Take this impostor to a bedroom and keep him secured there."

————

Keela sat on the hard wood chair by the simple round table. Against a wall was a bed with a thin mattress and a blanket. The door was closed, and he was sure there were witches on the other side guarding.

After what seemed to Keela a long time, to the point where he was feeling thirsty and hungry, Keeper Rehoat entered with a tray with two cups. She placed the tray on the table.

"Life is a journey of choices. Some are good choices, some of them are a mistake. Perhaps you would like to tell us how you came into the situation of pretending to be Altus Rector Carlton."

"I don't want to say anything." He looked at the teacups.

"I see. Just so you understand, you cannot leave this room until you have drunk from one of these teas. One is safe to drink."

"The other is poison?"

"I have a choice for you. Tell me what happened to the real Altus

Rector Carlton, and I will tell you which teacup to drink from. Refuse to answer my questions and I will refuse to tell you which teacup to drink from. Take as long as you wish to decide." Keeper Rehoat smiled. "I'm sure the person, or persons, who hired you would prefer you make the wrong choice. What is your real name?"

"Keela." He looked at the keeper, and back at the tea cups. *Damn, I don't want to die for this.*

"Are you getting thirsty? A tea would taste wonderful right now."

"All right, I'll tell you what I know." Keela related everything he knew, including the name of the woman who hired Darla and he. "She called herself Wizard Crimson, and she serves another called Master Diablo."

"Is that everything you know?"

"Yes. I beg you for forgiveness in my part of Altus Rector Carlton's death. I didn't know Darla planned to kill him."

"Witches do not seek revenge. I doubt it was Darla who killed Altus Rector Carlton, but rather it was you. It matters not. After you drink your tea, you are free to leave."

"Which one is poison?"

"Neither." Rehoat stood and walked out of the room, leaving the door open.

Keela followed her. "I can leave?"

"Yes, and don't return here."

29

The kitchen took up half of the living area of Wizard Crimson's cabin. Its location just outside of the town gave her enough isolation while still making it easy to travel to the town. She had added a yellow powder to a wood bowl containing a green paste when the outside door opened. She frowned and went to push the door closed. The door resisted her efforts.

Crimson checked to see what was holding the door open and saw four witches in dark robes standing outside.

"What are you doing here? Leave at once."

Instead, the witches advanced, holding their hands in front of them.

Crimson now felt the force that pushed the door open. First, she took a step back, and then another. She retreated as the witches advanced, unable to resist the force they used on her. Pinned against a wall, she struggled to breathe.

Three witches stood in front of her, while the fourth walked around the cabin looking inside cupboards.

A witch spoke, "Wizard Crimson, you have been aiding evil. Who else has been helping you?"

She shook her head.

"We can it make more unpleasant for you. If we increase the pressure on your eyes, they will become permanently damaged. One last time, who are the others you are with?"

"Master Diablo, Wizard Templet, and two other warlocks. I don't know their names."

The witch held a metal cup in his hand. "You will drink this."

"You can't make me," she gasped out. The pressure increased on her chest.

"You will drink this. If you refuse to do so, we will force you to. In addition, if you don't drink this yourself, we will remove your youth spell." He held out the cup.

"What is it?"

"It will remove your memory of spells."

"Please, I need my spells to survive."

"Drink or lose your youth spell."

Tears rolled down from her eyes as she took the cup.

A fourth witch returned to the others. "I found the book containing the spells. Has she told us what we needed?"

"She has."

"She drank the tea?"

"Yes."

The witch looked at the youthful looking wizard. "You are lucky we are allowing you to keep the youth spell. You have caused the death of a witch and have done other harm. Using spells to increase your power is no longer something you can do."

The four witches left, leaving Crimson sitting on the floor exhausted. The spells that made her strong eluded her memory. She had written the spells in the book the witches took, making the loss a disaster. Crimson hoped Master Diablo would not find out the witches had overpowered her.

30

Alric tried not to show any nervousness as he walked with Dorian and Ayleth to the Darkrose Terradomus. He wasn't sure what to expect inside, but after he entered, he saw similarities to the one he lived in. There were differences as well. In the Whiterose Terradomus, the front entrance branched in two directions. One led to a large chamber where the public could attend to hear a weekly sermon. The other side was a dining room.

The Darkrose Terradomus didn't allow the public inside, and the front entrance led to an open foyer. Around it was two hallways that disappeared into the enormous building and a dining area.

Alric received curious looks as he made his way across the foyer to the dining area. He felt his arm being held by his daughter, and looked at her, noticing her smile was tight.

"Don't worry. We're here as Dorian's guests."

"I know. But everyone is staring at us."

"They're probably wondering how an old warrior such as myself could have such a beautiful daughter."

She laughed. "Actually, I think you're the attraction. You're in the Book of Redemption and the Book of Destiny as the red-headed warrior. Now they can finally see you with their own eyes."

Alric sat with Ayleth in the dining room while Dorian went to obtain tea and food. As they waited, Orienla came up to them.

"Brother Alric, Sister Ayleth, welcome to our terradomus. May I join you?"

"Of course," Alric answered. "It is good to see you again."

"Dorian is very excited that you agreed to visit us." She looked around the spacious room, noting the stares of the other witches. "I apologize if you feel that every move you make is being watched. You are a bit of a legend." She grinned at him.

"That's okay. It's great to visit here and spend time with Dorian, along with Ayleth and you."

Dorian brought a tray with cups, a teapot and dark bread with cheese.

Alric saw he was looking very pleased. As he drank tea, he saw they were receiving fewer looks from the other witches, although a few witches came over to say hello and mention how great it was to meet him. One visitor was Altus Rector Truman, who joked the dining room was rarely this busy between mealtime.

"Father, can I show you the library?" Dorian asked.

Alric looked at Ayleth and Orienla.

"You go with Dorian. I want to chat with Sister Orienla."

Alric walked with Dorian to the library, where Dorian pointed out several books and scrolls that he liked to study.

As he looked around the library where a dozen witches sat studying, Alric was aware Dorian was watching him closely. "This library is like the one in the Whiterose terradomus. I'm struck by the similarities of the two terradomus."

"Do you like our terradomus?"

"Yes, of course."

"I asked the altus rector. We could provide a room here for you to stay in. It would be a large room because you're an important man."

"I see, but I already have a place in the Whiterose Terradomus."

"I know, but you could also have a place here. You could spend some time there and other times here. Mother and I could be with you more often."

"Son, that is something I need to think about."

"You mean Sister Ululla may not like it?"

"I cannot speak for her. What you are offering is something that needs due consideration."

———

Ululla listened to Alric's explanation of what transpired when he visited the Darkrose terradomus as they sat in the dining room.

"I don't know who else Dorian discussed this with, but I assume Orienla knows of this request as well. I didn't want to dismiss this right away. That may hurt his feelings even more."

"You're not tempted to have a room at the Darkrose terradomus?

"Tempted, yes, but that is not an option."

Ululla took a drink of her tea and raised her eyebrows. "You're certain of that?"

"Yes. You are my wife and I belong here with you."

"Good. Now, what are you going to tell Dorian?"

"It won't be a simple no. I need to word my reply carefully and explain to him my perspective."

They continued to sit, and Ululla brought up a new topic.

"Our daughter wants to visit the king and queen and to let them know Prince Terrowin is safe."

"Say again? She wants to travel to visit the king and queen? How does she know Prince Terrowin is safe?"

"She said she talked to him in her dreams."

"Are we going to let her travel to the castle? Would they even let her speak to the king and queen?"

"It is difficult to stop Ayleth from doing what she sets her mind to. She is of adult age, as well."

"If she insists on going, we need to make sure she has protection. I could go with her."

"I agree, but she said she wants Brother Bruhamoff to go with her."

"Why him?"

"She said he needs to go there. I don't know why."

A female witch approached their table.

"Excuse me, but this note is to be given to Brother Alric. It was left by our front door by a man in a dark robe."

Alric unfolded the paper and read out loud the message. "Teahouse by the blacksmith. Pastor Immin." Alric looked at Ululla. "Blackrain. This pastor, I've met him before."

"If you're going to meet him, I'm coming too."

————

The teahouse was located several blocks away from the Whiterose terradomus, and away from the chief market centre. The teahouse served those who worked with horses, such as stable hands, leather harness manufacturers and blacksmiths.

Alric and Ululla entered the teahouse, adjusting their eyes to the dim interior. Alric didn't see Pastor Immin as he looked around. He noticed they set more tables in the back area outside of the teahouse. Alric ventured through the inside area and saw the Blackrain pastor sitting alone at the far boundary. Beyond his table was a simple dirt road.

"Pastor Immin, this is my wife, Keeper Ululla."

"Of course, we know of her. Please sit and join me."

"What do you mean, we know of me?" Ululla looked at the man with a beard and a dirty face. His eyes were expressive, implying knowledge and wisdom.

"The Whiterose has the Book of Redemption that provides philosophy and predictions. We have a book as well. Your name is mentioned several times. It is an honour to meet you."

"You asked to meet with me," Alric stated.

"Yes. We are approaching a time when the different orders of witches must join forces. Your son and daughter have taken the first steps to the rejoining of the Whiterose and Darkrose orders to become the Umbravox. We must take the next steps quickly. Master Diablo is looking for the best time to strike. If the Whiterose and the Darkrose remain divided, Master Diablo may attack them despite his own weakened position.

"How is he in a weakened position?" Ululla asked. She had heard of Master Diablo before, but only as an evil entity trying to create havoc in the world.

"When he used the Dwykath forces to attack the Allisure Kingdom. Master Diablo wanted to kill Prince Terrowin, who is the reincarnation of King Terrowin. When Prince Terrowin awakens to his full powers, he will be instrumental in defeating Master Diablo. Master Diablo sacrificed the Dwykath army in trying to murder Prince Terrowin. In the end, he resorted to using werewolves to attack the royal family. Master Diablo used much energy using the dark magic and needs to rest before launching another attack."

"The werewolves failed to kill Prince Terrowin. That was fortunate." Ululla commented.

"It was because of failure in Master Diablo's spell. They instructed the werewolves to kill the sons of King Grayson. Prince Terrowin is not of his bloodline."

Ululla gasped. "The queen had an affair?"

"The royal family is human, and all humans have failings. We are now in a situation where Master Diablo is looking at the Whiterose and Darkrose witches as a weakness to exploit. He has never penetrated the Whiterose order but has in the past infiltrated the Darkrose. Fortunately, the Darkrose altus councillium discovered the imposters and corrected the problems they caused."

"What do you want us to do?" Alric asked.

"Talk to your son and daughter. They have the ability to convince the two orders to join. I understand that the two orders are exchanging visits, but they need to become whole again to realize their full potential. It is time. They must also prepare for a battle with Master Diablo."

"May I ask what Blackrain is doing to help us?" asked Alric.

"During the battle between the Dwykath and Allisure forces, we caused a heavy rain to fall, limiting the Dwykath's army's ability to cross a river. We put a concealment spell on Prince Terrowin, making it difficult for Master Diablo to find him after he left the Whiterose Terradomus. We have also put a concealment spell on Dorian and Ayleth. The spell, I will point out, doesn't prevent others from seeing them, but blocks other spells from finding them."

Ululla took a drink of her tea. "May I ask why Blackrain exists? The Whiterose and Darkrose witches believe in peace and strive to help all people. What does Blackrain do?"

Immin took a moment to consider her question. "Blackrain's purpose is to stop Master Diablo because we believe that peace cannot be achieved until he is defeated."

"What would Blackrain do if Master Diablo is defeated?"

"A good question. Perhaps there wouldn't be a need for us to exist."

———

During their walk back to the terradomus, Ululla asked Alric, "Do you think we should ask Dorian and Ayleth to push for the unification of the two orders of witches?"

"It wouldn't be wrong to suggest that to them."

"Do you believe what he said about Prince Terrowin not being a true son of the king? Pastor Immin is a strange man. I have a feeling he knows a lot more than he revealed to us."

"The Blackrain are secretive, but I don't believe Pastor Immin would lie about Prince Terrowin."

"I never expected we would take advice from Blackrain."

"War can bring together different allies."

31

Queen Elissa strolled down a wide marble hallway on the third floor of the castle. She ignored the guards stationed at the tall columns at intervals along the walls but paused at the doors at the entrance of a room, waiting for a guard to open a door for her.

The study room she entered was not large for the castle but was on two levels. A catwalk along the perimeter gave access to the books and scrolls on the shelving. The lower level contained tables and chairs. The few chairs were well-cushioned and next to small tables. In the centre of the room, eight chairs accompanied a large rectangular table. The walls on the lower level were devoid of books. The view of the royal courtyard was displayed through the windows on one of the walls. The other walls held paintings.

The room was nearly empty. A guard stood at the inside of the entrance and a servant approached her, carrying a tray of refreshments. Queen Elissa waved her away, looked around, and spotted King Grayson sitting in a chair. She walked over, noticing he was staring at a painting of King Terrowin sitting on a horse. King Terrowin held a double-bladed sword up high as he gazed at a distant horizon.

"Is this your favourite painting of him?"

King Grayson looked up at her. "Yes, it is. I admire the determination in his eyes despite his face showing weariness. You can tell by the dirt and blood on his uniform that he had just been in battle. His raised sword shows me he was victorious."

"I knew I would find you here. When you're troubled, this is the room you often go to." She studied the painting. "You are victorious, too. The Allisure army defeated the Dwykath Kingdom."

"True, but I do not feel triumphant. Three of our sons died in battle and Prince Terrowin has been forced to go into exile. Now I have difficult decisions ahead, and I'm hoping to find inspiration from King Terrowin."

"What is troubling you the most?"

"I'm feeling tired and old. The evil that used the Dwykath forces to attack us is still there, lurking in the darkness. Prince Terrowin may never return, and I must consider who would be my successor. Our daughters are next in line after Terrowin, but whomever they marry could eventually be king. Should I allow them to choose with their heart? My advisors suggest an arranged marriage would be best, one with a prince from a kingdom we are in good terms with."

"It is good to look for inspiration from King Terrowin. Truly, he was a great king and much loved. Come with me. I want to show you one of my favourite paintings."

Queen Elissa led King Grayson to another part of the study. She pointed at the painting of a seated King Terrowin. Standing next to him, with a hand on his shoulder, was Queen Lethya. The painting showed an older King Terrowin. His face showed calmness and contentment, and none of the fury in the earlier painting. Queen Lethya, a slender woman with long, silver hair, had a small smile on a beautiful face. A green emerald ring adorned the queen's finger that rested on the king's shoulder.

"I love this painting. It shows the king and queen relaxed and happy with their journey in life."

King Grayson nodded. "They appear to be pleased. This was the last painting of him. An assassin killed him shortly later. A truly evil, treacherous act." He paused as he scrutinized the figures. "Do you believe the rumours they were witches?"

"I don't know if it makes a difference on how they ruled. From what I understand, Queen Lethya was a Whiterose witch and later converted the king to one as well. Witches don't believe death ends who we are, but it is part of a cycle of birth, death and rebirth."

"Hmm. Perhaps that's the secret to their relaxed view on life. Thank you for showing me this painting. There is another way of being a king than just thinking of battles."

———

Alric went to the Darkrose Terradomus and waited at the front entrance while they summoned Dorian. He stood patiently and the witches watched him again. When Dorian arrived, he pointed to the front doors.

"Let's go for a walk. Too many eyes are watching me inside."

"I understand. What did you want to talk about?"

Alric walked with Dorian along the stone walkway. "A few days ago, you asked me about having a room at your terradomus."

"Yes, I think it'll be great when you have a room there."

"Dorian, I want to tell you something about me that you know, but perhaps don't fully understand. When I wasn't much older than you are now, I joined the army. I had visions of adventures, not realizing those adventures comprised sleeping on cold, wet dirt." He heard Dorian laugh and continued. "One other thing I didn't realize at the time when I left my parents' home was how much I would miss having a place to call home. Later, I left the army. That part you have read about in the Book of Destiny, the warrior who fakes his death to escape being a soldier."

"You lived on a farm after that. That's when you met my mother."

"Yes. I was happy living on the farm. It was a place I could call home. After what I lived through in the army, the word home had a very warm meaning to it. Later, after I met Keeper Ululla, I could call the Whiterose Terradomus my home."

"I understand. A place to call home is important. Now you can also call my terradomus home as well."

"Dorian, It's not quite that simple. If I were to cut an apple in half, we each would have half an apple to eat. We could say the same for a lot of things. If you cut it, it still works as before. But, if you were to cut a table in half, it can no longer function as a table. A half table is not a table. We cannot use a chair cut in half as two chairs. Dorian, a man can only have one home. Many years ago, I made a commitment to Keeper Ululla and the Whiterose order. It would be wrong for me to break that commitment."

"But it would be just occasionally you would stay with mother and me."

"I hear what you are saying, but how does one break a commitment occasionally? What would your altus rector think if you and your mother were to stay at the Whiterose Terradomus occasionally?"

For several steps, Dorian remained quiet.

"You are right. I just wanted to spend more time with you. I guess when I'm with mother and you, I see ourselves as a family."

"Dorian, we are a family. Your mother, Keeper Ululla, Ayleth, you and I are a family. It may not be the usual family, but we all care for one another."

"I guess that's important, too."

"Dorian, sometimes all we have is family. But it's what makes us strong enough to carry on."

32

Terrowin felt it strange to wear clothes again. He left the beach and made his way around the short bushes. Feeling nervous, he took out his sword as the green foliage became thicker as he made his way.

There was a pathway of sorts that he followed, although he wasn't sure if humans or animals made it. Birds chirped constantly and insects buzzed around him. To his left, he saw a rocky hill converging toward the path. The side of the hill was almost vertical, although it looked the rugged side would allow it to be climbed.

Terrowin became aware of something in the bushes pacing him. He took several glances, but only saw the ripple of plants. He deduced whatever it was; it wasn't likely to be too large. Still, he didn't know how dangerous it was, and since it was following him, likely considered he was prey. He looked at the hill that was getting closer and noticed the plant life on his left was becoming thinner. Terrowin moved away from the pathway, moving toward the rocky hill directly.

As the ground became open, he turned and walked backward for a few steps to see if the animal continued to follow him. At first there wasn't a sign of the creature, but as the leaves parted, Terrowin could see the head of an enormous cat, covered with yellow fur with black spots. The cat bared its teeth but didn't charge out from its hiding place.

Terrowin held up his sword and continued to walk backward, nearing the hill.

The cat gradually left the vegetation and advanced slowly toward him. It appeared unsure whether to attack and studied him.

Terrowin kept his sword at the ready. He avoided the urge to rush towards the hill and instead made consistent progress until he arrived at its base. A trail was visible to him, appearing to wind up the steep side, switching several times before reaching the top.

Waving his sword slowly side-to-side, he continued his backward progression. Then he turned and began the climb up the trail. The cat continued to follow him but didn't draw closer. Despite the narrow and steep trail with several large rocks interrupting the way, Terrowin didn't find the climb difficult. The cat advanced only as far as a few steps up the trail before turning around and going back to the bush.

Terrowin decided he might as well continue his journey up the hill, not wanting to find out if the cat was waiting for him if he was to return. The trail wasn't natural, and he hoped he may find people; specifically friendly people. The top of the hill was flat, with the trees clustered together along the edge of the hill. He walked along the grassy, but rocky, surface. Small trees littered the landscape, with patches of flowers and grass between them.

He was wondering If he was all alone when he saw smoke rising from among the trees. He slowed his pace, listening for sounds. Satisfied only the smoke was showing nearby activity, he ventured forth, carrying his sword down by his side.

Amongst the trees, Terrowin found a group of men, women and children camped around a fire. There were several buildings, made of tree limbs, surrounding the fire pit. He slowly advanced. When he was within an earshot, he raised his hand and shouted a greeting.

Immediately, the men stood and grabbed spears and bows and arrows. Women rounded up the children, pulling them behind the men. Terrowin continued to wave.

"Hello, I mean no harm. I'm just a traveller."

One man stepped forward. He, like the others, had black hair and dark skin. He was shorter than Terrowin, but slightly heavier. "What do you want? Who else is with you?"

"I'm alone. I seek only food and conversation."

"Step closer, so we can talk."

Terrowin put away his sword and slowly approached. He noticed that the men had lowered their bows and were pointing their spears to the ground. "Thank you for allowing me to step into your camp. I'm Terrowin."

"Tell us where you came from. The Metal people?"

"No, I came from across the water. The ship I was on sank and I swam ashore."

"You speak our language."

"I was given a way to converse with others. Please, I mean no harm. If you don't trust me, I shall leave you alone. I saw the smoke from your fire and desire only companionship."

The man used his hand to signal him to approach the camp. "You may call me Tallut. Come. Let us sit and share a drink."

———

Terrowin sat on a log stump, holding a wood cup containing fermented juice. The juice was warm and had a bitter taste, but his hosts seem to believe it was important to share it with him. He didn't give all the details of the shipwreck, only that a sea monster attacked it, and he didn't mention his encounter with the mermaids.

He learned the village was one of several that existed on the series of hills, with the hills getting progressively higher further away from the sea. A stream flowed through near their village, ending in a water-fall that emptied into a valley lake. The villages were all on good terms with each other, trading and occasionally going on hunts together. Collectively, they called themselves the people who rule the valley, or more often just the Valley people. Past the hills, the valley took over. Beyond the valley, mountains appeared. Terrowin was told he appeared like the Metal people, tall with a pale skin. He was dressed similar to the Metal people, who wore layers of clothing as a protection from the cooler climate.

"We trade with the Metal people. We have hides and dry meat; they have metal tools and weapons."

"How often do you trade with them?"

"Not often. It is a long journey. Several moons between visits."

"You live on the hills, but hunt in the valley?"

"Yes. There are many dangerous creatures in the valley. We never go there to hunt alone. Usually, four or more men will hunt together. We hunt in groups during daylight and return before dark because there are many dangerous creatures in the valley. Sometimes a hunter gets killed. We are prey in the valley. The hills provide us protection against danger and the creatures don't enjoy coming up here."

"How often do you hunt?"

"Only when we must. Every five to ten days. You may join us on the hunt if you wish, but your sword may not be that useful. Bow and arrow are the best for hunting."

"I only have my sword and a knife."

"The Metal people use such weapons, but they also have to fight against other men. We have extra bows. I will give you one to use."

"Thank you. I will join you in hunting."

Terrowin declined an offer of another drink, and after they added more wood to the fire pit, one by one the villagers went to the wood huts.

"You may share my space to sleep," Tallut offered.

Terrowin followed Tallut to one of the wood buildings. The doorless opening led to an open interior, with grasses and leaves spread on the floor.

"Pick a spot." He smiled. "This is how we sleep. Simple bedding compared to the Metal people."

Terrowin saw a woman and two young children looked at him while he chose a spot.

"I'm sorry if I'm intruding."

"Not at all. We don't get many visitors, so the others are curious about you."

Terrowin tried to sleep on his back at first, but found it more comfortable on his side, using his arm as a pillow. It didn't take him long to fall asleep.

———

In the morning, Terrowin asked Tallut if he knew anything about black-watcher birds. "They travel in pairs and are large."

"No, but there are many strange creatures here. I'll let you know if I see them."

Terrowin walked to the edge of the top of the hill and looked at the valley. It seemed quiet below, but he knew it was still a dangerous place to be, especially alone. He wondered how long he could stay with the villagers. *If those birds show up, I best be moving on. After those birds saw me on the ship, that monster attacked it. I want nothing to happen to these people.*

"What are you thinking about?"

He turned to the source of the soft voice, seeing a young woman.

"I'm Kala."

"Terrowin. I'm just wondering where I go from here."

"You don't have to leave. Our village is small, and we need more men."

"Thank you. But someday I want to return to my home."

"Is there someone waiting for you?"

"Yes. I promised her I would return." He frowned. "I didn't expect the ship I was on to sink."

"You were lucky to survive. You must be a strong swimmer."

"No, I grabbed a hold of a crate to help me stay above water."

"May I ask how you can speak our language? The Metal people speak a different tongue. There are mermaids in the sea, and they speak a language we cannot understand. Yet you, who lives far away, can speak our language."

"I was given the ability to understand others, no matter what language they use."

"A spell?"

"Yes. When I went on my journey, I was given the ability to understand others."

"Do you have other abilities?"

"No, other than being able to eat a lot."

Kala laughed. "You're a big man. Therefore, you should eat plenty."

Terrowin walked back with Kala to the village. A pot of stew was being cooked, and Terrowin accepted a bowl of the steaming dish.

Tallut came up to him. "Tomorrow, we hunt. Today, I show you how to use a bow."

———

Terrowin remembered the lessons his brother gave him with a bow and arrow. They were not as refined as the one he was familiar with, and the arrows were shorter. He noticed the arrows had a barbed metal tip on them and suspected those had to have been traded for with the Metal people. The end of the arrow used a feather at the end to help stabilize it in flight.

"Take your time to shoot. We try to make every arrow hit our target. We don't like losing any."

Terrowin looked at the large hide tied to a tree limb. A white dot was painted in the center.

"Try to hit the buck skin. It's difficult to do. Just takes practice."

Terrowin pulled on the arrow, feeling the tension on the string. He sighted along the arrow to the white dot and raised his aim slightly, remembering his brother's instructions. The wind was light, but steady. He turned slightly to account for the breeze. He slowly released his breath and let the arrow fly. It struck right next to the white dot.

"Great Moon! That be an excellent shot. You have done this before."

"Yes, but it was a long time ago." *Maybe it wasn't so long ago. So much has happened since then.*

"Still, a fine shot. I doubt you will lose many arrows."

33

Terrowin followed Tallut and four other men down the narrow path down the hill.

When they reached the valley, Terrowin was instructed to walk next to Tallut as much as possible and to watch for any danger in front or his side. The others followed behind them, with the last man protecting against any attack from the rear. Besides the bows and arrows, the men carried spears, save for Terrowin, who preferred his sword.

They travelled through the vegetation and arrived in an open area. The travellers could see deer-like animals grazing in the distance.

"We need to be careful now," Tallut whispered. "We don't want to cause the jessel to run away, so we approach slowly and quietly. But there are other animals watching us, thinking we would make a good meal."

They broke into two groups, with three men making a long walk along the perimeter of the field to ambush the game while the rest of the men were to chase the game toward them.

Terrowin waited with the other two men, bow and arrows ready for any jessel that came close. They also kept watch for any predators, knowing the trees that protected them also hid other creatures. Fingering the arrow, he examined how it was made. It appeared a knife was used to shape the wood into a round shape. The metal cap had a sharp point with several barbed hooks along the side. The arrows were precious, so they gave him only three.

Terrowin took a drink of water from the leather water pouch he was given. The tropical sun was making him feel uncomfortable, partly due to his clothing was designed for cooler climates. The other factor was not being sure of what was going to happen. He had never had to face charging plant-eaters before while worrying about predators behind his back.

A cloud of dust indicated the herd racing toward them. Then the thunder of hoofs before the first sight of tan and white jessel appeared. Terrowin placed the arrow against the string of the bow, drawing back as he locked his sights on the closest jessel. The fleet-footed animals raced toward him, and as a unit, turned as they neared his group.

"Shoot!" Tallut yelled.

Terrowin fired an arrow, striking his target in the neck. The jessel stumbled slightly, and Terrowin loaded a second arrow. Before he could pull back the arrow, two more arrows flew. One struck the jessel in its hindquarters; the other bounced off its back. Terrowin fired a second arrow. This one went true, hitting just behind the shoulder where the heart was. The jessel ran a few more steps and collapsed.

"Very nice!" Tallut slapped him on his back.

The three men ran to the fallen jessel. After they retrieved the arrows, a rope was tied around the hind-legs and two men began dragging the dead jessel. Terrowin examined the animal. As tall as a man at its shoulders, the deer-like creature was covered in fur. The head had a pair of dark, curved horns. There was a tuft of white fur at the end of the slim tail.

"This is the dangerous part. Other creatures will want to take the jessel from us. Keep your sword ready." Tallut spoke as one man searched and found the arrow that had missed the target.

They pushed through the green foliage, and the other three members of the hunting party soon joined them. It impressed Terrowin by how quickly they could drag the jessel. He noticed the men took turns pulling the jessel, moving at a fast walk showing a determination to get out of the forested area as soon as possible.

Terrowin saw movement at his side, glimpsing an enormous cat. He pointed it out to Tallut.

"Don't worry, it is not likely to attack. Cats avoid attacking a group of men. If you be alone, then watch out."

"Then why are we rushing?"

"Deholes. They hunt in packs and will attack us."

Terrowin took a turn pulling on the rope and they made it out of the forest with the hills in sight. He noticed the cat had not followed them past the forest. He wondered why the cat had stayed away, rather than follow them, when he saw the first of the deholes, light brown carnivores. *Wolves. Or at least something like them. Shorter snout, but it looks those jaws could crush a bone.*

The pack of deholes approached cautiously from the forest, surrounding the hunters and their kill in a semi-circle. The distance decreased even as the men dragged the jessel.

With growls and bared teeth, the deholes circled around the men. The hunters held spears pointing at the deholes, trying to keep them at bay. One dehole crept closer, ignoring the hunter as it focused on the carcass.

Terrowin stood next to a hunter who was using his spear to jab at a dehole. The creature snarled and snapped its jaws. Terrowin heard a curse, and the hunter thrusted the spear at the dehole. The predator locked its jaws on the shaft of the spear, getting into a tug-of-war with the hunter. Terrowin reacted quickly with his sword, whipping it downward on the neck of the dehole. The creature dropped, releasing the shaft.

Another dehole stepped forward and Terrowin swung his sword, nearly slicing off the dehole's forelimb. It yelped as it crumbled to the ground.

Terrowin took a step forward, swinging his sword side to side, forcing the deholes to back away. He moved to the front, clearing a space for the hunters to pull the jessel again. Another approached too close, and Terrowin's sword cut open its neck. Blood immediately appeared and the dehole quickly fell away.

The deholes didn't retreat, but stayed far enough away from Terrowin's sword, allowing a steady progression toward the hills. When they reached a pathway that led to the top of the hill, the remaining deholes lost interest, returning to the forest.

Terrowin helped drag the jessel up the pathway, grunting with from the exertion. When they reached the top of the hill, they celebrated him as a hero in the village, first as the killer of the jessel, and then ensuring the deholes could not steal their game. He tried to be modest, accepting the best cut from the jessel. *Maybe I can stay with these people for a while. This is better than journeying alone.*

34

Terrowin felt pleased when the Valley people built a hut for him in the weeks that followed, giving him a place to sleep alone and be by himself. He hoped when it was time to sleep, Ayleth would appear in his dreams. It was unpredictable when she appeared, and he learned he didn't have any control over her visits. *Except it's more than a dream. She really does visit me.*

He stared at the ceiling, wondering when he would see her again. He fell into a restless sleep.

———

Terrowin woke up with a slight headache. He blinked at the morning light and walked toward the area where someone had restarted the fire. He took a wood cup and filled it with a mixture of hot water and dried berries, resulting in a flavourful, if bitter, drink. The tea had a positive effect, eliminating his headache and gave him a minor increase in energy.

"You look tired."

"Good day, Tallut. I guess I am. Strange dreams."

"Bad omens?"

"No, just different. I think I'll go for a walk."

"I go too."

The uneven ground made for slow travelling, but Terrowin found the view from the hills interesting as he gazed at the valley below.

"How far does the valley go?"

"This is just the beginning of it. It goes longer than a man can see in two days of travels to the ocean. It is also very wide and goes to mountains."

"Do people live down there?"

"Yes, small villages by the sea. It's not safe to travel there." He pointed at the green valley. "There's a river that flows to the ocean. On the other side of the river are true monsters. We don't go there. Too dangerous."

"What about the Metal people? How difficult is it to visit them?"

"It is a long journey. It would be shorter to cross the valley if it wasn't so dangerous. The journey takes half a moon to get there. To get to the Metal people, you have to go through forests and climb as high as the clouds."

"That sounds difficult. Are there any predators along the way?"

"Some smaller creatures that we don't worry about. But there are creatures that look like gigantic men but with fur. They dislike people and will attack."

Terrowin listened to what Tallut said, deciding that to leave the valley people would require a long and dangerous journey. *Eventually, I need to return home. Do I go to the mountains or through the valley? Or is there another way home?*

———

The next day clouds changed quickly from white to dark, joining to block out the sky. When the rain came, it fell in a torrent, turning the ground into a slippery mud. Terrowin peered out of his hut. It surprised him the roof leaked little water. In the distance, over the valley, he saw three bolts of lightning. Each zig-zag strike was copies spaced closely together against the black clouds.

The rain gradually slowed down and stopped. The clouds opened up, revealing the blue sky.

Kala approached him after he stepped out of his hut. "That was a powerful storm. Did you see the god's light?"

"Yes, lightning."

"There were three flashes of god's light. That means a change is coming. It may be good or bad."

Terrowin didn't comment on whether he believed her or not. He decided if there were such things as werewolves, anything was possible. Kala stayed with him as he walked around on the muddy ground. He could see water vapour lifting off the ground, making a thin fog.

"Do you often get storms like this?"

"Just around this time of year. We will get two or three powerful storms."

Terrowin continued to stroll around on the wet ground. He reached the edge of the hill and peered down at the valley. Steam rose from the dense foliage. Near the horizon, he saw two black dots. Moments later, they resolved into birds. "Damn."

"What is it?"

"Black-watcher birds." Terrowin sprinted to his hut, causing splashes of muddy water.

"What are they?" She hurried after him.

"Birds sent by an evil entity to look for me."

"What are you going to do?" She watched him grab his bow and arrows.

"I'm going to kill the damn things."

Terrowin crouched, positioning between huts, watching the sky. Kala stood behind him, peering over his shoulder. Terrowin suspected that the black-watchers would circle the village, looking for him, and his suspicion came true.

The birds circled lower, occasionally making a cawing sound. They flew over the cluster of huts, staying close together.

Drawing back the bow string, Terrowin took aim at one bird. As the birds moved into his vantage point, he let an arrow fly. He watched as the black bird let out a screech and pummel to the ground. Terrowin reached for a second arrow, but as he placed the it into position, the second black watcher bird attacked.

Terrowin felt a blow from a wing at his head, causing him to fall. The bird made a quick pivot in the air, extending its talons and with the hooked beak open. He saw the fury in the yellow eyes and rolled, pulling out his knife. As he moved to a kneeling position, the bird attacked again. The talons reached for his face and he twisted his head to the side as he extended his arm.

He felt pain along his arm, but also the resistance of his knife as it plunged into his attacker. Terrowin twisted his knife, pushing as wings flapped around his head. He stood and used a hand to grab at a wing, trying to force it to the ground. Terrowin could feel the strength in the wing fading. He pulled out the knife and struck again. The bird stopped struggling.

Terrowin gazed at the creature with the wings spread out, blood seeping out of its chest. He looked at his own arm. Blood dripped from deep scratches.

"Are you okay?"

Terrowin took time before he responded. "Yes, I think so." He stared at the dead black-watcher bird. The creature was enormous, and the talons showed it was also a formidable hunter. "They're dead. Maybe I can stop hiding now."

Kala left, hurrying to her hut as Tallut walked over.

"I saw the bird fall from the sky. Very good aim." He kicked at the dead bird. "Evil looking thing."

"They were looking for me. No more."

Kala returned with a small clay jar. She used her fingers to apply the yellow cream on the scratches on his arm.

"This will help it heal."

"Thanks."

Tallut and Terrowin dragged the dead birds to the edge of the hill and tossed them over it.

"Terrowin, you showed much skill in killing these birds."

"Thanks."

"Perhaps you would now like to accompany us on a journey to visit the Metal people."

"I would be honoured to do so."

———

When they decided to visit the Metal people, Terrowin wasn't sure about the preparation. Tullut, and another man named Nahat, stacked animal skins on poles. The tree limbs were joined at one end, forming a V shaped sled.

After breakfast, the three men started on the journey. Tallut took the first turn, dragging the furs. Although the load wasn't easy to pull, Tullut didn't appear to struggle and could carry on a conversation as they marched uphill.

Terrowin noticed the trees grew smaller as they travelled, but the grasses still covered the ground. He took his turn pulling the wood sled and late in the afternoon, the three men arrived at another village. Terrowin noticed a familiarity with the villagers, whom he learned were also referred to as Valley people.

The second village celebrated their visit with food and drink, with Terrowin the object of interest. He learned the villagers traveled only a little further up the hills, preferring to hunt in the valley. They informed him the hilly region dropped in altitude before ascending again. It was the lower area that was the most dangerous, he was told, with the thick forest hiding large, hairy men and aggressive predators.

After sleeping in one hut, Terrowin and his companions left in the morning. They were given more fur skins to take to the Metal people, making the sled heavier.

"They gave us more furs to carry." Terrowin commented as he pulled the sled.

"We will give them arrow heads for the furs after our trading with the Metal people. This village is smaller than ours, and it is more difficult to hunt. They rarely visit the Metal people."

Terrowin was feeling an ache in his shoulders when they stopped for the evening. After a small meal, they slept around the small fire they made. Terrowin was hoping Ayleth would appear in his dreams, but instead were visions of black-watcher birds circling. In the morning, they resumed their journey, climbing the last of the series of hills. Ahead of them was a forest of thick trees and thick grasses.

"Are there a lot of creatures down there?" Terrowin asked as he viewed the green foliage. He decided the land, while lower than the hilly region they just traverse, still had higher elevation than the valley.

"Yes, some strange animals. Big, hairy men, and large four-legged creatures with powerful jaws. There are also animals to eat, but it is risky to hunt for them."

"Why is that?"

"The hairy men. They are very protective of the forest. You will understand as we go through."

Terrowin pulled the sled, finding it easier to drag it over grass than the rocky ground of the hills. He looked at the nearby forest, noticing the trees were thicker than the high regions. He heard a few sounds from the forest, bird chirping, whistles and a thumping sound.

Nahat held up an arm. "Stop."

Terrowin stopped. "What's going on?"

"The hairy men are nearby," Tallut explained, "they are warning us not to approach."

"Do we just wait here?" Terrowin wondered if he should draw his sword.

"Yes. In a little while, we can start walking again. If we hear them again, we stop." Tallut peered at the forest. "It's hard to see them, but sometimes we can smell them."

Nahat took a few steps forward. "No warning sounds. We can travel again."

"What do you do if those hairy men attack?" Terrowin asked Tallut.

"Run. Our arrows don't hurt them. If they attack us, we are dead."

35

Ayleth walked with Bruhamoff along a wide dirt road that led out of Jital. She looked at Bruhamoff, who remained silent and appeared to be deep in thought. He first appeared to be shocked at the suggestion of going to Allisure Castle, but after a day of thought, agreed he should. Ayleth didn't say why he should accompany her, just indicating it was time he returned.

"You are a silent traveler, Brother Bruhamoff."

"I don't know what there is to say. We are both seeing the same things."

"Do you enjoy travelling? I've noticed that you hardly ever go outside the terradomus.

"I only travel with a purpose in mind. I know some witches like to wander around Jital and go to teahouses to converse with others, but I like the quiet of the library and researching the Book of Redemption."

"Does Sister Tersica study the Book of Redemption with you?"

"Sister Tersica prefers the teahouse to the library." He laughed. "She takes Selkirk with her, and he enjoys being able to run outside. Sometimes, I convince her to come to the library and learn more about what the book provides us. She's smart but needs to spend more time with the written word."

"I can tell she loves you very much, Brother Bruhamoff. She is making an effort to teach your son the practice of being a witch."

"Sister Tersica and I agree Selkirk needs to learn at an early age. She reads to him the Book of Redemption and he enjoys listening to her. At least for a short time. He gets bored easily."

They continued their journey, and after a period of silence, Ayleth asked, "Did Sister Tersica ask you why you're going to the Allisure Castle?"

"She did, of course. She wanted to come along as well. But I informed her it was best I do this without her this time, and that it would be a difficult journey for our son. I didn't explain why I was going, just that it was something I needed to do."

"Why did you name your son Selkirk? I understand you choose it."

"When I was a young man, and travelling with your mother, I was attacked by a madman. A seaman, Selkirk, saved my life. Unfortunately, he was killed in the attack. I shall never forget his sacrifice."

"He must have been a very brave man. I understand why you would want to honour him."

"It is odd how paths cross with others, and sometimes a meeting can have long lasting consequences."

"Brother Bruhamoff, I don't know why I asked you to accompany me. When I decided I had to meet the king and queen, I felt the need to ask you to join me. I don't know why, but it was a powerful feeling."

"It was good you approached me to go with you. I know the reason, but I don't want to reveal it."

"That is fine, Brother Bruhamoff. I understand that not everything needs to be spoken. I am enjoying your company, even during the quiet periods."

———

The shadows lengthened, and Bruhamoff pointed to smoke rising in the sky. "Knavemire. It is a fair-sized city and will have a large terradomus where we can spend the night."

"Have you been to Knavemire before?"

"Yes, but I didn't stay at the terradomus."

Ayleth looked at him, wondering why he hadn't stayed there.

The city sprawled out, with most of the streets wide enough to facilitate the movement of manufactured goods. It was known for the production of horse carriages and metal works. The air had the faint odour of smoke as Bruhamoff and Ayleth made their way toward the interior market.

"The terradomus should be six blocks to the east of the market." Bruhamoff recalled the written directions to the terradomus they read before leaving on their journey. "A square building with two upper levels and two lower ones. I believe most witches arrive using a tunnel, but I'm glad we traveled in the open air. As Sister Tersica has informed me, I spend too much time in enclosed areas and should see the sky more."

"We all must balance our needs."

The terradomus stood in a middle of similar shaped buildings, and Ayleth assumed the others were for those looking for boarding rooms. They approached the twin front doors and waited until a door opened.

"I am Watcher Krillian." The young man stepped back. "Please enter our terradomus and make yourself comfortable."

"Thank you." Bruhamoff introduced themselves and asked for lodging for the night.

"Of course. Our guest rooms are located one floor down. The directions to the rooms are easy to follow." He pointed in another direction. "The dining area is there. I'm sure you will want some refreshments."

Ayleth saw Bruhamoff was quick to head to the dining area. The room was large and filled as they had arrived shortly after the normal dinner time. They went to the front counter, receiving a generous amount of stew, bread, and cheese. She sat with Bruhamoff at a long table that could accommodate ten witches. The six other witches at the table quickly welcomed them, recognizing them as newcomers to the terradomus. Ayleth did most of the speaking, with Bruhamoff adding only a few comments.

Ayleth and Bruhamoff visited the room that the terradomus called a reading room, but it was actually more like a common room where witches drank tea and socialized.

While drinking tea, Ayleth conversed with several witches whom she found to be friendly. Some questions directed to her were personal, but she attributed that to the curiosity of a new witch. That was until Bruhamoff stood up.

In a louder than normal voice, he lectured, "I am surprised that as witches, you are placing your needs over another witch that is visiting. Under the guise of being friendly, you seek to further your own gains. I believe you should apologize and let Sister Ayleth relax in peace." He pointed a finger at a tall, dark-haired male witch. "You should be more careful in the words you use when describing your own abilities. It comes close to bragging."

Ayleth watched as several witches stood, apologized, and left the area. The dark-haired witch lowered his head and then looked at Bruhamoff.

"You are correct. I did not consider Sister Ayleth's feelings fully. I will now leave the two of you in peace." He stared at Ayleth. "Please forgive me for my lack of judgement."

Ayleth spoke to Bruhamoff after they were left alone. "Brother Bruhamoff, I am confused. I thought they were just being friendly."

Bruhamoff sat. "Did it occur to you why they were all male witches and being friendly? Sister Ayleth, you are young and smart. You are also very attractive. At the Jital Terradomus, you are not usually subject to scrutiny by male witches. The reasons are your mother, Keeper Ululla, has a powerful influence on the witches. Your father, Brother Alric, was a former warrior. Even though he is now a witch, few would want him upset with them. Here, the witches see you as a desirable companion and do not know of your mother and father. Sister Ayleth, these witches wanted to share your bed tonight."

"I didn't realize that."

"We always need to be aware of our surroundings. I often remind Sister Tersica of this, but she seems to believe she is impervious to difficult situations."

"Perhaps I have the same problem." Ayleth knew she could use the turpis force, an ability to move objects by thought. Her brother, Darian, could move heavy objects, such as furniture. Ayleth hadn't reached that level but could still push a person away from her. What she hadn't considered before was the influence her mother and father had in protecting her in the Jital Terradomus. "I didn't consider before I was being protected in our terradomus."

"One cannot know all that is around us. According to the Book of Redemption, we see only in one direction at a time. It would be incorrect to believe we can see all around us at the same time. Sister Ayleth, do not be hard on yourself. You are learning, and that is what we all must strive to do during our life's journey."

"I understand what you mean."

"Good. Perhaps it is best that we get some rest. We have another walk tomorrow to complete."

She stood. "I am feeling tired."

Bruhamoff escorted her to the bedrooms below. The bedrooms were simple, with a single bed and a small table with a chair. The door wasn't lockable but was closed with a simple latch. If the door was closed, it meant it was occupied.

Ayleth rested on the straw stuffed mattress. She reviewed what happened in the reading room, deciding Bruhamoff was right, that the male witches were being friendly for a reason. She also considered she had received protection at the Jital Terradomus. To regulate her breathing, she closed her eyes. In her mind, she felt herself floating, moving in the darkness. She focused on Terrowin. The darkness turned into a heavy fog, and she gradually made out objects. Trees and rocks came into view as fuzzy, dark features. A yellow light drew her attention, and she moved closer, making out the flickering flames of a campfire. She saw Terrowin sitting on a log. She saw others sitting around the fire but couldn't make out their features. Ayleth moved in front of Terrowin, and he seemed to react by shifting his head to the side and brushed the air in front of him with his hand.

"Can you hear me, Terrowin?"

She waited, but he didn't react.

"I guess you need to be almost asleep for us to engage. I'm glad to know you're alive and have companions."

Ayleth withdrew, returning to her bed. Her breathing slowed, and she went into a deep sleep.

36

Ayleth and Bruhamoff ate a large breakfast and headed back on the road to the Allisure Castle. Once more, Bruhamoff was quiet as they walked, and Ayleth was content to enjoy the silence between the cities.

"I shall tell you the reason I want to go to the Allisure Castle." Bruhamoff suddenly announced. "This is for you alone. Please do not reveal what I'm to tell you to anyone."

"I promise, Brother Bruhamoff."

"The altus rector sent me on a mission many years ago, before you were born. I was to travel to the Allisure Castle and apply to be employed as a guard. I didn't present myself as a witch. Rather, I pretended to be a peasant."

"Were you told why you were to work as a guard?"

"No, just that I would accomplish what I needed to do by being there."

"What did you accomplish, if I may ask, Brother Bruhamoff?"

"They gave me the title of a royal guard and appointed me to protect the queen. My duties involved protecting the queen included the time she was in her royal chambers. Her bedroom was separate from the king's." He took several steps before resuming his tale. "I became friends with the other royal guardsmen and a member of the cleaning staff. I also visited the queen during the night at her request. Refusing her was something I didn't know how to do."

"Oh. Is that why you want to return there? If I may say so, you also appear to be reluctant to go there."

"That is true. I left without properly saying goodbye. I also feel I should have told them I was a witch. By withholding that information, I feel I was not telling the truth to them."

"The truth serves us well."

"Yes, but that isn't the main reason I need to return to the Allisure Castle. I am Prince Terrowin's father."

Ayleth stopped walking. "You're Terrowin's father?"

"Yes." Bruhamoff stopped as well. "I ask you not to reveal this to anyone."

"I won't." She studied Bruhamoff's face, suddenly seeing the similarity with Terrowin's.

They continued their journey, saying little as they passed the outskirts of the farms and vendors surrounding the castle. They reached the first gate to the castle courtyard where two guards stood by an iron gate.

Ayleth went up to a guard. "We are here to see the king and queen."

The guard didn't react, acting as if he hadn't seen or heard her. She walked through the gate, with Bruhamoff following her.

"Did you use a spell on the guards?"

"No, it's something I always could do. I focus on believing I have the right to go somewhere, and people let me. Maybe it is a spell or magic. I'm not sure, but it works."

They gathered a few looks from others in the courtyard, not used to seeing witches inside the castle grounds. Past the courtyard, Ayleth and Bruhamoff proceeded up the wide marble steps to the grand entrance to the castle.

Bruhamoff walked with Ayleth as they approached the four open doors, each one with a royal guard standing by at attention. None reacted as they went past the doorway. Ayleth went to a desk situated just past the entrance. The royal guard looked up in surprise at her approach.

"How did you get here past the guards?"

"We have come to see the king and queen about Prince Terrowin. We have news about his welfare."

The guard studied her for a moment. He rang a handbell, and a servant hurried over. "Inform Steward Trennis there are two witches that claim to have information about Prince Terrowin. Make haste!"

The servant ran.

"You two will wait here. I've got nothing against witches, but I can't have you wandering around here."

Ayleth smiled. "Your son is sick with a fever, but don't worry, he'll be fine soon."

"How, how do you know this?"

"I just do. I thought I should tell you."

Ayleth looked around and saw an older man in a cloak coming toward them.

"I am Steward Trennis. Do you truly have new information on Prince Terrowin? I warn you, if this is a ruse, you will certainly regret it."

"Witches do not lie. We have information on Prince Terrowin that King Grayson and Queen Elissa will want to hear."

"Follow me." The steward turned and led the way up a set of stairs to the second level. They travelled down a long hallway, reaching a room with two guards standing outside. Inside the room, the major feature was a single long table with several chairs on one side and two large chairs on the other side.

"Sit. His majesty will be here at his convenience."

Ayleth and Bruhamoff sat, while Steward Trennis and a guard stood near the door.

Shortly later, a group of servants entered, placing plates of food on the table, along with goblets containing wine and water. The servants later stood at attention at a wall.

Ayleth took a small portion of food and wine. Bruhamoff ate like he hadn't eaten for several days.

Just as they were finished eating, Stewart Trennis entered the room again.

"Stand. The king and queen are about to enter," he ordered.

Ayleth stood and faced the doorway. First, the queen entered, followed by the king. They went directly to the large chairs at the table and sat. King Grayson looked at Ayleth.

"You claim to have information about Prince Terrowin."

"I do, King Grayson. Perhaps it is best I tell what I know privately."

"Very well. Steward, clear the room except for yourself."

King Grayson tapped on the table with his fingers until the door closed. "Now speak. Is Prince Terrowin alive and well? And how do you come by this information?"

"King Grayson, Queen Elissa, my name is Sister Ayleth of the Whiterose order. Prince Terrowin and I are close, and I'm able to visit him during my dreams. Prince Terrowin is far away, living in a village."

"In your dreams? You're merely dreaming of him, and you claim this as information we can trust?"

"I do not deceive you, King Grayson. I truly do visit him, and he is doing well. Prince Terrowin will return, and will accept the role of king, if you should choose to him to be your heir." She paused. "Your daughters are free to choose with their hearts."

The king grunted. "I do not doubt witches have special powers. You say you visit our son in your dreams. Tonight, you will be our guest. Perhaps you can tell us something to help believe Prince Terrowin is indeed safe. Steward, show them to the guest rooms."

"Wait," the queen spoke. "What is the purpose of your companion here?"

Ayleth saw Bruhamoff swallow, looking transfixed on the queen. "He travelled with me to provide me with protection. Although I am a witch, it is still wise to have a strong man accompanying me."

"I'm sure he provides adequate protection," the queen smiled.

Ayleth looked around her spacious guest room. A servant had left a tray of refreshments and Ayleth relaxed with a tea and biscuits. A guard stood outside her room, ensuring she wouldn't be able to wander around the castle.

As the evening progressed into night, Ayleth stretched out onto the enormous bed and closed her eyes. She believed she could reach Terrowin, although it wasn't for certain. If he was alert and not resting, all she might do is to observe him.

She drifted into a fog-filled room. She peered around and found

Terrowin sitting, appearing like he was preparing to rest. Ayleth moved closer.

"Terrowin."

"Ayleth? Are you here?"

"Yes, I'm close by."

"Why can't I see you?"

"Your mind is awake. But at least we can talk. Lie down and close your eyes." She watched him as he laid down. "I spoke with the king and queen today about you. I told them you are well, but they are reluctant to believe I have been able to visit you."

"My parents, are they okay?"

"Yes, they are good, but are worried about you. Tell me something that only you would know. I want to prove to them I can speak with you."

"The ring I gave you. It is from my grandmother, Queen Lethya. When I was very young, my mother told me to give the ring, to the one... He stopped. "I gave it to you to show you I care about you."

"Prince Terrowin, I love you. Do not fear sharing your feelings."

"I can see you now. Ayleth, I must confess I am in temptation living so far away and unsure of my return to home."

"I do not judge you, Prince Terrowin. I am a witch and understand everyone has failings. It is how we deal with our own weaknesses that determines our path."

"When I was a child, I had a toy horse that I called Master Frederick. If you tell my parents this, they will believe you're telling the truth."

"Thank you. Sleep well."

———

Bruhamoff opened his bedroom door and saw the guard standing by it. "I am bored. May I go to the library? The small one on this floor."

"Normally, I'd have to get permission to allow you to leave the room, but I remember you, Bruhammy when you were a fussy cheeked youngster. Come, I'll take you to the library."

"Thanks." Bruhamoff thought for a moment. "You're Royal Guardsman Eliot."

"That be me."

Bruhamoff chatted with him until they reached the library, where he settled at a table with a book.

He was jolted from his reading when a figure stood in front of him. He looked up and saw the queen. Bruhamoff immediately stood.

"I'm sorry, Queen Elissa. I did not see you enter."

"That is all right. You always did love the library." She turned to the guard. "Leave us."

She sat at a chair next to the table. "I am suspicious why you have decided to return here."

"I do not have any desire to cause problems, Queen Elissa. I am here for two reasons. One is to provide companionship for Sister Ayleth. The other is for me to visit the place where my... Prince Terrowin grew up. I left when he was just a baby. I just wanted to return here one last time."

"Are you married, Bruhamoff?"

He smiled. "I am married and have a son named Selkirk."

"That is good." She stood. "While it is nice seeing you again, I hope there won't be too many more visits in the future."

"No, there won't be. I am now at peace with my earlier time here. It was good to see you again, Queen Elissa."

"Take care, Bruhamoff."

———

Ayleth joined Bruhamoff in a dining room for breakfast. The tables were small and formally set. Numerous servants took care of the royal court. While they were eating breakfast, Ayleth asked Bruhamoff how he had spent his time yesterday.

"A guard accompanied me, but I went to a library. It was enjoyable reading books, and these differ from the ones in our terradomus."

Ayleth laughed. "I believe you are the most read man I know."

A royal guard approached their table, wearing insignia that showed he was of high rank. "Bruhammy, it is you! And you've become a witch!"

Bruhamoff stood. "Captain Hawkins, sir. It is wonderful to see you again, sir."

"Stop that sir nonsense. I heard rumours you had returned, and I had to see for myself. I'm most pleased to see you're of good health." Hawkins looked at Ayleth. "Is she be your daughter?"

"No, just a companion. This is Sister Ayleth."

"I should have guessed. She's far too pretty to be of your blood." Hawkins laughed.

"Please join us, Captain Hawkins." Ayleth stood and indicated an empty chair. "It would be an honour for me."

Ayleth listened to Captain Hawkins talk about the time when Bruhamoff was a royal guard. The impression she had was that Bruhamoff was a shy, but well-liked guard.

"What brings you here, Bruhamoff? You want to reenlist as a royal guard?" Hawkins chuckled.

"Sister Ayleth has never travelled far from the Jital Terradomus before. She expressed interest in going to the castle, and I was asked to join her. I was glad of the chance to visit here again. I have many fond memories of my time here."

"That's good to hear. May I assume you have no regrets about becoming a witch?"

"None. Are things well with you, captain?"

"Yes, although there is a dark hanging around the castle since the attack that killed three of the princes and with Prince Terrowin gone missing. We are fortunate King Grayson is a strong and wise ruler, but we could use some good fortune."

"As a witch, I believe good fortune arrives from a positive outlook. I will meditate for positive energies for the kingdom and the people."

"I admire witches' ability to stay calm, even during war. For myself, my temperament is more toward using the sword. As for good fortune, your visit here leads me to believe good tidings have returned."

———

Ayleth and Bruhamoff returned to the same room as before. This time, the king and queen were waiting for them. They were not invited to sit.

King Grayson peered at Ayleth. "Well, do you have anything to tell me this time? I'm wondering if this is a ruse to get my hopes up."

"Your majesty, I spoke with your son last night. I asked for information to help prove I am telling you the truth."

"Go on."

"When Prince Terrowin was a child, he had a toy horse he called Master Frederick."

Queen Elissa gasped. "That is true."

Ayleth extended her hand, showing a green, emerald ring. "Prince Terrowin said this ring was given to him by Queen Lethya. He gave it to me, knowing how it important it was."

The queen stood. "Let me see that ring."

Ayleth pulled the ring off her finger and passed it over the table.

"It is her ring. Terrowin did not tell me he had given it to you." She passed the ring back. "He was told the ring was to be presented to the one he wishes to marry."

"I've always known I shall marry Prince Terrowin."

"You were the little girl who ran up to him during our excursions in Jital."

"I was."

The queen continued to stare at her. "How do you spell your name?"

Ayleth told her.

"I believe you're telling the truth, that Terrowin is alive and well."

37

King Grayson walked with Queen Elissa down a hallway to the study.

"Why are we going here? You said it was great importance."

"It is. And it explains why Terrowin and Ayleth are so close." She led the way across the room to where the painting of Queen Lethya stood next to a seated King Terrowin.

"I don't understand what you're trying to show me."

"Queen Lethya is wearing that same ring with the green emerald."

"I see that."

"Look at her face, her hair. She looks like an older version of Ayleth."

"I suppose that's true. Both have fair skin and long hair. The features are similar."

"Yes. You know of the rumours the king and queen were witches."

"A likely fact and not just rumours."

"The letters in Ayleth and Lethya are the same, just rearranged. Ayleth is the reincarnation of Queen Lethya. Prince Terrowin is King Terrowin. They have found each other after death."

"My Lord. That is why the evil wants to kill Prince Terrowin."

38

"Are you going to tell Sister Tersica about Prince Terrowin?" Ayleth asked as they walked on the road to Knavemire.

"You mean I am his father?"

"Yes. That is an important part of your life. If you are serious about Sister Tersica, then holding back that secret would make a fuller relationship with her difficult."

"You are correct. Sister Tersica is a wonderful woman. She sees the world differently than I do. She's smart and not afraid to express her thoughts. She also dislikes long periods of silence and is prone to speaking about anything just to break the silence."

"You're worried she would reveal your secret."

"Yes. She wouldn't knowingly betray me or the secret but may invertedly reveal a detail that could lead to speculation about Prince Terrowin. I must consider that any additional information about Prince Terrowin, such as my being his father, could jeopardize his life. I do not wish to hide this secret from her, but Prince Terrowin's safety is paramount. I do not enjoy being in this dilemma."

"Prince Terrowin is not aware you are his father?"

"That is unlikely, as the queen would not reveal that secret to anyone."

"Then perhaps it isn't right for you to tell others before Prince

Terrowin himself knows the truth. Brother Bruhamoff, I know you study the Book of Redemption and follow its teachings. There is a passage about truth that may help you."

"A good point. One must ask who benefits when speaking the truth and if the truth is even beneficial. My obligation to tell Sister Tersica the truth about Prince Terrowin must wait until he knows. I feel relieved."

"Good. I am glad you're feeling better.

———

The Knavemire Terradomus had a different energy to it when they entered. At first, Ayleth could not discern the cause of it. As Bruhamoff and her approached the dining room, Ayleth came to a halt.

"Brother Bruhamoff, are those Darkrose witches sitting with the other witches?"

"Yes, I believe they are."

"I can't believe what I am seeing." She hurried over to one table where three witches on each of the two orders were drinking tea and sharing a plate of biscuits. She didn't know what to say, standing in disbelief at the two orders of witches enjoying conversation together.

One Whiterose witch looked up at her. "Sister Ayleth, please join us. We have important news to share with you."

Ayleth sat, searching for clues in the friendly face.

"Our altus rector received word from the altus councillium that the Whiterose witches are to open the terradomus to the Darkrose witches. The two orders will work together to become one again. They have also invited the Whiterose witches to visit the Darkrose Terradomus. A new era of peace has begun among the witches."

Ayleth sat with her jaw slack. *My brother did it. He has stopped the fighting between the orders. We can now join forces and defeat a common enemy.*

39

Terrowin surveyed the land before him. The trees looked different, becoming lighter in colour and not as thick. Yellow, tall grass covered the areas where the trees didn't grow, and he noticed a slight rise in altitude. He ventured closer to the edge of the pathway and peered at the valley below. The jungle appeared less dense as the valley below became narrower.

There was silence among the three men until Tallut's arm went up and he pointed.

"The Metal people live there."

Terrowin looked. In the distance he saw a mountain, separated by deep crevasses from the surrounding hills. The layered hill had green terraces, with men and women working the soil on the different layers.

"How do we get across?" Terrowin asked.

"The Metal people have made a crossing."

As they approached the Metal people's home, Terrowin saw two bridges, each made with rope and wooden boards. One bridge went to an unfamiliar area from where they came, but the others joined the path they were on. The downward slope was steep as they approached the bridge, and Terrowin was hesitant when they reached it, seeing it sway gently above the valley below.

Nahat laughed as he saw Terrowin stand at the bridge entrance. "It is safe. No one fall yet." He stepped lightly on the first board, using one hand on the waist high rope to maintain his balance.

Terrowin followed suit, remembering the feeling of being on a ship as the bridge swayed from the added weight of the three men walking. He looked down, seeing the once green valley was a mix of red and brown soil with one scraggly looking tree. He held the front of the sled while Tallut lifted the rear.

"Looking down not good. Look straight ahead," Tallut advised.

"Why did the Metal people live on that hill? It seems like a strange place to make a home."

"For safety. Hairy men won't cross bridge. Other enemies of Metal people cannot attack easily."

"There are more people beyond? Some are Metal people enemies?"

"Yes. There are several other tribes of people. Some are peaceful, some are not." He pointed to a distance hill that was higher than most, resembling more of a mountain. "Spirit people live there. They be peaceful, but not trade with others."

Four men and a woman, all wearing furs dyed in different colours, greeted Terrowin when he reached the end of the bridge. They were almost his height with pale skin. Terrowin now understood why Tallut had asked him if he was part of the Metal people tribe.

Terrowin stood in silence as Tallut used hand gestures and words to convey they had brought fur skins to trade. The Metal people responded in kind and showed them a room, dug out from the hill. The walls were straight, with bricks lining the interior. In the centre of the room was a fire pit. Terrowin looked up and saw a hole in the ceiling where the smoke could escape. The furniture comprised of low wood benches covered with fur.

Terrowin listened to Nahat and Tallut discuss the upcoming trade negotiations. Nahat was of the opinion they would get eight to ten arrow heads and a knife for the furs.

Tallut disagreed. "Maybe six arrowheads and ask them for a spearhead."

Two women entered the enclosure and presented food and drinks. They spoke a few words about the refreshments, although Nahat and Tallut didn't appear to understand.

Terrowin, however, understood.

"Fresh from our gardens. The juice is from crushed berries. Welcome and enjoy."

After the women left, Terrowin tried the food. They rolled the chopped vegetables up in a leaf. Spices enhanced the flavours, and he tried the juice, finding it sweet with a hint of fermentation.

Between bites, Terrowin asked, "What happens now? Do we just wait here?"

"Yes. The Metal people leader will come by later and offer us metal pieces for the furs. We will try to get more. It is hard to do because they know only the Metal people can make arrowheads and knives."

"I have knowledge of metal-making and their language. May I help with the trade."

"Yes, if you can speak their language, please help us."

After they ate, two men and a woman entered the chamber. One man pointed to the furs they had brought and opened a cloth roll with six arrowheads and a knife. He used his hand to show that was their offer.

The woman whispered. "Those are very good furs, and we need them. Don't insult them by offering too little. We can make lots of metal objects, but we don't have skins."

Terrowin stood. He considered the Metal people were dependent on plants for food but had trouble raising animals on the terraces. The hairy men limited hunting, and thus furs were hard to obtain.

"That is a very poor offer."

"You speak our words?" The woman asked, astonished.

"Yes. I will make a counteroffer. But first, let me tell you how the Valley people get the furs. They do so by hunting in a jungle, using a few arrows to kill an animal. It is dangerous and difficult to do. If they had more arrows, knives and spears, they could kill more animals and have more furs for trade."

The male leader nodded. "That is reasonable."

"Arrowheads are easy to make. I know how metal work is done." He passed over his own knife. "You can see it is even better than the knife you offered."

The male leader passed the knife to his companions. "Yes, it is better than what we make."

"I suggest a fair price for the skins should be twelve arrowheads, two knives and four spearheads."

The male leader swallowed. "That is a very high price."

"It is a fair price. You underpaid before. Now you must give more. If you don't, I will teach the Valley people how to make metal and they won't need to trade with you again."

"We will talk about this offer." The leader gave back the knife, and the three left the chamber."

Tallut asked, "What did you say to them?"

"I told them their offer wasn't good enough. I asked for much more."

"That would be good. What if they won't?"

"Then we keep our furs. They want the furs more than we do."

Terrowin drank more of the juice as they waited.

The male leader returned with the woman, carrying another cloth roll. He opened the cloth to reveal the dozen arrowheads, two knives and four spearheads.

"This is what you asked for. To keep the Valley people as our friends, we will not argue with you."

Terrowin observed that Nahat and Tallut were excited at the presentation. "Thank you. We accept your generous offer."

––––––––

The celebration of the trade started shortly afterward, with the fermented juice adding to the event. Terrowin was careful not to overindulge and was the centre of attention. When asked about his origin and presence with the Valley people, he provided only ambiguous responses. He showed off his knife but was careful not to relinquish control of his sword. The sword wasn't his own handiwork, he explained, but was made by skilled craftsmen.

The next day, Terrowin saw a tired-looking Tallut lead the way back home. Tallut spoke little, but again thanked Terrowin for the extraordinary amount of metal goods they got. "There will be much celebration when we return, thanks to you."

40

The three men passed by the forest, but this time didn't encounter any of the hairy men. Without dragging a sled with furs, they made better progress on the return journey. They arrived by late evening to the second village, sharing several arrowheads and a knife with the inhabitants. They spent the rest of the evening eating around the fire, where Nahat retold how Terrowin negotiated for additional arrowheads, knives and spearheads.

"He spoke their language and you could tell he was forceful with his words. Terrowin has shown to be a remarkable man."

Terrowin held up his hands. "Thank you, but I merely explained to the metal people that if they wanted to have more furs, then they should provide the valley people with better tools to kill the wild animals."

Nahat nodded. "It is correct what you say, but now the metal people understand this."

———

Tallut, once again, took the lead on the journey home in the morning. Before mid-day, he spotted two dark spots in the sky and pointed it out to Terrowin.

"The birds have returned."

"Damn." Terrowin watched as the spots became larger, resolving into birds. The black-watchers flew high, pivoting in a circle. "They have seen me."

"Maybe we can kill them again."

"They would keep coming, I'm afraid." Terrowin cursed under his breath. "I may have to leave."

"Why? They are just birds," Nahat replied.

"The birds are from an evil man. He will cause evil things to happen to those around me. For your sake, I need to leave soon."

The black-watchers continued to follow them, occasionally going lower and close enough for Terrowin to make out their yellow eyes. Then the birds left, flying away.

———

When they arrived back at their village, there was an initial celebration of the extra supply of metal weapons, but then quiet as Terrowin announced his intention of resuming his travels alone.

"I'm sorry, but there isn't any reason to put your village at risk. I don't know what will happen, but someone wants me dead and will do anything to ensure it happens. Tonight, let us celebrate. In the morning, it will be time for me to go."

"Where will you go?" Kala asked.

"I think into the valley. They won't find me there."

"That is dangerous for a lone man."

"I have my sword and knife. I will be okay."

Nahat shook his head. "That is not wise. We will go with you until you reach the big waters. Then you can travel along the beach. There's a fishing village. Good people."

"Let me think about that in the morning." Terrowin tried to smile and show he was confident, but he was not looking forward to going into the valley where there were many unknown beasts.

———

Terrowin was in a light sleep when he heard the first warning cries. He quickly rolled toward the hut opening, picking up his sword.

From the light of the fires, Terrowin saw several of the deholes approach the village. They hunched low to the ground as they approached.

Tallut yelled, "Get ready to shoot!"

Terrowin raised his sword, wishing he had brought his bow and arrow instead.

Tallut shouted again, and several arrows flew into the dark. Yelps responded as the arrows hit their mark. More arrows flew, and the deholes turned and retreated.

"You scared them off." Terrowin approached Tallut.

"Yes, we may have killed a couple of them. Strange. I heard them howling earlier in the night, and it seemed they were getting closer. Deholes rarely climb up the hill, and it is rare for them to attack at night. Maybe the evil man sent them here."

"I think he did. This is not good. Maybe next time he sends the hairy men instead. In the morning, I will leave."

Tallut nodded. "I understand. But we will help you be safe."

———

There were three dead deholes between the village and the trail that led down the hillside. Nahat sneered his disgust at the creatures.

"Their fur isn't even worth keeping." Two men assisted him in dragging the creatures to the edge of the hill and allowing the bodies to tumble down the slope.

High above, black-watcher birds circled.

No one said anything as they observed the birds but walked along a worn trail.

Nahat spoke to Terrowin. "We will build you a raft and help you avoid detection by the birds. I wish you could stay, but we now know the watcher-birds will not let you be."

The trail to the waterfall was steep. At the bottom, where the water splashed into the river, white and grey tree trunks and branches rested in the rocky shore. Terrowin watched as the men selected several pieces of wood. They used vines as ropes to secure the logs together.

Tallut spoke to Terrowin. "This will float, but we will also put a cover over the raft to stop the watcher birds from seeing you."

They finished building the raft by the time the sun reached its high point in the sky. Branches with the leaves still attached formed a canopy.

They gave Terrowin dried meat, water in a skin pouch and well-wishes as he climbed onto the raft with several other men. The men waited, and then one by one left the raft, hoping to fool the black-watcher birds on where Terrowin was.

Terrowin hid underneath the canopy when they finally launched the raft. He peered upward between the leaves, observing the pair of birds circling. They appeared to be following the Valley people as they climbed back on the trail, not paying attention to the raft.

Good, maybe I got rid of them.

———

Terrowin used a short branch as a rudder to keep the raft in the middle of the river. He noticed movement in the trees that lined the river and a few noises from creatures that hid partially in the water. Other than the fish he spotted near the boat, it appeared most of the creatures preferred the sides of the river.

The raft drifted with the river and Terrowin settled in, watching the passing scenery. He noticed there were several types of birds flying from tree to tree. Their colourful feathers made them easy to spot. Several species had oversized beaks, and he wondered what purpose they served. *Too large for their heads. That would be a very large bite for them.* His attention went higher in the sky, and he saw several enormous birds with brown feathers circling. *That would explain why the black-watchers haven't appeared. They would be prey to those larger birds.*

The raft jolted suddenly and turned to face one shore. Terrowin watched as the rough, scaly back of the creature twice as long as himself went by, mostly submerged under the water. Terrowin found he was holding his breath; thankful the creature wasn't interested in the raft.

Terrowin turned the raft to face forward and spotted the wide, blue water of the ocean. He let out a sigh. *Okay, soon it'll be time for the next step.*

The raft slowed its journey as it entered the ocean. Terrowin looked down into the shallow, clear water. He considered staying on the raft for a while longer, but decided it was likely to only drift further out from shore. *I might as well leave now and follow the shoreline. I hope the fishing village isn't too far.*

The water was warmer than he expected, and he stepped lightly on the gravelled bed. He waded toward the shore and followed it, keeping watch at the green jungle that stopped only a short distance from the water. A few trees with overhanging branches dropped roots into the water, making the shoreline difficult to distinguish where they dominated. Terrowin saw several small animals and birds among the thick leaves.

Terrowin splashed along the shoreline, finding his travel easier staying in the shallow water than the sandy beach area that disappeared into the jungle at irregular intervals. He was mindful of the grey-coloured fish that reached half his body length swimming near him. Their movement made him believe they were predators, and he was leery of larger versions, seeing him as a meal.

The thin clouds tempered the sun's strength, but he was too warm with the humidity, making his clothes uncomfortable. As sweat dripped off his forehead, he plodded on. He drank from the water pouch, wishing he could get out of the sun.

A screech from the jungle startled him. Seconds later, he heard a splashing sound behind him. He turned, seeing a dark creature partly swim and partially run in the swallow water.

That's a panther. What can it be running from? Another panther?

He watched the cat swim out a short distance and look back at the dense green growth on the shore. Terrowin saw the green brush part and first one, and then three ugly bird-like heads appear. The beaks of the colourful, feathered heads looked more like jaws with numerous pointed teeth and were attached to thick necks. One creature stepped into the water, revealing the almost human height reptile. It stood upright, with the arms ending with four, black clawed fingers. A short, thick tail looked stiff. It stopped a few steps into the water and let out a screech that caused Terrowin to sink low beneath the surface.

He wanted to run away from the monsters, but hiding in the water seemed a better option. *Please don't see me.*

After a few seconds, the creatures returned to the bush, leaving Terrowin to wonder what to do next. He stood, and saw the panther swimming parallel to the shore, ignoring him, as it paddled almost submerged under the water. Terrowin continued his journey, watching the water and the shoreline. He took the last drinks from the water pouch, draining the contents.

He marched through the water and saw the panther make its way back to shore ahead of him. It stood in the shallow water and shook its body, sending water spraying. It raised its head and sniffed the air, then plowed back into the jungle.

Terrowin continued his journey, noticing the clouds were filling the sky, blocking the sun more effectively. He tried to conserve his energy, not knowing how far he had to go. His thirst was getting stronger, and he looked at the jungle, wondering if there was any fruit he could eat.

He peered into the green foliage. *I don't know if anything is safe to eat, but if I don't get something to drink soon, I'll be in trouble.*

His vision caught a long, dark shape, a fin sticking out of the water. The gleaming fin was jet-black except for a touch of white at the tip. The body was longer than he was tall, and more massive. It swam past him and circled back.

Terrowin quickly moved to the shoreline, reaching a small area of sandy beach. He stood watching the white-tipped fin move toward him. Suddenly, the head broke the surface. The jaw opened to reveal hundreds of sharp teeth. The fish lurched toward him, the shallow water not allowing it to swim up to him. Terrowin retreated into the bush, watching the frustrated fish struggle to return to deeper water.

Cautiously, he stepped back on the beach. He spotted the fin moving rapidly away. He touched the handle of his sword. *I wonder what good that will do against something like that.* He brushed away a few insects around his head and examined his surroundings. The growth of the foliage was too dense to travel through easily, but he thought his sword could help cut a path. Still, he knew of the panther and the strange reptiles he had seen. *They may not even be at the top of the kingdom here.* He saw small berries, but decided they wouldn't likely provide much relief to his thirst, even assuming they were safe to eat.

He pulled out his sword as he studied a plant with a thick stem slightly taller than himself. Small pale-yellow flowers covered the mushroom-shaped top. The stem glistened with watery liquid and was thicker than his leg and covered with small spines.

Maybe there's something inside the plant stem that I can eat and quench my thirst. In the smooth motion, he swung the sword, slicing at waist height. The top fell as water poured out from the opening. He cupped his hand in the stem, still standing, bringing the clear liquid to his mouth. It tasted slightly sweet, with an after taste of green vegetation. After a few more gulps, he turned his attention to the fallen top, the open end upright where it leaned against the still standing stem. Using his sword, he sliced off the thorns on the outside, revealing the pale green interior. After removing most of the thorns, he picked up the stem and turned it above his head. He gulped the liquid as it poured down, washing over his face.

He went back to the water after satisfying his thirst, being careful to watch out for creatures on land and in the ocean.

The warm air tired him as the sun crossed the high point in the sky. He decided to return to a beach area and find another pale-yellow flowered plant to drink from. The plants weren't uncommon but hid under the larger trees and plants. The yellow flowers gave off a pleasant scent, but only if he went close to them. On closer inspection, he saw numerous dark flies crawl among the flowered top.

This time he stripped off thorns first, then most of the top. When he cut the stem near the bottom, he tried to control the outpouring of the liquid to a speed where he could absorb it with less wastage.

Feeling tired, he sat on the beach with a tree at his back. *This is as safe as I can get right now. I'll let the sun move a bit before resuming my journey. Since I don't know where I'm going, there's no rush to get there.*

He partially closed his eyes, listening to the sounds of the jungle. Birds and insects made most of the sounds, but there were also growls and screeches. None of the more worrisome sounds seemed to be close by, and he tried to relax as much as he could.

The clouds thinned out, and the sun warmed the air more. Terrowin found he wasn't getting any more rest, and resumed his travels in the water, submerging himself periodically to help keep cool.

One of his glances to the open water caught the image of what he thought at first were two large birds. On closer inspection, the low-flying birds looked odd. They had feathers, but their heads were too large, with the oversized beak counter-balanced by extension at the back of the skull. Both creatures seemed intent on what was in the water. First one, and then the other, dived below the surface. Each reappeared carrying one of the large fish he had seen close to shore. The fish wiggled helplessly in the jaw. The large birds turned back toward the land and Terrowin saw the birds were just as ugly closer by. Their feet dangled below looked like those of a large hawk.

Resuming his walk, Terrowin knew he was likely too big for the birds to attack him. He went around another rocky bend, watching for sharp rocks, when he came to a series of logs standing vertically and tied together. The logs extended into the ocean past the shallow area, with the tops only an arm's length above the surface.

He looked where the logs went to the shore and saw they continued their barrier. The logs were spaced further apart but thick vines grew between them, effectively blocking an easy entrance past them. The area between the logs and the forest was cleared, leaving only short grasses.

I don't think I want to swim past that barrier or break through those vines. Maybe I'll try climbing over and see what's on the other side.

Terrowin reached up to the top of a log and pulled himself up. Past the log barrier, he saw a village with numerous huts. Dark-skinned people were working at the shoreline, pulling in a large net from the water. He saw children running around. The men and women wore only cloths wrapped around their waists.

They don't look warlike. I hope they like strangers, otherwise I'll be in trouble.

He pulled himself high enough so he could sit on the log and observe the village. *If they see me and come charging out with weapons, I'll make a retreat.*

41

After a few minutes, one of the male villagers pointed a finger at him and gave a shout. Several villagers stared at him. Terrowin waved. Two villagers waved back. A male villager, carrying a spear, entered the water and advanced toward him. He held the spear vertically, not appear threatening.

Terrowin lowered himself into the water and moved slowly to meet him, careful to keep his hand away from his sword. He waved again. "Hello," he shouted.

The approaching villager grinned. "Hello, stranger. What brings you here?"

"I'm a traveller." He stopped and waited until the other man had made his way to a spear's length away from him.

White teeth showed as they surveyed Terrowin. "I can tell you are not from around here. Come, you must need rest and food."

"Thank you. My name is Terrowin."

"You must be important to have such a big name. I am Jat."

They reached the shore and Terrowin saw he was the tallest person in the village, easily standing a head taller than the men nearby. The women were slightly shorter than the men, and usually slim. Both men and women wore their dark hair long, with the men cutting their hair shoulder length. The women left their hair uncut, but often braided or secured with colourful beads.

Children were the first to get close to him, touching his legs before running away, giggling as they did so.

A young woman took his arm. "Come. I'll take care of you."

He allowed her to lead him through the small crowd, who stared at him.

"You look very uncomfortable in your wet clothes. Why do you wear so many clothes? Are you cold?"

"No. It is what I always wear." He paused as he looked at her. Fine bones gave her face a delicate appearance.

"That is strange." She took him to a large round hut, round but divided into several smaller rooms. A doorway led to another hut.

"My name is Terrowin."

"Hawn," she said and gave him a smile. "A big name for a big man."

The cooler air and being out of the sun felt good to him and let out a sigh. "Thanks. I've been out in the sun too long."

"Your face shows redness. Perhaps you're not used to the sun being so strong."

"That's true."

"Take off your clothes. I'll make you a drink that will help you regain your strength." She busied herself with fixing up a cot in one room. "You can rest here." She looked at him. "Your clothes are wet and heavy. Take them off. I can help you if you wish."

"No, I can do it. But I'll leave my pants on."

She went to a basket near the entrance. "Here. Something for you to wear." She handed him a long, green cloth.

He took the garment. "I'm not sure about this."

"I am sure." She smiled. "The cloth wraps around your waist twice, then tucks under at the back. Bring the loose end between your legs and tie it at the front. Now change. I'll bring back a drink and you can rest."

Terrowin watched the slim woman leave the hut. Her dark hair was made up into four braids, with blue and red beads inserted. Reluctantly, he undressed and put on the cloth as per instructions. He felt exposed, although more comfortable, and retreated to where the cot was, carrying his wet clothes with him. The cot was low to the ground, using thin branches to support a thick blanket on top.

Hawn returned, briefly stopping at the entrance to view him. She smiled, as if holding back a laugh. She carried a large wood vessel and a smaller cup.

"We have seen men like you before. Sometimes they were dead when they floated to our shore. Sometimes they were alive but wanted to leave right away. I doubt any of them returned to their home."

"Why is that?"

"I'll tell you later. Drink this. It will help you."

He took the wood container and peered at the yellow liquid. A tentative drink showed it was a sweet, pulp filled liquid. The taste wasn't bad, and he finished the rest of the drink.

She took his clothes from him and placed them on the floor. "Good. Now lie down. I will put a mixture on your face to help it heal."

Terrowin went on his back on the cot as it groaned under his weight. He placed his hands protectively on the cloth as she applied a yellow cream to his face.

"Rest. You'll feel better soon." She picked up his wet clothes. "I'll dry these in the sun."

Terrowin watched her leave. *I guess I have little choice but to trust her.* He closed his eyes, and the exertions of the day pulled him into a deep sleep.

———

Some time later, Hawn entered, giving him a smile. "Hello, Terrowin. Was your rest good?"

"Yes." He quickly added, "Where are my clothes and my sword?"

"Your clothes are outside being dried. One of our men took your sword and rubbed oil on it. The ocean water is hard on metal, and he didn't want the blade to tarnish."

"Oh. What do I do now?"

"It is soon time to eat. Come." She held out her hand. "Tell me where you came from."

He considered trying to explain his journey but decided on a simpler explanation. "The ship I was on became damaged by a storm. I used the remains of the ship to float to shore. I followed the coastline to here."

"The storms here can be very strong."

"What are the creatures that I saw in the forests? They look like giant birds."

"They are from another world that journeyed through time to live here. The gods placed them here to make sure we do not stray far from our home. In the waters, there are other enormous creatures that can eat a person whole."

He thought about the barrier around the village. "Does your village get attacked by those creatures?"

"Yes. The toluck are the worst. They are likely the bird-like creatures you saw, and they hunt in packs. Sometimes they try to climb the barrier and get at us. They are also larger beasts, but they rarely attack. We shoot fire arrows at anything that approaches our village, and most creatures leave us alone. Except the toluck. They avoid the arrows, and attack, usually late in the day."

She led him to the barrier, where a wide ladder made of uneven sticks allowed two people at a time to climb to the top. When they reached the top, she pointed at the grass.

"We cut down the plants so the creatures can't hide among them. Those dark spots are where our fire arrows burn the grass."

"What are fire arrows?"

She pointed at his side at a cluster of arrows. "The arrows have a cloth soaked in oil. We light a fire to the end and shoot at the creatures. If an arrow hits one, it hurts them much more than just a normal arrow would."

"The toluck attack anyway?"

"Yes, when they get hungry, they attack despite being shot at. At dusk, they attack while avoiding the arrows. Our men injure them by pushing spears through the gaps as they attempt to climb the wall. They usually retreat. A few time times, one will get to the top and it will jump down. Then we have a battle to kill it. A few people died from such an attack. They are hard to kill with just a spear."

They climbed down from the ladder.

"Come. It is time to eat."

Hawn led him past the huts. Most of the huts were of similar size, and about half were joined together. The huts didn't seem to have any order in their placement. After passing several huts of similar size, about half of which were connected, Hawn led him to an open area. Several clay pots sat at the edge of a fire.

Greetings were called out to him, and he sat on one of the larger rocks that circled the fire. They handed a bowl to him, along with a wooden spoon. He sniffed at the thick mixture. *Fish.*

He was hungry, and after finishing the meal, accepted a second bowl. Several villagers came over to say hello to him. Hawn remained near him, and whenever a woman approached to greet him, she placed a hand on his arm.

After the meal, and drinks of water, he walked with Hawn around the village.

"You were very brave to survive the storm and make it to shore." She reached over to hold his hand.

"It was more luck than anything else. I floated to shore and turned in the right direction."

"I'm glad you made it here."

Terrowin said little, unsure what to do with her handholding.

She showed him where the villagers went swimming and washing by the ocean. At a different, far corner of the village, was a grassy and clay ground on a rocky hill.

"The men use the lower part. The women the higher part." She explained the etiquette of the facilities.

The stars appeared, and they sat, looking out at the ocean.

"You seem nervous, man with a long name."

"I don't know where I am. I guess I don't know what I'm supposed to do next."

"You will find out when the time is near. Come, it is time to sleep."

He walked with her to the hut, learning she shared with her brother, Jat.

"When my brother finds a partner, he will move out. When I get a partner, he will move in with me."

"You said your parents live in the next hut."

"Yes, I stay next to them for when they need help. You met them during the dinner."

"How old are they?" He couldn't recall which ones were her parents of those he met.

"How old? I do not know. We only keep track of passing moons."

They entered the hut, and Terrowin saw Jat kneeling, his hands clasped over his face.

"Is he all right?"

"Yes, he is praying to a god. Perhaps thanking her for the fish we caught today."

"Where do I sleep? The same cot as before?"

"Yes. I will be close by, along with Jat."

He went to the cot, resting on his back. Sleep didn't come easily. He thought about Hawn and Ayleth. *I promised Ayleth I would return to her. But what If I can't?*

42

Terrowin ate breakfast with the others. The past few days, he did little but observe the quiet life in the village. He spent one afternoon helping repair the fishing nets. Another afternoon was used to help gather wood for the fire. The wood was outside the walls protecting the village, and Terrowin and the others had to transverse the open field to reach the edge of the forest. Two men with spears came for protection as Terrowin and another man quickly gathered the dried branches.

Tea came from a large pot heated by resting on large rocks where a fire had burned down. Fruit and dried fish were available in large bowls. The villagers took what they wanted and relaxed in the morning sun.

Jat approached Terrowin. "Would you like to go fishing with us? It isn't difficult, although we could use your strength to help pull the nets."

"I would be glad to help." He followed Jat and two other men to a carved-out log. A pair of wood shafts attached to another log supported the dugout, forming a crude outrigger.

Terrowin helped load a net into the boat and noticed the men carrying spears. He wondered how they would use them for fishing in the ocean. He decided his knife would be sufficient for what he knew about fishing. With a paddle in hand, he took a seat behind Jat who was leading the way. To maintain the proper direction, he switched paddling sides, copying Jat.

"How far out do we go?"

The man behind Terrowin, Min, answered. "It depends. The fish like certain areas of the ocean, but they move around. Jat has a strong vision of where they are likely to be. We have a long way to go yet."

"Do you come across people that live in the ocean? People who look like fish?"

"Yes, but we stay away from where they swim. They used to kill us if we got too close, but we made peace with them. If we stay away from them, they leave us alone. In the past, they have given us an infant to raise as one of our own. I don't know where they got the baby from, but it is good they didn't kill it."

Terrowin didn't explain the baby was actually from a mermaid that kept human characteristics. "I have come across them as well. We call them mermaids. You are right. It is best to avoid them."

Jat stopped paddling and stood, looking around. "I don't see any dragonfish."

"What are dragonfish?" Terrowin asked.

Jat answered. "Big fish with teeth that can eat a man. Some look like large fishes, other types have a long neck. They sometimes attack the boat as well."

Min continued. "That's why we brought our spears. Not to fish, but to fight back."

Terrowin heard a splash and saw the rear most paddler, Loe, had dropped into the water and was pulling the net, spreading it out.

Loe was heavy-set, but he swam easily in the water. He displaced the net and returned to the boat. Slowly, the crew paddled, disturbing the water as little as possible.

Terrowin looked over the side and saw flashes of the silver bodies of fish. Jat gave a wave, and the crew pulled ropes from the net, reeling it in, closing it.

Jat secured the ropes and led the crew back to the shore.

"Good catch today," Jat shouted. "Today we have a big feast."

Hauling the net out of the water was harder. The wet, heavy load took a lot of effort, but the fishing expedition was deemed a tremendous success.

"You brought us luck, man with a big name," Jat exclaimed. "Sometimes we get nothing. Sometimes a few fish. But this is many, many fish."

———

Terrowin enjoyed the evening party. Fermented juice helped make the celebration louder than normal. Hawn spent much of the time close to him, but he was careful not to encourage her, reminding her he had someone waiting for him.

"But she is not here. I am."

"I must be loyal to her, as I'm sure she is waiting for my return." Terrowin went to his cot, deciding to continue to party could cause problems later. "I'm going to bed now. Good night."

Hawn reached up and gave him a kiss on his cheek. "I understand. Sleep well."

———

In the morning, Terrowin joined several other men to a secluded area. The rocky beach area faced the south-east, making the shallow water warm. Terrowin, like the others, left his loincloth on the rocks to dry after washing it. All the clothes were distinct in colour and pattern, making it easy to identify for the owner.

As Terrowin swam in the water, he saw a woman come by, inspect the cloths, and pick one up. She looked at the men in the water, smiled, and walked away.

Several of the men laughed. Jat pointed at Min. "Corrol has chosen you!"

It puzzled Terrowin as Min waded out of the water, turning to where the women had their beach area hidden from the men. "What's going on?"

Jat explained, "Women get to choose who they want as a partner. A woman will take the cloth, or something that belongs to him. He then follows her to get it back. She normally goes to a secluded area where they can have privacy."

Terrowin finished washing and re-wrapped his cloth, reflecting on the social custom of women starting contact with men. Making his way to the main fire pit, he took a cup of tea and a piece of dried fish. He found a quiet spot near a tree and sat against it, staring out at the ocean.

After finishing his meal and tea, he became absorbed in his thoughts as small waves lapped against the shore. His breathing slowed and his eyes closed.

"Hello, Terrowin."

The voice was familiar, and he refrained from opening his eyes. "Ayleth." As he said her name, her ghostly shape appeared in front of him, sitting on the edge of a bed.

"How have you been?"

"I'm good. I'm staying with people in a fishing village."

"Let me tell you some good news. Your parents are doing well. They know we are meant for each other and do not oppose our union." She held up her hand, showing off the emerald ring.

"That is wonderful to hear."

"The witches. Our two orders are becoming one. My brother had forged a way for the witches to unite."

"That is great news. Ayleth, I miss you. I worry when and if I shall be with you again."

"You will return to me. Do not ask me how I know, I just do. Terrowin, you will prevail. I love you and would never lie to you. Trust me, you will come home again."

"Thank you. I believe you. I needed you to tell me I can make it home."

Ayleth reached out with her hand.

Terrowin felt fingertips light as feathers graze his cheek. "I love you, Ayleth. I will come home to you."

"Are you dreaming?"

Suddenly, Ayleth disappeared. He opened his eyes to Hawn. He blinked, wishing Ayleth was still there. "Yes, in a way."

"You were talking to someone in your sleep."

"Yes, the woman I promised myself to. She talks to me in my sleep."

"So, it wasn't real then."

"It felt real to me."

Hawn smiled. "Come. We are going to cut the grass outside our walls." She held out her hand.

Terrowin took it. "Who are we?"

"Almost everyone."

Terrowin saw the adults had gathered near one of the two doors that opened past the wall to the grass.

Most of the adults held poles with a white bone attached to the end. Terrowin recognized the bone as part of a rib of a gigantic creature. When he looked closer, he could see the edge had been ground down to form a large knife.

Jat handed him his sword.

"You and a few other men will walk in front. If the toluck sees us, they may attack. We will protect the cutters until they can get back to the village."

Terrowin nodded. He walked between four other men with the cutters behind them. He kept watch at the edge of the forest, listening to the sound of the cutters sweeping the blades across the grass.

Some rodents, insects and birds scattered as they marched. Occasionally, Terrowin hacked a spindling within his reach, denying the tree a chance to grow.

They continued their advance. When they reached the half-way point to the forest, Terrowin saw a striped cat step toward them. It paused and made a retreat into the forest.

Terrowin observed the forest as they approached the edge. Other than the cutting of the grass behind him, all was quiet. He had expected to hear sounds from the trees where small creatures and birds made their home. Instead, there was silence. Then, chirping and birds flew through the branches. Chatter from animals suddenly rose. *Something's happening.*

Jat waved at the cutters to stop. He pointed his spear at the green foliage. "Something is hiding in there. Everyone, step backward slowly. Don't run."

Terrowin took a step backward with the others, maintaining an even line with the other men holding spears. He saw movement in the forest, branches bending as something pushed their way through to the edge. He took another step backward. The first of four creatures revealed itself.

This wasn't like the large bird-like beast that chased the cat into the water. It was bigger, with a long neck. But it still had bird characteristics, with bright green and yellow feathers. Terrowin thought it stood a head taller than himself when standing upright, but was leaning forward, shifting its head from side to side as it surveyed the humans. The other three creatures were slightly smaller and stayed behind, but they were also shifting their heads on their long necks.

"This is another type of toluck," Jat called out. "They rarely attack us when we're behind our walls."

Terrowin readied his sword as the large toluck advanced.

Jat moved closer to Terrowin, jabbing his spear toward the toluck. "This is their leader. If we can prevent it from attacking, the others will leave us alone."

Suddenly, the toluck snapped at Jat's spear, revealing rows of sharp teeth. Jat pulled the spear away and jabbed at it again.

Terrowin watched the toluck. It appeared to be uncertain of the danger of attacking the humans, but clearly knew the spear was a weapon. It was hesitating a full attack but continued to snap at the spear. Occasionally, it let out a deep-throated growl. The men took a step back, and the tolucks advanced again. The lead toluck was acting more aggressive, sending turfs of grass with a clawed foot behind it. Terrowin raised his sword, waiting for the toluck to reach for Jat's spear again.

The toluck twisted its neck in a quick motion, locking its jaws on Jat's spear. Terrowin swung his sword as he stepped forward, connecting just behind the creature's head. Blood squirted out as the toluck squealed. Terrowin rotated and struck again, slicing at the throat. It fell to the ground, its legs kicking as blood continued to rush out of the open wounds.

Jat let go of his broken spear. "Keep retreating."

The other tolucks stared at their fallen leader, now just twitching on the ground.

Terrowin was the last to enter the door back into the village and was immediately surrounded by the joyful villagers.

"You killed a giant toluck! Such bravery!" Hawn hugged him. "Man with a big name has much courage in his heart."

The people wasted no time and began the festivities, quickly preparing and sharing food and drinks, and proclaiming Terrowin a hero for killing the toluck.

Terrowin learned there were several types of toluck, and the ones that normally attack the village are much smaller, but more numerous.

Jat took Terrowin to a vantage point along the wall and pointed to where the large toluck was killed. A dozen or more small tolucks were feasting on the remains.

"Those are the tolucks that attack us. The walls guarding our village can be scaled by them. They don't care if we kill many of them. They keep attacking, usually during the evening or night."

"I wish I had an answer for you. They look like they could cause problems."

"It is not your problem, but I wanted to show you what they looked like."

Terrowin returned to the celebration, wondering what they could do to help protect the village. He enjoyed more drinks and food, forgetting about the tolucks until he went to retire for the night.

He relaxed on his cot, reviewing the day, especially his confrontation with the toluck. *I hope I don't have to fight one of those again.*

43

Dorian met Ayleth in the lobby of the Darkrose Terradomus.

"Welcome to our terradomus. It has been a while since I've seen you."

"Yes, I went on a trip with Brother Bruhamoff to visit the royal family."

Dorian walked with Ayleth to the dining area.

"I understand the trip went well."

"It did. Now they understand the closeness between Terrowin and me. They were also relieved to know he was alive and well."

At the front counter, they were served by a young woman with dark hair and complexion.

"Brother Dorian, how nice to see you again." She looked at Ayleth. "You must be Sister Ayleth. I'm pleased to meet you. I'm Sister Bethena."

"It's good to meet you as well. Peace be with you."

Ayleth and Dorian each took a tea and a plate of bread and cheese. They sat at a table near the centre of the dining room, talking about the change that allowed the two orders to reciprocate visits.

"What are the next steps for the reunion of the witches?" Ayleth asked.

"The altus councillium of the two orders have met and discussed how to ensure the altus rectors help, rather than hinder, the mixing of the witches. Here, it is fine. But in some of the smaller towns, there may be resistance. The altus councillium has become one. They separated into two groups, each with former members of the orders. The two groups are travelling to as many cities and towns as possible to ensure the union of the two orders. We refer the new order to as the Umbravox."

"That is great news. I'm so proud of you." She touched his hand. "I need to ask you something. Are you seeing anyone?"

Dorian used hand signals to answer. Ayleth and he found their hand signals more efficient than words to convey thoughts and also prevented others from eavesdropping on their conversation.

"Because you're my brother and I care about you."

He used more hand signals.

"Not enough time? That I don't believe. We're sitting by ourselves, and no one has stopped by to say hello."

Dorian answered again with hand signals.

Ayleth answered back also using hand signals.

Dorian replied, "My mother is isolated, too. The witches don't like to associate with us."

"That's not true. Your mother refuses to see male witches because she wants to protect you. You need to show her you can live by yourself so she can feel comfortable meeting others."

Dorian frowned.

"Your mother and you are both isolating yourself, so the other isn't alone. It's time both of you started making new friends." She used a hand signal, telling him he knew she was right. "You don't need your mother's protection anymore, and she needs to meet others."

Slowly, Dorian nodded. "Maybe we have protected each other from attacks for so long, we forgot what being a witch is all about."

"I'm going to get more tea." Ayleth took her cup and walked to the counter where Bethena greeted her.

"Do you want more tea? Instead of refilling your cup, how about I give you a pot instead?"

"That would be nice. If you like, why don't you get a cup and join us at the table? I'm sure Brother Dorian would like to talk to you more."

"All right." She smiled as she answered. "Sister Nola, I'm going to take a short break," she called to the back of the kitchen.

Ayleth saw the surprise on Dorian's face as she approached the table with Bethena.

"Sister Bethena accepted my invitation to join us." She used a hand signal to tell him to be nice.

Dorian stood. "It is kind for you to join us."

Ayleth sat back, listening to Dorian and Bethena converse. She learned Bethena's parents moved to the terradomus when she was an infant, and this was the only place she knew. "But I remember seeing you all the time around here. I wanted to say hello to you, but you always looked so busy."

"I'm sorry, I should have been more friendly. To tell you the truth, I felt like an outsider in the terradomus, so I kept to myself."

"I understand. Your mother treated you differently because your father was a Whiterose, I heard. That was wrong. I always thought you were nice, but not treated well by others. I remember seeing you smile a few times and knew that was who you really were."

"Brother Dorian, I need to leave now, as I have some errands to do. But why don't you ask Sister Bethena to visit the Whiterose terradomus tomorrow afternoon? You could show her around and we can meet up for a tea afterward."

"I would love to visit your terradomus. I'm curious what it looks like inside."

Ayleth grinned at Dorian. "Good, I'm glad that's settled."

———

Ayleth was pleased how she introduced her brother and Bethena and get them to share a visit to her terradomus. *He looked annoyed at me, but also pleased. He needs friends and a companion.*

"Ayleth."

She turned and saw her mother approaching her from across the foyer. "Yes, mother?"

"Were you visiting your brother?"

"Yes, I felt he was in need of companionship."

"I'm sure you are right. But we are meeting soon. Altus Rector Howrand has a major announcement to make."

"Okay. Do you know what's about?"

"I do but can't say anything more right now."

Puzzlement overtook Ayleth. Her mother didn't normally keep any secrets from her, and her expression showed it was something important.

They filled the auditorium with the sound of a hundred conversations. Ayleth saw there were several Darkrose witches sitting on the circular benches. She took her place near the front, next to her father.

"Do you know what's going on? Why this meeting was called?"

"Yes, I do, and no, I won't tell you." He smiled. "A key to life is understand patience."

"But it's all right to keep secrets from your daughter?"

"Are you telling me you don't keep secrets from me?"

Ayleth frowned. "That's different."

"Only because you're the one holding the secret."

Altus Rector Howrand approached the podium. He paused as a hush fell across the room. "I understand many of you are wondering why this meeting was called, and on short notice as well.

"We are living in a time of change. In the years I have been the altus rector at the Jital Terradomus, we have seen the fulfillment of a prophesy stated in the Book of Redemption and the Book of Destiny, namely the arrival of the red-headed warrior that chooses to become a witch." He paused as a murmur went through the crowd.

Ayleth looked up at her father. His cheeks became flushed at the mention of the red-headed warrior.

"That was not the only event I have observed. Some I cannot speak about, others are obvious, such as the joining of our two orders. There are more changes coming, and we must be prepared to meet them with all our strength." He stopped speaking again and stepped around the podium.

"I am what you see. A man who still has wisdom, the strength of his convictions and is ready to do what is required to bring about peace. You may also see an old man, one who no longer has the strength of youth.

"I have given a lot of thought to what I should do. Not for me, but for what is best for the witches. I approached the altus councillium with my thoughts, and they agree with my plan of action."

"To meet the evil that is threatening our people and the peace, we need a leader who posses strength of character, is intelligent and has energy of youth. I believe it is time for a new altus rector to take may place."

Gasps came from the audience, and he raised his hands for quiet.

"I now have the privilege of introducing my replacement. Please, let us welcome Altus Rector Ululla."

Ayleth watched as her mother approached Howrand to the standing ovation of the crowd. She felt a nudge from her father, and quickly stood and joined in the applause.

Why didn't I suspect this? How did this happen without my knowing? She listened to her mother speak.

"Thank you for your warm greeting. I will do my best to follow Brother Howrand's leadership."

Ayleth listened to the rest of her mother's speech and later approached her in the throng of people wanting to congratulate her.

"You kept this from me!"

"I had to, dear. It was for the best."

"You told father."

"He is my husband. We do not keep secrets from each other. Someday, you will appreciate that."

"Okay, I'm happy for you. Let's talk later."

I was so focused on Terrowin and Dorian that I didn't pay attention to what was going on in my terradomus. The altus rector. That is really great.

44

Altus Rector Ululla waited at the front entrance of the Whiterose Terradomus. Normally, the front doors were kept closed and only opened them when visitors approached. This time, the twin doors were open. Ululla watched the approach of Altus Rector Truman and two other members of the Darkrose order.

Ululla smiled and opened her arms. "Welcome to our terradomus."

"Thank you for your invitation. I brought two of our senior witches with me. They were most curious about seeing your terradomus, as was I," Truman answered.

Ululla walked with Truman, while a pair of Whiterose witches escorted the other two Darkrose witches.

"It is wonderful you agreed to visit us, Altus Rector Truman. It will help bond our two orders together."

"And I thank you for the invitation. It is pastime our orders worked together to achieve our mutual goal of peace and contentment for all people. Together we can accomplish much. In many respects, we personally already have common ground. I have known Sister Orienla before she became part of our order and have remained friends with her."

"She is my friend as well. She spoke highly of you and was excited when you became the altus rector.

Truman pointed at a table in the dining area. "Do you mind if we sit? My leg causes me discomfort if I walk too long."

"Of course. You sit and I will bring tea for us."

Ululla obtained a pot of tea and two cups, carrying them to the table from the front counter.

"Thank you for bringing the tea. I apologize for my lack of mobility."

"Not at all."

"I was observing the other members of the Whiterose in the dining room. At first, it seemed similar to our facilities. However, I have observed a minor difference, or perhaps a significant difference, depending on one's perspective."

"What did you see?"

"Seeing isn't exactly right. I saw and heard a difference. The people in your terradomus don't speak in hush tones and even share a loud laugh now and then. My terradomus reflects the years of strict control and order from the previous altus rector. Our members are more reserved in their conversation. I hope I will change that. We have opened the doors between our orders, but it will take time to share the way we do things."

"It may take time, but we should encourage the exchange of witches between the terradomus. Your visit here is a good start to show our doors are open."

Truman stood. "I can continue our journey now. I'm eager to see what the rest of the inside of your terradomus looks like."

Ululla escorted Truman through a hallway and down a set of stairwells.

"Altus Rector Truman, this is where we have our living accommodation for witches. The ones on our right are usually for our long-term residents, while on our left is more for short-term visitors. A few years ago, we increased this underground area and opened up another lower level. It has increased our accommodation for new members."

"That is not unlike our method for our members." He pointed to two reinforced wood doors. "May I assume those are doors to tunnels? They are like our own."

"They are entrances to tunnels. We also have tunnels at another lower level."

"We at the Darkrose, also have two levels of tunnels. It is amazing our network of tunnels has not intersected with yours. Jital is an ancient city and has more tunnels than any other city. Some tunnels were constructed a thousand years ago, before what we call the first order of witches, the Umbravox."

"This is a very ancient city we live in. My husband..."

"The famous warrior, Brother Alric?" Truman grinned.

"Yes, that would be him. He spoke with a member, a pastor, of Blackrain." She paused as she heard Truman take in a small gasp. "Alric was told that Jital was an ancient city, that it existed before it was called Jital. It is the centre of powerful forces and will be the centre of the next great battle."

"Then it seems we are in the right place for the next great battle. Perhaps destiny has put us here for a reason."

Ululla heard his subtle reference to the Book of Destiny. "Perhaps it was. However, Brother Dorian was the leader in bringing our two orders together. Was it not his choice to defy the previous altus rector that led to him being replaced by yourself? You made a choice to appoint him, leading the way to make use of his abilities."

"An excellent point, Sister Ululla." He chuckled. "Can we ever be certain our choices are not part of destiny? Or, conversely, do our choices shape destiny? And does it matter when we arrive at this point?"

"I agree with you there." She noticed he changed their status to a less formal one, one that suggested they were now acquaintances or friends. "Brother Truman, you seem to be a bit of a philosopher."

"I do like to read the thoughts of others about our world. I think the truth is not something that is set in stone. Rather, the truth is from one perspective that others may not share. For example, is wood a better material to sit on that stone? One may be more comfortable, but the other is more durable. With destiny or choices, either can be true. Perhaps both. Consider, no matter what choices we have made, it leads to the Whiterose and the Darkrose joining. Something like travelling through a maze, but each time we arrive at the same exit."

"An interesting perspective. In both our books, we have passages about the warrior who later becomes a witch. Yet, neither book predicts which order he chooses. Could it be that destiny does not have an exact ending?"

"I see there is a library ahead. Can we go there so I may sit for a while?"

"Of course. I wanted to take you there as well."

"In my view, and it is just the thoughts of myself, destiny is just the probability of something happening. People claim destiny was correctly predicted if it happens. If it doesn't, it will be forgotten or claim it hasn't happened yet. The prophesy of the warrior is an interesting example. The prediction was that a red-headed man would fake his death and become a warrior. That writing is hundreds of years old. If one waits long enough, eventually a red-headed warrior will do as predicted. I muse sometimes how many dark-haired warriors have done the same thing?"

Ululla laughed. "Probably a few. On a more serious side, Brother Alric has brought about other changes. His son, Brother Dorian, has brought our two orders together. Our daughter, Sister Ayleth, appears to have unique abilities. So, his arrival differs from the ordinary."

They reached the library and Truman quickly sat at a table. "I do not disagree. With the Book of Destiny and the Book of Redemption, neither say what happens after the ultimate battle with evil." He smiled. "We need a new chapter in our books to be written."

Ululla sat with him at the table. "I have a story to tell you. It starts when I was much younger and travelling between regions. I had a special mission given to me by the altus councillium and it was in that role I came across Sister Elwendia of the Darkrose order. Years passed while I was in the company of a young man, Brother Bruhamoff. As we travelled from one city to another, there were at least two attempts on his life. Brother Bruhamoff was nearly killed in the last attempt by a horse and cart, and they took him to recover in the Newharken Terradomus.

"Newharken is a large city. There would be a lot of horses and carts there."

"This wasn't an accident. Someone used a spell to cause the horse to charge down the street at him. I was nearly killed as well."

"I see."

"At Newharken, a witch befriended him, Sister Sybbyl. It turned out Sister Sybbyl was a spy, sent by the Darkrose order."

"A spy? I'm sorry we lowered ourselves to such a point of deception."

"That was in the past. I'm sure we don't have to be concerned about it now. However, it turned out that Sister Sybbyl was to give Brother Bruhamoff a poison. Fortunately, Sister Elwendia intervened and stopped the poison from being administered. To do so, she had to leave the Darkrose order and asked to join the Whiterose order."

"That is rare for a witch to change orders. I can understand why she had to do so. This troubles me greatly. The deception and the attempt of poison. I recall at one time those who wished harm on others who infiltrated us. Fortunately, we have purged them from our order."

"After Sister Elwendia joined our order, she inspected a copy of the Book of Destiny we kept in our library."

"You keep copies of the Book of Destiny in your libraries?"

"Yes. When Altus Rector Bercthun left the Umbravox to establish the Whiterose order, he took a copy of the Book of Destiny. He believed it had value, even though we follow the Book of Redemption. We make copies of it and send them to our libraries. I want to emphasize these are copies of the original Book of Destiny."

"I understand. Altus Rector Bercthun left the Umbravox long ago, so it would be one of the first copies."

"Sister Elwendia said there were differences in the book compared to the one she read in the Darkrose terradomus."

"Really?!"

"Yes. I don't know the significance of the changes, but I believe Sister Elwendia was correct." Ululla stood and approached a pedestal where they kept a copy of the Book of Destiny. She carried the thick volume back to the table. "This is now yours."

"Thank you. I will investigate the wording compared to our own book."

She saw him open the leather cover tentatively. "I'll get us some tea while you look at the book."

When Ululla returned with two mugs of tea, she saw Truman's red face as he read a passage in the book.

"Are you all right?" She placed the tea on the table as she sat.

"If this is truly a copy of the original Book of Destiny..." His voice broke. "Why did they change the wording later? I don't understand," he said. "Blasphemy."

"I'm sorry to see you're upset. Please let me know if I can be of any help."

"Thank you." He closed the book. "The changes I have noticed are minor, but they are still there." He stood. "If you don't mind, I need to reflect on this and try to determine why these changes were done."

————

Truman sat at his desk with two copies of the Book of Destiny open in front of him. He frowned and went to his secretary. "Brother Karyte, would you have Brother Dorian come and see me?"

Truman returned to his office and waited by pacing until his leg felt sore. He sat at his desk, pondering the word differences in the two books.

A knock at the open door caused him to look at the entrance. "Brother Dorian, please come in."

"What did you want to see me about, Altus Rector Truman?"

"I understand you have the Book of Destiny memorized."

"I have."

"That is impressive. The reason I have asked you here is that, as you can see, I have two books, each called the Book of Destiny. But there are minor differences between the two. One is likely older, and thus be the more accurate copy. Although I compared the differences, I couldn't find out the purpose behind the changes. They are not significant changes. I am puzzled why someone would change the wording."

"The changes, are they near the beginning of each chapter?"

"Yes, how did you know?"

"I know why the changes were done."

"You do? Please explain."

"Sister Ayleth discovered spells hidden in the Book of Redemption. If one knows how to read certain passages, these spells are written out. When I looked for similar spells in the Book of Destiny, I couldn't find them. At least at first. But they were there as well, just hidden due a change in the passages. Someone distorted the spells by changing the beginning of each chapter, making them difficult to decipher.

"You deciphered them, regardless."

"I knew what I was looking for, thanks to Sister Ayleth's description. I would guess the changes made in the Book of Destiny were to hide the spells and not to change the teaching of the Book of Destiny."

"Perhaps that is the case. But who did this and why hide those spells?"

45

Terrowin observed that the boat lacked speed and agility in its design. He paddled with the other men as they took the boat to a location determined by Jat, who steered the outrigger. They paddled further out than the last time he went on fishing expedition, going to a spot that appeared to be calmer than the rest of the ocean.

Terrowin and another paddler unravelled the net into the water. Terrowin knew the next step would be to slowly paddle to spread out the net.

Suddenly, a webbed hand gripped the bow, causing the boat to rock. A woman with long, dark hair appeared. She gave a smile of pointed teeth.

"Hello, Prince Terrowin."

"Hello." His mind went back to the time when the mermaids held him captive. "Estelle, why are you here?" Terrowin saw the frightened faces of the men.

"To speak with you, of course."

"What about? How is Carassius?"

"She is fine and still talks about you. We want to warn you. Those two dark birds have returned and seemed to be looking for you. They circled above us for a full day and then went inland. A second big boat appeared on the horizon, but we couldn't lure it close to the rocks. Later, it disappeared. We are worried they are looking for you."

"Thanks. I know those birds are still looking for me, but I haven't seen them around here yet." Terrowin looked past Estelle and saw several more mermaids swimming nearby. "The men in the boat are worried you may attack them."

She shook her head. "No, we won't harm them. They keep to their fishing waters, so we leave them alone."

"How did you know where to find me?"

Estelle laughed. "We have our ways. We observe the coastline and one mermaid saw you in the village. But we also have a special sense of where our members of our pod are. Carassius feels close to you and told us where to find you."

"Okay, it's nice to know she cares about me. Please tell her I hope she is doing all right."

"I will. Stay safe, Prince Terrowin." Estelle slipped under the water.

"Were you talking with that mermaid?" Jat asked in disbelief.

"Yes, I can speak their language."

"What did they want? Are they angry with us?"

"No, they're not angry with you. They wanted to warn me about some people that are after me."

"Are you in danger?"

"No, not right now. Let's get back to our fishing."

Terrowin saw the appearance of the mermaids and his ability to converse with them unnerved the men. There were no further incidents during the rest of the fishing trip and not much conversation either. The net was filled with sufficient fish and when the boat returned to the dock, there was a celebration for the catch.

Word about Terrowin conversing with the mermaids spread rapidly. Hawn approached him.

"You can speak with the mermaids?"

"Yes."

"Do you have special powers?"

Terrowin considered denying it, but then couldn't think of another explanation for why he could talk with mermaids. "Not exactly. A spell was put on me that allows me to understand other people, no matter what language they have."

"That is very powerful magic."

"I guess so. But other than the spell of letting me speak other languages, I don't have any magic."

"What about your sword? Was that made by magic?"

"No, men who know how to form metal made it."

"Just don't use dangerous magic against us. We are peaceful people." She walked away, leaving Terrowin feeling worried.

Jat walked over to him, placing a hand on his shoulder.

"Don't worry about what she said. Hawn is always worried about the village. We know you're a good man. Come, it is time to enjoy the fish we caught and share a few drinks."

Terrowin enjoyed the feast and celebration with the other villagers. He found he had to explain to everyone that a spell allowed him to speak different languages. No one seemed to be concerned about the spell, other than Hawn's earlier questioning. Terrowin finished the night, enjoying a drink of fermented juice as he chatted with Loe.

————

The morning came too soon for Terrowin. He yawned and made his way to the main campfire for a cup of tea. He spoke little to the others gathered around for tea or breakfast and afterward made his way to the secluded spot reserved for men to wash. Several other men were already in the water, and after he washed his garment and left it on the beach to dry, he joined them.

"How are you feeling this morning?" Loe laughed.

"Tired, but that will pass."

Terrowin was glad the mermaids had taught him how to swim. He wasn't as adept as the other villagers but could dive and search out the plants and fish in the clean water. He broke the surface and saw Hawn walking along the beach.

"I wonder if she's going to pick up a cloth?" Loe speculated. "He be a fortunate man."

Hawn looked at the group of men and bent to pick up one cloth.

Terrowin saw it was his.

Loe gave him a pat on his back. "It looks like you're the chosen one."

Reluctantly, Terrowin made his way to the shore. He saw Jat raised his eyebrows but didn't comment. As he stepped out of the water, he tried to speak to her. "Hawn..."

Instead, she turned and walked away, carrying his cloth.

He followed her and they went past where the women were bathing. He heard a few of them laugh and call out, but he ignored them and continued after Hawn. A few minutes later, they arrived at a secluded spot. The ground was bare with a reddish dirt. A simple wall of clay bricks offered protection, with a doorway with a pathway that went to the village.

"Hawn, I told you..."

"I know what you said about waiting for your love. I won't make you do anything. Several women are interested in you. If I didn't pick you, another soon would. If you reject a woman who selects you for intimacy, it is considered offensive and an insult. I understand your reluctance, but another woman wouldn't. I'm doing you a favour by picking you."

"Oh. Thank you." He stood as she walked around him.

"Another woman may still pick you but is unlikely to do so if we act like we are together. You may find it uncomfortable to do so, but that means you should show attention to me in the village."

"I can do so."

She stood in front of him, looking amused at his discomfort. He reached for his cloth, but she refused to return it. Instead, she walked around him. When she returned in front of him, she looked him up and down. She laughed at his discomfort.

"Are you sure about refusing me? You look ready for a woman." She grinned at him.

"Please. I want to keep my promise to Ayleth."

"All right, but before I'll let you have this, I want you to tell me the truth about why you're here. You're keeping secrets. I can tell. Tell me everything, or you'll be walking back to village naked."

Terrowin decided telling the truth was easier than making up a story. He described how attackers had assaulted his family and how he had to escape to save his life. He told her of the shipwreck and how the mermaids befriended him, and the later time he spent with the Valley people.

"The black-watcher birds keep finding me. When they find me here, I will need to leave."

"Where will you go?"

"I'm not sure. Perhaps the Spirit people. I guess I need to find a way past the toluck."

"There is a way to go there that avoids where the toluck live." She passed him the cloth. "I will tell the other women you were very nice to me, and we are together. But someday another woman will pick you. In our village, it is not uncommon for a woman to choose a man, even if he is with another."

"All right." He retied the cloth. "Thank you for your understanding."

"Your woman sounds powerful."

"She is. I have known her for a long time. We are meant to be together."

Hawn took his hand. "Come, it is time to return to the village."

————

Terrowin occasionally held Hawn's hand and gave her a kiss to show the other villagers they were a couple. He was becoming fond of her and related more details of his past when she asked him.

"What duties did you have to do being a prince?" Hawn asked as they sat at the dock.

He took a length of string to repair a tear in one of the fishing nets. "To tell you the truth, I didn't have to do much work. I was supposed to study, behave properly, and get ready to be the future king. I was the youngest of my brothers, so I didn't expect that honour to go to me. But, as I told you earlier, they were killed."

"When you return home, you will be king?"

"My father is king, but I am next in line. I hope he will still be alive when I return."

"It must be difficult to be so far from home." She touched his arm.

"Yes, but I believe I'll make it back there."

"You must miss your woman. You refuse to get close to me, or the other women, in our village."

"Ayleth. I miss her. Thanks for pretending to be with me."

"Are those the birds you were talking about?" She pointed to the sky above the ocean.

Terrowin looked where she pointed. He immediately identified the pair of black-watcher birds. A pit formed in his stomach. The birds flew closer to shore. "Damn!" He stared at the birds, knowing they had seen him. The black-watcher birds continued their journey toward him and finally pivoted away.

The black-watcher birds suddenly had company. A larger, green feathered bird with blue trim flew from inland above them. As the black-watcher birds headed out to the horizon, the larger bird struck. It dived, knocking one black-watcher bird down, causing it to pummel to the water. The new bird continued to fly, and using its talons, gripped the second black-watcher bird. The struggle was brief as the captured bird flapped its wings desperately until a bite from the green bird ended its life.

As the green feathered bird carried its meal back to shore, Terrowin was hopeful both black-watcher birds were dead. The hope was short-lived when he spotted a black-watcher bird slowly fly close to the surface of the water.

"One of them is still alive. I wonder how much time I have before I have to leave."

"We will protect you. You don't have to leave."

"Thanks, but if I stay here, the village will be at risk."

46

Terrowin repeated his visit to the wall protecting the village. It had been several days since the black-watcher birds had seen him. He assumed the surviving bird made it back safely, and now wondered how and when there would be another attack. He thought the most likely attack would be from the toluck, perhaps a large group of the smaller types that could climb the wall.

He climbed down the ladder and returned to where lunch was available, grabbing several pieces of fish.

"You look tired."

Terrowin turned and saw Hawn. "I'm having trouble sleeping. I know I'm going to be attacked, but I don't know when or by what."

"I understand. But maybe the attack won't happen at all. Maybe that black-watcher bird also died."

"While I hope so, I'm still worried."

"You need to relax. Being worried won't help you prepare for an assault."

"You're right. I'm going to try to stop thinking about it."

"Go for a swim. Take your thoughts elsewhere."

Terrowin went to the men's beach area. He washed his cloth and left it to dry on the rocks. Terrowin waded into the shallow water and soon drifted on his back, staring at the puffs of white clouds. His eyes closed as he relaxed.

"Terrowin."

"Ayleth." He saw her as a shadowy image with a light outlining her.

"I need to warn you about a danger."

"I know. I just don't know what will attack me. I think it will be tolucks."

"It's not the tolucks. The attack will be from a giant snake."

"A snake?"

"Whoever is sending creatures to attack you, finds it easier not to use numerous creatures. This snake is very large. Please be ready for it."

"I will."

Her voice changed in pitch. "You're naked."

"I am resting in shallow water."

"That explains the ripples in my vision. Still, it is a pleasant view."

Terrowin tried to cover himself with a hand, and he heard her giggle.

"Perhaps you could visit me naked as well."

"That is very unlikely. Peace be with you, Terrowin."

"And to you" He waited, but Ayleth's voice had gone silent.

Terrowin left the beach, returning to centre part of the village. He saw Jat and called out his name.

"Hi, Terrowin. You look excited."

"Are there any enormous snakes that live here?"

"Only in the jungle. They can grow pretty big. They will eat tolucks."

"How big do they grow? Big enough to eat people?"

"Some, although it's rare."

"I think one is going to attack me. What's the best way to kill one?"

"I don't know. We leave them alone." He thought for a moment. "We need to keep guards around you. Your sword will be an excellent weapon. We can also shoot arrows at it."

"Not too close. I can fight better when I don't have to worry about others."

"Okay. Hawn wants to be with you. She's near the water."

"Okay, I'll go and talk to her."

Hawn walked with Terrowin along the beach, watching the ocean under the late afternoon sun.

"Aren't you nervous about when the snake will attack? You don't act worried."

"I remember my father telling me that a leader can show emotion. He can show anger, sadness, happiness, or even determination. But one thing a leader must never show is nervousness. That is a character flaw for a leader."

"I understand. But does that mean you're actually nervous but won't show it?"

"No, I'm not worried or nervous. I believe I will survive any attack."

"You are very brave." She looked up at him. "With your height and beard, you look like a great warrior."

He laughed. "If only appearances won battles."

Terrowin heard a shout from a villager standing on the upper walkway of the wall. He looked at where the villager was pointing at the beach used for washing. The pale yellow and red snake approaching from the beach area was larger than he expected, big enough to swallow him whole.

"Run! Get to the wall and climb a ladder!"

Hawn looked at him. "I want to help you."

"I fight better alone. Now hurry."

The gigantic snake slid toward him, and Terrowin stepped back, looking at where he might strike as he held his sword. The monster was as thick as half Terrowin's height. Arrows struck the snake, but the monster ignored the attack, and its gaze stayed on Terrowin.

Stepping to his side, Terrowin wanted the snake to turn, exposing more of its body to those shooting arrows. Although the creature appeared to be determined to attack him, he suspected the arrows had to influence it as blood dripped from its skin.

The snake tried to curl around him, moving with surprising speed for such a large animal. Terrowin jumped over part of its body as he sliced his sword at the reptile skin. Blood squirted out. Terrowin struck again with his sword. This time the cut was deeper with more blood pouring out. The snake twisted, trying to encircle Terrowin again, but he rolled under part of the coiling body and sprinted toward the beach.

Terrowin thought the snake had to be in agony from the arrows and cuts, but it kept moving toward him. *Time to finish you*. He ran into the water and swam until it was deep enough where only his head would be above the water if he stood. Taking a deep breath, he paddled to the bottom, lying on his back. He saw the yellow and red body glide through the water, leaving a trail of blood as it looked for him.

When the snake came close to him overhead, Terrowin pushed off the ocean floor with his sword raised. The blade pierced the jaw of the monster. As Terrowin twisted the blade, a gusher of blood poured out. The snake pulled away, thrashing in the shallow water. Terrowin raced to shore, barely avoiding being struck by the withering body.

He heard the cheers as he stepped onto the beach and looked back at the corpse of the snake floating in a sea of red.

Hawn hugged him, giving him kisses. "I feared you were dead when you disappeared into the water."

Jat placed a hand on his shoulder. "This will be talked about for many seasons. Tonight, we have a big feast."

"That would be great. But tomorrow I must leave. More danger will arrive here if I stay."

47

In the morning, Terrowin carried his original clothes into the hut where he was staying. He saw Hawn was waiting for him.

"You don't have to leave. We can protect you from any new dangers."

"I believe you will try, but some villagers could be hurt or killed. I need to continue my journey, regardless. Eventually, I must return home. This is the right time for me to go."

She watched him change his clothes. "I'll miss you."

"I'll miss you and everyone here. But I need to leave."

———

Terrowin looked behind him and waved at the figures standing at the open gate. He continued his progress, turning to his right to climb a slope. Along the hill, there was a rocky path that started from the sandy ground.

The trail led to a cave opening, as Jat had informed him. Terrowin carefully ventured toward the dimly lit cave's left side and stumbled upon a set of narrow stone steps. Gradually, he climbed the stairs and observed the light was intensifying. He stepped out into the open and looked around. Standing on a narrow ridge that extended toward the mountains, he looked out. On either side of the ridge, he saw a green jungle. *At least I'll be safe from those tolucks. They won't be able to climb up here.*

Terrowin began his journey, hoping the black-watcher birds didn't return. He saw the pathway varied from being narrow enough to see the green foliage far below on either side to wide enough to see only the horizon.

As he looked at the stony path, he recalled Jat telling him the journey to the Spirit people was one-hundred thousand steps. *Did someone really count their steps or is that an exaggeration? At least it doesn't appear I have to worry about any wildlife.*

He walked, establishing a pace that wouldn't exhaust him but would also not be so slow as to lengthen his journey too much.

The first day went well, but as the sun set, a cool breeze chilled him. He rested against a large boulder. He tried closing his eyes, but the wind refused to let him fall into a deep sleep. When the morning sun arrived, he reluctantly resumed his walk, yawning as he followed a path that seemed to repeat itself.

The next night was similar, with a cool wind starting up near sunset. This time he tried lying down on the rocky ground, hoping to find sleep. As he drifted off. Ayleth's voice stirred him.

"I am close by. Stay strong."

"I will try. How much longer must I travel?"

"It doesn't matter. You will reach your goal."

"You sound more confident than I feel."

"That is because I know you will succeed. Believe in yourself."

"Thanks. I wish I could sleep."

"Then you shall."

Terrowin woke up the following morning feeling refreshed from a deep sleep. He was still chilled but didn't feel sleep deprived. *Thanks, Ayleth, for the night's rest.*

———

Terrowin climbed another rise in the path. He had lost count of the number of times he had crested a rise, only to face another. He had run out of food two days ago and was on the last of his water. The nights were cold and sleeping on the harsh ground caused his back to ache.

Finally, in front of him, a wood walkway held by rope reached over a chasm. On the other end of the walkway, Terrowin saw a flat mountain face with many openings cut into it. Men and women wearing robes moved slowly along pathways between the openings. More people were seen working in terraced gardens, tending plants and small animals.

He hesitated at the wood walkway, placing a hand on one of the two ropes at waist height. As far as he could tell, no one was observing him. The suspended walkway swayed as he stepped across.

Just as he reached the other side, a man wearing a pale-yellow robe stepped out of an opening and approached him.

"Welcome. What brings you here?" He clasped his hands together in front.

"My journey led me here. I don't know why. My name is Terrowin."

"I am Masc. Come with me. Later, you will understand why you are here." He turned and walked toward one of the cave openings.

"May I ask for food and drink? I'm worn from my travel."

"Of course. Rest and nourish yourself." He gestured for Terrowin to enter a cave. Inside, a single candle lit the walls with a yellow light. Near a wall a cot waited with a single sheet.

"I will have someone bring you refreshments. Rest. I will contact you later."

Shortly later, an older woman brought in a tray of food and tea. He quickly consumed both, grateful when she refilled the tea pot. After he had his fill, he collapsed on the cot, falling asleep.

He woke to sunlight entering the cave, and for the first time, he examined the interior. What at first, he thought was a solid wall of rock, was actually curved to hide an entrance to another cave. The second cave was larger and appeared to have several doorways along a back wall. The center of the cave contained several stone blocks that he suspected were used for sitting. Sunlight came from the main entrance and from an opening in the ceiling. As he walked around the room, Masc entered.

"Did you rest sufficiently?"

"Yes. I must have slept through the night."

"Your body and mind need to recover from your journey."

"I guess I did. Thank you for giving me a place to rest. I'm uncertain why I'm here."

"You are here to learn and to take your next step."

"I don't understand."

"Terrowin, we knew of your arriving here many months ago. We will help prepare you, and to bring your spirits together."

"My spirits together?"

"You will understand later. Come, I want to show you our garden."

———

Terrowin used a wood trowel to cut around the plants. It had been three days since he had found the Spirit people, and though they didn't ask him to do any labour, he found a sense of peace helping with the chores. He worked in the garden, did water collection, and cooking of meals. There wasn't any indication of any disapproval when he stopped to rest or just view the mountains.

He sought out Masc at the end of the day.

"Tell me, is that all we do here? It seems repetitious."

Masc chuckled. "If you are referring to our labour, that is only a small part of our purpose here. It is our spiritual journey that is of most importance to us."

"What do you do on this spiritual journey?"

"Follow me. I will show you the first step."

Terrowin climbed a narrow path to a cave entrance with Masc. From there they travelled to a tunnel at the back that led to a cavern. The square shaped room had several stone blocks arranged in a straight line, facing a wall with a single white dot in the centre.

"There are different ways to reach the quiet time." Terrowin watched Masc walk around the room with his eyes focused on the floor. "When I was a boy, I had trouble learning how to focus. The white dot didn't work for me." He bent down and picked up a stone. "This is what I used."

Terrowin accepted the small stone, with dark grey and cream colours. He rubbed his thumb on the smooth surface.

"Sit and close your eyes."

Terrowin sat on the floor cross-legged, closed his eyes and waited as he heard Masc walk around him.

"Feel the stone with care."

Terrowin rolled the stone in his hand, teasing out details with his fingertips.

"Now picture the stone in front of you. Let it float, turn and tumble. Breathe slowly and focus on your stone. Nothing else is within your vision but the stone."

Terrowin pictured the stone, watching it slowly tumble.

"Relax. Breath. Watch the stone. Wait."

Terrowin focused on the stone. Nothing else mattered. He felt a hand on his shoulder.

"It is time to reawaken."

Terrowin opened his eyes, staring at the dim interior of the room. "How long?"

"It is now time for our evening meal. Come with me."

"I have been here the whole day?"

"You have done well. You have great potential to reach your true self."

"Thanks. What is the next step?"

"Food." Masc chuckled. "Then perhaps your destiny."

48

"Altus Rector Truman and other members of the Umbravox are concerned about the changes done in the Book of Destiny." Ululla spoke to Alric as they sat in bed. "They wonder why it was done. The changes were minor, but that begs the question why change any of the script at all."

"Good questions. I don't have the answer."

"Dorian said the changes made it difficult to find spells hidden within the text."

"That could be the reason to make the changes, but that doesn't answer your original question about who did it. Also, did they know that would hide the spells?" Alric answered.

"I don't know for certain, but there is one group that could be behind this."

"Who?"

"Blackrain."

"Blackrain? Why would they do that? They keep to themselves most of the time."

"That's true. But I have a feeling they maybe behind this. Can you arrange a meeting with them?" Ululla asked.

"I can, if that's what you want."

"I do. We are now all Umbravox. What is a concern to Altus Rector Truman is a concern of mine as well."

———

Alric guided his horse along a trail he had used before, arriving at a log cabin. As with his earlier visits, he waited at the perimeter of the grassy area in front of the property. Shortly later, an older man in a dark robe exited from the only door.

"You have come here seeking answers again."

"Yes, Paster Immin. Do you mind if I approach?"

"It would be preferable to shouting across the open field."

Alric slid off the horse and walked to Immin. "Actually, I am hoping you would agree to meeting my wife, Altus Rector Ululla, at a teahouse. She has several questions she would like to have answers to."

"That is possible. May I ask what she is curious about?"

"One is the change of passages in the Book of Destiny."

"I see." Immin sighed. "Very well, I can meet with her. I am pleased she is the new altus rector. The witches need strong, intelligent leaders as the final battle approaches."

"Ululla will ask this same question. I hope you will give me an honest answer. Will my son and daughter survive this battle?"

"I'm sorry, I cannot say."

"Because you don't know, or don't want to tell me?"

Immin gave a tight smile. "If I told you, that information could change the outcome of the battle. A second consideration is I do not know the absolute future, only the most likely outcome. Telling you the details of what I know could cause you to act differently and making my prediction less reliable."

"All right, I understand what you are saying."

"Good. Let us meet at the same teahouse as last time in two days' time."

———

Ululla walked with Alric inside the teahouse, quickly scanning the interior for Pastor Immin. It didn't surprise her he was sitting outside at the back. What did surprise her was he was sitting with a woman about his own age, also wearing a dark robe.

Immin looked up at Ululla's approach.

"Altus Rector Ululla, Brother Alric. Please join us. This is my companion, Pastoress Isabel."

Ululla and Alric sat, waiting to speak, until a pot of tea and two more cups were added by a server.

"I asked you to speak to Ululla about the changes in the Book of Destiny," Alric stated.

"Yes, I should tell her myself. Perhaps it would be beneficial to speak with Altus Rector Truman as well, but I doubt he would be comfortable meeting me." He took a drink of his tea. "One thing you must remember the change in the Book of Destiny occurred long ago, during a period of turmoil. The Whiterose had split from the Umbravox, and it was still small. That made it difficult to add someone undetected into their order. However, the Umbravox, being large, made that task easier."

"What task was that?" Ululla asked.

"Blackrain was aware of the spells written in the Book of Destiny and the Book of Redemption and was concerned if the wrong entity would discover them. Thus, we changed the wording enough to make the spells difficult to find. Blackrain did not want to change the meaning of the Book of Destiny or the prophesies within it."

"Regardless of your reasons, the Umbravox would consider it unacceptable to change any wording of the Book of Destiny. I'm not sure Altus rector Truman, or any member of the Umbravox, would forgive Blackrain." Ululla spoke quietly, but directly, to Immin.

Pastoress Isabel spoke, "Blackrain didn't wish to interfere with the teachings of the Book of Destiny but couldn't allow someone with evil intent to find those spells. The prevention of evil is more important than the exact wording of the Book of Destiny."

Ululla's voice increased in volume. "Any good done by deceit will ultimately undo that good. The end never justifies the means."

Immin placed a hand on Isabel's arm before she could reply. "We hear you. We did not ask to meet with you to argue with you, nor do we apologize for what was done. As you wanted to know how and why the Book of Destiny's wording was changed, we have given you the answer. The witches are striving to bring peace and to fight evil. That is commendable. Blackrain has a different purpose. Our order is older than the Umbravox. Unlike the Umbravox, we do not share our presence, preferring a solitary existence. Our purpose is not so much to bring peace, but to stop an evil man, Master Diablo. Whatever means we can bring, we will use to stop him. His intent is to rule the world and turn all his subjects into slaves. He is a demon in human form."

"Perhaps your efforts would be more effective if Blackrain worked with Umbravox."

"Possibly, but Blackrain long ago decided this was the path they needed to take. To be sure, one reason we have not worked with the Umbravox is that Blackrain will do things that witches would find abhorrent."

"What would be more abhorrent than changing the wording of the Book of Destiny?" Ululla stared at Immin.

"We discovered the names of the wizards that were helping Master Diablo. The witches had rendered Wizard Crimson powerless when we found her, and fortunately for her, we allowed her to live. We did not give the other wizards the same opportunity and eliminated them. We know the witches refuse to do harm, but Blackrain is not under those constraints."

Alric frowned. "Those are words a warrior might use. As I have discovered, doing harm usually leads to more harm needing to be done. There is rarely an end to it."

"Brother Alric, a warrior fights when there is a battle. Do harm or be harmed. Isn't that one thing a warrior knows in his heart?" Isabel asked.

"Yes, when we are in battle. We are not at war now."

"You are wrong, Brother Alric. I assure you we are in a battle. Just because you are not using your sword doesn't mean others are not." Isabel paused and took a drink of her tea. "Sister Ululla, I wish we could be friends. I admire you, but you seem to think because we are of Blackrain, we are not to be trusted. You will know that you can trust the Blackrain when the ultimate battle is in front of all of us.

"That may be true. Sister Isabel, I do like you as well. You have strength of character. However, Blackrain uses dark magic and will kill. That is something very much against Umbravox beliefs."

Immin responded, "That is true, but your beliefs are not the only ones that are valid. You say you do not wish to do harm. But consider, by not acting against those that will kill innocents, are you not causing harm to be done? Blackrain only strikes those who have evil intent."

"You make a good argument, Brother Immin, Sister Isabel. I ask, who judges those who would do harm? How does one know they will do harm before it happens?" Ululla asked.

"A good question," Immin responded. "Blackrain has methods to see darkness and predict outcomes. I cannot provide more detail than that. Sister Ululla, I wanted to talk to you regarding our intrusion in the Book of Destiny and offer answers. We're taking action to fight the evil that's endangering everyone, including your daughter. As for using dark magic ourselves, as you know, there is a price for using it. Blackrain has paid that price and will do so again in the future. We will sacrifice our physical and mental health to do what must be done. We hope our efforts will be worth it at the end, which is coming soon."

"How soon?" asked Alric.

"We are nearly at the end of the book we use."

"What is the name of your book?"

Isabel gave a tight smile. "The Book of Sacrifice."

49

Terrowin was used to a routine of labour, whether it be the garden, gathering water, or helping dig part of the mountain. He also relented in giving up his clothing and weapons for a robe.

"To continue your journey," Mask explained, "it is necessary to shed barriers. Weapons can not help you. Clothing that protects or gives an air of importance, will slow your journey. We prefer no clothing, but we all have a duty to be modest.

After another morning of using a metal tipped tool to cut away at the interior of a cave, Terrowin returned to a room where he practiced his meditation. He slowly moved the stone in the palm of his hands, closed his eyes, and envisioned the stone in front of him. His breathing slowed.

"Terrowin." A soft voice spoke.

"Ayleth."

"How are you?"

"I'm fine. I hear you but cannot see you."

"You have your eyes closed."

Terrowin opened his eyes and saw her stand in front of him. "There you are."

She smiled. "I was here before, watching you. I didn't want to disturb you because you looked so peaceful."

"Is everything all right?"

"Yes, other than I miss you. The two orders of witches are drawing closer together. The Allisure Kingdom is getting stronger. Whatever evil that wants to destroy us is keeping to the shadows. Eventually, it will strike. But it may find we are no longer vulnerable. I am hoping you will return before the final conflict happens."

"I will do my best. For now, it seems my journey requires me to complete this spiritual meditation."

She laughed. "Perhaps you will become more witch than warrior at the end."

"That would be all right if I have you by my side. My destiny is to return to Allisure to be king, but that doesn't mean I will only be a warrior."

"A witch and a warrior?"

"Perhaps." He chuckled. "Your image is fading. I believe my meditation time is nearing an end."

She vanished, and he felt a hand on his shoulder. He looked up and saw Masc.

"You were speaking during your meditation."

"I received a visit from my love. She is a witch and has the ability to appear before me."

"She must be powerful in spirit. Is she young, like yourself?"

"Yes."

"Then she may only be young in body. I suspect she has had a long life previously."

————

The days seemed endless to Terrowin. The weathered varied little, usually with a few clouds under a strong sun. Rainfall, when it occurred, happened in the late evening. He did his share of labour, taking time each day to meditate. He was pleased there had been no sign of the black-watcher birds.

"Terrowin, how is your day?"

"It is well." Terrowin saw Masc approach, and he rested on the shaft of the hoe.

"How is your meditation?"

"It is something I look forward to, although I don't seem to progress much past what you have taught me."

"It takes many years of study to climb the ladder of knowledge. However, there is another path you should take. There is a method of using drink and smoke that allows one to see all that one is. I believe you are ready for this step and find your true being."

"What kind of drink?"

"It is special." He smiled. "It doesn't taste good."

Terrowin went with Masc through a tunnel to a small room. A single chair and a small table waited in the centre. Terrowin saw items on the table, including a cup, and was prepared to sit on the chair.

"No, the chair is for me. Sit on the floor."

After he sat on the floor, Masc gave him the cup, filled with a dark orange liquid.

"Sip it."

Terrowin found the taste bitter, spicy, with a flavour of rotten fruit. He would have preferred to down it quickly. "That tastes like something rotten."

"An appropriate description." He passed over a clay vessel with white smoke rising. "Breathe in the smoke slowly. Relax. You will begin a dream that will take you on a journey. Do not worry, I shall be here and will revive you if you get too confused."

"What do mean..."

"Quiet. Follow your path."

Terrowin took long, slow breaths. He felt light-headed as the smoke obscured the surrounding room. Grey patches formed in the white smoke, becoming darker. He watched as the dark areas formed a shape of a person. Slowly, details of the human became clear. The figure reached a hand toward him.

"Come with me."

Terrowin sat transfixed. He recognized the royal figure in front of him. "King Terrowin."

"Yes, that was who I was. Shall we?" He gestured with his hand.

Terrowin stood and stepped toward where the king stood. The smoke dissipated and Terrowin was standing on a road. People, horses and wagons went past and through him. In the distance, he saw the Allisure Castle.

"We are in Allisure."

"Yes, and not really. This is just an image, like a dream."

"So, we haven't travelled anywhere."

"That is true. I am an illusion as well." The king took a step to his left, and another figure appeared to his right, a young man in peasant clothes. "This is Terrowin. He died shortly before you were born."

"We are all named Terrowin."

"Correct." The king indicated to his left, and Terrowin stood, wearing his royal clothes of a prince.

"That's me? How can I be seeing myself? Is this just part of the illusion?"

"Yes. The three of us are one and the same. There are others as well, but we all share the same soul. When we die, we leave one body and search for another." The young man and the king merged into Prince Terrowin. "We are still here, residing within your mind. Now that you know we are part of you, memories of your past will start returning to you."

Quickly, the smoke returned to a white haze. Terrowin felt a hand on his shoulder, and he opened his eyes to see Masc.

"How do you feel?"

"I'm not sure. Dizzy. Headache." Terrowin tried to stand and lost his balance, placing a hand on the chair.

"You need to rest now." Masc used his arm to support Terrowin.

Terrowin didn't argue, glad for Masc's help as they returned down the tunnel, eventually reaching a cot. He closed his eyes and fell into a deep sleep.

––––––––

Terrowin was barely aware of being supported as he was given a cup of water, returning to sleep immediately afterward. He noticed light in his room and a woman sitting close by.

"Hello."

"Oh, you're awake. How do you feel?"

Terrowin sat at the edge of the cot. "Weak, but okay. How long was I sleeping?"

"Four days. We were getting concerned. That was much longer than normal. Are you hungry?"

"Yes. And thirsty."

"Wait here. I'll get Masc and food for you."

Terrowin waited. He wasn't sure if his experience of seeing King Terrowin was real or not. *Am I supposed to remember past lives? What good would that do me?*

Marc entered the room, smiling. "Welcome back. You slept a long time."

"Yes, I guess so. I don't remember any dreams."

"Your mind was adjusting to the recent memories. That takes much effort."

"I remember nothing different."

"You will."

The woman brought in a large bowl and a cup. "You should eat now."

Terrowin was left alone, and he consumed the food quickly, finishing by gulping down the water. He left the room and stepped into the sunlight. *I wonder how Lythea is doing. I miss her.*

———

Terrowin returned to work, tending to the vegetables. In the morning, he helped transport the water in containers that collected in the rocks above. He heard a scream and crying and hurried to see the source of the noise. A child, a girl of only a few years, had fallen on the rocky path and was clutching her ankle as concerned adults gathered around her.

A man commented to him. "They like to run and play, but the mountain paths are dangerous. That looks like just a sprain. She is lucky she didn't fall down the slope."

Terrowin advanced to the child. "May I look at your ankle?"

The girl nodded, with tears streaming down her face.

He bent to one knee and placed his hands around the swollen ankle, mouthing words in an unknown tongue.

"It doesn't hurt no more!"

"Good. Now be more careful."

Marc approached him. "What did you do?"

"A simple healing spell. I didn't know I knew how to do that."

"Your memories are returning."

Terrowin nodded and returned to the room where he slept. He sat on the floor and closed his eyes.

"Terrowin! You surprised me. You have discovered the ability to visit me."

"Hello, Ayleth. Yes, and I have learned other things as well. I have good news. I have decided it is time to return home." He watched her expression as she sat in her room. "I have to travel to the port first to find a ship. But my journey has served its purpose."

"I can hardly wait for your return." She smiled. "You look so different from when you left. Bigger and with a beard."

"And you look as lovely as ever."

50

Altus Rector Truman peered at Altus Rector Ululla.

"I can tell you are feeling stressed. When I received the note you sent earlier requesting a meeting of importance, I thought it may be something to do with the joining of our orders. However, your expression is not one of worry, but one of telling me unfortunate news."

"You are very perceptive. Yes, I have unpleasant news, Brother Truman. I was in a meeting with two members of the Blackrain, a pastor and a pastoress. Their names are not important, but they have been in contact with my husband, Brother Alric, previously. They informed me Blackrain was the one who had changed the wording of the Book of Destiny."

"They had infiltrated our order and changed the wording? Did they give a reason? I suspect I may know the answer."

"It was to prevent hidden spells from easily being read. They claimed they were worried an evil entity may find those spells. I'm not sure of the truth of what they said, but I thought I must pass that information to you."

"Thank you, Sister Ululla, for sharing this information. Brother Dorian speculated that the wording of the Book of Destiny was altered to hide those spells. This may confirm that."

"You are accepting this intrusion by Blackrain rather well, Brother Truman. I was worried you would be extremely upset by this news."

"Before becoming a keeper, I spent several years as a watcher. I learned to observe and not to judge. The previous altus rector was quick to punish those of minor indiscretions. I often decided not to report the activities that, while not strictly within the required behaviour of our order, were harmless. This was especially true of the younger members." He chuckled. "One night I took in a young, drunk woman and secreted her to our surgeon's room. I told our surgeon I had seen someone attack her, and she needed our protection. The surgeon, to her credit, ignored the fact she was under the influence of too much drink and let her rest. That woman was Sister Orienla. The lesson here is sometimes doing what you believe is the right thing, even if it is against the rules, can have a positive outcome."

"That is a good point. So, you believe what Blackrain did may have a positive outcome as well?"

"It is too early to say. But if they truly believed it was to prevent spells from being known by the wrong people, I can accept why they did it. It bothers me how they hid their subterfuge for so long."

"Has the altus councillium decided what to do with the alterations of the Book of Destiny?"

"It is not a simple solution, I suspect. Our two orders are now one, and the altus councillium has merged into one another." He grinned. "Twice the members mean twice as long to arrive at a decision. To change the Book of Destiny to the original writing would be an enormous undertaking, and what purpose would that serve? The teaching within the book would be essentially the same. Thanks to your daughter and Dorian, the spells have been discovered. It may they decide not to change the Book of Destiny back to the original script. I am glad it is not my decision to make. I have heard they are planning to have a Book of Redemption available in all Umbravox terradomus'. That will require considerable effort and resources."

———

Ululla returned to her terradomus. Ululla felt relieved she informed Truman about the rewording of the Book of Destiny. It surprised her how well he had reacted to the news. She crossed the foray toward the library, deciding it would be good to review passages in the Book of Redemption. *Perhaps I can find something that will help guide me under similar circumstances.*

She carried a copy of the Book of Redemption to a table, quietly acknowledging a few other witches reading as she went past their tables. After going through several chapters, she came across wording that fit what she was looking for.

"One caveat of being a witch is to help others. Sometimes, this can be spontaneous, such as when one sees another struggling to carry a heavy load. Other times, it may be a case where a woman is pregnant, and they decide to help provide meals or do household chores. However, sometimes a gesture to do good does the opposite.

"A simple example of this is when a child picks flowers to give to their mother, but the flowers were from their neighbour. Should the neighbour be upset? Scold the child? Be angry with the mother? If someone takes those actions, they will create unease between neighbours and a child will be upset. Instead, let us trust the neighbour will laugh at the child's effort to please the mother. Remember, the flowers will grow back, but memories last a long time.

"When incidents happen, one must consider the intention of the perpetrator, not necessarily the result. Try to be generous in appraising the efforts."

Perhaps this is what Brother Truman was considering when I told him about what Blackrain did. I shall try to learn from his example when I receive difficult news.

Ululla closed the book and returned it to a shelf. As she exited the library, she heard her daughter's voice calling out.

"Mother! I have wonderful news!"

She saw Ayleth hurry toward her. "What is it?" She noticed Ayleth was slightly out of breath.

"Terrowin is returning home!"

"How do you know this?"

"He came to visit me. Mother, he looks so different from when he left. He has a beard and has gained weight. I can hardly wait for his arrival."

"That is wonderful to hear, Ayleth. Come, let us have a tea and you can tell me exactly what he said."

Ululla saw Ayleth was eager to share the details of her encounter with Terrowin as they shared tea.

"What surprised me was he started the contact with me. All the other times, I had to search for him, and he had trouble seeing me. And he seemed so confident, like he knew exactly what he was going to do."

"I can tell by your expression you are very much in love with him."

"I am. He will be my husband."

"Ayleth, if you were to marry him, do you understand you will have to leave the terradomus and live in the Allisure Castle?"

"Yes, I will be a queen when he becomes king. I understand that, Mother. As a witch, I will help ensure we live in peace. If we win the great battle, which will happen soon after Terrowin arrives home."

51

Terrowin changed back into his own clothing. As he returned the robe to Masc, he thanked him for showing him how to meditate. "It has helped my journey in remembering who I am. Thanks to you, I am now much wiser and can see my destiny." He held up the stone Masc had given him to help meditate. "I shall keep this as a reminder of my time here and know the answers to our problems lie within ourselves."

"May your journey lead to contentment. I wish you well, Terrowin."

Terrowin looked ahead of the narrow, rocky path ahead of him. *The solitude will be good. Time to think and walk.*

———

Terrowin noticed the pathway slowly declined as it curved around the mountainous slopes. As he stopped for the evening, Terrowin was delighted to see signs of small green plants. He stretched out, not worried about his journey, and fell into a deep sleep.

The following morning, he woke to a bright sun. He stood, feeling refreshed as he sipped from a waterskin. He resumed his walk down the path. Grass and scrubs became frequent, and eventually a few small trees appeared.

Terrowin passed the occasional traveller going the opposite direction as himself, and he caught up to an older couple going his way.

"Hello. Can you tell me how far the next town is?" He saw the couple were wearing worn clothing and carrying a cloth sack each.

The man, his lower face covered by a grey beard, studied him before speaking. "You're dressed oddly. That means you're not from here."

"I'm from beyond the mountains."

"The next town, Burksy, is a half day walk."

"Thanks for the information."

The woman broke her silence. "You hungry?"

"That I am."

They stopped walking, and the woman pulled several carrots out of the bag she was carrying. "Here. Not much, but it will get you to Burksy."

After thanking the couple, Terrowin continued on the path. It was now wider, allowing for people to pass by easily, along with the small wagons he saw pulled by various animals. The horses were smaller than the ones he was used to, and he wondered how well they could carry a fully equipped warrior. Besides horses, some carts used oxen to pull the carts.

Terrowin reached Bursky, feeling hungry and thirsty. He noticed the town was spread out, rising along a hillside, the buildings using grey stone for walls. He walked down the flat stone road and found a market where food and goods could be purchased. Terrowin entered an inn and sat at a table and waited.

A woman, middle-aged and heavy-set, arrived at his table.

"We have ale or tea. Food is ox stew, bread and cheese."

"I'm sorry I don't have coin to pay, other than these." He held the few coins he had left. "Is there work I can do in exchange?"

She sighed, frowning at the coins. "I don't know what those are worth, if anything." She stepped back and peered at him. "At least ya told me before you ate." She sighed again. "I'll get ya food. My brother needs help, so ya can work there."

Terrowin had two helpings of the stew and finished several cups of tea.

The woman returned.

"That was a lot of food ya had."

"I was hungry. It was a long journey to arrive here. Thanks for the food. It was good."

"Ya can help my brother now. After you finish, ya can have a bed here."

Terrowin took directions to where her brother worked, a blacksmith. He saw the short man use a hammer to work a piece of metal.

"Excuse me. Are you Han? Your sister sent me to give you a hand."

Han appraised him.

"Good. You look strong enough to help."

Terrowin followed Han's orders. Han's instructions were not spoken loudly, but rather with a matter of fact. After adding wood to the fire, Terrowin helped pour the liquid copper into ceramic molds. The work wasn't hard physically for him, but the heat tired him.

After pouring the copper into the molds, Hans questioned him.

"Where ya be from?"

"Originally, from across the waters."

"That be far." He eyed his sword. "Your sword is made of white metal. Very rare."

"It isn't uncommon where I come from."

"I wish I knew how to make white metal."

"White metal is what we call steel, which comes from iron. Your kiln isn't hot enough to melt the iron. Back home, the blacksmiths pump air to make the flames hotter. They also used a black fuel rather than wood."

"Thanks, I'll give that some thought. Makes sense. Hotter flame."

After finishing work, Terrowin was given another meal and a room to sleep in by the inn.

At breakfast, he asked how far the next town was.

"Lariby," the server told him over breakfast. "It's about a day's walk."

"Is it as big as Bursky?"

"Bigger. We trade our copper for food with them. They raise livestock."

———

Terrowin walked along the well-used trail, occasionally keeping in step with other travellers. He noticed several carts carrying goods both to and from the two towns. He wondered at first about robbers on the road, but summarized the traffic was too heavy for thieves to attack. *Safety in numbers. It might be different at night.*

As the server told him, Lariby was larger. It still used stones as the primary building material. He entered the town, but instead of inquiring for a meal in exchange for work, Terrowin went to the outskirts of Lariby, where farms and ranches were located.

He knocked on the door of a farm, where an older man answered.

"What do you want?"

"I'm looking for work for a few days. Food and lodging."

"Why would a soldier want to do work on a farm?" He laughed. "Doesn't the king feed his men?"

"I'm not part of the king's army, just a traveller."

"A traveller with a sword? Sorry, I don't trust no one like you. Be off my farm."

Terrowin left, considering he looked intimidating with his weapons and his size. *I'll try another farm, but I may need to look for another way to get food.* He looked at the small herd of sheep. *Maybe they won't miss one of those.*

He went to the next farm. It looked larger than the previous one and he hoped he would get a better reception. Dogs immediately started barking at his arrival and soon a blonde woman older than himself came from the stone walled farmhouse. She acted relaxed as she approached him.

"How can I help you?"

"I am looking for work for food and a place to sleep."

She studied him for a moment. "Why do you have a sword?"

"I have journeyed from far away. I needed it for protection."

"Are you willing to move rocks?"

"Yes."

"Come with me. What's your name?"

"Terrowin."

"Really? That's an odd name. I'm Beth."

Terrowin followed her to a small stone house, not much larger than a shack.

"This is where my husband and I lived in at one time. We keep it for when one of our kids gets married and needs a place. You can sleep in here. Food is in the main house. Best you leave your sword in here when you're working."

"Thank you."

She smiled. "After you move rocks, you may not be thanking me."

After she left, a boy and girl in their teens approached him. "Ma said to fetch you. I guess we gotta move rock," the boy reluctantly announced.

A horse and cart transported the trio to a field where goats and sheep were grazing. Rocks were scattered throughout the field.

The girl picked up a stone. "Jef and me will get the small ones. You're supposed to pick the big ones."

"Sounds fair. What's your name? I'm Terrowin."

"Cara. Terrowin, that is a funny name. Why is it so long?"

"I don't know. They named me after my grandfather."

"Okay, but that's still a fancy name, like you were important or something."

Terrowin laughed. "If I was important, then why would I be picking up rocks?"

It wasn't long before Terrowin took off his shirt, finding the lifting of stones into the cart hard work. After the cart had as many rocks as the horse could pull, they went to another part of the farm where a barn was being built. He could see where one wall and part of another were built using rocks.

"This is hard work for a meal," Terrowin grunted. He placed a large flat rock into place, extending the wall. He saw how the two teens were working slowly to conserve their energy and copied their style.

Jef picked up a small boulder, dropping it into place. "You must have offered to work. Ma will give a meal to anyone who stops by and asks. She even let them stay a few days."

"Where's your father?"

"He took some sheep into town. He'll be back by sundown."

Terrowin was admitted into the main house to eat, where he met the husband, Seth, and two more children. There was plenty of food and Terrowin was happy he could take a second helping.

Seth asked, "Where are you heading to next?"

"I'm not sure, but I need to reach New Kireland Port."

"What's in the port city?"

"Hopefully a ship to take me back home. I'm originally from across the ocean."

"That is far, indeed. We heard there are a lot of battles going on there."

"That is true. I hope it will end soon."

Terrowin stood. "Thank you for your hospitality. I think I need a good sleep after today's work."

"You're welcome. Peace be with you."

Terrowin stopped at the doorway and turned around. "Are you witches?"

Seth shrugged. "I'm not sure if that is what you can call us. We try to follow the teachings, but it has been many years since witches were active around here. I think there's a terradomus in New Kireland Port, but I'm not sure if it is still in use. Are you scared of witches?"

"The lady I shall marry is a witch." He smiled. "Peace be with you."

———

Terrowin spent the next several days working on the stone wall. Seth worked with him, applying a layer of mud and straw in the gaps between the stones.

"Why did you decide to continue to help us build the barn walls?"

"The task had to be completed. I didn't think Beth, Jef and Cara could move the large rocks, which meant you would have to do all the heavy lifting. Your family gave me food and a place to sleep. I want to repay that favour."

"We have an old book in our home called a guide to the Book of Destiny. Truth be told, some pages are missing, but we use it as our guide for life."

"That is good. The Book of Destiny has valuable teachings in it."

"It does. It also mentions a fable about a red-headed warrior who returns from the dead."

"That actually happened."

Seth grunted. "Well, I said it was an old book. Lots of stuff happens,

I guess, over the years. It also mentions the name of King Terrowin. Same name as yourself." He gave Terrowin a focused stare.

"He was my grandfather."

"That would make you Prince Terrowin."

"Yes."

"A royalty picking rocks. No one would believe me, even if I told them."

Terrowin grinned. "I'm a prince only back home. Here, I'm a traveller."

"Traveller or prince, we sure appreciate your help." He passed a few coins to Terrowin. "You may need to buy your next meal."

"Thanks. I'll remember your generosity."

———

Seth shook his hand as Terrowin prepared to leave the farm.

"Remember, take the long road to get around the Jasic Kingdom. They'll take your sword and demand to know where you got it. You may not get out of there alive."

Beth added, "They charge every wagon that goes into Jasic a fee. A tax. That king is an awful man."

"Thanks. I'll avoid the town."

"Once you get past Jasic, it's another day's walk to New Kireland. Beware. There are wolves in these parts."

Terrowin resumed his journey, finding the stiffness in his back lessened as he walked. He came to a fork in the road and chose the path that led upward into the hills. He noticed the trail was well-used but would be more strenuous for those with carts.

The strong sun was tempered by a cool wind swirling around the uneven landscape. From the pathway, he could see the city of Jasic below. *It looks like a city made of stone. Not very inviting.*

He caught up with an older man pulling a cart piled high with potatoes.

"That looks like a heavy load. Do you want some help?"

"Sorry, I can't afford to pay for your help."

"My help is free." Terrowin took over the handles on the cart. "You need a break."

"Thanks. The toll at Jasic makes it too expensive to travel through there. The toll is less if you bribe the guards, but it's also a crime to bribe the guards. It's best to avoid Jasic completely."

After pulling the cart up a steep rise, Terrowin stopped. "I think it's mostly downhill from here."

"Thank you for your help."

"Is there a king that rules New Kireland?"

"Yes, King Davan. Good king. Doesn't overtax his people. I wish he would challenge King Eric of Jasic, but he doesn't want to interfere with the rulings of another kingdom."

———

Terrowin entered New Kireland. The guards posted at the entrance to the port appeared to be there for appearance rather than restrict access. Terrowin suspected the guards to be part of the royal guards due to their height and clean uniforms. The Allisure Kingdom selected the royal guards based on their appearance, but they were also trained to be excellent fighters.

He stepped between the guards along with other travellers, not expecting any objection to entering the city.

A guard's voice called out, "You, sir, stop!"

Terrowin turned around and looked at the guard, who was pointing a finger at him.

"What is it?" he spread out his hands from his sides.

"Your name, and where are you from?"

"My name is Terrowin, and I'm a traveller from far away."

"Hand me your sword."

Terrowin considered resisting. *If I fight these two guards, that will make it even more difficult to get a passage on a ship later. I best comply and hope they won't hold me for some crime I didn't know about.* He passed over his sword.

The guard looked impressed. "This is a fine sword. White metal, but of a quality that even the Metal people couldn't produce. Where did you get this sword? Are you a warrior? Which kingdom do you represent?" The questions had the sound of authority behind them.

"The sword was a gift to me from a warrior who no longer had a use for it. I am from the Allisure Kingdom that is across the ocean. I am a traveller, but now want to return home by finding a ship that crosses the ocean."

"I have heard of this kingdom. A rich kingdom but is at war with others. Since you carry a sword, that makes me believe you are part of the army." The guard frowned. "Follow me. I will have the captain deal with you."

Terrowin reluctantly followed the guard along a brick walkway, eventually leading to an enormous castle. The castle was not high but spread out over a large area. They presented Terrowin to another uniformed man working in a large office on the main floor of the castle. He didn't have a desk, but a large table with several maps on it. A man and a woman were also in the office and appeared to be his assistants.

The mustached captain with dark hair eyed the sword as the guard presented it. "What is this?"

Terrowin watched the captain examine the sword. He wasn't as tall as Terrowin, and with a slimmer build. "This is a work of extraordinary craftsmanship. He looked at Terrowin. "You must be a warrior of considerable distinction."

"He said he was from the Allisure Kingdom, sir."

"That would explain it. Would you be a royal guard?"

Terrowin wondered how to answer, not wanting to reveal his true status as a prince. "I am associated with them. Captain, I appreciate your curiosity about where the sword came from, but I am only here in New Kireland to find passage on a ship to return to Allisure."

"That may well be, but I believe I should bring this matter to King Davan." Guard, take him to a guest room and ensure he has food and drink."

Terrowin sighed and went with the guard up a set of stairs.

"What is your name?"

"Royal Guardsman Jerit."

"What is the king like?"

"He is a wise and generous leader."

"I'm sure he is. But how long am I to be kept here?"

"That would be his decision, but I believe it will be only a few days."

Terrowin entered the guest room and heard the door close behind him. He assumed the guard would remain outside to ensure he stayed inside. The large room featured a bed that looked well padded, reminding him of the time he lived as a prince in the Allisure Castle. *That seems a long time ago.*

After knocking on the door, a servant entered carrying a tray of food and drink.

"For you, sir. Is there anything else you wish?"

"No, this looks fine." He watched as she set the tray on a table.

As soon as she left, he dug into the food, devouring it. He suspected by giving him a choice of chicken and pork, he was to pick one or the other. Instead, he consumed both portions.

The ale was of better quality than he had recently, and he had his fill of that as well.

Satisfied, he slumped in a chair and dozed off.

———

"Sir? Sir?"

Terrowin woke to the guard standing in front of him. He blinked several times. "I'm sorry. I fell asleep."

"Yes, sir. The king will see you now."

Terrowin stretched. "Of course." He followed the guard up another set of stairs, down a wide hallway and finally to a room that had the appearances of a library. At a table, the king sat, along with three other men and a woman. Terrowin summarized the other men were likely advisors and the slim brunette was the queen. The king had a grey and red beard, trimmed close to his jaw. Terrowin guessed the king was of average height and heavy-set. The king's face seemed friendly, despite the creases of age on his forehead. As he kneeled, he saw his sword lying on the table.

"Rise."

Terrowin stood. "Thank you for seeing me, King Davan."

"You said your name is Terrowin."

"That is correct."

"As you can see in this room, Queen Juliet and I are collectors of books. I have studied the Allisure Kingdom and tried to model my rule in a similar fashion. Of special note, there was a King Terrowin. You have the same name. I wonder about the relationship."

"King Terrowin was my grandfather."

"Then you are Prince Terrowin. Why are you travelling in our land?"

"Allisure is under attack by an evil source. They killed members of my family and I was sent away to protect me from their attacks. My time in exile has come to an end and I must return to Allisure. The purpose of my visit to New Kireland is to find a suitable ship that can transport me home. I am ready to fight the evil that attacked Allisure."

The king nodded. "Interesting. You believe you are now ready to fight the evil now, but weren't before? What has changed?"

"I was a boy when I left. Now I am a man."

"King Terrowin was a powerful man with special powers. Some say magical. Looking at you, I feel I am looking at him."

"He is part of me. I feel him within myself."

"I believe you. It is my command that you shall be our guest here until an ocean ship arrives. We will ensure you passage on the next ship going to Allisure. You may have your sword back, and I will have new clothes made for you. A prince should be dressed better than a peasant."

"Thank you, my lord. Your generosity is most appreciated."

"Not at all. I hope, after you safely arrive back at Allisure, you will recall our friendship. I wish to exchange greetings with the Allisure Kingdom."

———

Terrowin spent the next few days wandering around the castle, occasionally visiting one of the two libraries. He found several references to the Allisure Kingdom, and while not always entirely accurate, showed a deep respect the New Kireland Kingdom had for the distance land.

One day, the king invited Terrowin to have dinner with him. Terrowin was not sure if he would be dining with a large group, but he was surprised to find only the king, queen, and two advisors present. He sat across from the king and queen, and next to the advisors.

"Thank you for joining us, Prince Terrowin."

"The honour is mine."

Several servants quickly filled the plates with several cuts of meat, vegetables, and bread.

During the meal, the king asked, "I am curious on your perceptions of the New Kireland Kingdom. Please be honest. We seek only your opinion and will not take offence for any criticism."

"Truth be told, I have only seen the inside of your castle. I can't find any fault with the castle's maintenance.

"May I ask your views about witches?" the Queen Juliet asked. "We have a growing population of witches, and we are not sure if we should tolerate them."

"You have had witches for a long time, as have the Allisure Kingdom. We have found they will harm no one, unless they are attacked. Their purpose seems to be one of peace. I suggest a meeting between the witches and the kingdom will answer many questions about their beliefs." Terrowin decided against revealing his own connection with the witches.

"Excellent advice." The queen smiled and looked at one advisor. "Chancellor Balet, arrange a meeting with the witches. It is time we had a formal meeting with them."

"Yes, my majesty."

"Prince Terrowin, you have been careful in your answers to us. I understand your reluctance to say everything on your mind, but perhaps you can share with us one area that we can improve upon." King Davan spoke quietly. "After all, we wish to be a kingdom as famous as the Allisure Kingdom."

Terrowin took a drink of ale from a tankard. "Allow me to share what I have observed, but I do not judge."

"Very well. Please continue."

"I understand New Kireland trades with several towns along the coast, but one of the most important ones are Bursky and Lariby. Bursky, I believe, is the major supplier of metals."

"That is correct."

"However, Jasic is between New Kireland and Bursky. I am led to believe the king of Jasic is ruthless and ambitious. Have you considered what would happen if Jasic were to attack Lariby and Bursky?"

King Davan frowned. "It would put us in a difficult situation. We depend on metal works from Bursky and Laiby. Prince Terrowin, our kingdom, strives for peace. Are you suggesting that we attack Jasic if King Eric tries to claim Bursky and Lariby?"

"King Davan, the Kingdom of Allisure, believes in peace as well. Sometimes the key to ensuring peace is to take action before a situation becomes worse. If you wait until King Eric attacks Lariby and Bursky, then the battle will be more difficult. Perhaps you may wish to consider the possibility of attacking Jasic first."

"Prince Terrowin speaks with wisdom, my lord," Chancellor Balet responded.

"I will have to reflect on your suggestion later. Thank you for your insight. Perhaps we can retire to the common room and enjoy drinks and company."

———

Terrowin slowed the pace of his consumption of alcohol, trying to be careful with his answers to the various questions put to him.

"With so many alliances, does that mean Allisure was always having to battle?" Balet asked.

"Actually, having alliance prevented many attacks. Unfortunately, there was one kingdom that was aggressive in enlarging its territory. They will resort to using dark magic to accomplish their goals. In retrospect, attacking this kingdom before they grew strong would have been better to minimize the destruction they caused."

"It appears we may be in a similar position. A battle with Jasic eventually will happen. Our only decision is if we attack first, or wait to be attacked."

"That may be true. One solution is to first make overtures to Lariby and to form an alliance with them. That way Jasic would be pinned between two adversaries."

"Good point. King Davan wants to maintain peace, but sometimes a firm hand is the best way to maintain it."

52

Terrowin sat on the floor in the guest room he was occupying in the late evening. He slowed his breathing, relaxing as he fingered the stone in the palm of his hand. Shadows in the room shifted, sliding across the floor as the light in the room brightened. The early morning light gave way to a room lit by candles and a lantern. He saw Ayleth brushing her hair.

"Good morning."

"Terrowin!" Ayleth quickly turned toward where he was standing behind her. "It's good to see you again. I was wondering when you may start your travel home."

"I am a guest of the king in New Kireland, waiting for an ocean vessel."

"Some ships were delayed on their voyage due to the recent war. But at least two ships left some weeks ago, so they should arrive in New Kireland soon."

"I hope so. New Kireland launched an attack on a neighbouring city called Jasic. King Davan of New Kireland was expecting a bloody battle, but it turns out the Jasic population hated their king. The battle was short-lived. New Kireland has expanded its borders, which will make trade a lot easier with the close by cities."

"That's an interesting development since you arrived in New Kireland."

"Truth be told, I did encourage an early attack on Jasic. I remembered the problems Allisure face because we assumed Dwykath would be satisfied with their earlier expansion."

"No one could have foreseen an evil force had taken Dwykath over."

"True. I do not blame anyone for the events that transpired, but rather use that knowledge. New Kireland is now stronger and not in danger of an attack."

"Your magic is becoming stronger. You appear to be almost solid. I can believe you are actually in the room with me." She smiled. "I like your beard. It goes with your look of being big and strong."

"Thanks. You look beautiful. My longing for you is greater than you can imagine.

My image here won't last for much longer. Seeing you and letting you know that I'm doing well is what I wanted. As soon as an ocean ship is available, I'll be returning home."

"All right. I love you, Terrowin."

He smiled. "I love you."

———

Terrowin made his way to a library, a favourite place to spend his time. He pulled a book at random from a shelf and took it to a table to read. He leafed through the pages, reading passages that interested him. As he read a paragraph, a guard approached him.

"Prince Terrowin, sir, King Davan requests your presence at a meeting with him and a representative from the witches."

"Very well. When does this meeting take place?"

"Immediately, sir."

"Then you best lead the way." He closed the book. "One should not keep the king waiting."

———

The king smiled at Terrowin's entrance.

"Relax, you do not need to bow."

"Thank you." Seated with the king was the queen on one side of a long table. On the other side sat a man and two women dressed in robes. Terrowin recognized them as witches.

The king motioned with his hand to sit next to him. "I would like to hear your perspective. We are exploring ways to improve our relationship with the witches."

Terrowin looked at the woman sitting the middle. She had long grey hair, a slim build and a pleasant-looking face.

"Are you the altus rector?"

Her chin lifted and her eyebrows arched. "Yes, I am Altus Rector Candice." She touched the arm of the man next to her. "This is Keeper Jond." Also with us is Sister Elani. She fulfills the role of an advisor. It's surprising that you're aware of the term altus rector.

My name is Prince Terrowin. I come from the land across the ocean called the Allisure Kingdom."

"We have heard of this place. It is where the original witches came from."

"May I ask which book you follow? The Book of Destiny or the Book of Redemption?"

"You know of our book? You continue to surprise me, Prince Terrowin. We follow the Book of Destiny. There is another, smaller order of witches that uses the Book of Redemption. They are heretics, and we rarely associate with them."

"I understand. Where I come from, the two orders of witches have put their differences aside. They are now one order, and freely visit each the terradomus of the other."

"That is remarkable. The two orders get along?"

"Yes, because they believe in peace. How can witches spread the message of peace if they themselves cannot get along?"

"A valid point."

"In the Allisure Kingdom, the royal family has a good relationship with the witches. They gave the witches freedom to carry out their work. In return, the witches support the king. It seems to me the witches here could enjoy a similar arrangement."

"That may be true, but the witches do not wish to be under the rule of the king."

"So, you feel the people can be under the rule of the king, but not the witches? The witches are superior to the people they want to bring peace to? Surely, that isn't the message the witches wish to convey."

The altus rector pursed her lips.

Terrowin spread his hands. "Look, you have an opportunity to spread peace by working with the king and the other witches. You do not have to agree with everything they do, believe or say, but you should try to find common ground."

"He makes a strong argument," Keeper Jond added.

"Sister Elani, what is your opinion?"

"Prince Terrowin has the advantage of insight of the Kingdom of Allisure. It is prudent to accept the notion that we should seek peace, and the means to do so. There are challenges ahead for us. The people of Jasic need our guidance now that the previous king has been removed."

The altus rector nodded. "King Davan, you asked for us to meet. The words you used were to find common ground between witches and the king's rule. I believe that is possible. King Davan, if the witches are to support your rule, what can you offer in return?"

King Davan chuckled. "You mean besides the protection all citizens under my rule have?" He held up his hand to forestall any reply. "My offer is this. I shall no longer require witches to pay taxes. I want witches to support the royal family actively in return. That means attending events with an attitude that shows support for the royal family."

"That is reasonable. As long as you understand our support does not mean we may not agree with every rule and decision you make."

"Not everyone in New Kireland agrees with every decision I make. That is understandable. But I expect compliance with all laws that I pass."

"We can respect all of your laws, except where it goes against the teachings in the Book of Destiny. If the government passes a law that goes against the teachings of the Book of Destiny, such as requiring all men to carry a sword, we cannot agree to it. If we are not put in such a situation, then I do not see an obstacle in supporting your rule."

"Then we have an agreement. This is good news for us and the witches. Prince Terrowin, I thank you for your help in obtaining a resolution."

"You are welcome. The Allisure Kingdom has benefited from the influence of the witches. I hope that will extend here as well."

———

Two days later a messenger interrupted Terrowin's lunch.

"Pardon the intrusion, Prince Terrowin, but an ocean vessel has arrived at port."

He dropped his fork on the plate and stood. "That is great news. What's the name of the ship?"

"The Benin. Sir, guards will escort you there later. The ship is currently being unloaded of its cargo, and there is no hurry to arrive there."

"Very well. Please keep me informed when I can view this ship."

Terrowin paced about the castle. He ate a late dinner and by nightfall concluded he wouldn't see the ship until the next day. His sleep was restless, and he woke up several times. Once, during a dream he missed the sailing of the Benin.

After breakfast, he spent time on a balcony, trying to view the harbour. Buildings and smoke obscured his sight lines, but he felt better seeing the ocean in the distance. *I'll be homeward bound soon.*

King Davan approached him. "Good news. It is time for you to visit the ship that will take you home. The captain has already been approached and will make sure you have adequate quarters to rest during the voyage. I have two containers placed on board for you. One is for your personal use, such as a change of clothes. The other is for King Grayson. I hope he will appreciate the small gifts we have for him, and it will be a start of friendship between our kingdoms."

"I am certain he will be most appreciative of your gesture of friendship."

Two guards led Terrowin to the harbour. He could smell the ocean and made his way through the twisted roads to the docks, where he saw several ships. At first, he didn't believe any of the ships were large enough to cross the ocean until he saw the Benin at the end of the dock. *That's more like it. Three masts. I'm going home!*

Terrowin walked up the ramp of the ship. He was greeted by a man almost as tall as himself, but with a bigger waist.

"Welcome aboard, Prince Terrowin. I'm Captain Nolis, and I assure you I will look after your needs." He led Terrowin to the back of the ship, opening a door on a second level. "This be your room."

Terrowin looked inside the room that looked to be recently vacated. "It would appear I've taken someone's quarters. I do not wish to cause a problem before we set sail."

"It is of no bother, I assure you. The king was quite clear about his expectations for your voyage."

"I understand."

"Excellent. We have placed your trunk in the room. The other container is secure in the hold. Please rest if you wish. We will leave soon and will try not to disturb you."

"I am most gracious about your hospitality." Terrowin entered the small room and tested out the bed, deciding it was better than he expected. A cabinet yielded a bottle of dark spirits and he helped himself to a small portion.

When he heard noise from outside the room, he exited and saw sailors hurrying as they pulled ropes that secured the ship to the dock. He made his way to the bow of the ship, making sure he didn't impede the crew.

For a while, the ship was quiet. The crew rested on the deck, enjoying a few minutes of rest.

"Raise the main!"

The crew sprinted to ropes as Terrowin watched the ropes being pulled taut. *I remember doing this, but that was long ago. A different life, perhaps.* He ran behind a sailor and gripped the rope.

"Hoist the sail!"

Terrowin pulled on the rope. He saw the white sail unfurl as the wind caught it.

"Pull fast!"

A sailor pulling on another rope gave him a curious look, and then a nod of approval.

The captain approached him after the sail was fixed. "Sir, you are not required to do work here."

"I know, but an extra pair of hands will make the work easier. Besides, I don't want to be both bored and a nuisance on your ship."

"Fair enough. Just don't get yourself hurt or I could never return to New Kireland."

53

Terrowin sat against the rail next to a crewman, sharing a ration of food.

"You be a prince and all that. Why do ya do work like the rest of us?"

"I would be bored to death if I didn't do something. That's why I choose to do useful work."

"You look like you been on a ship before. Ya be no landlubber."

"I learned to sail in a previous life." Terrowin chuckled. "I've been around a few places."

Terrowin looked at the sky, watching the tall clouds for signs it might rain. Silhouetted in front of the white cloud were two dark specks. He studied the two images, watching them resolve into two birds. *Black-watchers.*

He stood and walked to the stern of the ship, focusing on the birds. He raised one arm and pointed his fingers at the black-watchers. For a short time, they flew toward him, but soon they dropped rapidly. Without flapping their wings, they plummeted to the water, disappearing underneath the waves.

One less problem.

———

Captain Nolis poured wine into the goblet in front of Terrowin. "One advantage of being a captain on this ship is I have access to better food and superior wine. It makes these voyages much more bearable."

"I must agree, this is excellent wine and fine food. You must enjoy life on the sea."

"I do. It can be lonely but there is nothing like the open skies to put the mind at ease. I noticed you spend a lot of time with the crewmen. It seems you share a common interest with the crew of the ship."

"I enjoy their company. They have stories to tell, and we can learn from the experiences of others."

"You seem wise beyond your years. May I ask if you're heir to the throne in Allisure?"

"I am."

"I believe you'll make a great king." He laughed. "Few people will believe I had the future king working as a crewman on my ship."

———

To Terrowin, time passed slowly, the days seeming long as they crossed the ocean to his home. The days slipped into weeks. Finally, the day arrived when Terrowin was looking up at the crow's nest and heard the shout of a sailor.

"Land!"

He hurried to the bow of the ship but saw only the edge of the ocean. Terrowin paced one direction then the other.

"We're going as fast as we can. Watching the ocean won't make the shore come any sooner." Captain Nolis spoke from behind him.

Terrowin turned around. "I know you're right, but it has been a long time since I've been home."

"If you want to pass the time, join me in my cabin. I have a very nice bottle to share with you. By the time we have gone through half the bottle, you'll see the land you long for."

Terrowin followed Noris to the captain's cabin. Terrowin had been impressed by the neatness of the cabin during his previous visit, and now followed Noris to it. Everything had a place to be kept or stored. He sat at the square table across from Noris, sharing the dark liquid.

"You know, I didn't set out to be a captain on an ocean vessel. I actually was a stow-away. Just a young lad who decided a ship would take him away from my troubles." He laughed. "Lesson learned. Another set replaced one set of troubles. What you do when you're faced with a problem? No matter what you do, take responsibility. After I figured that out, I found my life had a lot fewer problems."

"Wise words. To be fair, there are situations beyond your control. We cannot feel responsible for everything that happens."

"True, but what do you do when the storm hits? You didn't cause the storm, but as a captain, what you do next will save the ship and lives."

Terrowin took another drink. "Thank you, captain, for your insight. I feel the need to check to see if land is visible."

Terrowin peered across the bow of the ship and saw the grey smudge. *Home.*

He watched as the grey outline slowly changed into a distinct shape with colours. He could see other ships in the water and his excitement grew as he made out the harbour.

"That be Edwin." A seaman spoke nearby to him.

"It's the same port I left long ago."

"There not be many ports where we can dock a ship this big. Edwin can handle the ocean ships. We be taking down the sails soon. Guide boats will pull us into the docks." He grinned. "I sure am looking forward to visiting those inns and women."

"You deserve some fun after being at sea for so long."

Terrowin helped with sails, with the captain using only one small sail to help navigate. Four rowboats came out to take the Benin to the dock. When they secured ropes to each small boat, they began the final, slow journey.

———

Terrowin changed his clothing, deciding he wouldn't hide being Prince Terrowin when he landed on shore. He requested the captain to send the two containers to Allisure Castle.

"Please have a messenger inform the king that I have arrived and am safe and sound."

"Of course, Prince Terrowin. Will you be going directly to the castle yourself? In that case, I can arrange for a horse to take you there."

"Thank you, captain. I will take you up on your offer for a horse, but I will go straight to Jital. My bride to be awaits me."

The horse, Terrowin guessed, was likely the best one available from a stable. It seemed agitated and ready to gallop. He looked down from the saddle at the captain.

"Captain Noris, I shall not forget you and the fine crew of the Benin. Your hospitality made my journey much better than I expected. May the winds always be fair to you."

As Terrowin rode the horse down the brick streets, on lookers pointed at him. At first there were whispers, and then shouts.

"It's Prince Terrowin! He has returned! Long live the king!"

Crowds pressed toward the streets, forcing Terrowin to slow the horse down for fear of running over the excited citizens. He heard the alarm bells from a terradomus. *The witches know I've returned. They will spread the word to Jital.*

Two guards on horses appeared, flanking him on each side.

"We will keep you safe, Prince Terrowin. Where do you wish to go?"

"Jital."

The crowd reacted to the guards and cleared out of the way. Two more guards on horses joined them, and after they reached the town's boundary, increased their pace.

They passed a village where Terrowin recalled spending a night in a terradomus. *We are nearing Jital.*

When they arrived at Jital late in the evening, Terrowin's entourage slowed down as they passed the main entrance. Four more guards on horses arrived to escort him on his journey to the terradomus.

As the distance decreased, he heard the alarm bells ring out. By the strength of the bells, he guessed both terradomus' were sounding the alarm of his arrival. Crowds lined the line streets, waving as they proceeded. Shouts of "Welcome home!" and "Long live the king!" merged into a drone of cheering.

Terrowin realized they wouldn't reach the terradomus, due to the crowd of common people and witches that blocked the final distance. Sliding off his horse, he hurried, pushing past the crowd.

Her blonde hair made Ayleth easily recognizable among the

others, and he spotted her. The only thing on his mind was the gap between them as he ran. A gap opened as people made way for him and Ayleth.

They collided, spinning in a circle as their arms wrapped around their bodies in a vise grip. They didn't speak any words, and no words were necessary.

———

Terrowin held Ayleth's hand as they relaxed in her bed.

"Are your parents going to be upset I spent the night with you?"

"Possibly, but I would not let you go anywhere else. You better get used to me being next to you."

"I best speak with them. Is your mother in her office?"

"Yes."

"Perhaps you can ask your father to join us."

Terrowin waited while the secretary checked with Altus Rector Ululla before admitting him into her office.

"Thank you for seeing me. Ayleth and Brother Alric will join us soon." He sat in a chair after she gestured him to sit.

"It is always good seeing you, Prince Terrowin. It has been an amazing adventure you went on. You certainly have changed. I recall you were a nervous young man during your stay here. Now, you're bigger and have confidence in who you are."

He laughed. "Eating a lot explains my weight gain."

Ayleth and Alric entered the office and Terrowin stood. "Altus Rector Ululla, Brother Alric. Ayleth and I have an important request to ask of you." He stepped by her side. "We would like to have your blessing to marry."

Alric glared at him. "Only if you can beat me in a sword fight." He laughed. "I forgot. I gave you my sword." He stepped forward and gave Ayleth and Terrowin a hug each. "Welcome to our family, Prince Terrowin."

———

Terrowin sat in the dining room with Ayleth's family, including her brother. There were several other witches at the table, with the Altus Rector Ululla sitting across from him.

"You have enlightened us with a few of your many adventures, but I am most intrigued by your revelation of witches in New Kireland. Were you able to interact with the witches there? Were they Whiterose or Darkrose?"

"They were Darkrose and were not aware of the joining of the two orders. I believe they would be very receptive to a visit from the witches here."

"That is good to hear. I will discuss with the altus councillium about sending a delegation to New Kireland. I am curious about your relationship with witches, in particular with my daughter. Have you considered becoming a witch yourself? It may prove beneficial in your role as a prince and possible king."

"I am certain you are correct in your assumption. I am in step with the teaching of witches and appreciate what you are saying. My duty is to the king, my father, first. I trust you understand my obligations may negate myself becoming a formal witch, but I still will use their teachings when I make decisions."

"That is a wise and fair answer. Just know that if you wish to complete the vows of being a witch, I will support your inclusion."

"Thank you."

"Tell them what you told me earlier." Ayleth prompted Terrowin.

"During my travels, I visited a group who lived on the side of a mountain. They were spiritual in beliefs and taught me how to meditate. One time they gave me a special drink, and I went into a dream where I met my previous lives."

"Lives? More than one?"

"Yes, I suppose there have been more past lives, but I met a young man and my grandfather, whom they named me after. Actually, I did more than just meet them. They became part of me. I have their memories."

"Their memories?" Ululla looked concerned.

"Yes. It turns out my grandfather, King Terrowin, was also a witch. That means I truly understand what it means to be a witch and I have knowledge of the spells he knew." He smiled at Ululla. "I do not have any ill feelings about any events in my past lives. They all contributed to what I am today."

Alric spoke up, "We appreciate what you have revealed to us. It will be wonderful to have someone who reflects the beliefs of witches' part of the royal family. We still have the matter at hand of when Master Diablo attacks and how to defend against him. We don't know what type of methods he will deploy to battle us."

"I believe I know when and where he will attack." Terrowin paused as the others focused on him. "When Ayleth and I are married, we will be a formidable force against his evil intention. Together, we represent a power greater than two separate individuals. Master Diablo will attack during our wedding ceremony." He heard a gasp from Ululla. "The place of attack will be in Jital. It is the city a thousand years old and holds enormous power."

"You are planning to marry in Jital?" Alric asked.

"Ayleth expressed a desire to marry near the terradomus. We will have a second ceremony at Allisure, that will be likely a long, formal affair. But we will exchange our first vows here."

"Yet you expect Master Diablo to attack during the service?" Ululla asked.

"It seems likely. He will mistakenly believe our full attention will be on the service and the attack will catch us off guard. We will be prepared for him. We will defeat him. I promise you this."

———

King Grayson sat on a second-story balcony. The cushion chair was comfortable, and he relaxed with a tea. Despite the bare sun keeping the air warm, he had a blanket over his lap. He heard someone enter the balcony and turned to see the queen.

"Are you enjoying the fresh air?"

"Yes, thank you. I am hoping Terrowin comes home soon. His two containers arrived here, but not him."

"I understand how anxious you are to see him again. He wanted to see that girl first, and can you really blame him for that? Ayleth will be queen someday and she deserves his attention as well."

"I know. I have little time left." He stopped looking at the far horizon and turned his attention to her. "I want to pass the crown to him while I can still stand."

"Grayson, you still have strength of character. You will be here for when he returns." She gave him a kiss.

"You are my strength now. I shall try to be patient."

"Would you like a cup of wine? It will help you keep warm."

"Yes, that would be nice." He watched her walk away and smiled. *My life has been full, but I still want one more thing. To pass my rule to Terrowin and see that the kingdom will be secure for another generation. Elissa has truly been good to me. I wish I knew for certain Terrowin is of my blood, even though I've always treated him as my own. When he was growing up, I never suspected he would be the last of my sons alive. Some things are meant to be.*

"Your wine, Grayson."

"Thanks." His hand shook as he lifted the goblet. *Hurry, Terrowin, hurry.*

54

Willis used a pitchfork to toss a hay bale from the barrack onto a wagon. The barrack was located at the outside of the village and where hay and straw bales were stored. The horse attached to the wagon waited as he added the small, hand-tied bales. The day was warm, and Willis stopped to wipe the sweat from his brow. *Hard work, but better than swinging a sword.*

The horse pushed against the harness holding it to the wagon and gave a snort. Willis recognized the sound; it was the same when horses felt danger before a battle. He carried the pitchfork to the front of the horse, expecting to see a wolf or cougar. Instead, he saw a mound of wet dirt, slowly rising as it took shape.

What the hell is that?

Willis watched as the mound began to form legs, oversized claws, and a head. The head held massive jaws with dagger-like teeth and the skull had a crest with a pair of horns. The ugly creature, gleaming from a wet reptilian skin, was the size of a large wolf. The horse snorted again and attempted to raise its front legs. Willis charged at the monster, impaling it with the pitchfork. It screamed and he pulled out the pitchfork only to bury it again into its neck. The creature fell forward, and Willis took a deep breath. He looked around and saw several more mounds of dirt rising. He turned and ran to the centre of the village. The horse ran past him, pulling the wagon, as startled villagers looked on in surprise.

"Sound the alarm! Monsters are attacking!" Willis shouted.

A witch tending a garden pointed with a hand and yelled, "go to the terradomus. We'll be safe there."

Willis turned toward the terradomus, a two-story stone building. He had been allowed inside only a few times previously, as a guest of Catelia for tea or lunch. The inside, he recalled, was open on the main floor, comprising of a kitchen, a dining area, a common area and a library. He noted there were stairs for the upstairs and a lower level.

The front door to the terradomus was open and people rushed inside as the alarm bell rang. Catelia met him at the door.

"You don't need the pitchfork in here."

"You didn't see what I saw."

"No weapons inside the terradomus."

Willis sighed and tossed the pitchfork away. "How will we protect ourselves from these monsters?"

"We will be safe." She took his hand and led him inside. "A spell prevents those with evil intent from entering."

"The monsters I saw were created by magic. Maybe the spell won't work on them."

Catelia paused. "Perhaps you have a point." She raised her voice. "Everyone downstairs."

Willis stayed with Catelia as others filed past them to the stairs.

"I'm not going downstairs until you do."

"Thanks, but I just want to make sure the spell holds them back. I'll be safe."

"Then so will I. I won't leave you."

Catelia looked at him. "I know that."

"What I mean is I'll never leave you."

"I know that too."

The front door splintered, and the head of a monster burst through. It screeched before going silent as it died in the doorway. A second creature climbed over the first, destroying the rest of the door. It looked at Catelia and Willis and began to charge toward them. Suddenly it dropped, laying dead. Two more creatures followed through the open doorway. One screamed as they focused their attention on the two humans. Catelia and Willis hurried to the stairs.

Willis heard the scraping of claws on the floor, and then silence. As he reached the stairs, he saw both monsters had died as well.

"The spell killed them."

"Yes, but they are getting closer each time. The spell won't be able to stop them if they continue."

"Won't they just follow us downstairs?"

"We won't be there. Trust me, we will be safe."

Willis saw the stairs went to not just one lower floor, but another. In the lower level he saw the witches and the rest of the villagers, including several dogs and cats.

"The spell won't be able to protect us for long," Catelia announced. "We need to make use of the tunnel to go to the Jital Terradomus."

Willis heard the murmuring of crowd as they moved to the far wall. As he walked with Catelia across the room, he saw where a heavy door had been opened. Beyond the doorway, the flickering light of torches lit the tunnel. He passed the door, thick wood with iron braces. Willis took a deep breath, slowing his steps.

"What's the matter?"

"Is it safe to go down here?"

"Yes, completely safe." She paused. "Are you frightened of enclosed spaces?"

"I'm more scared of those monsters."

Willis was surprised the tunnel barely deviated from a straight line, other than in one place it forked to another direction. He followed the troupe, hearing their whispered comments and shuffling of footsteps.

They reached the end of the tunnel where another thick door was opened to admit them. Willis was amazed at the size of underground room, thinking it was more like a cavern.

Willis saw Catelia conversing with a tall woman as he looked nervously around. He saw Catelia point at him, and then wave him over.

"Willis, this Altus Rector Ululla. She is most interested in your description of the monsters and when you first saw them."

Willis related his encounter with them, adding "it was like they born out of the earth. They smelled awful too. Like decaying vegetation."

"Thank you. I'll pass this information on. By the way, you know my husband."

"I do?"

"Yes, Brother Alric."

Willis laughed. "Well, at least I know now the reason he became a witch. A pretty woman can cause a man to change directions."

———

Brother Howrand smiled as he looked past Terrowin and Ayleth standing in front of him. Ayleth had changed into a pale-yellow robe, the closest colour a witch could wear to white. Prince Terrowin wore a military uniform, including the sword given to him by Alric. Near the entrance of the terradomus, witches of the combined orders filled the nearby street. Dorian stood close by, also with his mother, Orienla. Next to the witches stood Captain Pickett with several royal guards and Lord Randle of Jital. Pickett tried not to stand too close to the witches. Even though Prince Terrowin was marrying one, he still felt apprehensive when he was near them. Many of the soldiers were still superstitious that witches would put a spell on them if they were annoyed. However, Pickett tried to take the modern view of the king and queen that the witches were not evil and should be given respect. He tried to look relaxed as he listened to Howrand.

"It is truly an important union of a wonderful couple when so many people come to witness their union. This union holds great importance for witches. It is the melding together of two souls and has special significance. Witches believe in the circle of life. Birth, death and rebirth. Our soul mate is not just with us in this life but will be with us in death and our rebirth. Our soulmate's life will always be near ours, from one lifetime to another.

"Join hands Sister Ayleth and Brother Terrowin." He paused as they held hands. Howrand noticed clouds had moved and blocked the sun, forming quickly with lofty peaks. "The vow you undertake today must be taken with the upmost sincerity. Do not agree with this if you have any doubts. Your words are your bond and must come from your heart. Do you understand this?"

"Yes, we do."

"You can no longer operate as an individual. Everything you do and say will reflect on your partner. Never do or say something that would cause harm to your partner. They are your true love, and you must cherish their love. Respect their wants and needs, as they must respect yours. Be open..." Howrand paused. The clouds had turned dark, and a chorus of growling sounds caused onlookers to gaze around. He frowned as he saw a hoard of creatures advance through the streets toward the terradomus. He tried to continue with the service, stumbling on his words. "Be open to them on your desires and, and, and failures. See them at, at their best, and hold them at their worst." A human scream from below interrupted him. Soldiers were trying to defend against an army of creatures, some half human and other creatures born from nightmares.

Howrand lifted his hand and signalled the witches. Moments later the witches chanted and held up their hands in front of them. The spell they cast held the creatures just in front of the smaller army of soldiers. He saw what looked like shimmering air between the soldiers and the monsters.

"I'm afraid we will have to continue the service later." Howrand looked apologetic as he spoke to Ayleth and Terrowin.

———

Terrowin gave a nod of acknowledgement to Howrand and turned to survey the surrounding area. Closest to him were the witches. The different hues of the robes identified which order they belonged to, but they intermixed, not concerned whom they stood next to. He noticed other robed figures that looked different from the witches chanting out their spell. Their robes were dark and looked worn. Instead of standing, these robed figures kneeled, clasping their hands as if in prayer.

His attention was drawn to where grunts, shrieks and howls came from nightmare creatures being held back by a transparent wall made by the witches. The air smelled of burnt dirt, acid, rotten eggs and mold.

Occasionally, one of the beasts tested the wall by charging into, only to bounce back into the throng of angry creatures.

After each charge, the guards reacted by either taking a step back or waving their sword at where the creature would have been if it hadn't been stopped.

Terrowin spoke to Ayleth. "We are under attack." He waved over Dorian. "We need to fight back against Diablo."

Terrowin stood with Ayleth and Dorian, pointing their hands at Master Diablo. The air glowed a faint blue light where their spell reached Diablo's own spell. Terrowin could feel the push against his hands, and he wondered how long Ayleth and Dorian could maintain their spell. He glanced at Ayleth and saw her forehead damp from perspiration, her arms trembling with effort.

"We must hold on." Terrowin tried to increase his concentration, hoping Diablo would tire.

"How long do you think you and your witches spell can last?" Master Diablo's voice bellowed out.

Terrowin saw a hooded figure float above the ghoulish army.

"Your witches will soon tire, and my army will break through, feasting on their pathetic bodies. And then it will be your turn to fall under my power."

Terrowin looked at the witches. They looked passive as they stood with their arms in front of them, but he knew the chanting of the spell and reaching out with their arms was tiring. The protective circle could be broken if a few witches lost their concentration.

A cool air descended on him, and he stared at the clouds, blocking out the sun. Directly above him, the clouds were grey, but further away, the clouds were darker. As he watched, the black clouds drifted over where he stood, pushing aside the lighter coloured clouds. The air temperature continued to drop as the black clouds, almost featureless, covered the sky. The clouds took a fuzzy appearance as streaks of lightning flashed above, followed by thunder.

Terrowin wondered if the black clouds were a spell made by Diablo, and what their purpose was. A bolt of lightening struck from the clouds to the ground, resulting in a loud thunderclap. He heard gasps from the witches and louder howls from the monsters trying to break the barrier.

A black mist fell from the clouds, and he saw Diablo look up in surprise. *Good, he doesn't know what it is.*

The creatures facing the guards reacted to the rain falling on them, trying to wipe the black liquid off themselves.

Lightning strikes led to the sudden spreading of fire. Black smoke rose as the creatures howled in pain. The protective circle was hit by the black rain, streaming down the invisible barrier. More screams and black smoke came as the yellow fire burned the creatures. Diablo's robe caught on fire as his arms flailed away.

As the rain stopped, so did the fire, with the wind dissipating the black smoke.

The witches stopped their chanting, and Prince Terrowin advanced through the witches and the army, holding his sword.

———

When the black rain fell, Terrowin scanned the area near the witches. nearby figures in robes kneeled on the ground, their heads bowed. *They look like the order of Blackrain. If they are the ones causing this rain to fall, their name really reflects their identity.*

"I need to finish this business with Diablo." He gave Ayleth a kiss. "I will return soon." Terrowin carried his sword and headed toward where the guards still stood. As he approached them, he could smell the decay of dead creatures.

"Prince Terrowin, these monsters were all killed by fire after the dark rain fell," Captain Pickette spoke. "But their bodies are dissolving right in front of us. They stink. I've seen nothing like this before."

"Magic," he informed him. "Now they're just returning to clay and earth."

"What should we do now, sir?"

"I'm going to find Master Diablo and ensure he is dead."

Terrowin lead the way with Captain Pickett and half a dozen guards following. His eyes watered from the heavy smell. His boots stepped on a mixture of mud, cartilage and bone, making an unpleasant sound. "Kill anything that is still alive and let me know if you spot Master Diablo."

They plodded through the streets filled with decay, slowly making their way to the perimeter of the dead creatures.

"I see something moving, Prince Terrowin!" a guard called out.

Terrowin looked toward the pointed arm. He saw a dark figure struggling to move over the corpses. Terrowin changed direction and quicken his pace. As he closed the gap, he saw it was Diablo in a burnt robe, trying to move with one leg dragging behind.

"Diablo, your end is near!"

Diablo turned and saw his approach. He raised a hand at Terrowin.

Terrowin felt a force pushing at him and used his hand to block it. "Your powers are now pitiful. Prepare to die."

"Please, mercy. I promise never to use my powers for evil again. I will swear allegiance to you."

Terrowin reached Diablo and saw the red blisters on his face and arms. Part of his hair had been burnt off. "You are ugly inside and out."

"Prince Terrowin, will you allow me to state my case for..."

With a swing of his sword, Terrowin sliced off his head. This is for Kumar!" He swung his sword down on the Diablo's body, nearly slicing off an arm. "For Nicholas!" The sword chopped at the body again. "For Rupert!" A final blow from his sword sliced into a leg. "Go to hell!"

Terrowin stood looking at the body, his arms shaking with anger. Long minutes passed, and he noticed the guards standing silently behind him.

"Captain Pickett, have this shit of a man chopped into pieces and scattered in the forest."

"Yes, Prince Terrowin. Anything else you wish done?"

"Only to complete my wedding with Ayleth. Thank you, captain, for you and your men who were prepared to defend us. Your men showed great courage in challenging these monsters and Master Diablo. We will never forget this day!"

———

Terrowin celebrated his marriage to Ayleth with a kiss. Grinning, he waved to the witches and the soldiers. After taking her hand, he made his way to those standing close by. After receiving congratulations from Ululla and Alric, he met with Dorian, and his companion, Bethena.

"Dorian, how are you feeling after our battle with Diablo? It can be tiring mentally using turpis force." He saw how Bethena clutched his arm and looked up at him as he spoke.

"No, I feel all right. Diablo had a lot of power, but it was you who really pushed back at him."

"Thank you, but it was the three of us together that was needed."

Dorian extended a hand toward his side. "Prince Terrowin, this is my mother, Watcher Orienla and Brother Trav."

"It is an honour to meet you. Your son was truly a hero in fighting Master Diablo."

"Thank you, Prince Terrowin. You are an inspiration to us all."

Terrowin laughed. "Well, I did run away a few years ago. I hope that wasn't the inspiration you speak of." He extended a hand to Trav. "Good to meet you, Brother Trav."

"We have read about you, and it is an honour to meet you, Prince Terrowin. As Watcher Orienla knows, you will fulfill the destiny of peace and hope."

Terrowin was taken back by the revelation. "Thank you, but I am just one of many who strives for peace."

Destiny. I hear that word often.

55

Terrowin spent the night with Ayleth, sleeping in late before deciding he couldn't ignore the hunger pains any longer. He received long stares and acknowledgement from witches as he accompanied Ayleth downstairs to the dining room. Word of his actions in the battle with Diablo had spread quickly, and he was perceived as hero, even among the usually reserved witches.

As they ate their breakfast, Terrowin brought up the subject of Blackrain.

"They helped to defeat Master Diablo. Pastor Immin told me that their order had no purpose after his defeat.

"What will they do next?"

"I do not know. I was wondering if the witches could approach them to see if there was an opportunity to include them in the Umbravox."

"They have different beliefs than we do."

"True. But they fought on the same side as the witches. Perhaps there is something to learn from their beliefs and the spells they use. Blackrain is not evil. If another evil force should arise, their knowledge may prove valuable."

Ayleth smiled. "Very well. I'll approach my mother with your views. You really care about the welfare of all those around you."

"I should and I must. If I am to be king someday, I must look beyond my own walls."

———

Ayleth received help from Terrowin to step up into the carriage.

"I hope you find the carriage comfortable."

"I have never been in one before. This will be quite an experience. Two carriages and it looks to be fifty guards on horses. I think this is the first time my parents have been in a carriage as well."

"My father insisted your parents come visit with us. You should, as a princess, get used to a distinct style of living."

"Princess. That may take a while getting used to." She laughed.

He grasped her hand. "You may find it comes naturally to you."

"Just because you experience past lives doesn't mean I do as well."

"I'm just saying some things are easier to adjust to because you experienced them before. Regardless, I am sure you will adopt to being part of the royal family easily."

Ayleth looked out of the carriage, seeing the throng of people cheering and waving as they went past. *I remember standing on the sidelines as carriages went by. It feels strange to be inside one now and watching people wave. Of course, I didn't just watch the royal procession. I really wanted to see Terrowin. I always knew we would marry someday. Maybe it was a memory from a past life. It doesn't matter; I'm happy with this life.*

The ride for Ayleth was exciting at first, but as the journey continued, she found sitting in the carriage tiring. The constant jostling made the rest impossible. *I guess it wouldn't be appropriate to ask if I could walk for a while.*

Ayleth was certain they would travel to the Allisure Castle directly, but because of the late start, they made a decision to stop at Knavemire, a halfway point to the castle. They chose the best inn and politely, but firmly, asked guests to find other accommodations.

"Why are we staying here the night? I thought we would travel all the way to the castle."

Terrowin replied, "Well, it is possible for us to complete the journey in one go, but the fact of the matter is that we need to arrive at the castle during the daylight. You are the new princess, and they must see you arriving at a decent time. Crowds will be there to see your arrival. We can't be doing that late at night."

"Oh, I hadn't thought of that. This will be one of the few times I have not slept in a terradomus."

"Something to look forward to, although most travellers do not call staying in an inn a memorable experience."

Ayleth entered the room, the largest available on the second level. The corner room offered views on two sides, although neither held her interest. The bed held the same comfort level as her own in the terradomus, although the blankets were not as clean. Shortly later, she forgot about the room's décor when Terrowin entered the room and kissed her.

———

The carriage ride the next day was uneventful until they reached the Allisure Castle boundary. Hundreds of people lined the streets, cheering as the procession went by. Ayleth was surprised by their enthusiasm, and the chants of "Long live the king" were especially boisterous.

After passing through gates where the royal guards stood at attention, the carriages stopped in front of the castle. Guards held a throng of people in check as Terrowin, Ayleth, Alric, and Ululla entered the castle.

Ayleth was shocked by how feeble King Grayson looked and was having difficulty standing to greet them. Queen Elissa looked to be in better health, but she showed the fatigue of poor sleep. She rushed up to hug Terrowin before turning her attention to the rest of the party.

"I will have our servants show you to your rooms, where you can freshen up after your journey." She hugged Terrowin again. "How I have missed you. My prayers for your safe return have come to pass."

Terrowin nodded and kissed her on the cheek. "Father, it is so good to see you again." He gently took the king's hand in his own.

"You have finally returned home." King Grayson wheezed. "None too soon. I have missed you."

Ayleth whispered to Terrowin as they ascended the stairs to their rooms. "Your father looks very weak. I am worried about him."

"Me as well. The stress of running the kingdom and fighting the Dwykath Kingdom has taken their toll on him."

A woman servant followed them into a spacious bedroom. "Princess Ayleth, we have several dresses made for you." She walked briskly to a closet, where several dresses hung. "I will be happy to assist you in changing."

Ayleth looked at Terrowin.

"I guess my robe is not suitable attire for the royal family."

"Protocol. A princess needs to wear fine clothes. I'm sorry if that makes you feel uncomfortable."

"You will need to change as well, Prince Terrowin," the woman servant announced. "Your clothes will be in the next closet."

———

Ayleth found her new garments heavy and restrictive. She appreciated the appearance of the dress yet questioned the need for such intricacy that a servant had to assist her in putting it on. Although it wasn't mealtime, several plates of food still sat on the table when she walked into the dining room. She saw Ululla and Alric were already seated and gave them a smile and a small wave of her hand. Her mother raised her eyebrows as she gazed at her dress.

"You certainly look like a princess now."

Ayleth grinned. "It may get some getting used to wearing so much cloth."

"You look beautiful," Alric commented.

"Thank you." She clutched Terrowin's arm as they went to the opposite side of the table to sit. Initially, she was taken aback by how regal he looked after changing and trimming his hair and beard. Unlike her, he seemed to be relaxed at the sudden change in clothing.

They waited at the table, making small talk and sipping wine, until the king and queen entered the room. Ayleth, like the others, stood. She saw how slowly the king moved with a guard walking close by in case he stumbled.

The king plumped on his chair at the head of the table, letting out a puff of air as he leaned forward, with his forearms resting on the table.

"Forgive me. The air seems thin to me lately." He took a drink. "I want to thank Altus Rector Ululla and Brother Alric for taking the time to journey to the Allisure Castle. It has been wonderful to meet you. You have raised a fine daughter, and I do not make such a claim lightly. As she will be queen of the Allisure Kingdom, it is important to have a woman who is strong in character and moral fiber.

"Our kingdom has had a history of close cooperation with witches. In fact, my father and mother were witches, but they kept it a secret at that time. I believe there is no longer any need to hide who we are, including our family history.

"I understand," he paused. "Perhaps, since we are family now, we can dispense with formal titles. Ululla and Alric, I understand you cannot stay here for long, so I will make sure the appropriate ceremony and celebrations that follow are not delayed. I have decided to abdicate the throne. My son, Terrowin, will be the new king."

Terrowin stood and bowed his head. "It will be my great honour to accept the crown."

The king gave a cough, recovered and smiled. "It is a privileged to have such a fine son and daughter-in-law to take care of the Allisure Kingdom. And now, I must take leave. I tire easily. Steward Trennis will make arrangements for the ceremony and the grand celebration afterward." He stood with the help of a guard and made his way out of the room, followed by the queen, who looked troubled.

Ayleth looked at Terrowin and saw a tear escape down his cheek. She reached out and placed a hand on his. "Are you all right?"

"My father, he looks so weak. How I wish I could have returned sooner. My time with him will be too short."

———

Ululla, after the meeting, walked to the queen's chamber, speaking to one of the two guards stationed by the door.

"Good day. I am Altus Rector Ululla. I would like to speak with the queen. Would you be so kind as to let her know I am here and want to speak with her about an important matter?"

"Yes, ma'am. Please wait here." The tall, dark-skinned guard entered the room. Shortly later, Queen Elissa appeared.

"Ululla, is there a problem?"

"It is King Grayson; I am worried about him."

"I know. The surgeon has told me he doesn't have much time left. He sleeps more than he is awake. The years have been hard on him."

"As a witch, I know I have to be very careful about the use of spells and potions. Indiscriminate use will cause problems, and I must weigh the consequences before considering their use. King Grayson is obviously important, but even more so is the wisdom he can pass on to Prince Terrowin."

Elissa nodded. "I'm not sure what you are suggesting."

"Give me access to the royal kitchen. There are ingredients I need to make a potion that will bring health back to King Grayson."

"He will be young again?"

"No, but it will heal his inside. He will only feel younger again."

"Then let us not waste any more time." She pointed at the guard. "Escort Altus Rector Ululla to the kitchen. She has my authority to take and use anything she needs."

————

Ululla noticed the royal cook was watching her as she added ingredients to the boiling pot on the stove. It wasn't with distaste, but from one of curiosity.

"If you want to know, these items help make a potion. They do nothing unless I add a spell to them."

"I was wondering if they would also act as a poison. Under the right conditions."

"Your regard to preserve the king is admirable, but they make this mixture from items you already serve to the king in various meals. I assure you, as a witch, we do not do harm using magic or potions."

"Okay. How does this potion work?"

"You have a curious mind. The ingredients, when activated by a spell, target certain parts of a body. The spell can only make a potion do certain things. A potion for making your hair turn darker won't be able to strengthen you."

"You need different ingredients for different potions?"

"Yes, like the ingredients for bread are different for stew." Ululla poured the yellow liquid into a clay vessel with a tapered neck. "Thank you for the use of your kitchen."

Ululla returned to the queen's chambers and waited for the queen to see her.

"Was your visit to the kitchen successful, Ululla?"

"It was." She passed over the container. "I have added the necessary spell. It will be most potent if taken during a full moon. That will occur in four nights' time."

"Thank you for this. How soon will it have an effect?"

"Several hours. If you give it to him at night, in the morning, he will feel much better."

"Ululla, this means so much to me, and all those who love the king. If there is anything I can do to repay you for what you have done, just ask."

———

Ululla walked with Alric through the courtyard.

"I wish we could return to the Jital Terradomus, but the ceremony and celebration is in just a few days. It makes little sense to travel home and return here again."

"One advantage in staying is we get to spend more time with Ayleth. After they make Terrowin king, we will not be seeing our daughter very often."

"That's true. I'm very proud of her."

"Where are we going, Ululla? You said you needed to go for a walk but didn't say why."

"Oh, I just wanted to walk until we came across a witch. I want to send word I will be away longer than I expected."

"It's a good thing you left Brother Howrand in charge during your absence. He certainly can handle any situation while we are away."

"There are a pair of witches just ahead. I'll ask them to send a message to Brother Howrand."

Ululla spoke with the two witches, who quickly agreed to her request. After she returned to Alric, he brought up a question.

"How certain are you the potion will work?"

"It will work. I have no doubt. This kind of magic is rare in practice. Witches believe indiscriminate use of such magic will cause problems.

Here, I considered King Grayson has the potential to help the entire kingdom."

"A wise decision. Terrowin is still a young man who still needs his father's advice."

"True, although Terrowin is not just a young man. His previous lives are guiding him."

56

Terrowin entered the study, smiling as he saw his parents sit in oversized chairs.

"I heard you would be in here. How are you feeling, father?"

"A little tired, but this room comforts me." He used a hand to point at the paintings that adorned the wall.

"There is a lot of history represented here," Queen Elissa added.

Terrowin sat and faced them. "I remember this room from when I was much younger. My favourite paintings were one with horses in them." He laughed. "I thought the other paintings were not as exciting."

"I liked the horses too." Grayson grinned. "One of my few regrets was not riding often enough. That, and not drinking more wine." Grayson waved away the guards and servants standing nearby. "Give us the room."

After they were alone, Grayson turned to Elissa. I apologize for asking, but please know that Terrowin will still become king regardless of your answer. It's important for me to confirm if Terrowin is my blood. I ask this in front of Terrowin, as he should know as well."

Queen Elissa took in a deep breath. She was about to reply, but Terrowin interrupted her.

"You are mistaken." Terrowin stood. "I am not your son, but you are

312

mine. Grayson, I have returned to carry on your rule. You should never doubt that we are related and share the same blood."

————

Queen Elissa had trouble falling asleep. First, the revelation of Terrowin claiming to be Grayson's father, saving her from confessing that she indeed did have an affair. She couldn't decide if Terrowin was speaking the truth or not. Part of her wanted to believe his fantastic explanation.

The second item was the potion she gave Grayson. She waited until the moon was full before administrating it to him. He complained the flavour was that of crushed pinecones but took it when she told him the surgeon prescribed it to help him breathe better. She hoped desperately it would help him feel better and prolong his life.

The morning came, and she was glad to be rid of the uncomfortable dreams. After getting help to get dressed, she ventured into the king's chambers, and saw the empty bed.

"Where is the king?"

A servant bowed and answered, "King Grayson arose early and left his room."

"Where did he go?"

"I am sorry, he did not inform me."

Elissa frowned and exited the room, going down the hallway until she saw another royal guard.

"Have you seen where the king went?"

"Yes, Queen Elissa, he went downstairs to the main floor."

She took the wide, marble steps to the main floor, where she asked another guard if he had seen the king.

"King Grayson went to the east wing. He was with two guards, and I believe they were going to the royal stables."

"Go, and find the king, and report back to me as soon as you find him. I will be having tea in the common room. Make haste."

"Yes, my queen." He bowed quickly and ran.

Elissa watched him for a few seconds and turned to the common room. The quiet, sun lite room helped her relax as she waited. A servant brought her tea and biscuits as she eased in a large, cushioned chair.

As she finished her tea, the guard came running up to her.

He bowed, and quickly informed her he could not find the king's exact location. "My apologies, Queen Elissa, but the best I could determine was that he went horseback riding with royal guardsmen. Where they went is impossible to determine."

"King Grayson went horseback riding? He was strong enough to do so?"

"The guard at the royal stables said the king looked hale and hearty, like he was twenty years younger. I do not know what to make out of this information."

She let out a sigh. "Let us be thankful he is all right."

———

Elissa observed how King Grayson enthusiastically attacked his lunch, even taking a second helping, and noticed that it surprised others at the table.

"You should slow down your eating, or you may get indigestion."

"I feel like I have been starving for a week." He took another drink of wine.

Elissa looked across the table at Ululla. She crossed her hands on her chest and mouthed "Thank you" to her.

57

Ululla recalled how the two orders of witches found common ground to form one order. When Ayleth told her Terrowin suggested the witches look for ways to work with Blackrain, she was at first surprised. On reflection, she decided it was worthwhile to try to establish communication with them.

One should try to see the positive aspects of others. It would not hurt to reach out to them.

She found Alric working to repair a wood chair in his workroom.

"Alric, will you set up another meeting with Pastor Immin? I would like to talk to him about a future relationship with Blackrain. Obviously, that would be the altus councillium's decision to make, but I would like to have a recommendation for them."

"Of course. It will be nice to take a ride out into the woods again."

———

Ululla and Alric arrived early at the teahouse but found Pastor Immin and Pastoress Isabel had already arrived and was sitting in their usual spot at the outside area of the teahouse. On the table was a book. The leather covered book was thick and looked worn and discoloured from age.

Ululla sat with Alric across from them. A glance at the book revealed its title. The Book of Sacrifice.

"Thank you for meeting with us again. And thank you for your help in defeating Master Diablo."

"It is good to see you as well, Altus Rector Ululla. As I told you before, the whole purpose of Blackrain was to defeat Master Diablo. Together, we succeeded."

"I don't wish to sound rude, but what becomes of Blackrain now? Is there a purpose for your continued existence?"

Immin frowned. "You have asked very straightforward questions. To be sure, our order is small, perhaps around fifty individuals dedicated to our cause." He placed his hand on the book. "The Book of Sacrifice. As the name implies, sacrifice is part of our purpose, even our belief system. To be part of Blackrain requires long study of our book, and to be prepared to sacrifice for the greater good."

"What type of sacrifice?" Alric asked.

"As a warrior, you understand sometimes it could be your life. That is true in our case as well. But there were other sacrifices made. One is our appearance. Pastoress Isabel are both younger than yourself, but we look older. We age faster due to the power we need to use the spell of blackrain. The second sacrifice we made was the spells cause us to be sterile. We cannot have children. That means each member of Blackrain must recruit new members to replace those who pass on. It is not an easy task to ask young men and women to give up their lives for the cause."

He turned the book around so it faced Ululla. "Our book. The final chapter has been read and fulfilled. There is no longer a need for Blackrain, but this book deserves to have a place in your library where perhaps others can learn from it."

"Thank you, but what of yourselves?"

"We have accomplished our task. Pastoress Isabel and I will live out our final years at our farm. With no great battle to worry about, it will be a peaceful place to be."

———

Three members of the altus councillium met with Ululla in the Hall of Sentential.

The elderly man sitting in the centre of a curved table. In front of him rested the Book of Sacrifice. "Please be seated, Altus Rector Ululla. Tell us how you managed to have this book in your possession."

Ululla explained her meeting with the Blackrain members in the teahouse. "At the end of the meeting, he left us with this book. I thought it was important to bring it to attention."

"That is a wise decision. Have you looked inside the book?"

"Yes, I read a few of the pages. The text was difficult to understand but seemed to be more of time frame of events rather than any philosophy. There were also spells, but I didn't investigate those."

"We have come to same conclusion. It's a very interesting book, describing events that have occurred long ago, and very recently at the end. Your name appears in the book. Are you aware of that?"

"I was told my name was in the book by Pastor Immin, but I didn't look for it."

"The book is remarkably accurate on events. It does end with the fall of Master Diablo. Is there anything you wish to add?"

"Yes. Pastor Immin and Pastoress Isabel truly sacrificed to help bring an end to Master Diablo. They have aged rapidly and cannot have children. We do not share the same beliefs as Blackrain, but I appreciate what they did to preserve our world.

"We have decided to combine the Darkrose and Whiterose orders, even though there's a difference in the books we follow. Blackrain is finished. They have few members and most live in isolated areas. I wonder if we might offer them a place within our terradomus."

"They are warlocks. Perhaps they are not the best fit with our witches."

"I don't disagree, but we do share a common history with them and had a common enemy. They have experience and wisdom they can share with us. I believe we can learn by having them live with us in their final years."

"We have learned to trust your judgement on many issues in the past. This seems unusual at first look, but perhaps you are correct we could learn from them and their long past. They gave us a copy of the

Book of Sacrifice, so it seems they have made the first gesture of friend-ship. We should at least explore the possibility of working with Black-rain. Perhaps we have room for their order within ours."

58

Ayleth stumbled slightly during a dance with Terrowin. Partly was due to the drinks she had consumed; the other reason was the unfamiliarity of a dance used in the royal court.

"Are you all right?"

"Yes, although I admit I feel clumsy. I have never realized dancing could be so complicated."

"Some dances are more difficult than others. No matter. You still look elegant and graceful."

"Liar." She laughed. "King Terrowin, is that how you wish to begin your rule, by lying to your wife?"

"Only if it makes her happy. And I was not lying. You look positively elegant."

"And you look most handsome as King Terrowin. Which Terrowin are you? The one I met, or the ghosts of the past?"

"Just I. My forbearers have receded from my thoughts. I remember them, but their presence now is like a distant dream. The spell I used to help defeat master Diablo has faded. I remember using it, but I don't know how to invoke it. It is something I would have to relearn again, although I don't see a need."

"I am a witch. I know enough spells for both of us."

"Ah, so you must have put a spell on me." He kissed her. "It is a most pleasant spell."

She walked with him off the dance floor. "I understand that we have to make a showing at all these various celebrations, but I would like some quiet time with you. I envy your mother and father. They seem happy and have a lot of time to do what they want."

"They have earned time for themselves. My father has rediscovered his love of horse riding. Let us bid goodnight to those who wish to continue to party and share a drink alone."

Terrowin said little as they entered their bedroom on the third floor. Unlike his father and mother, King Terrowin didn't want a separate bedroom from his wife. He helped her sit at a table while a servant poured a tea for her and a wine for himself.

"That was a good celebration, but I'm enjoying this quiet time with you."

"Me as well. You have made some unusual decisions as king."

"Such as?" He gave a crooked smiled.

"You know very well. The ship you sent to New Kireland with gifts and a blacksmith who knows how to make steel. You send two more ships to map coastlines. You also have sent a ship to where you met the merfolk and gave them a message you want to speak with one of them."

"Yes, I want to increase trade with New Kireland. I believe having a map of the lands and oceans is needed. I also want to ensure we have peace with the merfolk."

"I'm guessing there's one mermaid in particular you may be interested in. Should I be worried?"

"No, I'm married to you. Period. But, if you wish, you can come along with me when I see the mermaids again."

"Oh, I'll be coming along. That is a promise."

———

The carriage bumped along the narrow road, although Ayleth was getting used to the harsh ride.

"All you have told me is you want to go to the edge of the ocean to continue to look for a mermaid. Why don't we go to a proper harbour?

"Because mermaids will not go where there are people and ships."

"But they will go to where we are going?"

"Maybe. I did have a ship leave a message where I'll be at the island where I met them." Terrowin shrugged. "I will call out to them and see what will happen."

"All right, but this is the third time we have travelled here. What if they don't show up again?"

"Then I will try again. I'm sorry. I feel this is something I must do."

"And I will go with you each time. Few wives would put up with their husband searching for mermaids."

"True, but my desire is one for friendship and to make the kingdom stronger."

The carriage came to a halt, and Terrowin helped Ayleth out of the carriage. They left the guards behind and reached the short beach area. Once again, Terrowin called out in the strange language of the mermaids.

Ayleth scanned the waters, looking for a sign of movement. It startled her when the head of a woman broke the surface close by. The mermaid called out in the language of the mermaids, speaking to Terrowin, but also staring at Ayleth.

Ayleth listened to the strange conversation. A second mermaid appeared; a very young female who stayed close to the other mermaid.

She heard Terrowin laugh and make his way to the water's edge. Slowly, he reached down and lifted the small mermaid, holding her gently in his arms. The small mermaid grinned, showing off sharp teeth as she pulled at his beard.

He turned to face Ayleth. "This is..." He paused. "In mermaid's tongue, it means Water Flower."

"She is beautiful. Is she yours?"

"Not mine, but I am her father. Are you angry with me?"

"No, I foresaw this. When it happened, I knew you were in danger. I forgave you long ago. I dream about future events. I had a feeling you'd encounter a mermaid during your journey. It was not something you could avoid."

———

Terrowin was silent for much of the journey back to the castle before speaking. "I told Carassius I have decreed that no ship shall fish within sight of land. I want to stop conflicts between us and the mermaids."

"Carassius? That's the adult mermaid?"

"Yes, sorry, I should have told you her name earlier."

"That is good. We should reduce conflicts between people and mermaids. Witches and the merfolk share a similar philosophy regarding living with nature."

"I was told that by the mermaids as well. Carassius asked me if you were pregnant. I said I didn't know. Are you?"

Ayleth smiled. "I was going to tell you when we returned home. Yes, I am. It will be a boy."

Terrowin grinned and kissed her. "That is fantastic news."

"It is. And to be clear, we will not name him Terrowin. We have enough males named after him all ready."

Terrowin laughed. "One more won't hurt."

"We should name him after one of your brothers."

"Which one?"

"It doesn't matter. We will have four sons and two daughters."

"Are you sure?"

"I told you; I can see the future. And it is going to be a wonderful future."

Don't miss out on your next favorite book!

Join the Melange Books mailing list at
www.melange-books.com/mail.html

———

THANK YOU FOR READING

Did you enjoy this book?

We invite you to leave a review at the website of your choice, such as Goodreads, Amazon, Barnes & Noble, etc.

DID YOU KNOW THAT LEAVING A REVIEW...

- Helps other readers find books they may enjoy.
- Gives you a chance to let your voice be heard.
- Gives authors recognition for their hard work.
- Doesn't have to be long. A sentence or two about why you liked the book will do.

ABOUT THE AUTHOR

Jack Wear began his writing career after he retired (the first time!). Boredom and a laptop led him writing a short story, which turned into a novel. He sent the story to a publisher and acceptance came, although it showed up as spam email. Thus the adventure of being a published author began.

Jack's other post-retirement interest is wine, and he began selling (and still does) it to various stores and restaurants. The truth is, he often writes his stories with a glass of wine. In fact, he suggests to appreciate the story he has written, having a glass of wine yourself will make it more enjoyable to read.

Family is important. Jack is married with three sons and two grandsons. He lives in Edmonton, Alberta and enjoys the long, warm summer days and survives the nasty cold winters.

www.jhwear.com

X x.com/JH_Wear

ALSO BY J. H. WEAR

Witches and Warriors

Witches and Warriors

Witches and Kings

———

Novels

Shadows And Sensations

Dragons in the Water

A Taste Of Murder

A Hole in the Universe

Play Dead

Back Stabber

———

Castle Series

#1 Fall to Domum

#2 The Curse of the Dacron Gem

#3 The New King